W9-ATY-459

THE GIRL THEY
LEFT BEHIND

This Large Print Book carries the
Seal of Approval of N.A.V.H.

THE GIRL THEY LEFT BEHIND

ROXANNE VELETZOS

THORNDIKE PRESS
A part of Gale, a Cengage Company

GALE
A Cengage Company

Farmington Hills, Mich • San Francisco • New York • Waterville, Maine
Meriden, Conn • Mason, Ohio • Chicago

Thorndike Press® Large Print Peer Picks.
The text of this Large Print edition is unabridged.
Other aspects of the book may vary from the original edition.
Set in 16 pt. Plantin.

LIBRARY OF CONGRESS CIP DATA ON FILE.
CATALOGUING IN PUBLICATION FOR THIS BOOK
IS AVAILABLE FROM THE LIBRARY OF CONGRESS

ISBN-13: 978-1-4328-6196-4 (hardcover)

Published in 2019 by arrangement with Atria Books, an imprint of Simon & Schuster, Inc.

Printed in Mexico
1 2 3 4 5 6 7 23 22 21 20 19

For my grandparents

Based on true events

According to the Wiesel Commission, between October 1940 and the end of World War II, as many as 380,000 Jews were massacred in Romanian-controlled territories. One of the most well-known incidents, the Bucharest Pogrom, took place in January 1941, when thousands of Jews were dragged into the streets to be tortured or killed.

ONE:
ANTON AND
DESPINA

1

Bucharest
January 1941

The girl sits alone in impenetrable darkness. Shivering, she wraps her arms around her tiny body and buries her face in the collar of her wool cardigan. Out here on the building steps, she tries to remember exactly what her mother had told her. Did she say how long she'd be gone? It was still light out when she last saw her parents rounding the corner, her mother with her shoulders slumped forward, trembling in her thin dress, her father shuffling down the frozen sidewalk just steps behind her. A chill tears through her as she places her palms on the icy concrete beneath her. The winter wind bites into her flesh, slashing mercilessly at her bare legs, and she wishes she had a blanket or mittens, or at least her bonnet, which somehow she has lost. Still, she'd rather be out here in the frigid cold than inside that dark, musty lobby. The smell of cooked cabbage coming from one of the apartments made her stomach growl with hunger, even though at home she always refused to eat it no matter how much her mother pleaded with her.

Drawing her knees to her chest, she looks up at the building's three stories and its vast, rounded balconies looming above. Certainly, she's never seen this building before. She has never seen this street, this vacant, dimly illuminated street on which a single lamppost casts a glint of light over the blackened snow. There isn't a person in sight. It is as if someone has turned out the lights on this once lively city, forbidding any strolling, greeting, or laughter.

Her parents will be back any minute, she thinks, glancing up the length of the street again. She tries to recall her mother's soft voice telling her not to be afraid, that if she is a brave girl, all will be well. Still, she knows that she shouldn't be out at this hour. Just the other day, she overheard her parents talking about the curfew, how the Iron Guard were patrolling the city, arresting anyone still on the streets after sundown. How they'd shot someone in front of their own building, right there for all the neighbors to see. She heard them talk about other things, too, things they didn't want her to hear, whispering in the room next to hers after she'd long gone to bed. Their words were muffled, indistinguishable, but the desperate edge in their voices made her shudder in her warm bed.

There are noises in the distance now — shouting, shrieking voices intermingled with the rhythmic thumping of boots and windows slamming shut in the night. This has been happening for the last few nights, but this time, the sounds are accompanied by a strange smell, something like burnt coal but sickly sweet, which makes her stomach turn. Waves of nausea rise inside her, and she pulls the edge of her cardigan over her face to get relief from the stench, forcing her thoughts to her home and her bed with the pink satin quilt, the familiar light creeping through the door left ajar between their two bedrooms.

Tears well up in her eyes, and she can no longer fight them. She is ashamed, because she knows she is not brave after all, even though she promised her mother that she would try her hardest. *I will be good, Mama. I will be patient,* she'd said, but now those words seem as if they were spoken a lifetime ago.

In the crook of her arm, her sobs spring

free, knifing through the silence and echoing through courtyards and alleyways. Although she knows she should be quiet, there is no way to contain whatever it is that has come loose inside her. She cries until there is nothing left, until even her jagged sighs have melted away, becoming one with the wind. Lying down on the concrete landing, she curls herself up into a ball and finally lets herself slip into a bottomless chasm.

Suddenly, sturdy arms embrace her, lifting her in the air. She is startled awake, and looking up, she sees the face of a woman she doesn't know — hair pulled back in a silvery bun, random strands falling about her lined, rounded cheeks. The faint scent of starch and perspiration envelops her as the woman folds her against her chest, so tightly that she cannot break free, even though she tries with all her might, flailing her limbs. Yet there is something tender in the woman's grip, something comforting, and the girl is too cold and tired and weak, so she buries her face in the woman's bosom and begins to weep. Opening the entrance door with her elbow, the woman carries her back into the lobby. The girl wants to ask if she knows about her parents, if they are coming to get her soon, but when she opens her mouth, only a long, sharp wail escapes from her lips.

"Shh . . ." whispers the woman in her ear. "I've got you. Shh . . . You are all right. You are all right."

In the transient light of a passing car, the woman's face shines pale and wide like a moon visible amid passing clouds, her eyes like that, too, sparkling and moist. As if sensing the girl's gaze, they lower to hers, but an instant later, the light is gone, and they disappear from her again, sliding back into nothingness. Only the woman's arms remain, soft and solid all the same, and that scent encircling her in waves.

"Such a sweet thing," she thinks she can hear the woman murmur as if to herself in the returning darkness. "Such a sweet little thing." There is a cluck of her tongue. "What a pity."

Twenty years she's worked as a concierge in this building. Twenty long years, during which she's gotten to know every family on the block, and so she can practically swear that this little girl does not belong to any of them. No, she is most certainly from a different part of town. Perhaps her parents were visiting someone in the building when the girl slipped away without their realizing.

But who would let a child wander off in the middle of Dacia Boulevard? Who would leave a child of three, maybe four, in the middle of gunfire and the curfew and dead bodies lining the streets? In disbelief, in disgust, she shakes her head. She isn't the most educated woman, but she does know human decency, and she realizes this is an aberration.

Even in her sleep, the poor thing is clutching her hand so tightly that she finds it impossible to move from the stairwell between the lobby and the first floor, where she's been cradling the girl in her lap. Just when she thinks she can try to lift her, the girl goes rigid, writhing and twisting, and all she can do is still her with her own failing body, folding over hers in a prayer. A prayer that she repeats again and again hours later, when she's managed at last to bring the child down to her basement room and the wavering light of a winter dawn trickles in through the sliver of glass that is her window.

The girl wakes and sits up on the narrow bed. Her eyes roam unfocused about the tiny space, taking in the old dresser with its peeling lacquer, the kitchen half visible behind the threadbare curtain, the rusted *soba* in the corner in which a few sputtering flames leap like overgrown moths. Gathering the blanket closer around her, she scoots over to the far corner of the bed, but there is no fear on her face now, only confusion.

"Where's my mama?" she utters after a silence. Her voice is small, hardly audible. "Is she coming to get me soon?"

The woman's hands are cold, so cold as she looks down at them, the way they keep rubbing each other as if they have a mind of their own. In the wood-burning stove, the embers flare and pop, and it is only when they've turned completely to ash that she raises her eyes.

"No, my sweet girl," is all she says simply. "No."

2

Anton and Despina Goza were known in their vast circle of family and friends for their promptness. They never arrived a minute late either for appointments or for social gatherings, regardless of the irregularity of the trolleys, the icy sleet glazing the sidewalks, the alarming state of the city in the weeks past. Despina insisted on punctuality as if it was the very thing that defined her. She was a woman with impeccable social etiquette, always on time and polished to perfection, from her hat fashioned in the latest Parisian style to her reptile-skin pumps chosen to match her handbag and a belt that accentuated her tiny waist. Although she towered by at least a head over her four older sisters, she was profoundly feminine, a vision of restrained, manicured beauty balanced by a sleek, powerful frame. The face of a Greek goddess, friends of her mother often said admiringly and perhaps a little enviously of her porcelain skin, sculpted cheekbones, and wavy chestnut hair that set off the creaminess of her shoulders.

To her dismay that morning, opening her eyes and looking at the pendulum clock on the bedroom wall, she realized that she had overslept. Yet she remained propped against her pillow a little while longer, listening to the world gradually awaken outside her window, like water swelling into a boil. Every morning, she was greeted by the sounds of early traffic on Vlaicu Boulevard, the footsteps and muffled greetings. She found comfort in the familiar, her husband sleeping soundly next to her, the slant of sunlight falling across the foot of their Victorian bed, the café au lait silk sheets shimmering all around her like fine desert sand. But on this particular morning, her tranquility was cut short. Thinking of the day ahead, her stomach somersaulted in an almost violent way. *What madness to do this now,* she thought. *What madness, with the war at our back door.*

Deep down, she knew there would never be a right time, that the *right* time for this may have come and gone long ago. That despite her good fortune and enviable life, she would never have the one thing she desired most in this world. God had turned his back on her, it seemed, for despite her pleas, her silent bargaining, she was still without a child of her own. And yet fragments of hope still existed in her heart, even though she'd have given anything to dispel them. Then all would be quiet. Quiet and still, a land at peace after a long war. *Stop wanting,* she chided herself over and over, but her heart would not listen.

At least she had given up praying for it. Truly, she should have stopped praying years ago when it became clear that her womb was not capable of sustaining life, when her bouts of self-loathing and hopelessness became so frequent that her sisters began visiting only as a unit, tiptoeing around her, trying to distract her with meaningless gossip. One hasty word, one careless sentence, was enough now to send her into a vortex of despair that lasted for days and from which lately it took all of them to pull her out.

"You are blessed in many ways, Despina. Focus on everything else that you have in your life," they would whisper encouragingly beneath knowing glances as they brought out boxes of chocolates and served her tea and rubbed her hands while she slumped in a chair, broken, devastated.

Four miscarriages. After each one tore a fresh wound in her heart and her body, after the disappointments had become so predicable that they had lost their bitter edge, her once ardent hope gradually eroded to a mere flicker. Yet the fire wouldn't die out, not entirely. And now this unexpected chance. The appointment had been set so rapidly she had barely had a chance to prepare herself for it.

In the mirror over the bathroom sink, she sighed at her own image, pressing her fingertips to the hollows under her almond-shaped eyes. Her face was but a white-washed mask, her Grecian features sharper than usual. In her sleeplessness, she must have bitten her lips, for they looked swollen and slightly bruised, like overripe fruit painted against the backdrop of a blank canvas. A splash of cold water seemed to revive her senses, returning her to the day ahead. Anton came into the bathroom, and they passed each other in the doorway.

"Hello, love."

He kissed her cheek, flashing her an absentminded but dazzling smile. Despina could not help thinking that he looked handsome in his striped silk pajamas, even at this early hour, his short-cropped hair rumpled, the faint smell of last night's

23

whiskey still on his breath. He began brushing his teeth, humming a tune to himself. Sometimes his boundless optimism rattled her a little, but it was part of his charm. And her husband was certainly a man blessed with undeniable charm. Even on this morning, watching the bright gaiety with which he performed this mundane task, she couldn't help smiling.

It wasn't just her on whom Anton had this effect but practically everyone who knew him. His lightness of being was infectious, irresistible. Women turned their heads as he passed them on the street, looking like Cary Grant in his suits tailored to perfection, a white angora scarf draped over his broad shoulders, hat in hand tipped ever so slightly in a gesture of hello. Underneath the hat, an unguarded smile, not flirtatious but open and cheerful, welcoming the beauty of life. Men patted him on the back and smiled, too, taken with his joie de vivre and prosperity and his arms open to the promise of a new day.

Ten years had passed since Despina met Anton, yet every detail of the day was still as crisp in her mind as if it was yesterday. She realized with amusement that they might have never met had her father not

24

run out of ink for his Montblanc that Sunday or had he chosen to go buy a fresh jar for himself. But her father had been particularly busy going over his accounting ledgers, and the air was brimming with the promise of spring, so when he'd asked her to go instead, she gladly agreed.

"Piazza Romana," he'd said, handing her several large bills. "You know the store. And don't forget to get some envelopes, too. The linen stock if you can find them."

This was their usual routine. She would buy whatever he needed and was allowed to keep the change. Her father never asked any questions, and there was always something that caught her eye in the display windows along the way — a pretty hat, a silk handbag, a colorful scarf that complemented her hair.

Deep in thought about how she would spend that day's change, Despina walked the few blocks to Piazza Romana, strolling along in no hurry. She crossed the streets absentmindedly, not bothering to look at the signs, for she knew the route by heart. Her father had been buying supplies there for years, and she was acquainted with the landlady, Mrs. Zoltof, almost intimately. Thus when she entered the store, she was startled to find not the old woman, but a young man perched on a ladder, arranging

25

cigarette cartons on the shelving over the register. Her first thought was that she'd entered the wrong shop, but just as she was about to leave, a confident, friendly voice greeted her from the top of the ladder:

"Good morning, miss."

There was a smile on the young man's lips, warm and slow, as if he already knew her. For a moment, she found herself staring, forgetting herself and her manners. A perfectly straight, Roman nose. Strong cleft chin. Light brown eyes, dancing with some unspoken joy, like cognac swirling in the bottom of a glass. As he came down the steps as if it required no effort at all, she glanced at his muscled forearms, dark as honey against the white of his rolled-up sleeves.

"Please, come in, miss," he said again. "Let me know what I can do for you."

She stepped in fully, closing the door behind her.

"Yes, I'd like some paper stock and some ink, thank you," she pronounced crisply, lifting her chin though she wasn't quite sure why. "I'm Mr. Papodopulos's daughter. Well, one of his daughters."

Instantly, she felt ridiculous. Why would he care who she was? She was here to buy paper and ink, for God's sake. But he seemed genuinely glad for the introduction. As he stepped out from behind the counter, raking a hand through his thick blackish hair, he flashed her that irresistible smile again.

"At your service. Whatever you need."

Feeling her cheeks grow alarmingly warm, Despina looked away, trying to pin her eyes on something that she might comment about, to distract from the fact that despite the elegance and social graces that had been instilled in her since she could barely walk, she was acting like an absolute oaf. *God, this is unbecoming,* she thought. *He is just a store clerk.* Quickly, she turned away and began leafing through the hundreds of stationery samples arranged in narrow wooden slots on the wall.

"I'd like five hundred of these envelopes," she said coolly, holding one out to him.

She had no idea what she had just pulled off the shelf, but it would do. As he took it from her, their fingers brushed slightly. The pink in her cheeks deepened, and she looked away again, began fidgeting with some miniature glass figurines on a display case. But she could feel his eyes still on her, smiling, amused.

From the very beginning, Anton fit into her

life like a missing piece of a puzzle. Her father, a wealthy Greek businessman who had moved his family to Bucharest after the Great War, took Anton under his wing almost instantly, surprising himself with how quickly he warmed to the young man. Yes, Anton was not nearly as educated as Despina and did not come from a prosperous family, but in the weeks since she'd met him, the changes in his daughter were so favorable that he found himself unable to form a single objection.

Overnight, his youngest daughter began shedding the armor that had cloaked her since their first few years in the new country. When they'd left Greece twelve years before, Despina was a young girl, with eyes like quicksilver and a personality to match. Now at twenty-three, she was somewhat of a stranger to him. She had undoubtedly blossomed into a beauty but one who exuded perpetual coolness, an indifference of sorts.

But now that light in her eyes had returned. She was floating once more through the rooms of their home, twirling around in her silk gowns, her arms outstretched to the sky, laughing, remarking on the beauty or uniqueness of things she had not noticed before. Her energy was contagious, unbounded, it rippled like wildfire. Thus, it was not long before the whole household came to expect Anton's visits with equal enthusiasm, buzzing around him as if he was a central character in all their lives.

Not a week passed without an invitation to dinner or tea. The young man began looking forward to the freshly baked phyllo pastries stuffed with cheese or spinach or plums, something different each time, and the thirty-year-old brandy that had been placed on the bar cart in the library just before his arrival. He was flattered by the sound of young female voices, delicate like chimes, greeting him at the door, pleased at the way they all crammed into the car next to him on the way to a party as if he was already a part of the family.

From Despina's father, Anton learned about world events, politics, and business. Art followed, along with a growing appreciation for the small luxuries that accompanied their way of life — crystal wine goblets and monogrammed silverware, the aromatic flavor of imported cigars, the exquisite feel of silk and linen suits that Despina showered him with despite his protests. He wore them when taking her to the opera or to the horse races on Sundays. He discovered how to augment his natural charm with studied finesse, how to kiss a woman's gloved hand, looking her in the eye for just a brief moment, how to shake a man's hand with confidence, how to speak in a way that commanded respect, admiration.

They quickly became the talk of the large Greek community in Bucharest, a vision of charm and elegance and undeniable beauty. In Anton's presence, Despina flourished, becoming ever more radiant. As the weeks passed and they began spending more and more time together, she became certain of only one thing. The life she was destined for truly began that morning her father had sent her to the stationery store that Anton now owned, along with three others in some of the city's most affluent sectors.

Many great pleasures had passed since. Many moments in time came and went, and the blissful ones far outweighed the disappointments that no lengthy marriage was immune to. And so they were the lucky ones, it seemed. But of all the memories they had built together, the one that Despina recalled with most vivid emotion was a day in the fall of 1935, when she and Anton emerged from the Patriarchal Cathedral on Mitropoly Hill, arm in arm. A photographer had waved for their attention — *Look this way, the light is perfect,* he'd said — struggling to break through the cheering crowd that lined the length of the stairs. Even now, when she studied the silver-framed photograph, her breath caught a little, not because of how striking they looked — she clad in an exquisite cream charmeuse gown, he in a crisp black tuxedo — but for what the lens had captured in their eyes on that day.

In their dining room, the pendulum struck slowly nine times as Despina took a sip of her coffee, barely noticing that it burned the roof of her mouth. Over his morning paper, Anton quirked an eyebrow at her, then set down the paper next to his plate.

"If only I was a mind reader," he said, taking a bite of his toast.

"Oh, it's nothing," she replied softly.

"Tell me."

"I don't know, Anton. What if this is another . . ." She winced, hating to use this word. "Another failure?"

"Then we will try again," Anton answered without hesitation, as if this was the only answer he could ever give.

She smiled faintly, feeling a little less anxious, grateful for his optimism. But she knew how hard this had been on him, too. She knew what was in his heart — that slight dullness in his eyes perceptible only to her — on those interminable afternoons when they found themselves in the company of her sisters and their parade of children. She almost suggested that they should forget the whole thing, stay home, make a fire. It looked as though it would snow again soon.

"Despina, look at me," he said insistently. "Darling."

"Anton," she began, "Anton, I think —"

"We will not give up," he interrupted her, and there was a sternness in his voice that she rarely heard. "We will not give up until you have decided that it's enough. Which, knowing you, my beautiful and stubborn wife," he added, chuckling softly, "means never."

Tears flooded her eyes, and she shook her head, partly to curtail them, partly because she did not know what to say. What she wanted to do was fall into his arms right there at the breakfast table, kiss him fully on the mouth, but then she glanced at the clock. If they were going to do this at all, there was no time.

When he pulled out her chair and raised her hand to his lips, she interlaced her fingers through his, squeezed them tightly. There under her touch was all that was real and true, all that would still be hers no matter what fate had in store on this day.

3

The city of their youth flew by in a blur. There were the white peaks of the art deco buildings, the Telephone Palace that was Victoria Avenue's crowning glory, Hotel Capitol with its delicate, belle epoque facade, where so many times they'd sipped frothy drinks on hot summer nights. No people in elegant garb graced its curved wrought-iron terrace, no lights in the vast windows came into sight, even the criss-crossing bridges bowing over the Dambovita looked as if they served no purpose at all. Soon the deserted avenue spilled into the city's largest piazza, and the Royal Palace with its endless rows of windows came into view. At the gates, a handful of guards stood like wax figurines looking indifferently over the majestic square, where cobblestones once pounded by a thousand pedestrian feet shone pristinely under a fresh layer of snow.

Few words were exchanged with their driver. It was hardly possible to make small talk about the unspeakable things that had shaken the city to its core in recent days, though Anton attempted to break the silence once or twice, commenting on how his business had slowed to a crawl. "Who needs the trifles I sell at a time like this?" he said, and the driver turned to him slightly and nodded. In the backseat, Despina leaned her head against the cold glass, watching the huge, heavy flakes land on the windshield and shrivel into tiny stars. She wished all she'd seen with her own eyes could disappear like this, turn to water, evaporate from her consciousness.

Three days of massacre, with neighborhoods on fire, bodies lining the streets, broken windows and broken souls, women screaming, and the smell of burnt flesh. And men going missing in the night, flying off buildings with loaded guns at their backs, the sound of gunfire in Cismigiu Gardens. People had been marching in the streets with placards that read, *Jews Are the Enemy* and *Solve the Jewish Problem.* Many had painted Christian crosses on their front doors so their homes wouldn't be vandalized, the facades desecrated. These were people she might have known, decent people, students and union workers, high school kids and gendarmes who had taken an oath to protect the citizens of Bucharest. And behind them, the mobs rallied with angry fists and angry voices, knowing that they were anonymous in their shared hatred. It had become nearly commonplace to see cars in flames in the middle of boulevards, to see men and women dragged into the streets, beaten, kicked with ferocity.

At night, the fury would subside, but the fear in people's hearts would become most acute. They would shut their windows early, draw the curtains, lower the shutters. They would turn on their radios to drown out the world outside. They would talk casually about acquaintances and children or what they should have for supper, even though outside the Legionnaires, the Iron Guard, marched up and down streets with sharp bayonets pointing up to the sky.

Rumor had it that the Nazi-backed Romanian military arm known as the Death Squads were the most feared in all of Europe. Night after night, they patrolled the city's quarters in their crisp green uniforms, bearing the triple cross emblem on their sleeves. From blocks away, one could hear the sound of their boots marching in perfect unison, their voices rising and falling together, humming their sinister hymn:

Death, only a Legionnaire's death,
Is our dearest wedding of weddings,
For the Holy Cross, for the country,
We defeat forests and conquer mountains.

Romanian people, Despina thought, had always been so spirited. But this was fueled by something else, something that her beloved country had embraced, something despicable that pulled at its heartstrings and slowly stole its soul. Hitler's arm was reaching into the depths of Central and Eastern Europe, without a presence on the ground. Without a presence yet. The arm was extending its way, slowly grabbing the throat of the Romanian people.

It wasn't long after the holidays that she'd witnessed it for the first time, returning home one afternoon with bags of groceries in hand. Most of the shops in her neighborhood had rolled down their shutters, afraid of the constant looting, and she had walked nearly two hours to find an open grocer that still stocked some essentials — flour, eggs, oil. On her way back, she felt tired dragging along the heavy bags and thought of a quicker way to get home, even though she had promised Anton that she would stick with the main boulevards and stay close to other pedestrians. But sooner than she imagined possible, she found herself in a maze of back streets covered in shattered glass and heaps of burnt rubble. Anton would have been out of his mind knowing that she had wandered through the plundered neighborhood unaccompanied, but she strode on, unafraid.

Soon she reached Negru Voda Boulevard, a quiet street lined with large, shady oaks a hundred years old. A benevolent district, where people once took their time greeting one another, smiling, and shaking hands as children chased one another around their parents' legs. But on this day, Despina stopped at the corner and gasped, turning her face away.

The Cahal Grande, the synagogue that was one of the city's oldest landmarks, was on fire. Legionnaires were dancing around the flames, roaring with joy, slapping one another's backs. They had used a fuel tanker to spray the walls, and the temple had been scorched to the ground. Nothing remained of its ornate architecture. Not the menorahs or the old scriptures. Not even the lavatories.

There was pure pleasure on their faces,

their gleeful smiles, illuminated, lengthened, grotesque in the flames of the burning building, as Despina stood there frozen, unable to take a step. One of them looked in her direction, measuring her with unconcealed appreciation, and gave her a lewd grin. Then he bowed to her, his arm sweeping low, almost touching the pavement. Despina turned away and broke into a near sprint, the frantic clicking of her heels echoing down the sidewalk. She was desperate to be home, desperate to shake the horror that had built in the pit of her stomach, the taste of bile that had risen in her throat. Even now, thinking of what she had seen made her shudder with disgust. And she wasn't the only one. Of that she was certain.

Hitler himself, some said, was concerned about the violence that had erupted in Bucharest overnight with such vigor, threatening to boil out of control. He preferred a more tactical approach to the advancement of his visions, and civil war was certainly not what he had in mind for Romania. But the Legionnaires had sworn allegiance to Germany, to Hitler's Fascist principles, and were willing to extinguish the lives of their very own people, their families and friends from childhood. And the good people of Bucharest, the mobs, followed in their wake, knowing they would be held to no account, cloaked in anonymity.

Despina was still deep in thought as the Buick stopped in front of a gloomy two-story building with patches of peeling stucco and cheap metal roofing. On the discolored stucco wall over the entrance, a dark blue placard indicated that they had reached their destination.

The driver came around to her side and opened the door, extending his gloved hand for her. Her heart fluttered as she stepped out and wrapped her coat tightly around her. They had waited so long for this visit, despite many attempts to get an audience with the institution's director. It wasn't until her cousin Maria intervened, practically begging for a single visit, that the gates finally opened to them. *We are not in the business of peddling children* was what she had been told. *Their money will be of no use here.* But then the little girl had arrived, and with the orphanage already at capacity and Maria's incessant pleas, Mrs. Tudor finally agreed.

Maria, with her voice of silk and her saintly soul, was able to get them passage. Maria, who spent three days a week here bathing the children, serving their meals, shaving their heads, and healing their wounds, despite her husband's protests, despite her friends' puzzled glances, their incomprehension of her unwavering commitment. *Why on earth does she do it?* they would ask one another as they lunched on terraces and went to horse races and visited tailor shops and bought sweets for their children in pastry shops on the bustling Lipscani Boulevard. *And what about her poor husband, his reputation?* they commented, as Maria churned gruel and warmed water for baths and soothed the souls and bodies of children who belonged to no one.

Despina knew what lay in the hidden corridors of her cousin's heart, her dearest friend, with whom she shared not only a striking physical resemblance but a bond that surpassed anything she felt for her sisters. She knew how Maria missed her own child, her only son, whom she had last seen when he was nine, lying in a hospital bed with typhus. The boy had gone so quickly she had barely had a moment to caress his trembling body, to soothe him with words of love in his final moments. It was because of him that she worked here, that she offered the remnants of her heart to these poor, lost children.

They would always have this in common,

she and Maria, and with this last thought, she grabbed Anton's hand bravely and led him through the wooden gate into this last realm of possibility, where their dream was not yet lost.

4

She paused, assaulted suddenly by a scent she couldn't identify, something putrid that hit her straight on, like a fist. Garbage, she realized, leaning against the wall, suddenly weak in the knees, her heart beating too fast, as she took in the bleak surroundings of what was the playground of Saint Paul's Orphanage. A metal bin rested in the center of the courtyard, next to an oak tree with barren branches raised imploringly toward the slate-colored sky. Running around it in a game of tag, dozens of children wearing the same shabby khaki uniforms squealed happily, as if the awful stench was no bother at all.

Covering her nose with the back of her hand, she inched forward, stepping unsteadily over the uneven grayish cobblestones, trying to fight off the apprehension that had suddenly overtaken her. Just looking at these poor children — all pale and runny-nosed, with their shaved heads and bruised knees, their vacant eyes — filled her with such sadness that all she wanted to do was flee. Why had they come here? What were they hoping to find in a place like this? Surely this was a mistake. *A mistake,* she wanted to whisper to Anton as she tugged on his arm. But when he turned to her, there was a smile playing on his face, as though he was observing children at play in a park on a sunny Sunday.

"Come, darling," he said, looping his arm through hers. "It's all right."

Gently, he led her across the courtyard toward what appeared to be the main building. They were nearly there when a lanky boy of around ten sauntered up to them, spooling and unspooling a yo-yo with impressive ease.

"So you're here for a tour of our lovely institution? To take a look at us kids?" he said, snapping his fingers shut around the wooden object. "I'm the best soccer player there is. And I can count change."

Anton searched inside his coat pocket and extracted a bill. Without looking at it, he handed it to the boy, who yanked it greedily out of his hand. His eyes widened in surprise as he flipped it back and forth, trying to identify how much it was worth.

"Thank you, thank you, sir!" he said, bending down to stuff it inside his sock.

"Sure," Anton replied cheerfully. "But can you do something for us, young man? Can you show us to the director's office?"

"That won't be necessary." A thin, curt voice greeted them from behind.

They turned, a little flustered to find themselves face-to-face with a wiry middle-aged woman with salt-and-pepper hair pulled back in a severe bun and a gray woolen shawl covering her frail shoulders.

"I've been expecting you," Mrs. Tudor said, examining the time on her wristwatch and abruptly shifting her gaze to Despina, who could not help but blush at the overt reprimand. "You must be Maria's cousin."

"Yes," Anton replied cheerfully in place of his seemingly speechless wife. He shook the woman's hand much too enthusiastically and felt a little embarrassed himself when she pulled it out of his grasp and placed it stiffly behind her back.

"Well, right this way, then," the woman said, with a smile of forced courtesy that did not reach her eyes.

Through a dim corridor that smelled of ammonia and fresh paint, Mrs. Tudor led them at a clipped pace, not glancing back. A moment later, she ushered them into a tiny office, no bigger than a closet.

"Please, have a seat," she said, indicating the chairs in front of her desk.

They sat, Anton taking off his gloves and leaning deeply into his chair, Despina perching on the edge of hers.

"First, I'd like to go over some facts," said Mrs. Tudor firmly, half vanishing into her own seat behind a large wooden desk. She paused to push her oversize glasses higher onto her nose and flipped open a file. "The girl you are inquiring about . . . she is extremely withdrawn. As I'm sure you've heard from Maria, she was brought here in late January under unusual circumstances. Apparently, she was found in front of a residence on Dacia Boulevard by the building's concierge. The woman took her in for the night and the next day brought her to the local police precinct, in the hope that someone might have inquired about her. It appeared that no one had, so the police brought her here."

She cleared her throat and took a small sip of water from a glass on her desk. "At the time she arrived, the girl looked quite normal, well developed and functioning, but . . . she has not uttered a single word. We were assured she can indeed speak — somehow the concierge was able to extract not only her name but the month and day of her birthday — yet here she seems" — Ms. Tudor paused as if searching for the right phrase — "utterly *absent*. The only thing she shows any interest in is an old piano we have long retired into the storage room. She just sits up there and hammers away at the keys for hours on end, refusing sometimes to even come down for supper. Well . . ." She closed the file and pushed it somewhat impatiently off to the side. "Do you still wish to see her?"

Mrs. Tudor wanted to get to the crux of the matter quickly. She was certain that once this couple took one look at the girl, their visit would come to an abrupt end. Certainly they wouldn't want a scrawny little orphan, especially one who seemed trapped in a world of her own. People like them, with their expensive clothes and private car parked outside at the curb, had no idea what it took to take care of all these children, to manage a place like this. She could not help hiding her displeasure, her lips curling downward in silent contempt.

"Yes, of course," Despina replied, taking her by surprise. "We certainly do. Right, darling?"

Anton nodded, displaying no other sign of emotion than his patient smile as he reached for her hand. It was all the reassurance she needed, and her gaze traveled back to Mrs. Tudor, boldly.

"All right, then. If you are *sure.*" The director emphasized the word. "I think she should meet you, madam, first. Alone."

"Alone? But it isn't my decision entirely. My husband —"

"Yes, ma'am, *alone* would be best. After all the poor thing has been through, I think we will spare her the experience of being scrutinized en masse."

Already she was on her feet, holding the door open as if in challenge.

"I will be right here," Anton said, as Despina followed Mrs. Tudor hesitantly out of the room, looking back at him one last time. "After all, my love, it is your heart that will tell you all that you need to know."

In another unventilated room, Despina paced back and forth. Through a small barred window, she glanced at the courtyard below, noticing there were no children now. They must be back in the classrooms, she thought, then realized that most likely there were no classrooms in a place like this. There were no books, no toys, no games here. There was nothing but a great void of time that stretched on endlessly. Taking a breath, she sat on a child-size chair and waited.

Some time passed — she had no idea how long — before the click of the door made her jump out of her reverie. "Come, come, dear," she heard Mrs. Tudor say with surprising tenderness, as a tiny silhouette appeared in the doorway. The figure inched forward, crossing the threshold, guided from behind by Mrs. Tudor's hands.

The girl could not have been older than four, Despina realized; she barely reached to her waist. It wasn't hard to see that despite the shaved head and dirt-streaked pallor, she was a pretty child. Her heart-shaped lips and high cheekbones — one of which was punctuated by a small, round beauty mark, like a period at the end of a sentence — gave her a delicate, doll-like appearance. And her eyes — Despina had never seen eyes like that. Deep mossy green, like a pond in the middle of summer.

"Hello," Despina said, smiling, rising in a fluster, nearly dropping her purse.

In the long moment that followed, she felt herself trembling, and the very air around her grew still. It seemed like the most monumental few seconds of her life, yet nothing was happening at all. The girl would not even look up from the plank floor but rather stood there swaying, with a discomfort that was almost tangible, sniveling and wiping her nose with the back of her uniform sleeve.

"Here, you might need this," Despina managed. She reached inside her purse, rummaging to find her handkerchief. She held it out, and it hung uselessly, like a limp white flag, and eventually she lowered her hand. It might have been enough to discourage her, to provoke a look or a gesture that would have ended it all. Yet all she could do was stare at the tiny creature, as if everything else in the room had receded into a fog.

But where was her Shirley Temple? Where was the child of her dreams, with bouncy blond curls and a smile that would light up a room? When they had decided to give adoption a try, that was what she had envisioned for herself. A little blond thing with round, ruby cheeks and dazzling blue eyes. A girl strangers would stop and smile at on the street, a vision of cherubic blondness and happy disposition. This girl resembled nothing of the sort. But something about her — this sickly, timid child who would not look her in the eyes — moved Despina in an inexplicable way.

Reaching out once more, tentatively, so as not to startle her, Despina let her fingers trace over the girl's shorn head. The girl flinched as if her touch had stung her, but a moment later, her striking green eyes drifted upward, shyly at first, then more boldly, meeting Despina's tearful ones, full of recognition. Anton had been right after all. Her heart *had* spoken; it had spoken as loudly as the church bells that had begun to strike somewhere in the distance.

For the next six weeks, Despina arrived at the orphanage well in advance of her appointed times. Mostly, she arrived alone, but when Anton could get away from the demands of the stores for a few hours, he came as well, and with the girl clamped firmly between them, they strolled to the neighboring park, just blocks away. In the wake of the violence, a somber peacefulness had settled over the city, and they could rest on a bench for a little while, share the fresh phyllo pastries that Despina had baked for the occasion the night before. Other times, they bought warm pretzels with poppy seeds from the street vendor at the park's entrance. Every time, Despina brought along a new book to read. As they delved into fairy tales and legends, the girl sat with her head leaning on Despina's shoulder, her hair now grown into a boyish pixie, the color of burnt copper. She did not speak, but Despina felt the need for words less and less. She was happy just to sit with her in Cismigiu Gardens, under the statues of famous poets and composers, and watch the swans glide across the lake. The days were becoming warmer, still crisp but with the sun comforting and soothing on their pale faces, and for a few brief moments, the devastation of the past winter seemed to belong to another world.

Years later, long after the changes that would come, the losses and new beginnings that would redefine her life in ways she never imagined possible, Despina would always return to that park bench, where for a glimpse in time, she had felt utterly and undeniably content despite the war that was raging in Europe. She would never be far from that glorious afternoon when, holding the girl's hand tightly in hers, she led her through the courtyard full of children and through the heavy wooden gates of Saint Paul's Orphanage for the last time.

5

Stefan was trying to find the most reliable wavelength on the radio dial, but the voice of the male announcer faded in and out, and he could not make out the precise words. He put on his wire-rimmed glasses and smoothed a few blond strands across his forehead out of habit to conceal his prematurely receding hairline. At barely forty, he looked and felt older than his years, much older than his wife, Maria, who had managed to maintain her youthfulness and boundless energy at only five years his junior. Just now, she was buzzing around him with fervent energy, dusting the mantel, moving around the potted plants on the windowsill, and rearranging plates inside the china cabinet as if her very life depended on it.

His wife had always been fastidious about her cleaning, but this had little to do with the house not being immaculate or objects not being in their proper place. She was doing it to keep busy and maintain some sense of normalcy, to focus on something other than the wretched sobs coming from the floor above. That woman's cries penetrated right through their ceiling, through every crevice of their house, at all hours of the day.

"How much longer will they be here?" Maria asked, knowing already that it was futile to ask, that once more she would not receive an answer. "I cannot take it a moment longer, I tell you."

Stefan looked up from his radio and shook his head as if to say, *Not now, we'll talk about it later.*

Maria sighed and went back to wiping down the champagne flutes. In all the years they had been married, she had always bent to his will, letting him control all the important decisions concerning their lives. She trusted him implicitly, for if there was one thing she knew about her husband, it was that he was a man with exceptional intellect and impeccable morals. In their ten years of marriage, he had been entrusted with life-altering decisions by some of Bucharest's most prominent families, who hired him to draft their wills and manage their investments and advise them in difficult personal matters. Each of their secrets he guarded faithfully, not simply because it was part of his job or because he was paid to do so but because he was a man of integrity.

However, Maria was fearful that this particular decision had been made with uncharacteristic haste. These were unpredictable and dangerous times. Stefan, better than anyone, knew that. Still, despite her endless protests, despite the enormous risk they were taking with the woman carrying on like that just above their living room, he would not send them away. Even when the woman howled as if someone was tearing out her limbs one by one, Maria could not get him to agree that it was all too much, that she needed him to defer to her on this one occasion when she had made her wishes so vehemently known.

"Please forgive me, Maria," Stefan said, coming up behind her and rubbing her shoulders. "I'm doing all I can, every day. But you know I can't put them out on the street. It would be like pulling the trigger myself."

She shook her head once more and closed the cabinet door softly. "I know," she whispered against the glass. "But we can't go on like this day after day. How much longer can they survive like this? No human being can live like that for long."

It had been difficult indeed to keep track of exactly how long the couple had been up there in the dark attic without fresh air, without bathing. There wasn't much food to part with these days, and still, Maria did whatever she could. Most days, she managed to scrounge up some fresh bread and canned vegetables, some leftover casserole that she placed near the door, along with a carafe of cold water and an occasional bottle of wine which always went untouched. At least three weeks, she thought, this had gone on. Three weeks of living in fear, of arguments that had divided her and Stefan like never before, even as she understood herself that the whole thing was really out of his hands, that he could not have acted any differently. Even as deep down inside, she loved him for his courage.

Days before, when the knock at the door had startled her out of a dead sleep, her first thought was that her husband was being called on to attend to some urgent legal matter. It would not have been the first time he'd been summoned in the middle of the night for a last-minute will revision, asked to come quickly for there wasn't a moment to spare. And so she had been utterly surprised when she opened the front door and found herself face-to-face not with the son or wife of some elderly client but with a couple who could not have been older than their midtwenties.

The woman was wearing no coat, only a thin cotton dress that was torn at the hem. It clung to her bare legs as the biting wind coiled around her slender figure, yet she made no effort to shield herself. At her side, a young blondish man was shivering in his shirtsleeves. His hands were caked in dirt, almost black, as if he had been stirring coals in a hearth.

"We are so very sorry to barge in on you at this hour," the man muttered softly. "I was hoping I might have a word with your husband, if he is still awake."

A car drove by, and Maria caught a better glimpse of the woman's face in the passing headlights. She noticed the anguish etched in her delicate features, the dullness in her round eyes fixed in the middle distance on nothing at all.

"Yes, of course." Maria smiled unsurely, a tremor passing through her as well.

Just then, Stefan appeared behind her in his flannel robe and slippers, adjusting his glasses. He squinted in the dim light, and a sudden pallor spread over his face.

"Come in, please, come with me," he said gravely, motioning for them to enter.

As they moved timidly past her, Maria thought for a moment that she recognized the young man. He looked vaguely familiar, although she couldn't quite place him. The woman, she was certain, she had never seen before tonight.

"Maria, would you mind bringing some hot tea to the study, please?" Stefan said, interrupting her quizzical stare as he led them up the steps.

She wanted to protest, to remind him that it was the middle of the night, but there was something in Stefan's voice that told her this was not debatable. When she returned shortly with porcelain cups and a steaming pot of tea, Stefan did not open the door, despite her insistent knocks. It was only when she pried it open herself and peeked inside the dimly lit room that she understood that whatever was unfolding before her was not business as usual. The young woman was sunk in the brown leather chair next to the bookshelves, with her head in her hands, resting on her knees, and her long auburn hair hung almost grazing the floor. She did not look up when Maria entered and placed the tray on the desk.

Later that night in her room, Maria could

still hear their voices as she tried desperately to fall asleep. But sleep wouldn't come. Hour after hour, endless thoughts raced through her head. She knew her husband had had to deal with many sensitive matters, to hide many truths under the veil of attorney-client privilege. But this she couldn't fathom. Whatever was going on under her roof at this hour had nothing at all to do with his job.

By the time Stefan had slipped into bed, the room was already bathed in the pink glow of early dawn. He made no particular effort to be quiet, for he guessed that Maria was still awake. Certainly, neither of them would get much sleep now.

Turning toward her, realizing that she expected him to say something, Stefan whispered next to her pillow: "I cannot explain the reasons why I must do this, but please do not try to talk me out of it."

"At the very least, I deserve an explanation," Maria muttered, her eyes fixed on a fissure in the crown molding over their bed. "Who are they? Why are they here, in our home, at this hour?"

"I will tell you everything," Stefan said. "I will tell you all there is very soon. But for now, I am asking you, I am begging you,

Maria, please let me try to help them. I owe his father my life, do you understand? *My life.*"

After an extended silence, during which Maria had not stirred or made a single gesture, he went on. "It will not be for long." It took every bit of effort not to blurt out the truth to her, to relate all that he knew about that poor man's family. But Stefan was certain that Maria had already figured out why the couple had shown up, looking the way they did, at half past midnight. "It's just for a short while, and then I will find a place for them to go. We just have to keep them here for a few days, a couple of weeks at most, until things simmer down out there. Until all this craziness has passed."

Maria could no longer restrain the anxiety that had been bubbling in the pit of her stomach all night. "Are you mad?" she shouted. "Have you completely lost your senses? How can you promise them such a thing? Don't you know that we will be arrested along with them, that we will be lined up against the wall and shot in the street, like stray dogs? Don't you know what will happen to our family, to anyone who is close to us? What will happen to you? None of your clients will ever come near you again."

In all their years together, she had never spoken to him in such a tone, but it mattered little now, for she no longer wished to be the sensible one, the one who never raised her voice, who never lost her temper. She did not care if the couple hiding out in her home could hear her, if the neighbors could make out her every word.

Stefan threw off the bedcovers and sprang out of bed. He began pacing the room, his feet shuffling softly over the thick Turkish rug. For a while, he said nothing.

"Listen, Maria," he blurted suddenly. "Do you hear her crying? Do you know why she hasn't stopped since the minute they got here?"

Still, Maria was silent. She wasn't going to give in to him this time.

"Because they have had to leave their only child behind," Stefan said slowly and evenly, delivering the one bit of information that he knew would change everything.

She stared at him, her hand going up to her mouth, then dropping away. Tears filled her eyes, and Stefan knew what she was thinking, that she was remembering her own child, their lovely boy, whom neither of them would lay eyes on again. Flooded with a sadness of his own, he sat next to her and took her hand in his.

"I will tell you, my darling," he whispered in a strangled voice. "I will tell you everything, if you will let me."

She listened silently while the hazy mauve light of dawn sharpened the silhouettes of barren trees and frost-covered rooftops across the street. As Stefan revealed the events that had led the young couple to their home, she saw at last what was at stake and knew that nothing would deter him from the path he had chosen.

6

It had begun the night before, just after supper, as the young couple was getting ready to turn in for the night. There were knocks at the door of their small flat. At first, the woman thought it might be the old lady next door looking to borrow something again. Some flour or a cup of sugar was the usual request, and she could never say no, even though money was scarce and they could barely make do with what they had themselves. It was late, and she figured if she did not answer, the old lady would eventually give up and go back to her apartment. But the knocks grew more insistent, until they could no longer be ignored. When at last she wrenched open the door, she was surprised to set eyes not on the woman next door but on a police officer in a dark trench coat and a cap pulled low over his brow.

"Good evening, ma'am," he said with a polite smile, removing his hat promptly. "Is your husband at home? If it's not too much trouble, I would like to speak with him for a few moments."

The woman regarded him cautiously through the cracked door, but his tone was courteous, almost apologetic, so she stepped aside and let him in. "Yes," she said hesitantly. "May I let him know your name, sir?"

"Good evening," the officer offered once more in place of his name, and it took her a moment to realize that her husband had appeared behind her. He had taken off his tie, and his hands were still wet from washing up after supper. Ambling toward them, he unrolled his shirtsleeves.

"Your wife was kind enough to invite me in. I hope it's all right, given the hour."

At the table, they settled like old friends sharing a glass of brandy after a hard day's work. The clock ticked behind them, in tune with the sound of their voices, even, uneventful. An hour had passed, maybe two, and neither had shifted an inch. Yet there was a fatigue that had overtaken her husband; he kept rubbing his eyes, and beads of perspiration had appeared on his forehead, on his upper lip. As they talked, she had finished cleaning the kitchen and had put their young daughter to bed. Now, in the other room, she was pacing the floor as quietly as she could, pretending that she, too, was asleep. There had been questions, endless questions, about her father-in-law, his former post in the Royal Parliament, how much her husband knew about the king's present arrangements. And that, she realized, could mean only one thing for them.

Mere months earlier, King Carol II's abdication from the throne had astonished all of Europe. He had run in a hail of bullets, chased out of the country like a hunted animal. Not that he had ever been popular with his people. But in the short time before his abdication, the people's distaste for Carol had intensified, fueled by his handing over of Romanian territories to Hungary and Russia without contest, without a single gun being fired. The thing that made the pot boil, however, causing riots to erupt on the streets, was his unwillingness to give up Magda Lupescu, his mistress of twenty years, for whom he would forgo his country and honor and rightful queen, the mother of his only child. People hurled obscenities and insults at them, and children threw stones at the royal convoy as their cars sped hastily through the streets of Bucharest, Magda and Carol hidden from view in the rear seat of their Rolls-Royce. *Death to the Jewish whore!* they shouted angrily as the two ran up the steps of the palace, where Magda had been living for years, a reigning queen in all but name.

When shots were fired at the palace windows, it had all become too much. Packing just bare necessities, Carol and Magda fled in the night on a train to Spain with just a few trunks and a handful of loyal friends. Romania was then run by Hitler's right-hand man, General Antonescu, with young Prince Michael a mere puppet king and Antonescu's Legionnaires, in their mad quest for blood, murdering sixty of Carol's former aides and turning the city into a battleground.

"I have already answered all of your questions, officer," she heard her husband say. "My father has never discussed professional matters with anyone, especially not with me."

"What about the excursions you took to the country when you were a boy? It is a known fact, sir, that your father was a childhood friend of Magda Lupescu. Was she there, on these long vacations?"

"Who are you speaking of?"

"The king's mistress, sir. The woman who

helped your father obtain a position in the cabinet, who brought other Jews like herself under his wing, who cost him the throne! Do you mean to tell me that you do not know who she is?"

The officer's voice was no longer restrained. It was just short of a yell. Even so, the young man regarded him quietly. "I do not remember any such excursions," he said. "I am sorry."

Leaning back in his chair, the officer loosened the top button on his collar and took a gulp of his tea. In the downturned corners of his forced smile, the young man saw it all: the disdain for his family, the hatred, the frustration with this interrogation that was going nowhere.

"You will need to come with me to the precinct. Just protocol, you understand. But we have a few more questions. Should take no more than an hour."

Nodding faintly, the young man looked down at his hands. There was no point in arguing, it would only make matters worse, so he stood without any resistance and began making his way to the door. But then the words he prayed would not be uttered were there, out in the open, hitting him squarely in the back.

"Your wife and daughter, they need to

come, too."

"Why?" he asked, not turning, not daring to. "They have done nothing. Our daughter is only three . . ."

They were beyond conversation now; it was done with, and he heard it in the silence that followed, in the sharpness of the officer's steps as he approached the window and motioned to the patrol car below.

"By all means, we will come with you," he said now. His head was spinning, and the panic that had risen inside him caused him to speak too fast. It took an effort to slow down, breathe normally. "If I could have just a few minutes to explain the situation to my wife. . . . She gets extremely agitated, you see. I think my talking to her first might make our visit to the precinct a little easier." He clasped his hands in a pleading gesture that implied, *We are both men, we understand how delicate women can be.*

The officer retreated from the window, looked at his watch. He did not like being in these situations. He much preferred marching ordinary Jews out of their homes. But this particular family had to be handled with care; those were his orders. Besides, the last thing he wanted to witness was the hysterics of this man's wife. Nothing displeased him more than a scene.

"You have ten minutes. Starting now," he spat, calculating that an hour from now, if she agreed to come along peacefully, he could be sipping his drink at the corner bar. "I'll be right outside." Then, placing his hat on his head, he marched out of the flat, slamming the door behind him.

There was disarray in his desk drawer — too many things, envelopes and bills that were still to be paid, a letter opener that sliced along his finger, making him wince. *Lei.* He felt them, a large stack of them, right where he'd placed them in a hidden compartment, there for an emergency or a last-minute trip, never something like this. He shoved them hastily into his shirt pockets, his pant pockets, too, inside his socks.

There was a look when he burst through the bedroom door. A brief, knowing look, no words, as he lifted the little girl out of her bed. From the corner of his eye, he saw his wife grab a shawl, a bonnet for the girl, her blanket. He saw her look around the room for her shoes, settling on the slippers. And then they were running. With his daughter in his arms, they were running toward the kitchen and out the back door leading to the service stairs, and his heart was pounding, pounding like it never had before in all his twenty-seven years.

It was warm in the boiler room. Warm and damp, and the water heater was churning along, which was a good thing, for it offered some insulation, cocooned them in a strange way. They had been lucky, given the circumstances, downright blessed that the guards at the front gate had their backs turned and were laughing, smoking a cigarette, as the three slithered right past them into the bowels of the building. But now that they were here, the momentary feeling of safety was quickly dissipating. They were not safe, not by a long shot, with the guards back on the lookout and the little girl whimpering in her mother's arms.

"It's all right," she crooned, rocking her, smoothing her face. "It's all right." And the way she smiled seem to indicate this was only a game, make-believe that they would laugh about later by the fireplace. But when her fingers touched her lips and went flat, there was something that appeared in those tiny, wise eyes, and the girl knew that she had to keep quiet.

From a dusty corner, he dragged a few wooden crates and stacked them high against the wall. It seemed desperate, unlikely to work, yet there seemed to be no

69

other choice, no other way out. Thus, he was almost surprised when he climbed on the very last one, stretching his arms as if he meant to reach for the sky, that he could touch the edge of the basement window. Wiping away dusty cobwebs, he cranked it open, careful not to make any noise. The opening was barely wide enough for a child to slip through, yet he tried not to linger on this fact as he wedged his way out one centimeter at a time, grabbing the iron bars on the other side of the window. As he collapsed on the sidewalk above, he had to remind himself that this was no great victory. He had to act quickly.

"Give her to me," he whispered down to his wife. "Give her to me now."

Through the cavity, he groped for his daughter, her tiny arms and soft little body, the hair so long and lush for her young age. When he pulled at her, a little too roughly, he heard her cry out, and his heart nearly shattered, but he did not relent. The blood was pounding in his temples, and he thought, *We will be caught now, we will be shot, she will not see her fourth year.* He feared this with every fiber in his body as he yanked her through with one final tug. Then his wife was out, too, and they were together again, huddled against one another, breaths and arms intertwined, trembling in the darkness.

Crouching in shadows, they fled, crawling along alleyways, interminable walls. The police were still everywhere, blowing on whistles, shouting orders, urging others to get moving, to move faster. The screech of tires and car doors slamming shut echoed from invisible cul-de-sacs like the peaks of a mountain, and from behind drawn curtains, a few faces peered through, trying to make out the commotion below. Someone opened a window to get a better look, and he had no choice but to pull his wife and his daughter into the nearest entryway.

An apartment building drew them into its shelter, one that he'd known from his childhood days, with a rusty old elevator that had not worked in decades. Even then, seeking refuge from his friends in a game of hide-and-seek, he recalled it was hardly dependable; often the residents groaned and cursed and yelled for the superintendent to come rescue them from the death trap of a cage as he hid in the alcove beneath the shaft. No one, he recalled, could ever find him there. No one even knew the alcove existed. Yet it was not as warm as the boiler room, this secret hideaway of his youth, nor was it as comforting. The only source of warmth here was an old woolen blanket that he found in a broom closet, smelling of gasoline and full of moth holes.

"We can't stay here," he said after the frenzy outside seemed to die down a bit. "We have to move on. They will be back, they may already be on their way now, and they will comb every square inch, every entranceway, every home. They will interrogate every neighbor they might suspect of harboring us. We have to get across town. Tonight."

To his surprise, his wife did not seem to hear him. She was crouched into a ball on the floor, rubbing her feet, her arms, hidden underneath a tumble of hair.

"Darling," he said, "darling," but she did not move, and he stepped back from her in utter exasperation. When he lifted her upward, she slid from his grasp like a fish, making a tiny sound. He grabbed her shoulders then and shook her forcefully, so much more than he intended or thought he was capable of. *"Please,"* he implored. "Please move. Get on your feet."

He did not wish to frighten her. This was his love, his girl, the woman he'd started a family with. Yet he was no longer a husband himself, no longer a man. He was a cornered dog, wounded, gasping for his own last breath.

"Get up. Now! Do you understand that if we don't move, we will not live to see the light of tomorrow?"

"All right," she said at last, and there was nothing but hollowness in her voice. "All right, we will do as you want, *as you always want.*" Then she stood, smoothing out her torn dress, and reeled away from him, walking into the darkness.

Back on the street, the little girl began to whimper again, which only made him pick up his pace. Normally, he would have stopped to wait for his woman, but if he walked ahead, he knew she would follow, and it was the only way to keep them going. Another siren came dangerously close, and they ducked into yet another lobby, this one an expansive, elegant one with a spiral staircase and a beveled-glass entrance. They had to put more distance behind them, but she wouldn't stop crying, his little girl, her tiny chest rising and falling, her tears wetting his neck. His wife, too, could not go much farther, that much was clear. On the stairs now, she lay bent at the waist, her arms splayed out to the sides in a stance of crucifixion.

"I cannot go on," she sobbed. "I want to

die here."

He inched toward her, wanting to comfort her, inundated all of a sudden with remorse for being so rough with her, so unrelenting. But his will was leaving him, too, his legs felt like lead, his arms were numb from the cold and from the weight of the child he'd carried for so many hours. He could not remember how long he had been thirsty and cold. And this was only a glimpse of what was to come. He envisioned himself on the streets of Bucharest with his wife weak and broken at his side, his little girl starving, freezing to death. Where would they get food, shelter? Who would take them in? They were vagabonds, runaways. Soon their stride would slow, their resolve would burn down like a candle, their bodies would stop moving. And one morning, maybe tomorrow or the day after, someone would stumble upon three mounds in the middle of the stark and frozen city, three heaps of lifeless flesh lining the streets like so many others.

"My love." He looked away. How could he look at her, knowing what he was about to say? He balled his fists and took in a breath, choked back his own tears. "We have to try to give her a chance. A small chance but *something*." He crouched down next to his wife, forced her hands away from her tearstained face. "If we could leave her here, in this lobby, there is a good chance that someone will find her. Then we can keep moving, going much farther on our own. We will come back for her in a couple of days when things are . . . safer."

Only confusion rose in her eyes. Her mouth twisted, wordlessly, and she laughed, or at least he thought she did. "What did you say?"

Despite the iciness of her palms, he brought them to his own face, sank his cheeks into them. The bile had risen in him so abruptly he thought he would retch.

"Please, please, just listen. No one knows who she is, who *we* are. If we leave her here in this lobby, she can stay warm for a while longer, until someone, maybe one of the residents, finds her. No one will turn away a little girl. No one could turn their back on her, and she'll have shelter and food and a bed to sleep in for the night, maybe a few nights. Just until we can figure out a plan."

His wife's eyes were no longer uncomprehending; they were dark, filled with rage. For a moment, he thought she would strike him.

"If the police or the Guard get us tonight, there's no chance," he went on, undeterred. "No chance for *her*. You know how it ends for people like us, don't you?" His voice was splintering, breaking apart. "I know a place we might go. There is someone I trust, a good man, a friend of my father's. He lives on Boulevard Bratiani, not far from here. He may agree to take us in for a few days. But he will not take us in with a child. If she made a sound, if she even so much as whimpered, it would mean the end for them and for us, too. We will come back for her in a few days."

Then there were no more words, for he was weeping alongside his wife as the girl watched, wide-eyed and silent, her small fist wrapped around the hem of her mother's muddied skirt. In his wife's eyes, the man saw things that he had never seen before. It was the look of the dying, of someone still here but with the lifeblood draining out of her veins. And yet there was something else, too. For an instant, he recognized it, that same shred of hope that had risen above all else in his own wretched heart, a trace of resignation in the path that left no other options open.

7

June 1941

Anton sat by the fire in the late evening, with the day's newspaper in his lap, his nightcap all but untouched. Romania, he'd just read in the headlines, had joined Nazi Germany in the invasion of the Soviet Union, delivering equipment and oil and more troops to the Eastern Front than all of Germany's other allies combined. There was no turning back now that Romanian forces were fully immersed in the fighting in Ukraine and Bessarabia and, closer to the heart of the bear, in Stalingrad.

On the glass coffee table, the reflected flames shimmered, warming the maroon walls to a soft red, drenching the room in a welcoming amber light. Yet despite the quietness of the hour, which he'd always cherished, an intense restlessness had settled in the depths of his being. *This is the last oasis,* he thought, imagining what was to come now that Romania was no longer neutral in this godforsaken war. Since the country had taken the side of Germany, it would only be a matter of time before the Allies would retaliate and bombs would fall on Bucharest — of that he was certain.

This country of ours, he thought, *has always been in the crossfire between two worlds, a threshold between Russia and the rest of the world.* This time, however, it would be for Germany and Hitler's vision that innocent people in his country would die. And without a rightful king, who would protect it in the days ahead?

The Legionnaires, despite being forced to disband in the aftermath of the Bucharest massacre, were back on the streets, inciting a new rampage in the city of Iasi, this time with the full support of the army. No one knew when it would end, how much worse it would get. The stories of last January alone made Anton recoil in disgust and feel ashamed to call himself a Romanian, a God-fearing human being.

Lately, he couldn't sleep thinking about the things he had heard; he could not expunge those images from his mind: homes stormed in the Jewish quarters, women raped in front of their husbands and children, men forced to write suicide notes before being shot in the street like stray dogs. Dozens, perhaps hundreds, were killed in Baneasa Forest in northern Bucharest, and the next morning, gypsies pounced on their naked bodies to extract gold from their teeth.

One account in particular made his knees buckle from horror, causing him to slump onto the sidewalk in front of the tobacco shop where he had stopped for cigarettes. It would remain with him for the rest of his life, like a permanent stain on his soul. Inside the shop, he had overheard a man telling the clerk that a group of Jews had been arrested and brought to the municipal slaughterhouse, where they had been tortured and then hung on the cattle hooks and left to die.

Anton folded the newspaper and set it down next to him. He needed to read no further, for he could almost predict what was to come. This was no longer about the export of Romanian oil, which had for several years supported Hitler's military efforts. Tens of thousands of Romanians would die now, not only on the Eastern Front but here at home. Even here in the nation's capital, they would die for the Führer.

He needed time to think, to figure out

how he could stay ahead of the changes that were coming their way. For if there was one thing that he needed to do, that he felt was his *duty,* it was to preserve his and Despina's newly found happiness. It had been a few short months since they had formed a family, and he could not remember a time when their lives had been more content. They were parents now, parents of a lovely and timid little girl who completed their lives in ways that he never imagined possible. But with the war at their back, there was no telling at all what the future might hold.

Most certainly, they would have to cut back on their extravagances. For that he was nearly alone to blame, for his main personal weakness was his tendency to overspend. For a while, at least, they would have to limit their parties and trips to the French tailor who fashioned his suits in the latest European styles and to the shops where he purchased the latest fur stoles and hats from Vienna for Despina, as well as expensive gifts for her sisters and their children. He would have to start thinking about gradually shutting down three of his stores and keeping open only the one in Piazza Romana, where he had worked from the time he was a young boy and where people in the neighborhood still greeted him by his first name.

With growing uneasiness, Anton thought about the priceless stamp collection he had amassed over the years, realizing it might be risky to leave it in his safe at the store. He would have to bring it home, where he could keep it near. His most prized stamp, the famous Boar Head, was alone worth more than all their other assets combined, more than the rental homes, their weekend home at Lake Baneasa, even his three beloved horses that were housed at the Bucharest Hippodrome. Of all these things, it was the stamp collection that meant the most to him, the one possession he could not risk losing.

Upstairs, his wife was sleeping peacefully, her body lost in a sea of pillows. He thought of her now, how happy she'd become in such a short time, how carefree despite the fact that she now was a mother. For him, too, the girl's presence had been a balm to his heart, and he couldn't wait to get home in the evenings, to break loose from the demands of the day, just to feel her arms around his neck. Even at the store, when Despina dropped her off in the afternoons, she was all he could think about, knowing that she was slumbering under his desk with a stuffed animal pressed to her chest, comforted by the comings and goings, the laughter and banter he exchanged with his customers. And the piano. Nothing had prepared him for her reaction when she received that old Steinway, a fairly beat-up baby grand which he had picked up for a bargain at an antiques shop and set up in the parlor as a surprise to unveil for her when she and Despina arrived home later that day.

There had been no overt display of emotion. She had not looked at him in gratitude or smiled but simply ambled over to it and sat on the red velvet stool. Under her raised hands, the keys had sparkled, pearly and just slightly yellowed in the sunlight, but no notes emerged from the open lid. Only light, featherlike movements caressed the ivory keys, her fingers moving from left to right and meeting in the middle, then higher, over the narrow black ones.

"For me?" she had said, looking up at him, and Anton realized he had never seen such delight on a human face and that those were the only words she had ever uttered in their presence.

But she did start to talk after that, to get her voice back gradually. She began asking for something to drink at dinner and then if she could go to Cismigiu Gardens and if he would buy her an ice cream from the corner vendor. Slowly, she was blossoming before his very eyes, her smile wider, her eyes more expressive, the life back in her gestures, a little more each day. Although she was too young for formal piano lessons, he nevertheless hired the best teacher he could find, for it became clear that day that she had a special gift, one he meant to foster.

That little girl was the reason he rose in the morning, and Despina smiled more, too, as they sat late in the evening by the fireplace, enjoying a nightcap, warm and content in each other's arms, knowing their lives were complete at last.

No, he could not risk losing it now. *What can I do, what must I do, to protect them?* he thought, knowing deep down that it was a question without answer, that despite his best intentions and focused efforts, he couldn't really fight whatever the war would throw in their path. The eye of the storm was at his door once again, as it had been many years ago when he was no more than a boy.

Anton had not always been blessed with unabashed charm and prosperity. He came into the world in a two-room cottage on a vast estate in the heart of the Romanian countryside, where his father was employed as an administrator. His mother, a petite and fragile woman who brought in a little extra money teaching the village children arithmetic in the back of the local church, regarded his arrival as an additional burden more than a blessing. It was perhaps for this reason that from the time he was six years old, Anton learned to take care of himself. He prepared his own breakfast, fed the chickens, and swept the front steps. He brought buckets of water home from the well at the end of the dirt road where their two acres stopped and the rest of the land began. After that, he was free to roam the hills that stretched out to the horizon, to rest in the shade of overgrown grapevines, to pluck apples and pears from trees whose branches bent invitingly toward him, heavy with the fruit of summer.

Finding himself with little to do in the afternoons, Anton often wandered up to the big house. The landlord, a widower in the twilight of his life, traveled nearly year-round, leaving his vast home in the care of an old housemaid whose only duties were to water the plants and dust the few pieces of furniture that weren't perpetually covered with sheets. And she, perhaps more than

Anton, was always eager for company.

"Come up, come up, I have something for you!" She would wave at him enthusiastically from an open window as Anton ambled up the graveled driveway, kicking pebbles in his path.

By the time he stepped through the curved oak door, a glass of lemonade would be waiting for him on the veranda and sometimes a piece of bread and marmalade or a scoop of sherbet, which he loved the most. Yet of all the special treats that awaited him inside the villa, none compared to the cool solitude of the master's library. Even though he could read little, there was nothing Anton loved more than spending the long hours leading to supper browsing through the hundreds of books lining the walls, taking in the scent of yellowing pages, feeling the surface of leather-bound covers beneath his fingertips.

The summers were long and languid, and days passed quickly this way until he was nearly ten. In the early months of 1907, just a week shy of Anton's birthday, a peasant uprising erupted in a nearby province. Seemingly overnight, the revolt spread across the countryside, and his father spoke of going away for a while, at least until the peasants' grievances had been worked out and their fury had simmered down. But a few days later, when the army was called in and began firing on the peasants, things grew out of hand.

On the estate where Anton lived, an angry mob marched toward the big house with raised rifles and pitchforks. From their own front porch, Anton's father saw them coming over the hillside, and a singular thought formed in his mind: he had not seen his son since noon. Grabbing his pistol, he headed up the dirt road leading to the villa.

Inside the library, Anton heard his name called out. It was just one time, and for a moment he thought he might have imagined it. Still, he set down his book and went out to the veranda. At first he saw nothing. Then his heart began thundering, and his legs grew weak.

At the edge of the graveled driveway, his father lay motionless in the grass. He didn't move when Anton ran to him and shook him gently, then with ferocious determination. His face was down in the gravel, and dark rivulets trickled alongside his neck, staining the collar of his linen shirt. When Anton finally managed to turn him over, his father's eyes sent him reeling backward. They were open, vacant. Something permanent fractured inside the boy. *Don't leave me,* was his only thought, but it was already too late.

Two months later, his mother became gravely ill and succumbed quickly to the fever that had already overtaken half the village. *Anton,* she whispered as he leaned over his mother's quivering lips. To Anton, it sounded like the wind whistling through the cornfields in the middle of a rainstorm. Then she was gone.

He had never been able to shake that vision of her from his head. He thought of her when he ate the last scraps of bread from the pantry, the last of the potato stew that had grown stale and slightly mildewed. When the food was gone, he thought about her when he fed on berries and mushrooms that he collected from bushes in the fields, knowing she would protest, for they might have been poisonous. He thought about his mother when he bathed in the small stream behind their cottage, washing himself with a block of soap that she had made just weeks before in an iron tub in their front yard.

It was only when hunger became greater than his dignity that he began sneaking up to the villa, looking for leftover scraps that the landlord sometimes left behind on the terrace, bread crusts and half-eaten pastries, browned fruit oozing onto a hot plate in the sun. He foraged through the garbage pail just outside the kitchen door, hoping to find more of the same. But he was embarrassed by his appearance and did not wish to cross paths with the housekeeper, so he only went up there when his hunger was so intense that his vision blurred and his body trembled.

One day, the old housemaid saw him sneaking around to the back of the house, and she gasped. Instantly, she knew that if she didn't help him, the boy's days on earth would not be many. He would die from scurvy or from eating poison berries, but the end was inevitable. That night, she couldn't sleep. She tossed and turned, and by the time the sun peeked over the horizon, she had made her decision.

Ten-year-old Anton was taken in as a box boy in a stationery shop in Bucharest that belonged to a Hungarian lady, a childhood friend of the housemaid who had recently lost her husband and was in need of help. In exchange for fifteen hours of work each day, Anton was given a cot to sleep on in the back room, two changes of clothes, and enough food to get him back on his feet. Every morning, he rose at four o'clock sharp to mop the floors and rinse the sidewalk, to sweep up the entranceway or shovel the snow that had collected in front of the store. Later he made deliveries on foot, carrying boxes and crates on icy boulevards in the dead of winter, in the suffocating, humid heat of the city summers. He developed muscles he never knew he had and along with them a spirit that was unbendable. He learned how to smile politely at patrons, how to make himself trusted with any amount of money. In short, he became skilled in making himself indispensable.

It wasn't until ten years into his apprenticeship that Anton began working in the front of the store. By then, the old lady's hands shook so badly that she couldn't scribble out a receipt or pour herself a cup of coffee, and she'd come to rely on Anton for even these simple tasks. Her vision had also begun to fail, and soon she could barely count the change in the cash register. That was when she began teaching Anton about bookkeeping and supply inventory, about managing cash flow and staying on top of vendors so that not one delivery came late or went unpaid. And all of it he did flawlessly. Anton was twenty years old, and business was booming.

Anton had never shared the details of his

childhood with anyone, not even his wife. Despina had asked several times if they could take a trip to his childhood village, but he'd refused her adamantly. The past was best left alone, buried along with his parents under the patch of wild grass at the back of his childhood cottage. What good would it do for her to know the bleak details of his early life?

His life truly had begun with her. God had given them the precious gifts of love, prosperity, and promise and so many things that he never thought possible. He would not dwell again on those days long ago, when in a short space of time everything that was dear to him had slipped away from his grasp.

8

They had been living in the attic for six months now. When she had come out of her shock, her debilitating stupor, when she had wiped away the tears long enough to look outside the attic window, she had started counting the days. She began marking them in a yellowed notebook she found in a cardboard box along with some old newspapers. Tick after tick, day after day, the hands of an invisible clock turned endlessly. At least it gave her something to do. She had long ago stopped reading the books that Maria had left for her up here. Now she simply sat on the lumpy mattress among dusty trunks and discarded furniture and wrote frantically in her notebook. The signs of a new season — changes in temperature, the lengthening of days, the chirping of birds, the blooming of cherry trees — were all meticulously recorded. Her husband just paced endlessly, traversing the length of the attic to and fro, day and night, the hardwood planks groaning under his bare feet.

"Stop it!" she would shout, glaring at him. "Stop it, you are making me crazy!"

Several times he paused and turned to her as if he meant to say something but ended up just staring at her. As the days passed, there was less and less of him. He lacked fresh air and good food. He lacked life. She saw no emotion on his face now, nothing other than the wild, cornered look of a stray dog. Perhaps he deserved it. Perhaps that was what their daughter had felt when they did not return for her that night, when she realized that she had been left alone in a city ablaze.

Needing food less, she let him have most of the bread and butter, the occasional ham or block of cheese they found outside the door. They never knew when the provisions would be there next or how much longer they would continue. Maria came up less frequently now, and when she did, she always knocked on the door softly, as if she was afraid to disturb them. As if she was a hotel maid dropping off room service.

"Leave it!" the woman would shout from her side of the door.

She did not intend to be ungrateful or rude. But there was little grace left in her heart. There was no strength for a polite exchange or a display of proper manners. She felt less like the woman she had been with each passing day, feeling her humanity eroding in that dark attic.

One morning, she awakened and simply did not care if Maria and Stefan put them out on the street. She envisioned herself running back to their scorched neighborhood, shouting out her daughter's name in the alleyways. Shouting at the top of her lungs, not minding if the Death Squad got her. At least that would be real, it would be honest. She wouldn't have to hide out like a hunted animal in a dark hole.

Her husband barely spoke now, but the silence between them came as a blessing. She hated him, hated what he had convinced her to do of her own free will. There was no solidarity for him and her anymore. Not in this lifetime. He could go to hell for all she cared.

Days and nights strung together interminably. There was no beginning, no end. She had almost forgotten why they were here, she had forgotten that she was still alive. She felt like a corpse buried in a tomb, in this attic from which she would never see the light of day. Then one evening, something changed.

The knock came just after suppertime. It was stronger than usual, more urgent, so she went to open the door. When she cracked it open as wide as the chain would allow, Stefan stood there holding some papers over his head.

"I have good news," he announced cheerfully. He was still in his work suit, and his hair was slightly disheveled as if after a long day. "Please, let me in. I must speak to you now. I must speak to you both."

With his well-meaning demeanor, he entered quickly, though when his eyes roamed over the space and he spotted his young friend on the mattress, the ruddiness of his cheeks drained away.

"I have great news," he repeated in a voice less buoyant. "You are leaving. In a couple of days. I was able to get you papers. Look."

Although the papers were not legible under the weak light, Stefan waited with an outstretched hand as the young man rose to his feet and came over to take them. He watched him amble back to his corner, crouch over them in a sharp, almost feral movement, then flip them front to back with only mild interest.

"Your poor father," Stefan went on explaining, "God rest his soul, still has friends in this town, still has some influence. And the money you gave me, it was also very helpful. I'm afraid there isn't anything left. I've had to use every last bit." He paused. "In two nights, there is a train departing for Geneva, from Gara de Nord. I'm afraid we cannot waste any time. We don't know when the borders will shut down, how much time we have left. Rumor has it that the Allies are going to bomb Bucharest any day. It could be tomorrow for all we know."

The entire thing had been delivered practically in one breath. "You have to leave on that train," he went on more sternly, emphasizing each word. "It's the only way out. Switzerland is a neutral country; it will be safe for you there. I have arranged for your tickets already. Under your new names."

Still, there was no response, no gesture of any kind. It was as if he'd spoken a different language.

"Look," he began again, "I'm sure that —" and then he was suddenly interrupted.

"I'm not leaving without my daughter. You of all people ought to know that. We have to find her first."

The way she had spoken, as if she was challenging him to a duel, caused a new surge of anxiety to stab at his insides. "I'm afraid that's not possible." He coughed in his fist. "Not right now. You will not be able to board that train with her. The papers are for you and him alone."

"I'm not going without her," she told him again in that defiant tone. "I will die here in your attic, I will die in the streets at the hands of the Death Squad, but I will find her. I'm not leaving the city without her."

It was too hot up there all of a sudden, and he had to yank off his tie, crumple it in his pocket. This was precisely what he had feared, the whole thing coming apart at the seams, after all he'd wagered for their safety, after all he'd risked. It occurred to him that if he became too forceful with her, she might do something foolish. He feared she might burst through the attic door and run out into the street. He pictured her throwing herself out of the window.

"You will come back for her later, when it's safe. When all this madness, this fury, has passed. I will help you. This is my promise. As long as I live, I will help you."

"How do you know that I will ever be able to come back? That the fury, as you call it, will pass? How will she be safe, a small child alone in a city where people like her, like *us,* are rounded up and killed by the hundreds? How do I know that I will ever see her again?"

"Please listen to me," Stefan implored. "I

cannot pretend to know how difficult this must be for you. But even with the new papers, there is still a good chance that you will not make it past the border. The noose is tighter than ever. The Legionnaires have gone mad again, and it isn't just them this time but Antonescu's full army. Every train is being inspected, especially ones headed out of the country, every identity card looked at with a magnifying glass. I've done all I could, but the papers, as you know, are not authentic. If you are caught, there will be no hope. No hope for her, either."

Again he paused, wiped the sweat from his forehead. How could he put in plain words that they may be heading to certain death and that still it was their best and only option? How could he ask them to sacrifice their only child, knowing too well what that would bring in its aftermath?

"If she is on that train without papers, she will most surely be taken away. And you two along with her. Do you understand me?"

The woman crouched on the floor and began to sob. "No. I will not go. We will all die together. Here, in Bucharest."

Every fiber in his body told him at this point to be quiet. There was nothing more to say, nothing that he *could* say without a breach of a different kind. He had been sworn to secrecy, and it extended much further than this wretched event; it branched to the heart of his family. But the way this woman looked, crouched there on the plank floor of his attic, made his chest tighten with sorrow, and as tears sprang to his own eyes, he could hold back no longer.

"I think I know where she is," he said finally. "I believe she will be safe. But only if you can let her go."

9

Gara de Nord was far busier than they had expected. Half the city's population seemed to have descended on it at once, even though the sky was just beginning to lighten over the glass-and-steel cupola. Families with babies and young children, soldiers in uniform, peasant ladies bundled in shawls, and men and women in elegant clothing filled nearly every platform. Children chased one another around mountains of trunks as their parents fanned themselves impatiently with pamphlets, ironing out details about their trips. The scent of diesel mixed with that of faint perspiration and freshly baked *covrigi* was almost too much to bear at such an early hour.

Stefan walked slightly ahead of the couple, ushering them through the swelling mass, past the endless row of ticket booths, vendors selling newspapers, gypsies who had queued up along the platforms with buckets of flowers. It was not easy for them to follow; all those months in the attic had atrophied their muscles, and there was a fragility about them that screamed of suffering and illness, despite the expensive suit Stefan had forced his young friend to wear and the dress of green velvet that, although one size too big, flowed elegantly around the wife's tiny frame.

He stopped and turned only slightly, waiting for them to catch up, pretending to be checking his watch. Now that they were here, his own uneasiness was mounting by the moment, yet he could not risk showing it. No doubt, if he did, they would abandon the plan and try to go back for the girl. Then all hope would be lost for them, and for him and Maria, too. Trying to block this last thought, he had picked up his pace again, when suddenly his own legs seemed to weaken, bringing him gradually to a stop.

"Please stand aside! Make way, please!"

The voice, when it cut through the crowd, had the effect of a blade, parting it in two. There were boots and the usual uniforms and a ripple in the air he knew well. A station patrol pushed open a swing gate to let the officers pass. Everyone watched as one of them flipped open the top of his holster and extracted a small black pistol. He motioned to the other men to do the same, and the whole troop jumped onto a train that had already begun to roll out of the station.

Forcing air into his lungs, Stefan reached inside his pocket and extracted the tickets.

"Platform six. Here, give me this," he said as calmly as he could manage, taking the valise from his young friend. He could not help but notice how ashen he looked, how a gust of wind would be able to knock him down. He had to get them on that Geneva coach. He had to do it now, before it was too late, and so he began walking again, trying to steady his own heart, his own step, even though he himself felt like running.

Near the edge of the concrete strip, he set down the suitcase and stood there with his hands in his pockets, whistling softly under his breath. Only minutes remained before they were to board, yet he had never felt time stretch with such stubbornness. There was nothing more that he could do for them now, except force himself to look ordinary, to keep calm. They were just an average family bidding their good-byes, he had to remind himself, just an average family. There were no other officers — the platform was clear — and he felt himself relax for a second, or maybe it was just numbness.

101

"Remember what we talked about," he said finally, keeping his voice low so that only the young man could hear him. He felt the thinness beneath the old jacket when his hand touched his shoulder, when his other descended further to deposit the tickets and a roll of cash into his pocket. "Remember what to do with that money. If it comes to that," he whispered, and pulled quickly away.

He watched them as they moved from his peripheral vision, inching toward the steaming locomotive. With effort, they climbed the steps, panting a little, pausing on each one. The woman was the first to disappear inside the car, and when she did, her husband turned, and a flicker of a smile passed over his face. It was a smile of gratitude, but there was so much more in the young man's eyes, so much more that Stefan had to look away. And then he was gone.

Pressing his hat to his chest, Stefan stood still a while, thinking that he would never see them again, that this last image of them would imprint itself on his mind forever. As passengers swarmed past him with their trunks and packages, he began moving slowly against the crowd, trying to catch a last glimpse of them. He finally spotted them in one of the end compartments. The woman was staring ahead, and her husband's arm lay limply around her. They did not see him wave from down below.

You are free, Stefan whispered to himself, feeling a knot form in his throat and, strangely, a smile. *Free.*

On the outside steps of the station, he loosened his tie and sat down. The sky was gray, with an indigo heaviness, and he imagined what the weather might be like in Geneva. In less than a day, his friends would be there, in their new city, in safety.

He picked up his hat and stood up. Never before had he missed home more or wanted to get back there so badly. His eyes traveled across the busy intersection, scanning for a cab, hoping that one might be dropping off passengers. And then he saw them.

For a moment, he thought it was him they were coming for, to arrest or shoot him right there on the spot. But then they marched right past him, up the row of stairs, and into the building. One of them brushed his shoulder accidentally.

"Pardon," he said, as he kept up his ascent.

But Stefan had come to a halt, and his arms had fallen to his sides. For a while he thought he might be able to distract them somehow, but he couldn't think of a way;

he couldn't breathe or move.

He ran instead. Not caring how he might look now, he ran after them back into the station, a vise gripping his chest. He thought he should shout out, but what exactly he didn't know, and then it was too late. The officer who looked to be in charge was already inside the train marked for Geneva, advancing along the corridor that connected one car to the next. "Papers out, please," was the last thing Stefan heard though an open window as the train began rolling forward with a loud clang.

10

January 1944

The first day of the year turned out to be the coldest one in nearly half a decade. The streets were vacant, for no one dared venture outside in the frigid wind that lashed and whipped about so fiercely that one could hardly draw a breath or take a step against it. Only the intermittent clatter of empty streetcars and the scrape of shovels clearing ice from the sidewalks sounded distantly beyond the frost-encrusted windows and bolted doors.

In the firelit drawing room, seven-year-old Natalia was displaying the fruit of her work, a Chopin piece she'd been practicing for the better part of the year. She loved the way it carried her on its wings, the way she could rise and dip with each shifting rhythm, though today more than once, she'd made a mistake and had to start again from the beginning. Normally, it would have

105

nicked her pride and made her want to scream with frustration, but at the moment, she wasn't concerned about playing perfectly, only playing. As long she did, her parents would keep talking, and she could eavesdrop on their exchange by the fireplace, their voices for once above a monotone whisper.

"Let's go to the Black Sea for a couple of weeks," her father suggested, lifting the poker iron to stoke the flames. "We could rent a small house right on the shore, ride horses on the beach, go on walks. It would be good for Talia."

"You want us to leave the city in the middle of winter, Anton? Why, that's just simply insane!" Her mother's voice rose abruptly, no longer restrained.

With shoulders perfectly squared, she glided over the thick Persian rug and stopped in front of the window. There was something across the street that caught her gaze, past the flurry of snowflakes hitting the glass at an angle. Silently, he came up behind her and, circling her slim waist, drew her near. Her tense features softened a little, giving way to a faint smile that she couldn't suppress despite her best efforts. As she let her head drop against his chest, her jet-black hair cascaded like a tide pool of ink against the immaculate whiteness of his button-down shirt.

"Why do we need to go on vacation?" Natalia dared to ask. She had stopped playing abruptly, and they both turned to her, startled, her father with patient tenderness, her mother with a look of surprise. "Is it because the Allies are going to bomb us?"

"Where did you hear this, Talia?" her mother said, paling a little, as if it had never occurred to her that at the age of seven, Natalia was old enough to grasp such things. "Where could you have possibly heard something like this?"

Swiveling around on her bench, Natalia smiled with a gleam of pride for being able to demonstrate such maturity. "Well, it's hardly a secret, Mama." She rolled an auburn lock around her finger and lowered her voice conspiratorially. "It's all over the radio, you know."

That was true indeed. One could hardly tune in to a station these days that didn't drone on and on about the Germans' chain of battlefield successes and how nearly all of Europe had fallen under Hitler's boot. War was coming their way, everyone was saying, and it was only a matter of time before the Allied bombs would rain over the city. But to Natalia, they were just words, empty words that held no meaning. The war had been going on for years, but in Bucharest, there was no sign of it.

Here there were still parties and afternoons at the horse races and evenings at the opera and the theater and weekends at the sea. People were making vast fortunes in the middle of war, as endless barrels of oil left Romania for Germany, fueling the unrelenting Nazi machine, feeding their tanks and military trucks single-handedly. And the train stations, including Gara de Nord, served as transit points for German troops departing for the Eastern Front in Russia, where they were to embark on their fiercest battle yet.

Even under their own roof, little had changed in the nearly three years that Natalia had been living with them. Even though her father talked endlessly about cutting back on expenses and how they needed to tighten their belts, their home was still constantly filled with people, so many relatives and friends coming and going that there was hardly a Sunday free. Every weekend was a repetition of the one before: thirty-odd people gathered around the dining table set with fine china and crystal glasses of all sizes, endlessly chattering as Sofia ushered in a parade of dishes and wine bottles, dessert trays, and then bottles of port and cognac. Later, as the pendulum struck midnight, the appetizer platters began again. Long past the time Natalia had gone up to bed, she could still hear voices downstairs, rising and falling, bursting into intermittent laughter, lulling her to sleep. As she wrapped her body around a pillow, she pictured her parents in the smoky living room, swaying in each other's arms, the sound of American jazz filtering through the candlelit haze like a sash of velvet, her mother in one of her beautiful silk dresses resting her head on her father's shoulder.

Why was it that she found comfort in such simple things? She did not know. Just as she did not know why just the thought of them being near filled her with such peace. Why hearing their muffled voices somewhere in the house was enough to calm the hammering of her heart when, late at night, she jolted awake from some terror that she could never remember.

"Talia," her father said now, coming to sit next to her on the bench and taking her hand in his. "Talia, you know that you are safe here with us, do you not? That we will never let anything happen to you?"

"I know, Papa," she said, smiling brightly.

"Good. Good, my love." He patted her hand and stood up. "I've got a call to make. Be back in a minute."

"I'll get some tea on," her mother said, following him out of the room and closing the door behind her. The conversation, she knew, would be finished away from her prying ears.

Alone in the parlor, Natalia closed the piano lid and moved to the sofa, plunked herself down with a sigh. There was a photo album on the side table, and she picked it up, flipped it open to the beginning pages. Her eyes passed lazily over the photographs that her mother had arranged chronologically and with meticulous care. Afternoons in the park. Picnics at their summer house at the edge of the lake. Lunches on bistro terraces, under red parasols. Her favorite was the one where she was seated at her piano, her cousins gathered all around her in a flurry of holiday velvet and white satin. She recalled the delight sweeping through her as she played "Clair de Lune" for the first time to an audience, the way they had all applauded at the end. Her tutor, Miss Eliade, a spinster who often found herself in their company around the holidays, had stood there and beamed proudly, as if she alone was responsible for the performance.

But Natalia had not minded. The notes had a way of flying from her fingers easily, as if they had a life of their own, so she didn't think she deserved to be the subject of such praise.

It wasn't just that occasion but also many others — her entire life, it seemed — that had been captured in those pages. In more ways than one, it had truly begun with that first one, for if there had been anything before that, another home, another *anything,* she simply did not remember. Somewhere along the way, her past had faded to black, and she had been more than happy to bid it farewell. It was only once in a while, when catching a long sideways glance from one of her mother's sisters, that a sharpness sliced through her. It was only then that she was reminded what she was, *who* she was, that they regarded her still as a late postscript to their perfect family. But her mother was never more than an arm's length away and embraced her so fiercely that the feeling didn't last long. Now she simply ignored those looks. She hardly noticed or cared, for nothing could alter what the three of them had become.

Closing the album now, she curled up into a ball and rested her head on a pillow. Her eyelids were heavy with sleep, and she felt herself drift into a pleasant slumber, co-cooned in warmth and the soft leap of the flames. In a matter of days, there would be no more lounging around in the afternoons. It would be back to school and that dreary old institution that her mother referred to as the best academy in the country, to long hours of math and English and French and that awful uniform that scratched her skin no matter how many times Sofia washed it. At least as a day student, she was allowed to come home in the evenings, unlike the majority of those poor girls who were forced to spend the long months leading to summer under the ever-watchful eye of Mother Superior. Oh, how she wished this holiday would not have to end! It had been the very best Christmas.

As sleep carried her off, she relived Christmas Day once more from start to finish. There had been the traditional horse-drawn sleigh ride after supper, and this time, her father had taken her and the other children to the Arc de Triomphe. Along the way, they had stopped for chocolate éclairs and hot cocoa. Later, as her father led the sleigh around the sleepy, cobblestone plaza, it had begun to snow, and she had tried catching snowflakes on her tongue as they fell in a curtain from the moonlit sky. But the best part had come after that, back at the house, where presents awaited them under the tree.

The one she had chosen was very small, so tiny, in fact, that it might have easily gone unnoticed among the larger, more elaborately wrapped packages. Yet when she tore away the paper, a delicate velvet box rested in her hand. She had opened it slowly, gingerly, almost afraid to peek in, not expecting anything so breathtakingly lovely. A pair of ruby earrings, each with three crimson buds encased in the most exquisite gold, glimmered like stars in the intermittent flicker of Christmas-tree lights.

Her cousins had flocked around her, oohing and aahing, shoving one another out of the way to get a better look. But the conversation among the adults had grown suddenly quiet. She'd caught an exchange of glances between two of her aunts as one of them strode to the bar cart.

"Really, Anton, does a girl of merely seven need such jewelry?" she had said with what was supposed to be a trace of amusement, refilling her port glass.

If her father had heard her at all, there was nothing in his expression that showed it. He had stood there, still in his coat, with his arms crossed, his eyes only on Natalia, twinkling mischievously.

"Thank you, thank you, Papa!" she had screamed, her own eyes glistening, auburn curls bouncing over the lace collar of her best holiday dress.

Then, right there, amid the raised eyebrows of her mother's sisters, she had run into his arms and rewarded him with the biggest, most unrestrained hug that her small arms were capable of.

11

The night she had received the earrings, Natalia couldn't sleep. She gazed at them the entire night, so small and delicate in the palm of her hand, the crimson stones catching the soft glow from the night-light over her bed. Early the next morning, she took them to her mother's room and sat at the vanity table, in front of the oval mirror. Carefully, she clasped them on and covered her face with her hands. When she withdrew her hands and saw them glimmering in her ears for that very first time, she didn't want to take them off ever again.

"You shouldn't wear them every day; they're for special occasions," her mother had said resolutely, standing above her with an extended hand, waiting for her to hand over the earrings. "I will put them in my jewelry box. They'll be safe there."

It was the first time Natalia had refused her mother any request. "Please, Mama," she had begged, interlocking her fingers, dropping to her knees on the rug in an imploring gesture. "Please let me keep them for one more day!"

Despina agreed, but the next day, Natalia pleaded with her again. One day turned into a week, then into a month, and the earrings never came off. Eventually, her mother gave up insisting that they be stored alongside her own earrings, her sapphires and emeralds and strands of pearls, which she kept under lock and key. She no longer scolded her about wearing them to school.

Oh, but how Natalia reveled in the envious looks she received from the girls in her class! Surely they had their own jewelry — all their parents were wealthy enough — but she'd never seen any of them wear anything quite as lovely. The nuns gave her long looks, too. But no one commented on them. At least not for a while.

One day, a spindly girl a whole head taller than her approached her in the school yard. Natalia had seen her around, but they'd never spoken before, so it caught her completely off guard when the girl stepped right in front of her, cutting off her path.

Hands on her hips, puffing her chest like an ostrich, the girl pronounced loudly enough for all to hear, "So our little orphan

116

princess has got herself a pair of nice earrings."

It felt like a blow to her stomach. Natalia stared at the girl, dumbfounded, feeling herself grow cold. There was a bitter taste in her mouth, and she swallowed against it. She had stepped to the side to go around her when she heard it again.

"That's right. *Bastard!*" the girl shouted even louder, cupping a hand around her mouth.

Something like a flame exploded inside Natalia's head. She didn't know what was happening. It was as if she was watching herself in someone else's body. The fist, curling tight as a rock. The feel of the girl's hair, her sleek ponytail almost sliding out of her grasp. The O of the girl's mouth, silent, her body pinned to the ground underneath Natalia's own weight. It felt good. Whatever she was doing, it felt good, and she couldn't even hear the girl's screams, and she couldn't stop until suddenly she was lifted up in the air.

Mother Superior never rose from her chair. Rumor had it that she suffered from some grave bone disease, which explained why only on rare occasions would she be spotted anywhere but behind her desk, where nonetheless she ruled the school with the efficiency of a dictator. So when she pushed her chair back, when she smoothed out her skirt and stood to her full height (taller, it seemed, than a mountain), Natalia's blood froze.

Her gaze dropped to the ground, and she felt herself shaking. Only when the old nun stood firmly before her did she dare to raise her eyes. A vein she had not seen before had appeared across the wide forehead of Mother Superior, and her face looked nearly purple against her perfectly starched ivory wimple.

"It is unfathomable, Natalia!" Mother Superior began. "Unfathomable that a girl of your upbringing, of your family's standing, should behave this way!" There was a wooden ruler in her hand, and she kept tapping it against her palm, which terrified Natalia even more than her tone. "To think that you'd conduct yourself in such a barbaric way, that you'd . . ." She shook her head as if no words were adequate to describe the horror of her actions. "Well, what do you have to say in your defense?"

Truly, Natalia didn't know what to say. The tears that she had counted on wouldn't come, nor did any pleas for forgiveness. She did not have an excuse. Yes, her behavior had been appalling, but how to explain to Mother Superior that even a meek little orphan like herself had boundaries? How could she explain that what that girl had spat at her had felt like a bullet? Before today, there had been no orphanage, no other life. Until today, she had been a girl like any other, a lucky little girl whose mother and father loved her enough to bestow beautiful jewelry on her. Now all she felt was a deep, ugly wound.

Mother Superior let out a long sigh, tapping and tapping the ruler. For a moment, Natalia thought she would ask her to extend her hand for the usual punishment, but she only stood there, appraising her with those beady eyes in which Natalia could see no saintliness.

"Detention after school for three hours. And that is just to begin," she pronounced soberly. "Since you have nothing to say for yourself, your parents will be called in, of course. Surely they will be ashamed, but maybe they can talk some sense into you."

For the first time that day, Natalia felt the sting of tears.

The street was vacant and dark when she stepped out through the school gates, dark and cold, and the wind pricked her bare legs, but she barely noticed. Even now, she could barely stifle the rage that swelled up inside her when she thought of that girl, that *name* she had called her. Now everyone knew, and her life could not be the same. Perhaps that was what she should have told Mother Superior. Then maybe she wouldn't have made her face a blank wall for three hours — she'd been punished enough.

Hoisting her bag under her arm, she came down the rest of the steps and headed up the cobblestone lane. The school was nestled away from the rest of the neighborhood at the end of a cul-de-sac, and there wasn't a soul in sight. At least walking in solitude for a block or two would do her some good.

There was, of course, the matter of her parents. What would she say to them when she got home, what excuse? No doubt her mother had come looking for her and — seeing the empty playground in the late afternoon — thought that she'd gone home with Clara, her one friend who sometimes invited her over after school. Surely as daylight waned, she'd begun to worry, and Natalia pictured her now in a full panic, pacing the length of the living room, calling everyone in the phone book, starting with Clara's parents and ending with the police.

Yes, there would be trouble to face when she got home, and she would have to do it one way or another. Wrapping her coat tightly around her, she had quickened her step when all of a sudden she heard someone call out her name.

"Natalia!"

She stopped and turned, surveying the street, but there was no one there. Surely she had imagined it. Quickly, she resumed walking, but only a moment later, she heard it again, louder, more distinct.

"Talia! Hello!"

The voice, it took her a moment to grasp, had come from across the street. There was a car there which she'd not noticed before, a black car about half a block ahead, with its lights turned off. She could see a ribbon of cigarette smoke wafting from that direction. Her father must have sent a car for her; it was dark, after all. But then, just when she'd sprinted across to the other side, she realized she'd made a mistake. This car was not her father's Buick. It was larger, and the back plate was different.

"Hello, Talia," came the voice again, as a tall figure stepped out of the shadow and into the light of a post. "Please don't run. I don't wish to scare you. I only want to talk for a few moments."

She couldn't look up from the ground. Her bones had gone suddenly soft, steeped in terror. All she could do was look at the pair of loafers moving toward her, stepping over a tiny puddle. But then he stopped at a distance, and his hand came up in a greeting gesture, and she saw that he was no monster; he was a man. A young one at that, and nice-looking. He wore a fur-collared coat and a dark fedora like the ones her father liked. He smiled a bit awkwardly, as if he was somehow afraid, too, as if all he meant was to introduce himself. Something about him seemed oddly familiar. Natalia couldn't pin it down right away, but a moment later, it came to her with crystal clarity. The tiny mole on the man's cheekbone was identical to the one on her own. They bore the same mark.

Her knees nearly buckled, and she took a few steps backward, clutching her bag. "I have to go," she mumbled, more or less to herself. "I have to go."

Then there was nothing but the echo of her steps striking the pavement, the sound of her breath, and her heart pounding in her ears. Her bag slipped from her grasp, but she did not pick it up. Only at the end of the block, where the boulevard that led home opened up like an oasis, did she stop for a second. A few cars whirled by her and honked as she darted across the wide thoroughfare.

On the other side, she felt a little less frightened. There were pedestrians and a peasant boy selling flowers wrapped in newspaper, shouting out the price to no one in particular. "Fifty *lei*! Only fifty *lei* for fresh-cut carnations!" The intersection looked as it always had. It would have been impossible for the man to try to lure her into his car here, not with all the zigzagging traffic, people walking by. She was safe. But something seemed unusual, something seemed *off*.

Just beyond the spot where the boy crouched near the flower buckets, the thick iron gates of the Swiss embassy swung open. Natalia had never seen them open before, except on the rare occasion when a limousine or town car rolled through, the guards posted at the gates checking papers and inspecting the passengers before letting them pass. But there were no guards there tonight. There were no cars, no officers, no signs of life. Yet the gates were wide open. Only a small window in the second story flickered faintly.

She did not know why at that moment she turned and glanced across the boulevard to see if that car was still there. She did not expect to see it. But there it still was, barely visible underneath the dim light of the post.

The man was leaning against it, arms folded over his chest. Even from this far, she could see that despite the long stare, his eyes were resigned, as if he had no intention of pursuing her.

Shuddering in the evening breeze, she broke into a full sprint, and this time she did not stop until she found herself directly in front of her home.

12

April 1944

In the Goza household, arrangements for Easter Sunday always began one week in advance. In her bed every night, Despina tossed and turned, going over the seven-course menu in such detail that by the time she drifted off to sleep, every pinch of salt or pepper was accounted for, every spice measured in her mind so accurately there was no chance this could be anything but an epic feast. By the morning of Good Friday, only the shortbread pastries were still to be sprinkled with sugar and arranged in neat rows on the silver trays, like worshipful angels with folded wings, welcoming the most festive day of the year. And this Friday in particular held the promise of a glorious Easter. A restless, effervescent energy swelled and bubbled over the city, causing perfect strangers to smile as they lined up for last-minute things — color for eggs, nutmeg, or white candle pillars to light in the church at midnight mass and carry home to burn in their windows.

With no other details to attend to that morning, Despina glanced inside the china cabinet and realized with a flurry of alarm that only ten wine goblets had survived their last dinner party. Ten matching glasses — not enough for the table, even if she was to combine them with a smaller set, which she would never do, not with a new guest joining them for the first time. There wouldn't be much of a point in protesting, Anton knew, nothing to say to deter her from going out at the last minute to hunt for new crystal. And so both he and Natalia had exchanged a look and followed her out into the crisp morning. Crystal or not, the day was indeed glorious.

It wasn't until a couple of hours later, after they had trailed her from one end of town to the other, that Despina's determination began to dwindle and a slight listlessness crept into her step. Even the famous Lenox storefront, once set in a spectacular ensemble of crystal and silver, lay barren and so poorly lit one could hardly make out whatever remained on the shelves.

"Oh, no, Anton. Look," she uttered with a tinge of despair, letting her hand drop from his arm. "They've closed, too. How is it possible?"

"Darling, it will be all right. It's just family, after all, and we can make do with what we have. It won't really matter."

"Yes, but it is Easter, Anton. What will your new friend think?"

Anton smiled and patted her hand. Under usual circumstances, he might have agreed with her, but his new friend, as she called him, would probably have been content to sip his wine out of a ceramic jug. "Victor will not be bothered in the least. Believe me."

Despina frowned and pursed her lips. All week long, she had fretted about the invitation. It wasn't that she wasn't used to Anton bringing new acquaintances to the house — he did it all the time — but never on a holiday. Holidays were strictly reserved for their extended family and children. Already they were so many in number it was a challenge to fit them all under one roof.

"Do you think this is the right time, Anton?" she asked again as they hurried to catch a cab that had pulled to the curb. "Why not invite him for a Sunday lunch, when it will be just the three of us and we can get to know him better?"

"He has no one, Despina," Anton said,

holding the door open. "He has no family, no friends. He will be alone on the holiest day of the year."

"All right." Despina relented, scooting in next to Natalia in the backseat. "But I hardly think he'll feel comfortable among twenty-odd people he's never met."

Anton had met Victor by chance. He was locking up the shop late one evening when he spotted a young man at the end of the block rummaging through a trash bin in front of a neighboring café. The young man seemed oblivious of his presence, as he poked through sodden brown bags and discarded boxes, cursing quietly under his breath. He was quite tall and lanky, all sharp edges underneath his unbuttoned trench coat, and Anton guessed that it wasn't the first time he'd had to scrounge for leftover food. Yet despite his hunger, evident in the intensity with which he peered inside that trash bin, there was an air of nobility about him, something oddly dignified that gave him the air of a poet more than a beggar.

From the corner of his eye, Anton stood there watching him. The young man brought back memories of a forgotten time. He looked vaguely familiar, too, although he wasn't quite sure why. Where had he seen him before?

Then he remembered. The young man was the occupant of a small loft above the store. They had crossed paths on the service stairs several times as he was hauling in deliveries or putting out empty boxes in the alleyway behind the building. They had never exchanged a single greeting.

After twisting the lock for good measure once more, Anton deposited the key in his pocket. The vertical shutters clattered noisily as he pulled them down despite his best efforts to lower them quietly, and the young man looked up from the bin. Dropping the lid on the sidewalk, he pulled his trench coat tightly around himself and began walking briskly in the other direction.

"Sir!" Anton called after him, but the man did not stop. He continued in large strides across the plaza, darting through the circling traffic and disappearing on the other side. Anton followed him, struggling to keep up. For a while, he thought he had lost him, but then he spotted him rounding the corner and practically ran to catch up.

"Sir, please, I didn't mean to startle you!" he shouted just as the young man quickened his pace again. He had trailed him for another block when the man came to a halt and swiveled abruptly.

"What do you want from me?" he spat. There was panic as well as a trace of rage on his angular face. "I haven't taken anything. I haven't taken anything that is yours," the man went on a little less sharply, and Anton did not dare come any closer.

"Of course not," Anton replied, flushing with embarrassment. His intentions had been completely misunderstood. "No, of course you haven't. I just wanted to help. To see if you need anything." He fumbled nervously with the key ring in his coat pocket.

"Need anything?" the man said with a sardonic half-smile. "Yes, I could use some food. Nothing fancy, you see. Any scraps, any leftovers would do. I haven't had anything to eat all day."

For a moment, Anton was silent. Then his hand came out of his pocket, and he extended his arm in an inviting gesture. "Come," he said. "Come with me. I know a place where we could get some *mici,* even at this late hour. I'm hungry, too, you see, and I could use the company."

They arrived at a well-known beerhouse on Stavropoleos Street. Despite being labeled a pub, it was the kind of place people flocked to for the setting more than the selection of beer. Catching the critical glances that greeted them the moment they entered, the young man considered turning around and walking out. But his hunger was greater than his dignity, and the maître d', a portly old man in coattails who seemed well acquainted with Anton, was already ushering them toward the back of the restaurant, where a perfect ensemble of starched white linen and gleaming silver awaited. As they passed a row of tables where the conversation had suddenly hushed, the young man scanned the mural paintings, the ambient light emanating from the delicate art deco sconces, and thought, *No wonder they're all staring.* Normally, he would have been chased away from a place like this if he so much as glanced through the window.

Yet as midnight neared, they were the last two patrons left. Anton ordered more *mici* and steak with fries, and they switched from beer to brandy. The waiter had grown visibly impatient, but he could not refuse Anton's requests. Anton and his wife had been his best customers for years. There was simply no way to rush him along, especially not at a time like this, when he seemed so engrossed in a conversation.

It was the first time Anton had opened up about his past. It took him by surprise how easily he confided in this perfect stranger, how he effortlessly shared the story of his humble beginnings. Little by little, he laid bare his soul and the inner workings of his heart to the famished young man, this student whose name was Victor and who worked all kinds of night jobs to pay for his university tuition, even if it meant not eating for days. Anton felt liberated while speaking to him, as though an invisible weight had been lifted from his shoulders.

At first, Victor did not understand why the wealthy shop owner from downstairs would take an interest in sharing a meal with him, much less reveal such intimate details about his life. He'd seen him nearly every morning, unlocking the shop in his elegant suits and silk scarves. He'd seen the black Buick that dropped him off every day, the dark-haired beauty — undoubtedly his wife — who stopped by several times a week, carrying an assortment of hatboxes and shopping bags, always in a cloud of expensive perfume. What would a man like that want with him? Why would he bother? Yet as the hours clicked by and Anton delved deeper into stories about his childhood, he began to understand a bit why he'd been invited here.

"No child should be forced to work under such conditions for the benefit of the wealthy," Victor declared when Anton had finished telling him about his days as a delivery boy sleeping in the back of the storage room. "There will come a day when no one will have to live through such atrocities." He leaned forward so his voice wouldn't carry. "The subjugation of the poor that has plagued Europe for hundreds of years will soon come to an end, mark my words. When the wealthy are stripped of their undeserved fortunes, when everything is divided equally among the people, that's when this country will regain its humanity. You will see, Anton. You will see."

Reaching across the table, he extracted a cigarette from the golden case that Anton held out to him. All the beer and brandy had fueled his candor, and he had forgotten that the man sitting across from him belonged to the very ranks to which he referred with such disdain.

"But it hasn't worked," Anton replied truthfully, placing the case back in his pocket. "It hasn't worked in Russia. People are living in communal apartments in Moscow and Leningrad, they have no food, no heat. And what about the thousands of people Stalin has killed to protect what he has created? No one is better off. Everyone suffers all the same."

"You are naive, Anton!" Victor declared, more loudly than he intended, tapping his fist lightly on the table. "Stalin *has* industrialized Russia. He has created more opportunity, more advancements than any other country in the world. And why do you think that is? Why?" He paused, though obviously not for an answer. "Because the Soviets are devoted to society as a whole, not just selfish gain. And that is why they will win this war." He finished the last of his brandy and put down the empty glass.

Anton could not help smiling. He did not remember ever meeting anyone who spoke with such conviction. Not that he agreed with much of what his young friend was saying, but his enthusiasm, that fire in his eyes, was certainly catching. There was a bit of an indignation flourishing in his own breast, thinking that someone this articulate and intelligent had to dig inside garbage bins for discarded food. It seemed inconceivable.

Anton motioned for the bill. "Are you free for lunch Easter Sunday?" he asked. He guessed almost with certainty that Victor did not have a standing engagement or much reason to celebrate, but he didn't know how else to extend the invitation. "It would be a great pleasure if you could join us. If you'd like."

"Anton, thank you. But do you think your wife would be happy entertaining someone like me in her home?" He shook his head. "No, Anton. I think we will keep this — our meeting of minds, if you will — just between us. And I thank you. I thank you again for your generosity."

With that, he stood and extended his hand to Anton, who, still sitting, took it and held it firmly for a moment.

"Come by the house," he said, smiling in the dim light. "I'd actually like you to meet my wife. I'd like you to see that you're wrong."

13

Maria was not a devout woman, despite the fact that everyone who knew her thought her to be without question fully and completely dedicated to God. Certainly, she believed in his supreme power; she never questioned that all matters pertaining to life on earth were decided by the Almighty. But what was puzzling to her was why God always chose her as a vessel for his work, why he chose to put such difficult matters in her flawed and mortal hands.

The letter fluttered ever so slightly as she held it up against the window and read it again. It did not take long to get through it. Only a few lines had been written in black ink on a flimsy sheet, as fragile as a butterfly wing. It slipped out of her hand and landed at her feet, just underneath the windowsill. She crouched down to pick it up, and as she did, her finger slid over its edge, and it cut her skin.

Gazing absentmindedly out the window, her mind drifted to the day before. She had barely arrived at the orphanage in the early morning when the director had greeted her by the entrance, saying there was an urgent matter she needed to discuss. At first, Maria assumed that it had something to do with the long hours she had been putting in. Even Mrs. Tudor had noticed that Maria had been spending every waking moment at the orphanage, that her obsessive preoccupation with the children was beginning to take its toll on her appearance. "I don't need you here night and day," she had told her once. "I need you to stay healthy. Take a few days off, get some rest, go out for a good meal."

Maria knew she was right. Her husband, too, had become increasingly anxious about her sudden pallor, her thinning frame. He was telling her the very same things. But whatever Ana Tudor was going to discuss with her had nothing to do with her health. She knew it the minute Mrs. Tudor had followed her into her office and closed the door behind them. Somewhere along the years, she and the orphanage director had become friends, bound by a sense of responsibility and concern for the children, their constant care. They were beyond formalities and closed doors.

"Would you mind sitting down, Maria?" Mrs. Tudor had said, walking around her desk and sitting as well. "How to begin . . ." She laced her fingers together. "This is very delicate. It has to do with the Goza girl."

"Natalia?" Maria had asked, unable to conceal her surprise. "What about her?"

"This."

Across her desk, Ana Tudor had slid a cream-colored envelope. "I received this last week. Because of its sensitive nature, I wanted to entrust it to you. You and the girl's mother are very close, no? And so I think you will know best how to handle it."

Maria had taken the envelope. Reaching inside it, she had extracted a single sheet of paper, folded in half.

"Maria, before you read it, please know that whether you decide to share it with the Goza family or not is entirely up to you. I make no judgment about it either way, because I know that you, my friend, will make the right decision. Either way, my involvement in this matter ends here."

Maria had nodded, then unfolded the paper and begun reading. It did not take long to get to the end. When she looked up again, her hand was trembling.

Now the hardest part lay ahead of her.

She shuddered, thinking about what she needed to do, what she *had* to do if she was ever to have another moment's peace. It seemed so simple yet impossible to fathom at the same time. Despina was Natalia's mother; she had a right to know about the letter, *what the letter said.* But Despina was also the person closest to Maria. They had shared everything growing up, including a bed at the family's summer house in Salonika and secrets whispered in the dark and promises that nothing would ever come between them. She was the last person on earth Maria wanted to upset.

But suddenly, Maria recalled another face, not that of her cousin but the *other* one's. That woman who had lived in her attic for half a year, who had by a mere miracle survived, only to resume an empty life, one undoubtedly filled with pain and remorse. She sighed, thinking about how she had looked that last morning coming down the service stairs bundled in one of her own old woolen sweaters. How her eyes had lacked life. Yes, she knew what losing a child did to a person, how little else mattered after that. And so what of this woman? Did she owe her anything?

And then there was Natalia, that sweet, beautiful auburn-haired girl, whose smile could light up a room. She seemed so happy with Anton and Despina, so content. How could Maria, of all people, risk coming between that? How could she risk destroying that blissful peace they had all found in one another?

Heavily, Maria sank into a chair. She sat there watching the sky darken in the window, then evening giving way to night, as she lingered over the possibilities, the consequences, going back and forth and starting again. It was pitch-black outside by the time a searing knowledge rose unflinchingly in her heart, like a pinprick producing a droplet of blood on the surface of her thumb.

At last, she understood. Ana Tudor knew her better than she knew herself. Maria let her face drop into her hands and her tears spring forth. She did not try to hold them back, as she was grieving for what she herself had lost so long ago.

14

In her sunny kitchen, Despina bustled around in an impeccably starched apron tied over her lilac silk dress. With one hand she brushed a few loose strands away from her face, while with the other she stirred milk, sugar, eggs, and butter in a large metal bowl, methodically adding raisins and shot glasses of rum. Only the slight frown line embedded between her perfectly arched eyebrows gave away her intense concentration as she stirred in ingredients and motioned to Sofia to bring more sugar from the pantry, more flour.

On a stool in the corner, Natalia sat and watched her mother, sipping a cup of hot chocolate. These were Natalia's favorite moments, the hustle and bustle in the hours before a party, when the possibility of a perfect day still lay before them, filling her with anticipation. It was only ten in the morning, but the fragrance of her mother's baking, of braids of dough and nutmeg rising from the oven, had already seeped into every corner of the house. From a small portable radio on one of the shelves, her favorite show, *The Children's Hour,* droned away.

"Why don't you go outside and see if you can find some of your friends?" Despina said, catching a glimpse of her daughter. "The fresh air will do you good. Go on, now."

Natalia's eyes widened in surprise. "Really? You mean it?"

"Well, why not?" Despina smiled, planting a kiss on her forehead. "Just be back before two. I'd like you to change into something more festive for lunch."

"Thank you, Mama! I promise to be back in time!" she exclaimed, jumping down from her stool, needing no further encouragement.

Ever since the day she'd had to serve detention at school, her mother hadn't let her out of her sight. She'd been hesitant even to let her go as far as the mailbox or step out in the yard. Not that Natalia could blame her. Weeks had passed, and she was still shaken with guilt thinking of all that had followed when she'd finally arrived home that night.

There had been no torrent of fury. No yelling, no punishments. No phone call, apparently, from Mother Superior, either. That much was obvious the moment her mother had wrenched open the door despite her best efforts to sneak in quietly, to explain that, in fact, she'd been in the attic the whole time, searching for her old train set, which she meant to give to Maria for the orphanage. She was relieved, of course, at not having to lie, but the way her mother had looked at her, pale and wide-eyed, holding on to the door as if it was some kind of a life raft, made her own breath cut short.

"Talia," she'd said in a voice that didn't sound like her own. "Talia, where? Where have you been?"

"I'm sorry, Mama, I am so sorry. I never meant for any of this to happen," she'd mumbled, and burst into tears.

Sometime later, after she had been bundled in a cashmere blanket, after she'd been brought a cup of tea and had her feet and her hands rubbed, Natalia found the courage to tell her the truth. Softly, nervously, keeping her eyes on the rug, she'd recounted the whole awful day, what that girl had said to her in the schoolyard, how she had not been able to control her rage, how she'd been forced to stand facing a wall through the evening.

To her amazement, her mother had listened patiently, not uttering a word. It wasn't until she got to the part — almost as an afterthought — about the man who'd approached her on the street that she sprang to her feet as if she'd been shocked by a bolt of electricity.

"It's all right, Mama!" she'd cried. "I'm all right. Nothing happened! It was nothing."

But her mother could not stop pacing the room after that, rubbing her temples in tiny, frantic circles, frowning at the floor, sitting and standing and sitting again. After a while, she took Natalia's hand in hers, but this time there was no excessive affection, only an endless barrage of questions that seemed to go on for hours. *How old was the man, Talia? How was he dressed, Talia? What, and I mean precisely what, did he say to you?* Natalia did her best to answer, but truly she did not know why that man had tried to speak to her. Or why he'd seemed familiar — a part she thought best to leave out.

At one point, her father had come into the room and, not wanting to interrupt, poured himself a cup of tea and went to stand near the window. He did not take a single sip from his cup. He just stood there with his hands curled around his tea mug, listening.

"All right, Despina. Let's finish this in the morning," he'd said after a while. "Talia, come with me to the kitchen. I'll fix you something to eat."

She'd wanted to run up and kiss him. Thank God they were done with it, at least for the night. Yet as she followed him out of the room, she paused in the doorway and turned to Despina one last time:

"Good night, Mama," she'd said softly. "I'm sorry."

But her mother did not seem to hear her. She was leaning over the back of the sofa, holding on to the backrest with both hands, her shoulders bent forward, as if some deeply troubling knowledge had hooked itself inside her heart.

Now, after weeks of keeping Natalia under lock and key and watching her with the attention of a prison guard, her mother was telling her that she could go outside to play. How funny she was. How unpredictable. But Natalia certainly wasn't going to question her change of heart.

"I'll be back in time!" she reassured her mother again as she sprinted toward the kitchen door.

Her hands suddenly froze when she grasped the smooth, glossy surface of the doorknob, and she retreated back a step. There was a sound coming from outside, a whining like that of an ambulance but louder, more insistent. It sounded like howling.

She turned instantly to her mother, searching her face, but it was blank as she stood there with the bowl in her hands. It was not the sound from outside but the clatter of metal — the bowl slipping from her hands, white dough splattering over the tiles — that made her cry out. On the radio, *The Children's Hour* was interrupted by the grave voice of a male announcer.

"Bucharest is under bombardment! The Allied forces are bombing the city! All citizens are advised to take shelter immediately!" There was a crackle, a pause, and then the voice returned more urgently: "I repeat, all are to take shelter immediately! God help the citizens of this country. God help us all."

15

It had come after all, without warning. The thing they had all feared had taken the city by surprise, on Easter morning of all days. A single siren had sounded, not far away from their house, perhaps in one of the central plazas. It had come late, much too late for Despina to do anything but grab hold of Natalia's hand and drag her toward the cellar door that Sofia had already pried open. They had barely made it halfway down the steps when their house began to shake and give way to sounds they'd never heard before. Still, Despina thought they had been lucky to be able to act right on the spot.

Down in the cellar, she did her best to comfort Natalia. Above the shrieks, the bone-rattling booms, the pop of fracturing bricks and blasted-out windows, her daughter's cries were the hardest sounds to endure. Despina hummed a tune in her ear,

147

telling her to think of something happy, telling her not to be afraid. What more could she have done? She might have prayed, as Sofia did, on her knees with her forehead pressed firmly against the wall. She might have, but it would have only terrified the child more.

When it ended, Natalia remained motionless, her head buried between her knees, her hands covering her ears. It was Sofia who finally carried her up the steps into the chalky haze that enveloped the house. It was Sofia who soothed the girl in those first terrible moments, for Despina was already on the phone, dialing frantically, redialing, grasping with a shard of terror that the line was dead.

Two hours passed, and there was still no sign of Anton.

"Sweetheart, why don't you go up and rest?" she kept urging Natalia, who wouldn't let go of her hand. There was so much debris, so much broken glass in the cellar, it wasn't safe, though it seemed pointless to ask. "I'm not going, Mama! Please stop asking. I want to stay right here with you!"

"Miss Talia, I'll stay with you for a while." Sofia finally interceded, even though she didn't much want to leave Despina's side, either. "Your mother needs to be alone for a bit."

Reluctantly, she went up with Sofia in tow. Watching her small frame move up the staircase, Despina breathed out a small sigh of relief. Now that she was alone, she needed to move. She needed to keep her body moving so that she wouldn't go mad.

"He is all right, he is all right," she muttered out loud, trying to calm the wild thrashing of her heart.

But then she remembered the arguments she and Anton had had in recent weeks. How he would not, *could not,* promise her that he would go into a shelter if this moment came. He had begged her to understand that he could not go into a coffin, that even their own cellar felt like a wooden box to him. And now, with the phone lines down, there was no way to reach him. But surely he would walk in any minute. Any minute, she would hear his voice in the foyer calling her name, calling Talia. All she had to do was keep busy until then.

At the threshold of the dining room, she paused, her fingers curling around the doorjamb. From the sight of it, it seemed impossible that their home had not been reduced to rubble. The Vanderbilt chandelier had fallen on the table with such force that not one of its crystal baubles remained intact. Everything in the room lay underneath a layer of glass so fine it looked like a sandstorm had blown through.

Struggling not to breathe in the dust, she crossed the room to open the terrace doors. Something sharp stung her foot, and she bent down to pick it up. It took her a moment to realize it was one of the candle-holders that she had inherited from her grandmother. It had been severed in half. Just this morning, she had placed the pair on the sideboard, alongside the good china for Easter lunch. There would be no Easter now, no lavish feasts, no colored eggs, no family celebration.

Her sisters. Maria. Were they all right? She realized that she had not spoken with any of them in nearly a week, since the Sunday before, when they had all met at Café Capsa on Victoria Avenue. That afternoon, there hadn't been a trace of suspicion of what was to come, as if war was some distant thing, something that had nothing to do with their lives. The five of them had squeezed in together at a table near the window, and, savoring an assortment of pastries and English tea, they had gone over details for Easter lunch. Ecaterina was to bring the champagne, Elena some hors d'oeuvres if there was enough time to pull it together. Her cousin Maria said she would do her best to be on time. Maria. There had been something strange about her that afternoon. She'd seemed out of sorts, troubled even, standing there in the hallway near the ladies' room, waiting for Despina to come out.

"Desi." She'd called her name in a whisper.

Startled, Despina had turned, and seeing Maria, she'd let out a breath. "God, you gave me a fright." She'd chuckled, reaching for her cousin's arm and squeezing it affectionately — but Maria had not smiled back.

"Can we talk, after the girls leave? Just you and I alone?"

"Of course! You and I always talk when they're gone," she recalled saying, expecting a laugh, but only a slight frown had passed over her cousin's face.

"There's something I want to tell you. That I feel I *need* to tell you. In private, Despina, just you and I."

But the afternoon had passed much too fast, and they'd lost track of time. The waiter, so diligent at the beginning of the afternoon, had grown visibly impatient. Ecaterina was the first to notice his exasperated look as he peeled away the last of the tablecloths, after sweeping the bread crumbs with a silver brush.

"Goodness, we should be going," Ecaterina said, checking her watch. "They are trying to close to prepare for dinner. It's nearly three!"

They'd collected their cardigans, exchanged hurried kisses, and flown out the door. Within moments, Despina and Maria found themselves standing alone on the sidewalk. It hardly seemed like the right time or place for a serious discussion.

"Let's talk next week," Maria had said as they embraced. "I will come and see you in a few days."

Whatever it was that her cousin had planned on telling her, Despina hoped it was not to do with her health. Maria looked pale and exhausted these days. She was spreading herself too thin, barely taking the time for a proper meal before flying off to the Red Cross headquarters, where she spent entire days on the telephone collecting funds for the hospitals and war orphans and families of wounded soldiers. Strangely, she no longer worked at the orphanage. Despina had never asked her why she had quit her job there, but she figured that Stefan had put his foot down at last, for Maria knew no personal limits when it came to those children. Poor Stefan, Despina thought. How was he to know that his wife would only find a new cause, an all-consuming endeavor to dedicate herself to?

Please, dear God, let her be all right. Please, let them all be all right, she prayed silently now as she made her way through the house, taking in the rest of the wreckage, thankful that at least Natalia's piano remained unscathed. In front of the sole window that was intact, she paused, but she kept her eyes downcast, unable to look out. Where was the sound of the traffic, of children playing at the end of the block? Everything was so still that she could hear the ticking of the pendulum clock. She could hear the jagged inhalation of her own breath. And suddenly, something else. Somewhere below, she heard the shuffle of steps, the jangle of keys, and she tore madly through the house.

Ten whole minutes had passed, and she couldn't stop crying. She hated this uncontrollable display of emotion, but she couldn't get hold of herself. Tears flowed, unstoppable, drenching his shirt as she buried her head in his chest.

"I'm right here, I'm all right," he whispered into her hair, kissing her head, her wet cheeks, as she slid down to the floor, pulling him along with her. On the tiled floor, he cradled her in his arms and rocked her back and forth until her sobs melted into long, deep sighs.

They were dusty, his hands, when she took them in hers. A deep gash spanned the length of one palm, and when she pressed her lips on it, the metallic taste of dried blood made her shudder. He winced, too, but said nothing, and they remained like that for a while, not daring to move, not daring to let go of each other.

"Where's Talia?" he whispered after some time.

"She's upstairs in her room, resting. She was so frightened, Anton. So frightened it broke my heart. What's this?" she said, gesturing to the briefcase he had dropped near the door.

"Oh, that. I've been meaning to move the stamp collection to the house. No better time than today."

She did not laugh, as he'd hoped she would, and he pulled her away from him then, gazed down at her with tenderness and a slight amusement.

"Despina. My strong, beautiful Despina. Don't you know by now that you need not worry about me?"

Her answer was barely a whisper. "I don't know what I would do if anything happened to you. I couldn't bear it."

"Nothing will happen to me or to us. We will go through this together as we always have. We will fight, and we will live, and soon enough things will be just like they used to."

"You're right," she said, because she knew that he was.

He was here now, safe with her, wiping the tears that had pooled underneath her eyes with the thumb of his injured hand. They were together; they were alive. It felt good, his warm hand on her face. The curtain of dread had lifted a little.

From the top of the stairs, Natalia watched them silently. Earlier, she had tried to sleep, but sleep wouldn't come, no matter how hard she tried. As the afternoon wore on, she, too, had become anxious about her father's absence. Now that she had heard his voice in the foyer, she wanted to leap down the steps, fly into his arms, and be pulled into their embrace. But at the top of the steps, something held her back. Whatever was passing between her parents at that moment seemed to be for them alone. Instead, she retreated back to her room, slipping quietly down the hall, past the stand from which her mother's porcelain figurines had fallen and smashed into a thousand pieces.

16

July 1944

The long, hot summer stretched on interminably in a predictable pattern, the sirens sounding at the same time each day, like clockwork. Despina and Natalia huddled in the cellar, waiting out the worst of it, lighting kerosene lamps and counting the rows of jars on the wooden shelves above them to make the time pass. Anton ran to the park across the street, where he and Natalia used to feed ducks in the pond before the war. There he sat on a bench, with his stamp collection in his lap and no more for cover than the thick branches of a sycamore tree. Heart pounding in his chest, he sat and watched the debris falling around him, obliterating parts of his neighborhood, praying that it wouldn't be their home that would be hit this time, praying that his family would be spared.

Despina had given up trying to persuade

him to go underground. After begging, crying, shouting, and threatening, all her efforts had been in vain. Now she just made the sign of the cross when the sirens began. At last, she had come to accept the idea that God alone would keep him safe out there on that park bench, and her efforts, too, were best spent on prayer.

But it wasn't just Anton's inability to go into a shelter that had been the cause of their recent arguments. For weeks now, Anton had been trying to convince Despina to join her sister Ecaterina on her family's estate, just outside Bucharest in the village of Snagov, where the bombs had not yet reached. All her other sisters, he repeatedly pointed out, had long left the city. One by one, they had taped their windows, rolled up their rugs, covered their furniture with sheets, and boarded trains that took them to remote places that the Allies had no interest in bombing. It was no longer safe to remain in Bucharest, he kept telling her, not with all the unimaginable rumors about refugee camps across the border in Poland. Not with the Führer scorching the earth so close to home.

"I cannot bear, Despina, to think of what I heard in line at the bakery this morning," he said one night as the two of them were getting ready for bed. "Don't ask. You wouldn't believe it. The Germans are such civilized people, how can they do such things?"

"Well, there's been nothing about it in the papers, darling," she replied, sitting at her vanity table and removing her pearl earrings. "And rumors have a way of proving themselves untrue."

"Perhaps, but it isn't safe for you and Talia to be here. Hitler's army is too close now. Too close. You know what that means, don't you?"

Despina placed her hands on the vanity table and shot him a look in the mirror.

"You know I'm not leaving without you. And since you are on call with the Army Reserves, I guess there is nowhere to go. Besides, we are not alone. Victor is still here. And what about Maria and Stefan? They haven't run off like frightened deer. Why should we?"

It was a pointless argument, Despina knew. True, Maria and Stefan were still just across town, but their existence — like everyone else's — had shrunk around the few hours in the day when it was safe to leave the proximity of a shelter. There seemed to be less and less time for the smallest of necessities — replenishing the pantry, picking up mail at the post office, or simply going outside for a short walk before the sirens sounded — and they rarely saw one another now. She still did not know what Maria had intended to tell her that afternoon at Café Capsa, before the first bombing. The last time she had tried bringing up the subject on the telephone, the line had gone out in mid-conversation. Since then, they had spoken once, but Maria was rushing off to the Red Cross, and she had promised she would come by to visit soon. Despina hoped she wouldn't let too much time pass. She could get by without the company of her sisters, but not having Maria around felt like some essential part of her existence had been amputated from her.

"Please, Despina, I beg you," Anton said now, coming up behind her and placing a soft kiss on her neck. "There is no telling what will happen next, what will happen *tomorrow*. I only know one thing," he went on, taking her hand and pressing it to his lips. "You and Talia are not safe here."

She laughed and traced his cheek affectionately. "Is this how you plan to convince me? With kisses? Your charm won't work this time!" She turned to him fully, then stood and draped her arms around him. "Aren't you the one who told me not

160

to be frightened? Things will turn soon, you will see."

Things did turn swiftly, overnight, but not in a way that anyone expected. The news came in over the BBC first, and Anton was one of the first to intercept it. When he burst out onto the terrace, where Despina sat reading a book, she knew instantly that something monumental had taken place.

"Come, come inside now," he said to her, motioning for her to follow.

"Why, Anton? What's happened?" she said, letting the book slip from her grasp.

"Antonescu has been arrested!" he shouted, already halfway to the parlor, where the radio rested on the credenza. "There's been a coup!"

He flicked the dial back and forth, trying to find a reliable wave-length. Just as Despina entered the room, a voice came on, one that she recognized instantly. It was that of young King Michael in an address to the nation.

"General Antonescu has been arrested and detained by the Romanian army. Today, Romania has declared its loyalty to the Allied Forces . . . and I have accepted the armistice put before me by Great Britain, the United States, and the USSR. We are at war with Germany."

"My God," Anton said. "My God." And he crumpled onto the sofa, taking a handkerchief from his breast pocket.

This was a complete reversal of allegiance, a colossal blow to German forces. Who would have ever imagined that young King Michael, a boy of merely twenty, would manage to pull off a coup against the man who had ruled Romania with an iron fist? That he would not only take back his birthright but deal a lethal blow to the crumbling Nazi power?

Anton recalled vividly all that had taken place in the months before they adopted Natalia. How after King Carol had abdicated and fled to Spain, young Michael — his only son — had been sworn in as king, even though the real power had transitioned into the hands of Marshall Antonescu. It had not been difficult for Antonescu to take over Romania as a military dictator, for in that he had Hitler's full support. It was understood, of course, that it wasn't so much a personal connection between the men as the fact that Antonescu had delivered Romania's natural riches for Hitler's war effort on a silver platter. Oil in particular was of utmost importance to Hitler as he planned the invasion of Russia. Oil and the fact that Romania had opened the gates wide for his advancing army sweeping east.

"No good deed goes unpunished," Anton remarked. "There will be hell to pay for Romania's change of heart."

This time, Despina could think of nothing to say, no way to disagree with her husband. What neither of them realized as they sat together in silence, sipping a brandy to calm their nerves, was that retribution would come sooner than they even thought possible.

Two days later, as Paris was liberated by American tanks, as Russian bombers raided Berlin, the attacks over Bucharest became more frequent, day and night and all hours in between. Only this time, it was the German bombs that were blasting the already crumbling city.

17

It took precisely one hour and twenty minutes reach Lake Baneasa by trolley. One hour and twenty minutes that Despina welcomed, for it gave her time to think. Riding at dawn with a sleepy Natalia at her side, watching people awaken to another dismal day, another day of dust and debris and diminishing food supplies, gave her a chance to collect her thoughts, to tally up her own life.

So much had happened in the weeks past, and yet it seemed that not much was different at all. The bombings had continued with no end in sight, and schools had shut down indefinitely. Despite the droning of the sirens, most afternoons stretched on with nothing to fill them save for Natalia's constant piano playing. Every moment when they were not in the cellar she spent at her keyboard, repeating the same pieces, going back to the beginning and starting over again, as if those sounds could sweep over everything like a giant swell, wiping the world clean. Sometimes Despina couldn't even coax her away with her favorite sweets, and soon she began fearing that those sirens had reawakened something in her daughter, some buried anxiety that she couldn't assuage.

So when Anton had insisted that if she wouldn't join her sister, she and Natalia spend their days at the lake house — at least away from imminent danger — she had agreed, not so much to appease him but because Natalia desperately needed a change.

Anton, too, had begun going to the store again, even though his daily treks through the scarred and broken city had more to do with his new friend living above the shop than with keeping business open. She knew that was the reason he insisted on going every day, even though no more than a handful of customers wandered in all week long.

What was it about the young man that fascinated her husband so? They were more than fifteen years apart in age and seemingly had little in common. More than that, on several occasions, Anton had hinted that Victor's political views were of a *modern* leaning, and that, she knew, could only mean one thing. Still, in Victor's presence, there was a side of Anton that she had rarely seen. When Victor came to visit — as he did every Sunday since the bombings had started — the bright gaiety with which Anton received his other guests was replaced by an introspective calmness of sorts, an ease of being that was foreign even to her.

Perhaps looking after Victor gave Anton a chance to heal the wounds of his own youth, she thought, gazing absentmindedly out the window. Perhaps that was why Anton dropped off food on Victor's doorstep when there was so little to spare, why he checked in on him nearly daily to see if he had enough oil for his kerosene lamps, enough ink for his pens, enough money to get to the university on the trolley and not have to walk on foot. Why he spoke of him with the affection of a father.

But what truly surprised Despina was that Natalia, too, had come to expect Victor's visits just as eagerly. Her daughter had never taken more than a lukewarm interest in any of their friends — or many adults, for that matter. Yet she was the first to greet him at the door when he knocked once, then two more times rapidly to announce his arrival, bearing the usual bouquet of flowers — lilies and daisies and wild roses that he had most likely collected from a park on his way. She shrieked in delight when he swung her overhead in the doorway and carried her into the house on his back as easily as he might a half-empty knapsack. A trace of pride gleamed in Talia's eyes whenever he crouched down next to her to watch her play various pieces that she was becoming quite good at, pieces from Beethoven or Chopin which she had practiced all day to impress him, to soak in the stunned pause between her ending and his applause. When she spoke, Victor's attention was on her, solely on her. No one ever treated her with such consideration or paid her as much attention. In a short time, Despina realized, Victor had done more for the girl's self-esteem than her family had in all the years she had been living under their roof.

Despina often wondered, how was it that someone as sensitive as Victor could be so utterly alone? Not lonely, for he hardly seemed the type to need anyone's company, but devoid of people in his life. Where were his parents? Did he have siblings or relatives? Certainly, he was good-looking enough to have attracted the attention of some young lady by now. With his sharp, decisively masculine nose, his high forehead, and full, sensual lips, there was no denying that he was quite attractive. But something about his wiry frame and slightly stooped shoulders, the pallor of his skin, and the exceedingly angular cheekbones gave him an air of fragility or ill health that at first glance might have inspired pity rather than awe. And he was always absorbed in thought, his eyes bearing the forlorn look of someone who was pondering a difficult problem or mathematical equation. No, Victor was not an open book, Despina knew, but she had no doubt that someday he would accomplish great things. She, for one, took great comfort in knowing that in a city that had gone up in flames, the devotion of a man like him was the one thing she could still count on.

The trolley lurched forward and came to an abrupt stop, catapulting Despina out of her thoughts. She grabbed her bag in one hand and Natalia's hand in the other, and they descended in a hurry, just as the trolley's engine revved up, ready to loop around the cul-de-sac and resume its trip back to the city. Despina wanted to get to the house quickly. A day like this was not to be squandered, and she intended to make the most of it, especially now with the scent of autumn already in the air. It was not until they actually arrived at the house and opened up all the French windows overlooking the lake that she knew the garden was where they needed to be, the garden filled with lilies and dahlias and rosebushes, all of which would be dormant in less than two months' time.

"Come, Talia," she said, grabbing a blanket and placing a makeshift lunch inside a picnic basket. "Come outside."

Underneath the glorious canopy of an ancient oak, they stretched out side by side, hair loose, shoes off, grass tickling their skin. Natalia was humming a melody, and soon her voice softened, until it stopped and only her breath hummed in Despina's ear. She was overcome with something in that moment — a feeling of ecstasy as much as certitude, that all the beauty in the world was here, in this moment, that she already had everything that could ever give her life meaning. Things would turn out all right. The war would pass, the sirens would eventually stop, the falling of debris would cease, and in the end, their lives — as Anton had promised not long ago — would get back to normal.

Sometime later, she would wonder if in that instant she'd tempted fate. To be so complete, so serene — had she tempted the gods? Had she drawn proof that bliss was a fleeting state, one that could vanish at the snap of a finger? It came so softly at first — surely no more than a colony of bees hovering over her rosebushes — and she closed her eyes against it, ignoring it. But then it grew and expanded, and soon there was no denying that what she was hearing was a siren.

Jolting upright, she tried to make out the direction. It sounded far away, not as acute as usual, and for a moment she thought it would not affect them after all, that it would pass. But she barely had time to shake Natalia awake before three tiny dots appeared above them. Circling in the flawlessly blue sky, diving down lower like eagles hunting for prey, the fighters came into view.

"Get up, Talia, get up now!" she screamed, pulling the girl upward, dragging her to her feet. "We have to go!"

Startled, Natalia scrambled to her feet, stepping on a sharp shrub. She yelped, but her mother kept pulling at her, and she had no choice but to hobble along even though her foot was bleeding.

"Where are we going? Where, Mama?" she screamed, for they were running not toward the house but toward the front gate, and she couldn't hear a thing.

"There's no time," Despina mouthed. "This way."

Up and down the sidewalk they scrambled, searching for a place to take refuge, an entryway, an alcove of any kind. It was a split-second decision, driven by panic or impulse, and Despina feared now that she'd made a mistake. But she couldn't think straight, her head was spinning, and her pulse was tearing through her like a freight train. Natalia was pulling on her sleeve, shouting something, and as a shadow passed through the sky, she looked up and saw the Luftwaffe come at them with such speed that she fell to her knees.

"Happy thoughts, Talia, remember? Think of something happy," she managed to utter, bringing Natalia down with her and covering her body with hers. As the sky exploded in a sheet of glass and roof shingles, in a cloud of ash, her only hope was that Natalia — as she had taught her to do in the shelter — was able to pluck from her memory something that had once filled her with joy.

When it was over at last, when the ominous silence had gone on long enough for her to know that the fighters had gone, Despina did not have the strength to rise. At first, she thought she'd been hit, but there was no pain anywhere, no blood seeping from any part of her body. Crimson rivulets ran down to her ankles over her torn silk stockings, but other than that, she appeared unharmed. *Breathe. Breathe. You are still alive,* she willed herself, struggling to get some air into her lungs.

Underneath her, Natalia was murmuring incoherently, saying something Despina couldn't understand. It was only when she brought her ear close to her daughter's lips that she realized the girl was mumbling a prayer. "Thy will be done on earth as it is in heaven," she heard her say.

In the end, when they stood and began ambling down the sidewalk like marionettes pulled by invisible strings, nothing looked the same. Despina could not recognize a single residence on this block, even though she had passed them all a hundred times before. Before the war, she and Anton often strolled down this very street on summer nights, sneaking away for brief moments from their constant weekend guests. Now she could not tell one house from the next. The facades had all crumbled, and large piles of stucco and cement had overfilled the sidewalks, burying the once ornate iron entrances. The broken windows were like gouged eyes, ugly and dark and pleading, and not a sound emerged through them. There were no voices, no cries for help, no barking dogs. Only silence.

Not quite at the end of the block, Despina came to a sudden halt and let go of Natalia's hand. She stood there in her chalky, ash-covered dress, eyes blank with incomprehension, staring ahead, coughing, choking on the smoke.

Through a gaping hole in the facade of what had once been her beautiful lake house, sun rays filtered through a cloud of ash, illuminating the ravished interior. On the back wall, an intricate Turkish tapestry still hung next to the green velvet chair, and on the side table next to it, the telephone rested unharmed.

"Mama?"

Despina stared blankly into the middle distance.

"Mama?"

Natalia watched helplessly as her mother crumpled at the edge of the sidewalk and wept in a strange way, a way she had not seen before. She wept without making a sound. When she looked up at last, her fingers had left tracks along her temples, where soot had collected like black snow against the ivory paleness of her skin.

18

There had been no choice for Despina but to agree to leave for the country. She cried and pleaded and threatened, kneeling at Anton's feet, but he would no longer relent. After Despina and Natalia had only by a miracle escaped the bombing at the lake house, he was no longer willing to compromise or take chances.

"You have to go. You have to take her and go. You owe it to me, to her, for Christ's sake!" He practically leaped from the sofa, his voice escalating with unusual force. "You cannot stay, not after what's happened, Despina!"

Despina went over to him and rested her hand on his shoulder, but he pulled away roughly. Then he tossed the rest of his cigarette into the fireplace.

Wide-eyed, Despina regarded him silently, then turned and headed for the door. She was almost out of the room when his voice followed, a little calmer.

"I will come and see you every weekend. No bombs can keep me away, you know that."

When she spun around to face him, her eyes were blazing. "It's forty kilometers, Anton! Are you going to travel that far on foot? Every weekend?"

"I won't need to walk," he replied softly. "I can catch a train, be there by lunchtime. We can go on picnics, we can watch Natalia swim in the river, we can laugh like we used to, breathe some much-needed fresh air. Why should all of that seem so uninviting to you?"

She laughed then, but it was a shrill, forced laugh. "Anton, we both know that the trains will stop running soon. And what if they bomb the train station? How will you get to us then?"

It was his turn to storm out of the room. Despina watched him whirl past her and slam the French door so hard that the glass squares rattled in their frames. She sighed and fixed her eyes on the ground. This was not her husband. This was not her peaceful, loving, accommodating husband. She had to do something.

It wasn't so much that Despina was ada-mantly against leaving her life in the city;

whatever remained of it now was hardly enough to keep her here. She knew it was the wise thing to do, the sensible thing. But the idea of parting from Anton at a time like this seemed inconceivable. Perhaps she should have listened to him earlier. If she'd agreed to leave months ago as he had wanted, he might have been able to join them. Now he was stuck here in this cemetery of crumbling, incinerated buildings in case the army needed him to take part in the war's dying throes. Not that it was likely that the Germans could sustain their efforts much longer. With France liberated after four years of Nazi occupation, much of Europe was quickly slipping from Hitler's grasp. But war was still war, and there was no telling how much longer it would go on. And while the war was still a reality, Anton could not leave the city for more than a couple of days.

It would be weeks before she'd see him again, this Despina knew in her heart. Yet he was more determined than her these days, and she could no longer resist his wishes.

The following Sunday, Natalia watched her parents say their farewells from the backseat of the town car her father had hired to take them to the train station. She listened to their voices whispering, rising and falling like waves crashing against a shore.

"I will see you and Talia in a few days," her father was saying, wiping his brow with a handkerchief. It was only midmorning, but the sidewalk was already blistering, the heat radiating off the melting asphalt. "Try not to get accustomed to getting on without me."

Leaning against the cool leather of the backseat, Natalia sighed and smoothed out her dress. It would be as wrinkled and sweaty as an old rag, and if they went on like this much longer, she'd have no choice but to go inside to change. This had to be the longest farewell in history. Even the driver had checked his watch more than three times and was drumming his gloved fingers on the wheel.

Feeling a tinge of embarrassment, Natalia rolled down her window. Trying to ignore her mother, who was now weeping openly in her father's arms, she shouted cheerfully, "Good-bye, Papa, we'll miss you!"

That got her mother into the car, where she slid in next to her and put on a pair of sunglasses. When the car pulled away, only Natalia turned to get a last look at her father. She saw him standing near the curb with his hand held up in a gesture of good-bye, growing smaller in the tinted back window.

"You are here! Oh, goodness, I was beginning to worry!" Ecaterina appeared in the massive oak entrance of her three-story villa, which resembled a medieval castle more than a country house, with its steeply pitched roof, half-timbered stucco walls, and massive windows. Pushing the servants out of the way, she hurried down the long, curved stairway. Climbing out of the horse-drawn carriage that had been sent to fetch them from the station, her mother straightened her skirt and fingered her pearl strand as if she was being deposited at a gala, not in the middle of a farmland. Natalia hopped down as well and embraced her aunt, who, despite the resemblance to her mother, looked like she belonged to another century in her leather slippers and peasant dress, which fluttered about her sturdy bare legs like a tent. Even her mother seemed shocked to be hugged with such ferocity.

"Hello, sweethearts," Ecaterina sang, clasping a hand to her mouth as she turned to Natalia. "Look at how much you've grown!" She clucked her tongue. "But too pale, too thin! Well, we'll have to fix that! At least you've come to your senses, Despina. How long have I been asking you to come out here? How long?" Motioning to one of the servants to unload the bags, she placed one arm around her sister, the other around Natalia. "Well, let me tell you. It will take a moment or two to get used to the country life, but it's really so much better! I mean, who needs all that dust, all that" — she stopped and made a forward gesture — "pollution? I will take care of you both, don't you worry! And the girls, they are so excited to spend time with Natalia! You will love it here, I promise. Don't you like this place already? Don't you?"

An hour later, as they dined on the outdoor veranda, Despina had barely spoken at all. She had not touched her plate, waving off whatever was placed in front of her by a florid young girl wearing a bright blue maid's uniform, and only taking small sips of her wine. Natalia and Ecaterina's girls — waifish twins who had studied their fingernails all through dinner — had decided to pass on dessert and went off to play cards and listen to records.

Now that it was just the two of them, Ecaterina was filling the space with endless stories, talking nonstop about things that for Despina held little interest. She was so tired and consumed, and she could not get respite from her thoughts, from what lingered constantly at the back of her mind. Just now, she realized, the sirens would be sounding over the city. Just now, the shells would begin raining down without much warning, obliterating what was left of Bucharest. The fighter planes would destroy more streets, more blocks, maybe theirs this time. An image sliced through her. She saw Anton shielding his eyes as he gazed in awe at an expanding sphere of light and smoke billowing over their terrace. She placed her napkin alongside her untouched dinner.

"Excuse me, Ecaterina, I think I need to go lie down. Would you mind?"

"Of course not, darling. Florina will show you to your room. You just need some rest, that's all."

Despina pushed her chair back and smiled sadly. "If that could only be the cure. Please make sure the girls don't stay up too late. I'll see you in the morning."

The first thing Despina noticed when she entered the guest suite was that it did not possess the same dark, oppressive aura as the rest of the house. Near a corner on the far side of the room, a spacious cedar armoire had been emptied and left open. A few of her favorite books had been placed on a shelf above the bed, and on the side table a bouquet of white lilies was carefully arranged in a vase next to a water carafe. She poured herself a glass and sat on the edge of the quilt. Ecaterina had gone out of her way to make this room as homey as possible, but it only made her miss her own home all the more.

Yet even back home, things were hardly the same. Their lake house was gone, and she was no longer surrounded by the company of her sisters, and she and Maria had quarreled. Just thinking about what had taken place the afternoon before their departure felt like a blade twisting inside her heart. It wasn't so much the words that had been exchanged when Maria handed her *that letter,* which threatened to ruin everything she had ever fought for, everything that made her life complete. It was the way Maria had regarded her with those soulful eyes when after reading it, she'd meant to tear it to pieces. But that look had been enough to stop her from destroying the one thing that could strike at the heart of her family. And for that she did not know how to forgive Maria.

The empty glass trembled in her hand as she went to the French doors. She flung them wide open and stood there leaning against the doorjamb, letting the evening breeze linger over her face. Could Natalia's biological parents come back for her? *Would* they come back, searching for their lost child, leaving no stone unturned, once the war ended? It wouldn't be difficult, after all. All they had to do was follow the thread back to where it had started, back to her very own cousin.

A while longer Despina stood there, staring out at the nearly black horizon. In the distance, over the city, the searchlights crisscrossed and moved in a rhythmic dance as the sound of antiaircraft gunners rose over the tireless tune of the crickets, far away but acute in Despina's ears. As the curtain of darkness fell deeper and more pronounced and the world sank into a bottomless slumber, Despina's heart pounded on, filled with longing for Anton and a new sensation that had imbued her, inexplicably. Her world was changing, and she couldn't control it, but she *would* try to rise up to it, with the last breath in her body.

19

Since early morning, Natalia had been waiting for her father at the estate gates. She curled up on the strip of grass lining the graveled driveway and rested her forehead on her knees. Perhaps he would not be able to come after all. The roads had been barricaded, and civilian trains had stopped running. Just this morning, she'd heard her aunt and her mother discussing it out on the veranda and knew it was true.

"I've seen them with my own eyes," Ecaterina had said. "There are lines and lines of soldiers waiting on the platform, waiting for the next transport back to Bucharest. You should see them, Despina. You should see the state they are in, dirty and hungry and without proper bandages."

Her mother had gotten up from her chair and begun pacing, but Natalia knew it was not the state of the soldiers that had gotten her so worked up. Even she understood that it would be nearly impossible to return to the city now that the railroads were used strictly for military transport.

"We are trapped, then," her mother had uttered with sheer frustration. "God only knows when we will be able to get back home."

"Perhaps it's for the best," Ecaterina had said in that elder-sister tone of hers. "Maybe now you will give up your crazy notions of leaving."

Despina had turned and shot her a look, then stormed back into the house, nearly bumping into the maid, who was carrying out a platter of cookies. Carefully, the girl had placed the arrangement on the table, then backed toward the door, wiping her hands nervously on her apron. Natalia had given her a small, sympathetic smile. *It is not your fault,* she'd wanted to tell her. *It is not your fault that she is like this.* The temperance her mother had shown thus far was fading. And they hadn't seen her father in weeks.

In the beginning, he did manage to come, traveling the forty kilometers that stretched between the capital and Snagov in any way possible. He took cabs, hitched rides to the outskirts of town, walked as long as his feet would carry him. Sometimes he was able to get rides from peasants transporting goods in their horse-drawn carriages along the country roads. He rode in the backs of animal wagons, with cows and chickens, happy for the chance to catch his breath, to rest a little without delaying his progress. Most Sundays, Natalia knew her father had arrived long before she could see him at the top of the gates. His presence was signaled by the squealing and laughter of small children who trailed him all the way from the main road, devouring the rock candy that he doled out for them from his rucksack as he made his way up to the big house.

But this Sunday, like the Sunday before, there was no sound of the children, and as the hours clicked by, her hope began to dissolve. Soon it was simply too hot, and she was too hungry, so she stood up and began walking back toward the house, kicking the pebbles in her path. Halfway there, she heard her name being called out.

"Talia! Hey! Want to come down to the river?"

Her face brightened, and she spun around. It was one of the village kids she'd befriended, poking his sunburned face through the slats of the gate. The time she'd spent in their company — climbing the vines of the church tower to ring the bell, sneaking into the neighbors' orchards — had been the most fun she'd had in this place, and today in particular, she could do with the company. At least she wouldn't have to be at the house, where her mother's anxiety would drown everything in its wake.

"Yes!" she yelled, and ran back toward the gate.

"Bet you can't keep up!" the boy taunted. He bolted down the hillside a moment later, knowing that she'd be right on his heels.

It was late when she rose the next morning. Close to noon, she could tell from the stark light that had invaded the room. It wasn't the first time she'd overslept, but where were her mother and her cousins? Why hadn't they come to wake her sooner? Throwing off her covers, she tried to get out of bed, but a heaviness held her in place. Her nightdress was wet, clinging to her skin like a sodden ship sail. Propping herself up, she noticed a haziness in the room — even the clock seemed to spin in her vision — and she couldn't make out the time. Certainly, the village kids had come looking for her long ago and had left. Deflated, she let herself fall back onto her pillow. Now she would have to pass the day with the twins or, worse, helping with chores around the house. But she couldn't even keep her head upright, put her feet on the ground. Maybe if she slept for a moment longer, her strength would return, so she closed her eyes again.

She heard her mother's voice. It was cooler now in the room, though she was burning and needed a drink. Something cold touched her forehead, making her gasp. *Talia,* she kept hearing. *Talia, sweetheart, are you all right? Are you all right?* Fire lashed at her throat, and she put her hand up against it, then, curling herself up, she turned to the wall. She watched the shadows of poplar trees play on the wall over her bed, their branches swaying and twisting in the breeze and slowly, slowly disappearing.

When she opened her eyes again, it was dark. No one was calling her name now, it was cold, and all she could hear was the clink of her mother's knitting needles, tapping, going around and around. There was no day and no night; there was only a chasm that kept pulling her into its depth, pulling her down. *Where was I?* she thought in that final moment, trying to hold on, to bring herself back to where she'd left off. All that came back was the end of that dusty trail, her thirst after the long run. And how sweet was the water she had drunk from the old well that all the kids said might be spoiled — how sweet and how cool.

20

Just before sunrise, Despina had dragged their trunk to the front steps, where Natalia's dolls had already been stacked haphazardly next to her traveling case. No more than an hour before, Ecaterina had returned to the house alone.

"I'm sorry, Desi, it's no use. All doctors have been deployed to the city hospitals. There isn't one left in the entire province. And I couldn't get anyone to take you back to Bucharest. It's simply too dangerous."

Despina looked at her incredulously. "It's forty kilometers! Forty kilometers that Anton has covered on foot on more than one occasion. How dangerous can it be?"

"The city has been blockaded, Despina. The fighter planes can be seen circling from here. Be reasonable," Ecaterina said, glaring at her in exasperation.

It was all true, Despina knew. Even Anton, with his determination of steel, had not been able to penetrate through the circle of fire in the weeks past. She could not forget the last time he had shown up, looking so haggard that she barely recognized him when he stumbled in the door at half past midnight. Only the smile buried beneath the thick stubble, the gleam in his sunken eyes, had kept her from falling at his feet, weeping. But how could she make her sister understand? How could she explain that nothing would keep her from doing what she *had* to do? That it didn't matter if the city was evacuated and the train station was abandoned, that she would get back to the city even if she had to carry Natalia in her arms?

"Ecaterina, look out there, at the field," Despina said, gesturing toward the predawn blackness that stretched out before them. "There are hundreds of peasants working on this land every day. Surely one of them will be willing to help."

Ecaterina wanted to protest, to point out that Despina wasn't being rational, but she knew it would do no good. A few times in the past weeks, she had seen this look in her sister's eyes. As she sat down next to her and examined her upright stance, her profile, steady and fixed on the horizon as if she was willing the sun to come up, Ecaterina had the sudden sensation that she was looking upon a stranger. Where was the fragile beauty who at a time like this would have fallen into her arms, weeping with despair? Where was the girl who always sought her advice, who hung on her every word? Whether it was the separation from Anton or the loss of her summer house or just war itself that had caused this shift in her, Ecaterina was sure of one thing: her younger sister did not need her advice or her arms to cradle her.

"All right, Desi. As you wish," she said, rising with an air of resignation. She went into the house, closing the door softly behind her.

Relieved to be alone at last, Despina sat on the porch and waited. She watched the workers gradually populate the field below, their straw hats bobbing over the sea of golden husks in the light of early dawn. When there were enough of them, she marched down the graveled driveway, the pebbles crunching under her steps. At the edge of the field, she took off her shoes and strolled on ahead through the freshly plowed earth, her sandals dangling at her side.

The first farmer she approached would not look her in the eye when she explained that her daughter was ill, that she needed a carriage to take them back to the city.

"I'm sorry, ma'am," he said. "There's too much work to be done here before the rains."

She got the same response from the next one and the one after that. Young ones and old ones and everyone in between, they all shook their heads and politely declined her offers. No amount of money seemed to be enough for what she was asking. One after the other, the peasants refused her, even as she pleaded and begged and threatened, her fury turning to desperation.

Soon there was no one left. *Cowards,* Despina thought. She wanted to scream it out loud. But just as she surveyed the field once more, she spotted a familiar face not far from where she was standing. It took her a moment to realize it was the same man who had given her and Natalia a ride from the train station when they had first arrived in the village. Straightening her back, she strolled toward him, slipping off her wedding ring along the way.

"Hello," she said, smiling.

The farmer turned, a little startled.

"Miss Despina," he replied politely. He remembered her name. This was a good sign.

"Yes, you remember me? Do you remember my daughter, too? Talia?"

The farmer nodded. He had to be at least sixty, Despina realized. Deep lines were etched in the leathery skin of his face, like scars from the slashing of a knife. Perhaps he wouldn't be as afraid as the others. Despina reached out and took his large callused hand in hers. She felt him flinch but did not let go of it. Without a word, she pressed the sapphire-and-diamond ring inside his palm and held it there for a moment. Tears spilled down her cheeks, but she could not look him in the eyes, afraid of the answer she might see in them.

"Please, please, give us a ride back to the city. My daughter needs a doctor."

The farmer regarded her for a long moment with his old, soulful eyes, then gently pulled his empty hand away.

"I will take you to the train station, ma'am," he said softly. "But that's as far as I go."

The station was deserted. Ecaterina had been right about that. Cradling Natalia in her arms, Despina sat on the sole bench on the platform. It was nearly noon, judging from the position of the sun, and her absolute conviction from earlier was weakening. For the first time, she wondered if she should have listened to her sister. If what she had done had indeed been foolish. Yet they were fairly close to the city, and a train of some sort was bound to come through sooner or later. Certainly, she was not expecting a civilian one, but there were still cargo and animal transports all over the countryside and soldiers returning from the front and Red Cross convoys bringing the wounded to the city hospitals. And even if there was no train at all, she would get back to the city somehow. She would carry Natalia along the highway until she found a carriage of some sort. For a moment, she believed it could be done. For a moment, before her fingers trailed over the hollow at Natalia's throat, where her pulse fluttered faintly, irregularly, like the wings of a moth.

Bending down over Natalia's tiny body, she placed her cheek close to the child's. Her breath was so shallow, a featherlike whisper grazing her skin. It reminded her of that first time in the cellar, when she had held her just like this in the dark, as a curtain of artillery rained down around them. She had been able to mask her fear then, to remain calm for her, even though she had been terribly shaken herself. Well, she was even more afraid now. The uncertainty of what would come next terrified her more than those bombs.

In late afternoon, when the sun beat down ferociously and there was no water left in the flask she had brought along, she looked around for a little shade. Across the rails, she spotted a patch of grass underneath an oak tree. Lifting Natalia, careful not to jolt her, she made her way toward it, stepping gingerly over the tracks. It was then that she felt it, a slight tremor under her feet, barely perceptible. There was a rustling of sorts, too, far off in the distance, like a tumble of weeds. It may have been no more than that, but she was already running, she was running recklessly, at full speed, toward the empty horizon, waving her scarf frantically in the air.

At first, she did not know if she was still alive. *Open your eyes,* she willed herself, feeling the heat from the engine so close that it was scalding her face. Her heel had caught on a rail just as the train came into view, and for a moment she had been terrified that it wouldn't stop in time. Perhaps it was only because she had been pinned in place, unable to move out of its path, that the locomotive had come to a screeching halt.

Shaking still, struggling to keep herself

upright, she began crawling alongside the windowless cars, banging on the metal walls with her fists. "Help! Somebody, help!" she shouted, her frantic voice slashing through the silence.

At last, one of the doors rolled open. Despina ran ahead and stopped in front of it, peering up into the partially open wagon. There had to be at least a hundred men standing shoulder to shoulder in near darkness. The wagon had no seats of any kind. A strong stench like that of sweat and dried blood wafted toward her, and she turned her head. She heard some words exchanged but could not make them out. Was it German or Russian? On the platform, a pair of black leather boots shined to perfection materialized. She took a step back on the gravel.

The officer could not have been older than twenty-five, but he was high-ranking, no doubt. She could tell from the way he jumped down onto the rails and strode toward her with his hand on his pistol. She recognized the symbol on his sleeve. The swastika.

"Madam, how can I be of service?"

Piercing blue eyes gazed at her from underneath his green cap. With great relief, Despina realized that she had understood him perfectly. For the first time in her life, she was grateful for her German-school education, for being forced all those years to learn a language she did not see much reason for knowing. Certainly, she hoped that she would remember enough of it now.

"Please, sir, my daughter is very ill. I must get her to Bucharest. She needs a doctor. Please."

For a moment, she thought he might not have understood her, for he just stood there with his arms crossed at his chest. But then he walked over to where Natalia lay motionless in the grass. A shadow of sadness or pity passed over his face as he looked down at her, cocking his head to one side. Perhaps he thought she was already dead.

"Madam, do you realize what you are asking? This is not a civilian train. These are soldiers retreating from the front! Besides, I don't think you'd want to ride among them. They've been on this train for days," he said, gesturing toward the cars.

"Perhaps you might find some help in the village," he went on when Despina did not move, when her eyes refused to leave his. Then he turned and began walking back toward the open wagon.

"Please, officer." Despina's voice broke behind him. She picked up Natalia and began half sprinting, half running after him. "Please, I beg you!"

But already he was inside the wagon, the metal door sliding shut. It clattered loudly, like a death sentence. A moment later, the train began moving out of the station.

This is her life, Despina thought as the last ounce of hope faded. *This is her life, and it's slipping out of my hands. This train is leaving and taking her life with it.* Then something changed, so unexpectedly that she could not make sense of it at first. As the train puttered by her, no more than an arm's length away from where she was standing with Natalia in her arms, she spotted the officer again on the gangway between two cars. Their eyes met for a moment. For a moment, he looked right at her, and she did not know why, she did not understand, until he leaned out and tore Natalia out of her grasp. His move was swift and decisive, like the slash of a sword.

And then it made sense all of a sudden, it came to her like a bolt of lightning, and she was running alongside the train, trying to keep pace with it, just long enough, just fast enough for the officer to reach down for her hand. *We live or die together, we live or die now,* she thought, catching a flash of terror in his eyes as the train picked up speed.

When he leaned down lower, his hat flew off, and she noticed the deep vein across his forehead from the effort. She closed her eyes, expecting the inevitable, expecting her knees to hit gravel, her body to tumble in the wake of the speeding locomotive, but instead, she felt herself being hoisted, extracted from what might have been her final moments. When she opened her eyes again, the station had vanished from view, and the officer's arms were wrapped tightly around her, holding her back from the edge of the platform.

"Are you all right?" he asked, panting, his disheveled hair flopping in the wind.

No words came when she tried to speak. No words, but the tears that had sprung to her eyes said everything. Beneath their feet, the ground passed like a shadow, an indistinguishable flash of gray.

The officer bent down to pick up Natalia and placed her firmly in Despina's arms. "I, too, have a daughter," he said, unlatching the metal door behind them. "A daughter younger than yours whom I haven't seen in two and a half years."

Then, placing his hand on the small of Despina's back, he pushed her forward into the airless cavity. The last thing Despina saw before the door slammed shut and darkness engulfed her was the heartbreaking sadness etched on the officer's face.

21

In front of Maria and Stefan's home, Anton paused to catch his breath. Although he'd become accustomed to traveling long distances on foot, these particular ten blocks had left him drained. The autumn breeze rustled the leaves on the sidewalk, and they swirled around him in a circular dance of red and yellow and burnt copper. Slowly, he climbed up the steps and knocked on the door.

He did not know, in fact, if Stefan and Maria were home, if they had perhaps left the city. It had been months since he'd seen them, since they'd had any contact, really. Certainly, he did not blame them. What was there to talk about these days, where was there to go, when bombs came unexpectedly now, often before the sirens? And then there was that *other* matter, that letter that had sent Despina into a tailspin, just days before she and Natalia had left for Snagov.

When she'd first shown it to him, holding it out as though she was passing a death sentence to be read in front of a jury, he'd nearly smiled, sitting next to her on the bed. "What's this?" he'd said with a slight amusement. Only too well he knew those vertical lines that crept between his wife's brows when some perceived peril loomed over their household. Each time, he would have to make her see how senseless her agitation was, how things weren't as grave as they seemed. But as his eyes lingered over the lines, his own hand began to tremble. That letter had left him speechless. For the first time in their married life, he was flooded with an equal sense of anxiety and confusion.

"How did you get this?" he asked.

"Maria, of course. Who else? Who else is at the crossroads of all this?"

"And what does she say about it?"

"Well, you know her," Despina replied irritably. "You can only imagine what she has to say."

The letter fell to his side. Curling his arm around Despina's bent shoulders, clearing his throat, he pronounced slowly the words that he knew she did not want to hear. "Maria is right, Des. It's the right thing to do.

Natalia should at least know they are still alive."

He flinched when she sprang from the bed. "Anton, are you telling me that you, of all people, don't see how damaging this would be to her? To us, as a family? Here," she spat, grabbing the paper out of his hand and crumpling it before thrusting it back at him. "I want you to take it and burn it. I know what you will say. I know what you think. I know what this makes me in your eyes. And I don't care, Anton. I don't care because I am asking you, no, I am *begging* you to do this one thing for me."

He stared at her, wide-eyed, astonished. Above all things, his wife was a fair woman, and this he had not expected of her. "Despina, how could I do such a thing?" It broke his heart the way she looked at him, his strong woman who would bend to no one, the pleading in her eyes, the fear. He could look at her no longer, so he stood and turned away.

"Then hide it," he heard her whisper coldly. "Put it somewhere where I never have to lay eyes on it again."

Then she'd stormed into the bathroom and slammed the door. Over the flow of the faucet, he heard her sobbing quietly.

Taking a handkerchief from his coat

pocket now, he wiped away beads of sweat from his forehead. The temperature had dropped abruptly, but he felt flushed from the walk. He still hadn't gotten over the shock of the call, the way he'd found them at the train station, and all that had followed — the taxi speeding recklessly along the cobblestone streets, his daughter's whimpering in the backseat, his wife, bent over her small body, not moving, as if she was near death herself. Then, at the house, Sofia wrenching open the taxi door, running upstairs from room to room to gather more blankets, to draw a bath and fetch the rubbing alcohol.

I should not have sent them away, he thought again, for the hundredth time. If he could only turn back time to when he and Despina had quarreled and he had insisted, no, he had *demanded* that she go to the country. He was the one who had placed that distance between them, those forty kilometers that now might cost them their daughter's life.

Like a madman, he'd been ringing the bell, again and again, and when he realized it, he stepped back, letting his hand drop away. *They are not here,* he said to himself. *You fool, they are not here.* And he had turned to go when the click of the door made him halt.

"Anton. My goodness!" Maria exclaimed through the cracked door. She swung it open all the way, and, tying her robe, she motioned for him to enter. "Come in. Come in, please."

"Thank you, Maria," Anton said, removing his hat. "Is Stefan here? I must speak with him urgently."

"Of course, Anton." She fumbled with the light switch near the door, and when the light went on and she saw his face, she paled. "Anton, what's wrong?"

"Maria, please, if I may speak with him."

She nodded quickly, patting the lapel of his coat before rushing into the house to find her husband. An overwhelming fatigue spread through him, and he wondered if it had done any good coming here. Yet where else could he have gone for help? Where else was there to turn when every hospital had refused to admit her? They were full, completely full, he was informed by every clinic in the city when he called them one by one, when he begged and offered any sum of money and in the end had threatened that he would just come with her, he would come and sit at the entrance until they agreed to take her. Wounded soldiers were being cared for on cardboard cots, he was told. The beds themselves were saved only for the gravely wounded, the ones who were not expected to make it through the night. There was simply no room for civilian patients, no room for a *case* such as this. But Stefan had connections; he had powerful friends. He was perhaps the only one who might be able to get them a doctor, to cobble together a small miracle.

"Anton." Stefan's voice boomed behind him, bringing him back to reality. He felt the firm hand on his shoulder and turned. They had been through so much together, he and Stefan, so many grave moments. But he couldn't speak now and simply held out his palms to him as if begging him to read the truth in his eyes. *My daughter is dying,* his eyes said, and he began weeping, right there in Stefan's arms.

"It's all right," Stefan said after a silence. "Whatever it is, it will be all right."

22

Dr. Vladimir took the stethoscope out of his ears and placed it back in his brown leather bag. He leaned over Natalia and picked up her wrist, checking her pulse again. Gently, he placed her arm back on the bed.

"I'm afraid I don't have very good news," he said somberly. "If I could have seen her a little sooner, perhaps . . ." His voice trailed off. Even after thirty years of practice, he still struggled with this sort of thing. There was simply no easy way to deliver such news.

"What do you mean exactly, Doctor?" Despina uttered, her voice hinged somewhere between disbelief and laughter. A tiny web of veins appeared underneath the white, nearly translucent skin at her temples. The doctor cleared his throat and glanced away awkwardly. He had to get through the next steps with delicacy.

"I'm afraid it's not good news," he repeated, taking off his glasses and placing them in the leather satchel. "She has an infection, perhaps she's had it for days, because it looks quite advanced . . ." Again, he paused, fumbling for the right words. "Judging from her high fever, the infection has likely spread, may already be in her bloodstream. I'm afraid there isn't much I can do at this point."

Stone-faced, Despina stared at the doctor. She couldn't move a muscle, yet all she wanted was to pounce on him, hit him with her fists. She wanted to gouge his eyes out, tear the last hairs from his receding hairline. She slid to the floor near the bed. Something opaque veiled her vision; it turned everything in the room an ugly, grotesque shade, like that of congealed blood.

Anton knelt down beside her, tried to put his arms around her, but she batted at him. When he tried again, she hit his shoulder, his cheek, and she scrambled away. Then she screamed. She covered her own ears and screamed, a sound so guttural that even Natalia's eyes snapped open.

"I'm so very sorry," the doctor said again, taking a few steps toward her but stopping halfway. He went back to his bag and began rearranging its contents. "Maybe if we had some penicillin, if we had it days ago . . ."

There was simply nothing more to say to

this poor woman, this mother who was coming apart before his very eyes. From his breast pocket, he took out his chain watch and looked at the time. There was nothing worse than this feeling of helplessness, of a battle lost. Of death beating down hope, winning.

"If we had what?" Stefan asked from where he stood motionless in the doorway. Now that he had brought the doctor here, now that he'd scoured the city and banged on the doors of people he'd never disturb in the night and paid in gold bars and begged on his knees for a semblance of help, he expected more than a declaration of defeat, a sentence passed without much of a fight. "If we had what, Doctor?"

"Penicillin," the doctor repeated warily, rubbing away at his temples. "It's a new drug that could cure a bacterial infection like Natalia's. A wonder drug, really, quite new and scarcely available. It's nearly impossible to come by these days. No hospitals in this country have it, and if they did, they would have run out of it long ago, using it on the men who are dying by the thousands —"

The doctor stopped in mid-sentence, realizing that he had ventured into a subject that did not concern anyone in this room.

That, in fact, it would make matters worse. But Stefan had a look of concentration on his face, as if he was already ahead of the conversation, as if he had long moved past his words.

"What if I could get it for you somehow? What if I could get it *to* you? How much time does she have?" He hated having to ask this in front of Despina, but there was no time to speak to the doctor in private. And they were all beyond measured words now.

"Two, maybe three days. Perhaps a week," the doctor replied in a low, somber voice. "But as I've said before, it's impossible —"

"Let me worry about that, Doctor," Stefan interrupted. He had already grabbed his hat from the top of the dresser. "Let me try."

This time, he was not addressing the doctor. He came to crouch down next to Despina at the foot of the bed and tried to pry her hands away from her face.

"Look at me, Des," he said, but she would not. She would not raise her head to look at anything in the room. "Despina," he said again, resting his hand on her shoulder. "I will do all I can. I will do all that's in my power. But I will need to unlock the one door that you do not want opened."

For a while, no one spoke. The only sound in the room was that of a tree branch tapping on the windowpane, as if it, too, demanded an answer. Despina buried her face in Stefan's collar and began to weep.

"Yes," she mumbled between sobs.

Her tears flowed freely like an open dam, and she no longer cared how she looked in the eyes of a stranger, for she had nothing else to lose. They streamed down Stefan's hands as she clenched them tightly against her cheek.

23

A day passed, perhaps two. There was no telling, really, the minutes and hours threading together endlessly, mercilessly, heedlessly. Without regard for what went on inside the walls of their home, Despina's desperation and cries, Anton's stunned silence, his frenzied pacing across the wooden floor, back and forth, back and forth.

Every few minutes, Despina leaned over to put her ear close to Natalia's lips, praying for the shallow sound of her breath. She did this mechanically, like a marionette being pulled this way and that by invisible strings, propelling her to move even as she felt dead herself, a moving corpse. Holding her own breath, she listened for Natalia's ragged exhale against her cheek. It was still there, delicate, like a butterfly's wing. The mere realization that she was still alive brought her such sweet relief. The fragile string connecting life and death had not yet unraveled.

So little time had passed since the doctor's visit, and Natalia's skin was already beginning to take on a bluish, translucent hue. She was so still it was difficult to believe there was still life inside her, that blood was still coursing through her veins. The night before, she had not uttered a single sound. Even her occasional sighs, her faint whimpers, had ceased.

For two days, Despina had sat at the foot of her bed, refusing to move, refusing the trays of food that Sofia brought in for her. Refusing to speak to Anton. Aside from getting up once or twice to get a glass of water, she had barely shifted since Stefan had left their home to chase down this unattainable drug, this penicillin that perhaps did not even exist. And if by some miracle he did manage to get it, would he make it back in time? Would it be too late by the time he returned? A few days, the doctor had whispered in Stefan's ear, but Despina had heard it louder than the church bells in the plaza at the end of their street. Two, perhaps three days, mere hours, was all she had left.

Despina lifted her eyes to the half-opened window framed by sheer fluttering curtains. She no longer had the strength to ask God for mercy or forgiveness, for she was screaming inside, her fists clenched so tightly that she drew blood from her own palms. *Do you hear me? If you are up there, if you exist, show me. Show me!* she shouted voicelessly to the perfectly blue patch of sky that seemed to smile at her innocently.

To keep busy, she began reciting poems from the children's collection that Natalia had loved when she was younger. She remembered reading them to Natalia when she was a little girl and the sound of Despina's voice was enough to lull her to sleep, to calm the nightmares from which she startled awake during those first months after they had brought her home.

As she had done then, she kept reading long past the time when the light of evening bathed everything in a pink-orange hue, long after darkness fell into the room and shadows swelled and moved on the wall above Natalia's bed. She turned on the side lamp and continued reciting poem after poem, unaware that her throat felt like sandpaper, that her voice was raspy and thick. She did not stop until daylight, until Sofia came in and dragged her away to her own room to get a little rest and wash up.

In this strange and austere household that

she had once known so well, Sofia had become uncertain of her role. No one seemed to have any desire for the food she cooked. No one asked about clean sheets or pressed clothes. No one seemed to notice that a leak had sprung in the kitchen ceiling and water was collecting in a pot underneath.

"Should I call the plumber, Mr. Anton?" she had asked, realizing now that the pot was filling so quickly it had to be dumped out every couple of hours.

Anton had just looked at her as if he had not understood one word of what she said. Sofia had lowered her eyes and closed the door to his study. At least he had finally settled down. For two days, he had been pacing the house nonstop, the rhythmic sound of his hard-soled shoes trudging back and forth, endlessly, for hours. Now he just slumped in that chair by the fire and stared into the dwindling flames. Tiptoeing around him, Sofia asked if he would like something to eat, if she could bring him the morning paper. He shook his head and went back to staring into the fireplace. Death had already permeated their home.

Another day went by.

Anton began to plan for what would

inevitably come now, in a matter of hours, a matter of days. A child lost. A child lost to them, after all they had been through. A child lost at his hands. He dropped his head against the sofa rest and began to weep. He did not hear the doorbell until the third ring. In dreamlike motion, he got up to open it.

"Anton, thank goodness."

In the doorway, Stefan stood holding his hat against his chest. He smiled and said something just as a tramcar went clattering by, drowning out his words.

Why are you smiling? Anton wanted to ask. *How can you smile at a time like this?* But he did not, for in his extended palm, Stefan was holding a small brown box.

There was no grace in Anton's movements as he reached for it, yanked it greedily. In one swift move, he tore it open, ripping through the thick cardboard as if it were made of flimsy paper. The box came apart easily in his hands, and just as it did, Anton saw the Red Cross emblem, bright red and distinct, like a gaping wound at the top of the box. A foreign address was scribbled underneath it in small print: *Geneva, Switzerland.* Inside the box, there were ten or twelve small vials containing a whitish, cloudy substance.

"She will need to receive it intravenously," Stefan was saying now. "Dr. Vladimir has arranged for her to be admitted today at the Coltea Hospital. But we need to hurry."

Anton nodded, dry-mouthed, stunned. Hope flooded through him with unexpected force, and it fueled his shattered heart, spurred on its wild galloping, and it began pumping too fast, too hard. *How?* he wanted to ask. *How did you manage this?* But the words were trapped in his throat, and there was no time for questions, no time to delve into what he already suspected, what he knew, in fact, must have been the only way. Tears spilled once more onto his pale cheeks, shaded in stubble.

"Now, Anton," Stefan said more firmly. "Go on and get her now. I will be waiting in the cab."

At the bottom of the steps, Anton saw a town car parked at the curb, its engine still running.

For three days, the sleepless hours threaded together like beads on a string, and there was no longer a beginning or an end, there was only now. He was only dimly aware of the presence of people in the hospital corridor coming and going, the clink of the metal clipboard as it dropped in a slot at the foot of Natalia's bed, the quiet drip of a fluid-filled bag attached to a metal pole, a sheer, frayed curtain billowing in the late-afternoon breeze. And silence. Long, interminable silence punctuated only by Despina's sobs.

Alongside his wife, in late evening, when the lights had been turned down and the hospital quieted, he found himself doing something he hadn't done since he was a child. On his knees, he prayed for Natalia, and for himself and Despina, too, and soon an unknown calmness descended upon him and with it some kind of understanding that had until now eluded him. This was what it must have been like for them, too, the people who had given Natalia life, when she had been snatched from their hands. They were sharing a common fate. Even though he had never known them and never would, the magnitude of what they had done to save her, not once but twice, hit him straight on, and he grasped with a start that they would always be bound by a common love for her. It was not fear they should be regarded with but thankfulness for the gift of Natalia, for the gift of her life, and ultimately, for their sacrifice.

Sometime later, as he sat in a corner of the room struggling to keep his eyes open, afraid that if he closed them for a moment, she would slip away, all of his life's defining moments unfolded before him, and he welcomed them with a new reverence. Like a horde of boisterous children, they paraded one at a time, bearing reminders of all that he had once felt — happiness and love and passion and pride and possibility and, ultimately, the hope in him that would not be stifled.

And then one searing memory:

"So I am to live with you, then?"

"Yes, sweet girl."

She clutched the doll to her chest and measured him from beneath her thick, dark lashes. Her green eyes gleamed like embers with relief and perhaps a little uncertainty. "For how long?"

"Why, forever. We are to be a family."

"A family?"

"Yes, a family. That means we will never part."

Her gaze traveled back to the doll. She ran her fingers over the long pale hair, the gold-threaded muslin dress, the smooth surface of the porcelain skin. When she looked up at last, a smile like one he had never seen lighted her face.

"And so I shall never leave you," she had said.

■ ■ ■ ■

The next morning, when Dr. Vladimir returned, holding his chart rigidly against his chest, the image before him made such an impression that without a word, he turned around and walked out of the room. For how could he have disturbed what unfolded before him? It was a miracle, indeed, one for which he himself had not dared hope. Yet there they were, at the foot of the hospital bed, the three of them in an unflinching embrace. It reminded him of something he had seen once that had stirred him deeply: a three-budded rose had sprung back to life among a tumble of weeds over a forgotten grave.

■ ■ ■ ■ ■

Two:
Natalia

■ ■ ■ ■ ■

24

September 1944

The crowd moved and swelled like a tidal wave, restricting the air between them. Inch by inch, the mob pushed forward, toward the roped wire that the police had put up to constrain the thousands of bystanders and keep them from spilling out onto the boulevard. To get home from here, they would have to reach the other side of the plaza, then take one of the side streets that radiated from its center like spokes on a bicycle wheel. An impossibility.

The smell of whiskey and cheap women's perfume wafted toward Natalia in a sickening swirl as she held on steadfastly to her father's hand. She buried her nose in the edge of his jacket and nearly tumbled forward as a heavyset woman shoved her absentmindedly from behind. Struggling to get past them, elbowing her way further into the crowd, the woman shaded her eyes with one hand while with the other she loosened the scarf tied under her chin and began waving it in the air.

A second surge of cheering erupted like an avalanche, and the bodies began to push forward with renewed force.

"Papa, I'm scared," Natalia whimpered, tugging on her father's sleeve. "Papa!"

"Don't be, darling."

His arms were sturdy enough that they could easily lift her onto his shoulders, where she felt safe. Safe and not nearly as frightened, for all she could glimpse now was a sea of handkerchiefs and hats and tiny flags flapping and twirling — until only a moment later, she followed the direction of the faces in the crowd, and she gasped.

They were smaller than she had imagined them to be. No bigger, really, than the armament trucks she'd seen bumping along the country roads. Motorcars flanked them on either side as they rolled down the center of the thoroughfare like a colony of centipedes, metal grinding the asphalt, flattening the littered debris in their way. On the platforms, hundreds of soldiers in green uniforms — packed so closely together that some could only hold on to the bars with one hand — waved their starred caps to the roaring crowd.

"It's over, the war is over!" someone shouted, and the excitement spread and rippled, carrying the crowd forward another pace.

A few women had brought baskets of flowers, roses and gardenias and lilies freshly plucked from their gardens, which they began tossing one at a time in the path of the tanks. A girl of barely twenty broke free from the barricade and knelt in the street, lowering her forehead to the ground. When she looked up again, her eyes glistened with tears.

Natalia looked down at her father for a sign that maybe they, too, should be weeping, or at the very least shouting out a cheer, but his face was a mask, betraying nothing. He brought her back down to the ground and clasped her hand tightly; then he began leading her through the mass, carving a path in the opposite direction. They were like a great big warship bucking the tide of cheering men and women and wailing, terrified children.

On the other side of the strangulated plaza, they cut briskly into a backstreet. A few vehicles with windows down lay abandoned at odd angles in the street, as if their passengers had run from a fire. Though it was relatively peaceful there, they still hurried along toward the end of the block, for that could change at any moment.

"Natalia, do not believe everything you see," her father said when they were out of earshot of any pedestrians. He paused momentarily as they walked past a dingy café with dirt-streaked windows in front of which three men were swaying arm in arm, singing a drunken tune. Bending down to her, he whispered, "Sometimes the truth is not altogether what it seems."

What do you mean? she was about to ask, but his eyes were pinned to the street, glancing up just long enough to check the street signs before they crossed. Perhaps he was trying to figure out a way to get home from here, now that they had gone in the other direction from the plaza. To get to the next main artery, they would have to cross over a maze of side streets and alleyways. They could hope there would be a bus or trolley of some kind.

Usually, she did not mind taking long walks with her father. It was the one time when his attention was undividedly hers and she could share with him whatever was on her mind. But today her father was not at all interested in her stories.

He had been like that a lot lately, practically since her return from the hospital.

Gone was his usual buoyant energy, the mischievous glimmer in his eyes as if every moment had been created for his enjoyment. Gone was the man who liked surrounding himself with people at all hours of the day. Even on the occasional evening when an old friend dropped by, he seemed eager for the visit to end so he could go upstairs and listen to the news. Mostly, he hung about just long enough to exchange pleasantries before excusing himself, complaining of a headache or some other ailment.

Maybe it was all the same, for even though the war had ended in Romania, their home was still as quiet as it had been during the bombings. Schools were to reopen soon, and all over town, lights had begun twinkling again — however timidly — in storefronts, in windows, but Despina's sisters and children had not yet returned to the city. Only Maria and Stefan still came by from time to time, but they never stayed long.

Natalia was puzzled by the chillier relations between her mother and Maria. Before the war, they had never spent more than a couple of days apart. But now Maria's visits were short. She seemed rushed, almost uncomfortable to settle in for long or delve into a conversation of any length. Usually, she left as quickly as she came, giving Natalia a quick peck on the cheek and a glance at her mother that spoke of something she did not understand. The air felt thick between them.

And Victor? The last time Natalia recalled seeing him was at Lake Baneasa, before the bombing that destroyed their summer house. The four of them were going to have a picnic by the shore, and she remembered how wonderful the sun felt after the long winter, how the scent of honeysuckle and lilac had enveloped her so sweetly. She had insisted on carrying the basket of sandwiches, and Victor followed her with a blanket and a bottle of wine, some plates rattling inside a matching basket. At the back gate, she'd paused, waiting for him to open it. "Bet you can't catch me!" she had shrieked, and bolted down the hillside through the tall, untamed grass.

He had run after her, so closely that she was sure he would beat her this time. But as usual, he did not. It was hard to imagine that all that remained of those days would now be contained in a handful of photographs on her mother's mantel. Just recently, she had heard her father say he wanted to level the ground and put the lot up for sale.

"Papa, are you sad because Victor hasn't come around in a while?" she found the courage to ask.

Her father slowed his step a little, surprised, it seemed, by the question or perhaps contemplating this very thing himself. "Well, you know he's busy, Talia. He has a job now and probably not much time for social visits."

"Victor has a job? What job?"

He shrugged. "He works for the Ministry of the Interior, that's all I know."

"Is that why he moved out of the loft?"

"Probably," he said, and something passed over his face, something that might have been melancholy or pride. "That place up there is hardly deserving of him now, you know."

It was clear he did not want to discuss it further, for he picked up the pace, and they continued in silence, weaving through the maze of honking automobiles and people hooting out of their car windows and from the balconies above. They had not been able to find a bus, and it was nearly nightfall when they reached home.

Alone in the parlor later that night, Natalia sat at her piano and dove distractedly into a

Beethoven sonata, her eyes fixed dreamily on the window, beyond which there was now only a patch of black. The room was imbued with the smell of gardenias her mother had plucked from their garden just that afternoon, and she inhaled deeply, feeling the knot in her belly loosen a little but not all the way. Even here within the walls of her home, she was haunted by a feeling she couldn't explain, a tilt of reality that deeply unsettled her.

What was it about her parents these days? She couldn't quite put her finger on it. Sometimes she felt as if she was living with a lesser version of the people she once knew so well. Unlike her father, who had succumbed to a fog of glumness, her mother fluttered about as if nothing had happened at all, as if their lives had not been in the least interrupted by war and illness and fallen bombs and now by the Red Army that was marching down the city's main boulevards.

Every morning, she appeared at the breakfast table in one of her silk dresses or peplum suits, her hair in her signature French twist. As she had done every morning before the war, she sipped her coffee on the terrace, straight-backed and unflinching, gazing down at the traffic below, the trolleys and tramcars that had just begun running again. Few people would have guessed that she brewed her own coffee now and prepared their breakfast. That she washed towels and sheets, leaning over the tub in the evenings, wiping the sweat from her forehead with soapy, reddened hands. That she mended the drapes and restored the gleam of the fireplace, scrubbing soot from every nook and crevice of their home.

Ever since Sofia had left them, she had done it all single-handedly.

It was ironic, really, that after being with them through the worst of the war, through the darkest days of the bombing, they would lose her now, of all times. But this year, Sofia had turned seventy and decided that it was time to return to her native village near the Hungarian border, to her roots and her grandchildren who were now fully grown.

"I want to spend my last days on the soil from which I've sprung, Miss Despina," she had said, and Despina had pleaded and offered her a raise, offered her anything to stay, but in the end let her go.

From her bedroom window, Natalia had watched them say their farewells as the rays of dawn shone over the rooftops on that Sunday morning. Even after the cab that was to take Sofia to the train station was gone, her parents stood outside in their slippers and house robes, holding on to each other under the lamppost, and Natalia was reminded of another time, another cab ride that took her and her mother from the burning city.

After Sofia's departure, her mother took all matters of the household into her own hands with the zest of a conquering army.

"Get someone else to help," her father kept telling her, but she would not. Her mother was loyal to Sofia even in her absence.

"I can manage, Anton, don't worry."

She had begun making peach and cherry marmalades and pickling red peppers, tomatoes, and onions. She prepared their meals, taking great pleasure, it seemed, in her old culinary skills, and their cellar was stocked again with hundreds of jars of homemade *zacusca* and eggplant spread and *tarama* — all labeled and dated in her sharp, determined handwriting. To Natalia, it looked as though she was preparing for another war.

And Natalia had had enough of war.

All she wanted to do was to open her arms to the sky, to breathe, to feel alive. For the first time in as long as she could remember, she woke up not feeling afraid of sirens and bombs, of the growl of fighter planes strafing the rooftops. She could step out onto the terrace and breathe in the morning air. She could wear her pretty dresses again, without fearing they would get soiled in a cloud of ash. She could stroll past the storefronts which had just opened again, to the pharmacy around the corner which still stocked a dozen or so shades of lipstick. The lady clerk pretended not to notice as she tried the samples, pursing her lips secretively in the counter mirror, and only smiled a little whenever she caught her eye. "Give your father my best," she would tell her on her way out the door. But nowadays her father had little interest in his old acquaintances, little interest in anything other than the presence of Russian tanks on the streets of Bucharest.

"The Soviets have just negotiated an armistice granting them military command of the country," he informed them one night at dinner, barely taking the time to fold the napkin onto his lap. "We are under their control, Despina, by *force*, by orders of Moscow. Are you aware what this means?"

Natalia put her fork down, suddenly not hungry. She wanted to run out of the room so she wouldn't have to hear this all over again.

"Oh, Papa!" she blurted out before she could hold herself back. "Why can't you stop talking about this? The Soviets, the Soviets, why does it matter so much?"

The look he gave her made her wish that she could push the words back into her mouth, though she wasn't quite sure what she'd done wrong. Wasn't he the one who always encouraged her to speak her mind, to not hold back her opinions? Yet there was no praise in his eyes now, only shock. Her mother, too, was regarding her wide-eyed, the forkful of food in her hand hovering over her plate.

"And how much exactly do you think that you know about all this, Talia?"

"I know enough," she replied. "I know that people are dancing in the streets and draping garlands around their necks and greeting them with fresh bread and flowers. So whatever it is that they are doing here, it can't be all that bad."

The silence was heavy and seemingly endless.

When he spoke again, his voice had dropped to a whisper. "You are excused, Natalia," he said somberly, rising from the table to pour himself a drink.

A knot formed in Natalia's throat. She swallowed hard against it. *Don't be angry with me,* she wanted to say. *Be happy. The war is over. Why can't you be happy?* But this time, no words came. Instead, she stood from the table, pushed her own chair out, and left the room without saying another word.

25

November 1948

Winter arrived much too early that year. Christmas was still seven weeks away, but it had already begun snowing, the days short and desperate, icicles glistening under roof eaves like broken daggers in the bleak light of the midday sun. In Palace Square, the bronze statue of King Carol I was toppled in front of a crowd of bewildered bystanders. As half a dozen tanks smashed mercilessly into the pedestal, a shout of outrage cut through the mass of people; it was joined by another, then another still, until all voices intermingled and rose like a great billow of smoke over the square. It wasn't until a militiaman fired a warning shot into the air that the chorus subsided and people began dispersing in clusters, bracing silently against the bone-shattering chill.

A new border stretched over the continent. A wall of barbed wire, behind which all the grand cities of Eastern and Central Europe found themselves hostage, ruled by checkpoints, guarded by watchdogs and Soviet armored tanks. In Bucharest, all the country's former leaders and members of the Royal Parliament had been arrested or imprisoned, some sent to work in forced-labor camps in remote Siberia. Many had vanished overnight without explanation. The winter before, King Michael himself had been forced to abdicate at gunpoint after the Royal Palace was surrounded by army units sent by Stalin. It hadn't been only him facing the end of the barrel; if he refused, he was warned, one thousand arrested students would die, and the bloodbath would not end there. Thus, he'd signed the decree, and in a matter of minutes, the last surviving monarchy in the Balkans was no longer.

"Do you know we are to be called a People's Republic?" the stunned citizens of Bucharest whispered on street corners, at bus stops, near flower stands where they could talk in whispers. "Do you know our new prime minister was appointed by Stalin himself?"

The new reality had been shaped around them not with the slow progression of change but with the sharp precision of the guillotine, severing them from everything they knew to be true and familiar.

On her way to school, Natalia was mesmerized by the constant activity as she passed the old Palace of the Senate and the Military Headquarters. Slowing her pace, she gaped at the parade of men in dark leather coats and fur caps — sturdy, square-shouldered men with sober faces — coming in and out of government buildings that now bore new names. The guards planted at the gates saluted them at attention, dashing ahead to open their car doors, carrying their briefcases and boxes filled with documents, and loading them into the trunks of cars with black, impenetrable windows. On the streets, people stood aside and looked timidly to the ground as these men marched past them in long, purposeful strides. They kissed their hands when they entered beerhalls and demanded bottles of vodka and fine delicacies that no one had a taste for any longer.

A new silence had descended on their home.

"Do not speak to anyone at school, Talia, about what we have in our home," her mother warned nearly every night. "Most of all, do not ever mention the piano, the leather-bound books. Do not talk to anyone at all. And remember, the walls have ears."

"I know, Mama, you've told me. Please don't worry," she would reply each time, not wanting to point out that her father had told her the very same thing just the night before. That she had practically memorized those lines.

Perhaps it was because of her parents' growing paranoia that she found herself eavesdropping on street corners as she pretended to tie her shoelaces or search through her backpack for something she could not find. The stories she heard terrified her, stories about homes being ransacked and looted, about Red Army soldiers breaking down doors in the middle of the night, waving machine guns, taking all they could carry — jewels, china, silverware, oil paintings, Turkish rugs. Stories about men dropping on their knees and kissing their boots, offering them their gold watches, their wedding bands. About civilians disappearing without explanation, by the hundreds, the thousands.

"They are drunk," she'd heard some say. "They are drunk on *tuica,* they are drunk on power and life outside the muddy trenches. They haven't forgiven the Romanian people for the siege of Leningrad, the

241

bloodbath at Odessa. How many thousands died at our hands? How many thousands?" they uttered, shaking their heads. It was all true, Natalia knew. The Germans had starved the Soviet people, they had forced them to eat cats in winter, they had forced them to eat corpses. And all along, the Romanian people had lent a helping hand.

"Is it true, Mama, what they say about the Red Army soldiers?" she asked one evening, but her mother brushed her off with the usual reply.

"Go wash up, Natalia. If you hurry, maybe you could get in a few minutes of practice before dinner."

Natalia sighed but did as she was told, knowing it was pointless to bring up the subject. Despite all the stories that circulated, despite the rumors that the Soviet soldiers surpassed even the Germans in their brutality, her mother never wanted to talk about them. Natalia suspected it had something to do with that time, during the last days of the war, when she had sat on the rail in Snagov with a sick child in her arms. It was a soldier then who had saved their lives. "War is war," she had told Natalia once. "It transforms human beings in unimaginable ways. But they are still human beings."

Four years had passed since that fateful day, four years that might have been a century, for that time had been eclipsed entirely by more pressing matters, things that weighed on their household like a gathering storm. For months now, her father had been coming home every night with news of businesses being confiscated, banks being nationalized, money being devalued. Of people like him, honest, hardworking businessmen, who had been marched into the street and shot for some careless, offhand comment against the new government. Of families much like theirs who were sent away on trains and were never heard from again.

"These are dangerous times, Despina," he so often remarked. "You should try to go out less often. And put away those furs of yours. It will draw the kind of attention we don't need."

"All right, darling." Her mother would try to appease him. "But please don't speak of it in front of Talia. Don't speak of it at all. I will do as you say."

Like the rest of the dwindling bourgeois class, the Gozas found themselves more and more confined within the walls of their home. Having little to do, Natalia spent most of her waking hours much as she had during the days of the sirens, at her piano. Her father had insisted on moving it up to her room, at the farthest end of the house, where she was least likely to be overheard by the neighbors. He was not particularly fond of noise of any kind these days, particularly the kind that might be construed as an aristocratic pursuit and get him arrested.

He had also had to cut back on her piano lessons, but Natalia did not mind. She felt freer than ever practicing on her own, away from the overanalytical eye of Miss Eliade, from her shrill voice that would often interrupt Natalia's playing to complain that she wasn't sitting properly or that her elbows were too stiff or that she needed to lower her wrists and not attack the keyboard like a vulture. Now she was free to improvise, to make up her own melodies, variations on classical works she had long learned by heart, even some less conventional pieces that would have had the old woman burning with rage.

Had jazz ever affected her so? In the years before the war, it seemed it was always there, trickling in the background of her everyday life as peacefully and uneventfully as a creek. Yet something had happened when she'd brought the turntable and records no one played anymore up to her room and sat at her own piano. Ever since, she'd felt guilty, as if she was somehow betraying the great composers, yet as she muddled along with those melodies, she felt as if she was somewhere else altogether, those chords and movements filling her up with a bubbling energy, like a fever. Sometimes she imagined herself to be that girl on the album cover, wearing a sequined gown in the dimmed lights of a stage, a handsome trumpeter in a white coat playing right at her side, their sounds twisting and entwining in a caress. It was a challenge at first to learn the unique syncopations, but after a while, Natalia found that it became less difficult, and she began being able to emulate those pieces quite well.

It saddened her, though, that she couldn't share them with her father, for so often now he was in his study with the door closed, and he no longer asked her to play for him before bedtime. He was preoccupied these days, sullen, quiet. He no longer ranted about the deteriorating living conditions or how it was a matter of time before all they had would be taken from them.

And something else. For the past few weeks, he had come home every night with a heavy suitcase in his hand. Muttering a quick hello, still in his coat and hat, he would drag the case breathlessly across the parquet floor and through the kitchen, all the way to the back stairs leading up to the attic. The old wooden door would creak open, and she would stand there and listen to the case slamming against the cement stairs, echoing in the stairwell, and wonder what was inside it. She wondered still when he came back downstairs with the empty case and tossed it near the front door, where he would pick it up again the next morning.

Whatever it was he was depositing up there, she knew better than to ask questions. It would only force him to make up some false reason, some half-baked answer that they both knew she was too old to believe. Then, once again, a discussion would follow, a long-winded discourse about their family's circumstances, how she was not to trust anyone, not to talk to anyone. How their very lives would hang in the balance if she divulged what went on in their home. No, it was best if she did not bring it up at all.

But it wasn't the fact that her father had not wanted her to know what he was hiding in the attic or that even during the heaviest days of the shelling, she had not seen him act with such systematic determination. It was the detached resolve with which he performed this routine every evening that told her this was worse than the bombings, much worse for people like them.

One night at the end of the winter, her father handed her mother a handgun. He held it out to her over the dinner table, over the potato casserole and meat stew, as if he was passing the salt. Her mother stared at it for a moment but did not reach for it. He placed it on the white linen cloth, and it sat there between them, its delicate ivory handle gleaming in the overhead lights like an enchanting porcelain yet with all the gravity of an undetonated grenade. It was a small, elegant pistol, a lady's model, small enough to fit into an evening clutch.

"I want you to carry this with you at all times," he said almost matter-of-factly, digging into his food. "Just for the time being. And Talia" — he raised his eyes to her sternly — "in case you should stumble upon it, I thought you should know what it is, so that you'll never touch it."

Natalia felt her mother shift slightly beside her. The fork clinked against the side of her plate as she set it down. She patted her mouth, which had stretched into a thin line, and took a small sip of water but said nothing.

A gun? Natalia almost blurted in astonishment, knowing how much her mother hated them, how she wouldn't even let him keep one locked in the safe. So many times she heard her say how they filled her with terror, but now, with one displayed on the dinner table as casually as a butter dish, her mother wasn't forming a single objection.

"We'll discuss it in the morning, Anton," was all she said quietly, and Natalia knew it was only for her benefit.

"All right, darling," her father replied, and they held each other's eyes with an understanding needless of words. "As you wish."

But the next morning, when he came down for breakfast, the first thing he did was to look inside her purse. Humming a tune under his breath, he clamped it shut, and with a satisfied look, he went to the sideboard to pour himself a cup of coffee.

All that afternoon and most of the evening Natalia spent in her room. She played and played along with that merry jazz music, riding on the wings of a fairy tale. She played until her back ached and her fingers cramped — until all that angst had washed away from her, drained clean like a streak of mud in a downpour of rain.

26

April 1950

Elena's house, it turned out, was the only one on its block that still bore its prewar facade. If the property showed any signs of the tumult of years past, it was barely visible in the fissured stone walkway, the slightly rusted iron fence, the wooden shutters that needed a fresh coat of paint. Overall, it still resembled a Greek villa at the edge of the Mediterranean, even on a gloomy street such as this, amid melting, mud-splattered snow.

On the light-filtered porch, Despina drew off her gloves. She shook the droplets of water from her coat and removed her rain boots which were such a stark contrast to the rest of her elegant attire. Natalia followed suit, doing the same.

"Remember what we talked about," she reminded Natalia. "I know they are family, but we are not to delve into anything but polite conversation, right?"

Natalia nodded enthusiastically, half listening. She had no intention at all, in fact, of delving into grown-up subjects of any kind. All she wanted was to see her eldest cousin, Lidia, whom she'd been missing so terribly. The entire winter, they'd been barricaded inside their house as if they were still in a war zone, and it was only because she'd begged and pleaded, and because the sun had decided to make an appearance, that her mother had agreed to go there. Just for an hour or two, no more. At least they were getting out of the house again.

At the side window, there was a flurry of curtain, and then the front door opened promptly. A sturdy pair of arms came up to envelope her, as did a powerful scent of a musky perfume, which must have just been applied moments earlier.

"My goodness, how long has it been?" Despina's eldest sister exclaimed, looking decidedly overdressed in a deep burgundy dress and lips painted to match.

There was something a bit desperate, almost hysterical, in her voice, as if she was faking her jubilance for their benefit. Even the way she hugged them seemed a little too forceful, a little too enthusiastic. Then again, everyone was acting strangely these days, and at least Elena had a reason. Her husband, who'd been stationed in Istanbul as part of a diplomatic corps for the past year, had refused to return when summoned, and there was no telling if they would see him again, much less be able to join him. Things between the families had come to a head long before that, their differences widening at each visit, each ghastly encounter. And the last time, Natalia would never forget the words spat from her uncle's lips, moist still with her father's wine, as he shot upright from the dinner table and motioned for his wife and daughter to gather their things, that they were leaving. "I'll see you hang from a pole!" he'd fumed, leaning over the dinner table with his eyes fixed ferociously on her father, yanking the napkin from his lap and throwing it into his half-eaten soup, splattering bits of finely minced vegetables over her mother's perfectly starched tablecloth.

But that was months ago, and in the time since, there seemed to be a truce at least between the sisters, even though the whole thing still hung between them like a dark cloud.

"Talia, darling, you're taller and prettier every time I see you!" her aunt was exclaiming now with an affection she'd never seen from her before. "Why, you are nearly as tall as your mother! Come!"

She pulled the two inside and locked the door behind them twice with those same quick, nearly jerky movements. In stark contrast, the sitting room greeted them serenely with a roaring fire that instantly seemed to soothe Natalia's nerves. On a large silver tray in the center, a Turkish coffee kettle and a soda siphon had been set out, like old times. As they settled amid the multitude of cushions on the velvet sofa, Lidia bounded into the room, all blond waves and peach lips and smelling too strongly of her mother's perfume.

"Hi, doll," she said, gliding up to Natalia with a brilliant smile and fondly pinching both of her cheeks. She dropped down onto the sofa next to Despina and reached for one of the compote-filled bowls, cocking an eyebrow at Natalia, making a face that nearly made her burst out in laughter.

Oh, but how she adored her cousin! Five years her senior, Lidia was not only charming and funny but also one of the prettiest girls Natalia knew, with her enormous blue eyes and golden hair that she wore tied back in a red ribbon. Natalia realized she wasn't the only one who thought so. She had seen the way boys fluttered around Lidia, the way other girls followed her around, asking her to go to the movies or if she could come to their house after school. It was Lidia who had schooled Natalia in the art of personal transformation, who had shown her how to comb her hair to bring out its shine, to glide about a room with the grace of a movie star. Before the war, they had spent many afternoons together, but now that there had been such a rift between their families, they did not get to see much of each other at all.

"Lidia, you look *très chic,*" Natalia said casually, catching an amused, sideways glance from her mother.

"And you, Talia, how is your piano coming along?" Lidia asked, pouring coffee into a small china cup and handing it to Natalia with that same playful naughtiness. "What are you playing these days?"

Natalia let out an exaggerated breath. "My tutor's a monster, *chérie.* She expects too much. I try my hardest, but the 'Moonlight Sonata'?" She rolled her eyes a little in a way that she hoped was dramatic. "I mean, I'm not even fourteen yet," she said, hoping that her mother's attention had shifted back to her own conversation, for surely she would point out that Natalia, in fact, had just turned thirteen the month before and that lately she was just clattering away at

God knows what — not Beethoven, to be sure.

"Oh, Talia, you're really getting better. The key is to stick with it and try to improve a little each time —"

A hammering at the front door stopped Lidia in mid-sentence, and the two of them exchanged a look.

"Are you expecting anyone else?" her mother inquired of her aunt, her eyebrows going up in surprise.

"No." Elena shrugged. She took a sip from her cup, and when she placed it back on its saucer, it rattled a little. "Though we have had" — she paused, swallowed hard as a hand traveled up to the base of her throat — "visits. Ever since Radu . . . well, you know."

Her mother lowered her eyes, and they said nothing for a moment. The knocks wouldn't stop; they were stronger, more determined, with every passing moment. Even Lidia seemed to have sobered suddenly and sat rigidly in her chair, biting her lip.

Natalia looked from her aunt to her mother, puzzled. "Well, isn't someone going to answer?"

"Yes, I suppose I should," Elena said, straightening up, rising to her feet ever so slowly. She smoothed out her dress with precise, measured gestures and ambled toward the door, leaning to the left a little as if she was in no rush to get there at all.

From the other end of the house, Natalia heard the dead bolt turning, once, twice. She listened, her heart suddenly in a leap, to the brief exchange of words, of voices she did not recognize, male voices, followed by boots clomping on the wooden floor, the jangle of some metal object. In the glare of the open French door, two darkish tall silhouettes approached. It wasn't until they paused in the doorway that she felt all her blood drain to her feet.

She had seen plenty of Red Army soldiers before, sitting in groups behind café windows or marching in formation down the streets with their hands on their holsters. Some had even smiled at her on the street, saluted her as she walked past them, touching their index fingers to their khaki caps with red stars, gaping at her shamelessly. But she had never seen them this close. Standing here in their mud-splattered uniforms, glassy-eyed and smelling of brandy, they looked grotesque to her, almost inhuman. All the stories she'd heard came rushing back, stories of Soviet soldiers pillaging and robbing homes, taking everything they could. Alarmed, she looked at her mother, hoping for a sign, a signal of some kind, but her face was a white canvas. Only her arm moved ever so slightly, almost like a nervous spasm, then, as it stretched out at full length over the sofa, grasping her purse, then bringing it close, right up to her leg.

"Please, officers," Elena was saying now, coming up behind them. That artificial, strained tone had returned to her voice, although she was trying hard to sound cheerful. "Would you care for some *tuica*? I have some fresh pastries, too. Right this way, please."

She gestured for the men to follow her to the kitchen, but they ignored her. Instead, they stepped further into the room and began inspecting various objects — a crystal ashtray, a Fabergé angel on the mantel, a silver tray on the sideboard — turning them this way and that, studying the engravings on the bottom. The older, stockier officer said something in Russian, and they laughed. Then both pairs of eyes fell on Lidia. The younger, broad-shouldered soldier gave her a smile, but there was something dark and ugly in his eyes.

Lidia stood up from the sofa and, averting the bold stare, headed toward the door. She was nearly there when he cut her off and stood before her, hands on hips, blocking her path. She tried to go around him, but he stepped in her way again. And again, two more times, the same sequence of movements. Lidia grew visibly flushed. Her breathing quickened. And then she did something unthinkable, something that made Natalia gasp in shock. Lifting her gaze, she looked right into the soldier's face and spat in it.

The room was as quiet as a tomb as he raised his hand to wipe his cheek. When he grabbed Lidia's arm, his movement was so sudden that she did not have time to react. It was only when he spun her roughly around and pulled her against him that she began flailing her free arm, clawing at his hair, his face, pounding her small fist on his unflinching chest like a trapped, frightened bird.

Lidia! Natalia thought she shouted, but no words left her lips. *Lidia!* And she instinctively closed her eyes. She squeezed them shut and covered her ears to drown out all that followed — her cousin's piercing screams, the sound of her blouse tearing, the eggshell buttons hitting the floor one at a time, her aunt shrieking, imploring, the pounding of blood in her own temples. And then a single sound, a single terrifying sound that rose above the others, and all fell silent.

No one moved as the smell of smoke enveloped the room. No one dared to breathe. It seemed that the air itself had stilled. The soldier took a few steps backward, his eyes wild with incomprehension before they traveled downward and an agonizing cry emerged from his throat. A crimson rivulet trickled through a hole in his uniform pants, just above his knee. When he crumpled to the floor, it was in stages, first dropping to his knees and struggling to pull himself up, then falling sideways, his shoulder hitting the wall with a loud thud.

"Leave her alone. Leave this house now." Her mother's voice rose in the silence, raspy and thick, unrecognizable.

Natalia's pulse began to race, and she felt suddenly dizzy. She was only dimly aware of the smear of blood on the pale lilac wallpaper where the soldier's hand had rested a moment ago, Lidia sobbing, clutching whatever remained of her blouse, the rug twisted at her feet, the men hunkered together now, in a fury of frenzied movements. From the corner of her eye, she observed the blithe figure beside her that was her mother, the way she held the gun steadily, waving it slightly between the two men. *Give me a reason to finish the job,* her steely eyes said, and there wasn't a trace of fear in them or even rage now; there was only cold, hard resolve.

And then the extraordinary. Grunting and cursing between clenched teeth, the wounded soldier drew himself up. He slipped and nearly fell, but his companion caught him in time and helped him back to his feet, sliding an arm underneath his shoulders for support. Without looking back, they stumbled out of the parlor, a three-legged beast receding from view, past the entry table and the framed lithographs in the foyer and through the front door that swung open in the evening breeze.

The entire time, her mother kept her pistol at eye level. She only lowered it when the men had vanished from sight, when the only sound coming from the street was that of passing cars and the screech of a tramcar coming to a stop at the end of the block.

27

Empty storefronts and poorly lit streets, the stench of garbage mounting on street corners underneath a blanket of grayish snow, that was all that remained of the old Paris of the Balkans, with its once pristine sidewalks and dazzling white modern facades, its lush parks and lively plazas. Natalia and her father walked in near darkness amid a backdrop of soot-blackened walls and half-toppled fences. Earlier, she had stopped by the store to help out for a few hours, as she did every Friday after school.

On their way, they passed a few shops that had gone out of business, their awnings torn, their windows broken and vandalized, even though there was nothing inside to steal. Passing by the only bakery that was still open, they glanced at the empty shelves behind the grimy window. A lonely placard lay against the cash register, reading *Out of Bread Today.* Natalia had seen that sign nearly every morning on her way to school, hours after the customers who had lined up early had dispersed empty-handed.

"I want to come to the store every day, Papa," she said. "I can get my homework done in the back and help out after. We could walk home together every night. Just like this."

A flicker of a smile passed over his face. "I don't know, sweetheart. I'm sure your mother would not approve of me breaking her rules. I am the last person from whom she would expect such rebellion."

She said nothing.

"Things are not what they used to be, Talia. They're different now, since . . . since . . ." He did not finish, but she knew what he meant. "We have to be careful, more careful than ever. Go home after school for now. It's for the best."

At the corner, they stopped. Just before crossing, her father dug into one of his pockets and extracted a few coins, which he tossed into the metal tin of a blind old gypsy who crouched underneath an awning.

"God have mercy. God have mercy, my child," the gypsy chanted, her cloudy, unfocused gaze trailing them toward the intersection.

"Let's go," her father said, taking her hand

and pulling her along to make the light.

He was always walking fast these days, Natalia thought, always dashing across changing green lights, and even red ones sometimes, as if he was in a mad rush to get somewhere. Always keeping his hands in his pockets and looking at the ground. His eyes had been darting about constantly ever since three weeks earlier, when she and her mother had gone to visit Elena and Lidia.

She'd never forget his look that night, wild with worry, pacing like a caged cat when they walked into the house at nearly midnight. The way he had stood before them, barefoot in his silk robe, holding his hands out, demanding an explanation. She'd wanted to fall into his arms and tell him how terrible the whole thing had been, how frightening, but he'd followed her mother into the parlor, where she collapsed onto the sofa and began to sob in her hands. What was it that he had said to her then?

"Tell me, Despina. Tell me, and don't leave anything out."

Her mother had looked at him for a moment, and then, with trembling hands, she'd reached for her purse and extracted the pistol. "Get rid of it. Hide it," she had said, holding it out to him.

It seemed like an eternity before he had

reached out and taken it from her. When he placed it on the coffee table, it made a clinking sound, soft and innocent, like the chime of a bell.

Since then, he and her mother had barely spoken about it. When it did come up, her father tried to make light of it, saying things like, "Luckily, Despina, they took you seriously and decided to leave when they did," but her mother never laughed, as she might have another time. She only drew in a long breath. Days turned into weeks, and they rarely spoke of it now. Lately, Natalia had begun to relax, to think of it less, but all along, she couldn't shake the feeling that despite the devastation of war, the fear of persecution, the endless food lines, and the rationed electricity, despite all that she and her family had endured thus far, this was the very thing that would unravel their lives. And still she could not expect how quickly it would happen, how swiftly the blade would fall.

There was nothing out of the ordinary at first. As she and her father made their way home through the clatter of streetcars and billboards of factory workers swaying joyfully arm in arm, she saw nothing unusual, save perhaps a looming shadow, a blur that hung loosely in the corner of her eye. For several blocks, she paid no attention, until the shadow gained forward momentum and came into full view, and she noticed it was a black town car, an unmarked automobile with tinted windows and no license plate. The car swerved out of traffic, coming to an abrupt stop, and a man — stocky and rather sinister-looking despite the expensive over-coat — emerged through the back door. He might have been any man, a stranger with whom they were merely crossing paths, but the way he stood before them — arms folded at his chest, feet splayed apart — made it clear that he was not.

Above his raised collar, his eyes were hard and fixed, and Natalia saw nothing in them, not even a trace of interest, as he mouthed, "Sir, are you Anton Goza?"

"Yes, yes, I am," her father replied, paling, though his head remained high. "How is it that I can help you?"

"Sir, you are under arrest. You will need to come with us." Placing a gloved hand on top of the car's back door, he opened it all the way, almost courteously, as if he was inviting him to step in.

Natalia's gaze darted alarmingly between the man and her father. This was not a police car. And this man was certainly not

wearing a police uniform. How could he arrest her father? She nearly smiled, thinking
it had to be some kind of a mistake. A joke,
perhaps. She did actually let out a sound,
something like a stunned chuckle.

"Papa?"

And then it came to her. The realization
hit her with such force that her knees nearly
buckled. This was no ordinary police; this
had to be the Secret Police. But what did
they want with her father? The Securitate
only dealt with crimes against the state. Her
father was not an agitator, an activist. On
the contrary, he kept to himself and spoke
to virtually no one these days. Why would
they want him? Then she remembered the
stories she had heard on street corners,
rumors of unexpected arrests and kidnap-
pings, of people disappearing in the night,
never to be seen again, and for no reason at
all.

"No!" she yelled, her voice raspy and
choked. "Papa, run!"

She tugged on his sleeve frantically, but
he just stood there, not moving, not running. As if he wasn't at all surprised. "Go
home, Talia," he said sternly, gripping her
shoulder. "Go directly home, and do not
stop for any reason."

With that, he took off his hat and climbed

into the backseat.

"Why?" she screamed. "Why? He has done nothing!"

But the man in the dark coat was already sliding in next to him, and the door was slamming shut, and all she could glimpse of her father as the car sped away was the back of his head dropping backward, as if he was taking a long breath.

A breath. She willed herself to breathe, too, aware faintly that across the street, several pedestrians had stopped to look, and above them, curious faces peered out from behind curtained windows. It took such effort to think; all her senses were pulled tight, like violin strings. What would happen to her father? Why had they snatched him like this? And where were they taking him?

There were other things she remembered about the Securitate, and she couldn't keep them at bay, much as she tried. This was exactly how they did their work. They pounced in the darkness, on an unknown street corner in the middle of the night, so there would be no scene. There would be no wild vociferations, pleadings, unnecessary emotions. Whatever her father was accused of, it didn't matter. Whatever the reason, there would be a sham trial resulting in a sentence without the right to defense or an immediate transfer to a forced-work camp. The Gulag, Natalia had heard people call this place, where people who had committed crimes against the state were sent and from which no one ever returned.

A violent cry, a spasm, emerged from her throat. *What will I tell my mother?* she thought absurdly. *How can I tell her he isn't coming home? That he may never come home?* She buried her face in her hands and shut her eyes, slid down to her knees. Suddenly, she felt the weight of a hand on her shoulder and looked up. It took her a moment to recognize old Mr. Enesco, their next-door neighbor.

"Natalia, what's happened?" he said, bending down beside her.

All she could do was fall into his arms and sob. She sobbed for what felt like hours in the arms of this kind old man who stroked her hair comfortingly with his withered, callused hands.

"Let me take you home," he said after a while. "Your mother will worry, and you should not be alone at a time like this."

Natalia nodded and wiped her eyes. She stood and picked up her bag, praying that it had all been a dream.

"Your father was a good man," Mr. Enesco said, shaking his head as they began walking toward home. "I don't know what he's done, but that is a fact."

My father still is a good man! Natalia felt like shouting in protest. *He is a good man, and he will come back to us!* But she didn't have the strength to speak. Instead, she took the man's hand, and they continued the rest of the way in silence.

28

Victor Dimitrov had indeed come up in the ranks. She hardly recognized him when he stood in their doorway, dashing, taller than she remembered, with his cap in his hand and an air of quiet authority behind the polite smile. He looked handsome in a dark leather coat, which he removed promptly before entering, for it had been drenched in a torrent of rain.

"Hello, Miss Despina. Talia," he said, smoothing his black hair which despite the downpour had remained perfectly intact. Green eyes that she remembered well held hers for a moment. He smiled, and one corner of his lips turned slightly upward, as it did involuntarily when he was amused by something or surprised. Natalia dropped her gaze. Something shifted inside her, a small leap, barely perceptible, stifled by her sudden embarrassment. She blinked, a little out of breath, feeling her cheeks grow warm.

"Please come in, Victor," her mother said, taking his coat. "Thank you for coming. I know how busy you are."

Hearing her say this brought Natalia back to reality. Victor had not come just for a visit; he'd come because her mother had asked for his help. It was, in fact, the very first thing she had done on that late afternoon when Natalia had come home alone without her father, without the words that were, after all, unnecessary. Paling visibly, steadying herself against the stairwell banister, her mother had ambled directly to the study, then flicked on the desk lamp and rummaged through her father's papers, opening and shutting drawers, knocking over a stack of files. At last, she had found what she was looking for in an old cigar box. Holding the small scrap of paper against the light, she'd dialed the number on it, slowly, steadily. "Yes, I realize this is a private number. He knows who I am," she'd heard her say. The conversation itself had been short, but when she hung up, a trace of light had returned to her eyes. And now Victor was here. He had come as promised.

How long had it been since they'd last seen him? Natalia couldn't remember. He was so thin then that the sharp contours of his shoulders were visible through the wool and angora sweaters that had once been her father's. He was coughing a lot, too, and his hands, perfectly manicured now, were then rough as sandpaper and cracked around the knuckles.

"Is there anything you can you do for him, Papa?" she'd asked once. "Could you give him a job at the store?"

Her father had smiled affectionately and patted her hand. "He doesn't want to work for the likes of me, sweetheart. But I'm helping in any way that I can. Don't worry."

He had no family, Victor had told them once over one of those long Sunday suppers that now felt like they belonged to another lifetime. He was an orphan, like Anton, but unlike him, he had never known his parents. He was raised by his aunt, his father's sister, who was a seamstress before the war. They had lived in a one-room flat in the back of a courtyard perpetually strewn with sheets and undergarments fluttering on crisscrossing clotheslines, and Victor had earned his keep by helping with deliveries around town. Through the windows of grand villas, he stole glimpses of a life he would never have, no matter how hard he studied, how hard he worked, how well he applied himself. He came to detest how he was often

271

greeted in doorways, told to wait outside, to not touch anything. He loathed the way butlers or housemaids removed the gowns from his hands as if they were dirty, even though he had helped in the making of those gowns — cutting out patterns, unraveling the rolls of velvet and silk, and preparing his aunt's needles. At night, he would rub her aching shoulders, her hunched back, as she worked late so they could buy food the next day. After a few years, her stoicism began to unnerve him, and soon he began to detest her a little, her quiet resignation, the overstated humility with which she accepted a few coins for an entire month's work, her unrelenting belief in a good and mighty God. The God she praised on her tired knees every morning at the church down the street and in the evenings in front of her homemade altar to the Blessed Mother.

"What has God given you to make you believe in him so?" he'd asked her once when he was fourteen.

She had turned around and slapped him. "Do not challenge Almighty God," she had shouted, shaking her finger at him. "You should be grateful for your daily bread, for all that he makes possible for us."

What daily bread? he had wanted to say,

but he knew it was pointless. That was when he decided that he'd had enough of her piety and saintly humbleness. Not long before, he'd met a young man, a schoolmate who brought him to a party one night, where he had his first drink of whiskey. There were other young students there, and they were talking about things that he'd never heard of before, things that made his spirit soar with excitement and indignation. They talked about liberty and equality, about the industrial revolution just across the border in Soviet Russia and how it was surpassing the advances of any other country five-fold. They drank late into the night, and by the time dawn rose, Victor felt free. The sudden optimism that had sprung in his young heart seared itself into his flesh like a permanent insignia, and he did not care if his aunt was worried about him, if she had to cut and sew her dresses all by herself. For the first time in his young life, he had hope, and on hope alone he could subsist for days, weeks, without food, without shelter.

The following month, he had moved into a converted attic above a store in Piazza Romana and begun attending weekly meetings, where his new friends treated him with respect and asked his opinions and listened to what he had to say. In their eyes, he saw the future — unfathomable possibilities for people like him who had only known a life in which they were insignificant, poor, broken, exploited. He routinely participated in demonstrations and was even arrested several times for disturbing the peace, but he kept going back out into the streets, always the first in a swell of workers and peasants. Often, he was held for a few days, but no charges were ever pressed against him, and eventually he would be let go. Soon bigger events had overtaken the city, and the police no longer bothered to break up the rallies. No one noticed them any longer as entire city sectors went up in flames.

Natalia recalled a time, not long after that, when Victor said that Anton had been as close to a parent as anyone he'd ever known. Victor had looked him straight in the eye when he said it at the supper table, his fork suspended in midair, his eyes blazing with gratitude and conviction. Her father had given him one of his hearty laughs and patted his back, but there had been so much more in his expression than flattery. It was as if a beacon of light had ignited between them, fleeting yet undisputable, connecting two kindred spirits in a bond that was theirs alone.

Where was that young man who once held such a special place in her father's heart? There was little left of him that she could see now. There was no semblance of him in the person who sat across from her mother, listening intently as she recounted the events that had led to her husband's arrest.

If Victor was in any way surprised or alarmed, there was nothing on his face to betray it. Not a muscle moved, not an eyebrow went up, not a tremor showed on his lips. He was as still as a marble statue. *How does he do that?* Natalia wondered as she observed him, mesmerized, from behind the glass door. *How is he able to feel nothing?* She retreated behind one of the semi-sheer curtains, afraid that he would see her, but she could not step away, not entirely. Her feet were held in place by an invisible magnet.

At one point, he stood and lit a cigarette, then, sweeping a hand through his hair, he went to the window and gazed at something outside. A few moments later, he walked back to the coffee table and put out his cigarette in the bronze ashtray. Out of his breast pocket, he removed a small notepad and a pencil and scribbled something on it.

An exchange of words followed, something Natalia could not hear, as he tore off the page and handed it to her mother.

In the brief moment that passed between her mother dropping her face into her hands and Victor touching her arm as if to comfort her, Natalia saw her do something she had never done before. Taking Victor's hand in hers, she raised it to her lips and kissed it.

29

The sun had not yet risen by the time Despina left the next morning. Natalia heard her gathering her things in the foyer, the clinking of keys, the front door slamming shut, then steps on the sidewalk fading away, short and precise. She leaped out of bed and peered through the half-drawn curtains, observing her mother's silhouette glide briskly toward the end of the block.

If she had passed her in a crowd, Natalia might not have recognized her in that oversize coat — her father's, no doubt — and a faded, floral headscarf tied under her chin. At least she'd given up her high-heeled pumps and fur coats. The month before, on the tram, someone cut a hole the size of a soccer ball in the back of her mink. She did not feel a thing, standing there holding on to the overhead strap. Only the chill on her back when she came off the trolley tipped her off that a large swath of her coat was missing. As her fingers felt around the crude dissection, a woman in a drab factory uniform and rain galoshes stopped to regard the spectacle. "It serves you right!" she cackled with a hand on her hip. "The time for your fancy coats is over!"

After that, Despina's furs were wrapped and placed in the back of her wardrobe, where at least they would remain intact and not be sold piece by piece on the black market. But in the weeks after her father's arrest, her mother stopped caring completely about what clothes she was wearing. It seemed that the mere act of getting dressed in the morning had become an impossible chore.

Natalia felt recently more like the parent than the child, reminding her mother daily that she needed to eat for she was getting too thin, rubbing her shoulders, bringing her tea in the morning as she lingered in bed, retreating into a place where no one could reach her. Natalia was the one to stand in line at the grocer's, to sort the mail, to answer the interminable phone calls from her aunts and explain that her mother was tired, she could not speak this evening, she could not move or breathe, she was simply *missing*. Until her father was released, Natalia realized, their days would unfold precisely like this, bleeding somberly into one another, suspended somewhere between despair and hope and marked only by a long list of chores.

But at night, when the house was quiet and Natalia went back to her room, her moments were entirely hers, and she could allow her mind to drift off. And it seemed that her mind was constantly fleeing her ever since Victor's visit. It was a mere distraction at first, something besides her piano to take away the longing she felt for her father, the fear. Yet lately, it was happening all the time. Lying back in her bed, waiting for daylight to come, she thought of him now — the glossy dark hair, the commanding stature, the intensity of his gaze, which had always been there and yet had transformed from something raw or desperate into a steely calmness. She thought of the way he'd smiled at her in the doorway as if he'd never really seen her before, and something drew up inside her tightly like a ball of yarn.

It was wrong, she knew it. This was the same Victor she'd known since she was a little girl — a little bit older, a little bit better dressed, but still, the same one. Everything in her recent life had weighted her with such heaviness that she couldn't resist this tiny seed of exhilaration, which bloomed in her heart like a scarlet rose in a dreary field. Besides, everyone was allowed a secret. This was hers, she said to herself, a small secret causing no harm at all, and she closed her eyes and caressed her own lips unknowingly for what she thought was only a moment.

The grandfather clock downstairs jolted her back to consciousness. She'd been lost in a dream, though she'd slept hard and couldn't recall it. Her room was flooded with a light so bright it hurt her eyes, and she sat upright, counted the strikes. She'd slept straight through the morning, it seemed, and her mother had been gone for nearly six hours. Six hours, and she had no idea where she was. Scrambling to her feet, trying to get her bearings, she threw on her robe and hurried downstairs, hoping that maybe she'd left a note. Halfway down the steps, the sound of the phone in the foyer caused her to leap over the rest of the steps, and she lunged for it urgently.

"Hello?" she answered, slightly out of breath, expecting to hear her mother's voice.

There was a bit of a crackle, as if the person on the other end had placed down the receiver and was again picking it up.

"Talia? Good afternoon. It's Stefan calling."

"Oh, hello, Uncle," she answered, the temporary relief of moments ago instantly evaporating. "My mother isn't here right now. Should I take a message?"

"Actually, no, Talia . . . it's you I was hoping to speak with. I need your help, you see. I'm afraid it is not something that can wait."

"All right," she murmured a little unsurely. "What can I do?"

"Talia, do you know how to get into your father's safe?"

The question stunned her. It was the last thing she expected. It took her a moment to think of how to reply, what to say. Yes, she knew how to get into the safe. She had seen her father do it plenty of times at the store, putting away petty cash at the end of the day. She'd even opened it for him once or twice. The combination was easy to remember. It was her birthday.

"Why, Uncle?" she hesitated. "Umm, my mother should be back soon."

"Talia, this is urgent. Please forgive me for having to be so direct, but . . . well, I don't know how else to say this, but time is running out. For both of them."

She felt an opening in the pit of her stomach. "What do you mean?"

"I cannot explain right now, my dear. All I

281

can say is that you'll have to trust me. You have to get your father's stamp collection out of the safe for me. Right now."

There was a silence while she tried to collect herself. "Uncle Stefan, I think my mother —"

"Your mother will not come home today unless we act quickly," he interrupted, and the tone in his voice flooded her with the realization that what he was saying was true. But he was talking too fast, and she couldn't keep up with all the details, couldn't quite grasp the whole thing.

"Look, a warrant for your mother's arrest was issued this afternoon," he pronounced now more crisply, slowing down a bit. "She is *there*, Talia; she is visiting your father right now, so chances are that they will detain her as well. I know this from Victor, who called me just minutes ago."

"Victor?" she repeated, and her grasp tightened around the telephone cord. "What's he got to do with all this?"

"Victor is doing all he can to get the charges dropped. Unfortunately, there will be a price for that, a substantial sum. I don't have that kind of cash on hand."

There was another pause. The silence was excruciating.

"It has to be done now. Do you understand what I'm telling you?"

Yes, she understood. She understood so well that she had to lean up against the wall. The image of her mother pulling the trigger flashed in her mind, and she knew now it was the reason they had come for her father. It was an excuse to punish him, to make him cower in fear. And now they would do the same with her mother. Only with her, they would not stop at that.

It paralyzed her senses, her ability to breathe. She could not lose her parents, her father and mother both. They were all she had in the world. Whatever it took to stop that from happening, whatever the conse-quences, she would deal with them later. Right now, there was no time to waste. Their future rested in her hands.

"What do you need me to do, Uncle? Just tell me, and I'll do it," she uttered shakily into the receiver.

"Can you get the stamps out of the safe? Can you, Talia? I can be there in less than an hour."

"Yes," she replied simply. Then, as if to reinforce this very fact to herself: "You can count on me."

30

A single shard of light trickled in through the narrow arched window, just below the pitched ceiling. So much time had passed since she had been up here that she had nearly forgotten what the attic looked like — the vast, dusty space filled with old furniture, her bed from when she was little in the corner, the mattress discolored and full of moth holes, her mother's salvaged stove from the lake house underneath a pile of old clothes. Things that had once been the minutiae of their everyday lives. Discarded, useless things now, things that had nothing to do with the present.

All of it she tried to block out, focusing on the task at hand. Forward three, back twenty-three, forward thirty-seven, the digits of her birthday conjured with the round dial, underneath her trembling fingertips. As she slowed to the last number, she wondered if her father had changed the combination and had to steady her wrist with her other hand to complete the turn. When the internal lock released with a resounding click, she nearly collapsed with relief.

For a moment, she rested her forehead against the cool surface of the metal door, waiting for her pulse to slow down. Then she pressed down on the handle.

With surprising ease, the door swung open, and a synthetic smell, something like burnt rubber, drifted toward her. Reaching inside the cavity, pushing aside the rectangular blocks wrapped in cloth that seemed to fill it entirely, she searched for the leatherbound case. It did not take long to find it, lodged between the back wall and one of the blocks. Gently, she eased it out, and just then, something else caught on its edges and tumbled out with it, landing on her lap. It was a cardboard file, tied around the middle with red yarn. She picked it up and was about to thrust it back inside when something unusual caught her eye. The tab in the corner, handwritten in black ink. *Natalia*, it said simply.

For a moment, she held the file, unsure of what to do. She fumbled with it, turning it over, then back again, staring at her name. *Put it back. Put it back now,* her own voice rang in her head, but her hands would not obey; they seemed to have a mind of their own. Already they were unraveling the yarn, once, twice, until it fell away and the file gaped open before her.

The first thing she extracted was a black-and-white photograph of her and her parents; it must have been taken just days after her adoption. Tilting it against the light, she gazed at a much younger image of herself — the enormous white ribbon on top of her head, the lace socks that were a little too long and bunched under her knees — and her parents, breathtaking in formal attire, standing on either side of her. Setting it down, she rummaged through the folder, hoping to find more photographs, but there were no others, just a bunch of envelopes of varying sizes.

The largest one contained some kind of a legal document. There, in the corner, was the state insignia and at the bottom her parents' signatures along with Stefan's, above the line that read *Attorney and Witness*. The decree of her adoption, she realized, setting this down as well.

The second envelope she plucked from the folder was much smaller, the kind that was used for everyday correspondence. Someone had scribbled a date across it:

February 20, 1944. There was no return address, only a strange, faded stamp which she strained to make out — *Geneva, Switzerland.* Whom did her parents know in Switzerland? Curiously, she reached inside and extracted a single sheet of paper. It was flimsy, almost transparent, and a little yellowed around the corners. Unfolding it, she held it up against the slant of light and began reading:

Dear Mrs. Tudor,
I am writing to you in regard to a young girl who was brought to your orphanage in January of 1941. At the time, she was not yet four years old. It is with overwhelming relief as well as undeniable heartache that I recently learned of her whereabouts. I understand she was adopted by a family shortly after she was brought to your institution and that she is much loved and cared for.

My intent is not to disturb the life to which she has undoubtedly become accustomed or to cause anguish to the family that has embraced her as their own. My only wish is to make it known to her, should she ever inquire of you, Mrs. Tudor, that leaving her that night was my only choice and her only salvation. It was with a heavy heart that I had to set her free so that she might live, so that she might have a chance at life, even as it meant the end of mine. I do not dare to hope that she and I will meet one day. I do not wish to foster such false hope in my heart. My only desire is that she know that I loved her with every breath and that I have spent my last moments on earth begging God for her happiness.

The note fluttered out of her hand. She placed her palm at the hollow of her throat, where a thick lump was obstructing her air passage. The piece of paper had landed right where she knelt, but she couldn't pick it up; she just kept staring at the date. And staring. Everything else seemed to have gone black.

Six years had passed since it had been written. Six years since it had been placed inside this safe, sealed in obscurity. Were her parents ever planning to show it to her? Were they waiting for the right moment? Could it be that they had simply forgotten? Certainly, much had happened since then, events that far eclipsed this, set it into the background. A war had been raging, with loss and illness, and their life resembled nothing of what it had once been. Yet another possibility crept into her mind. Maybe they had deliberately kept it from her. Maybe that was why she was coming upon it now, like a thief stealing in the night.

She took in a long breath, forced it into her lungs. Guilt seared through her, guilt for trespassing, but also a sharp, indisputable awareness that this was the truth. Her mother in particular would have done anything to guard what was hers, the family that she'd so badly wanted. This was why she'd always been so protective of her, why she had kept her so close all those years. Why she'd been so deeply affected — terrified even — when that man had stopped on the street after school. Natalia shuddered now at the memory. It had taken place about the same time as when this letter was written. Had he really intended to kidnap her? Was that why the gates of the Swiss embassy were open so late in the evening?

All the pieces of her life were reassembling themselves in a new light, like a movie she had already seen but whose meaning she had failed to grasp the first time. Even the abrupt cooling between her mother and Maria suddenly made sense. Maria worked at the orphanage; she had been there when Natalia was brought in. Maria knew too

much, and so it made her mother uncomfortable having her nearby, feeling like she
was being judged every minute of every day.
And something else, something Natalia had
long put out of her mind, a conversation
she'd overheard just days before she and
her mother left for the country. "Tell her,
Desi," she'd heard Maria say that afternoon
as Natalia walked by her parents' room,
where the two women had retreated from
the heat after shopping. "She has a right to
know." No doubt, they were speaking of this
letter. That had to be the reason why at the
sound of her footsteps, her mother had appeared in the half-open doorway, and when
she caught sight of her standing there, all
the blood had drained from her face.

Carefully, Natalia folded the paper and
placed it back inside the envelope.

Everything contained in those lines was
absolutely true. She *was* indeed loved, even
worshipped, by the best parents any child
could hope for. What would she have been
if it weren't for them? An orphan, a stray,
someone who might have ended up selling
flowers in the plaza alongside the gypsies.
These parents had saved her from a life of
ruin, and to them she belonged. This other
woman, this *stranger* who had written this
letter with such pathos, had left her on a

doorstep to freeze in the middle of winter. She did not have to look far for the truth.

And so it was really quite simple: she would not give this letter another thought. There was no room in her life for question marks, for what-ifs. There was only here and now and her parents who needed her this very moment. Whatever awaited at the end of this chapter, whatever was to come, it would always be just the three of them.

The relief was extraordinary, sweeping through her in waves, bringing her back to the attic with its flurry of dust, the stamp album with the glossy leather cover that gleamed at her — a reminder. She ran her fingers over the smooth surface, wanting to open it one last time and flip through its pages, admire each gorgeous stamp like she used to do under her father's desk at the store, but the doorbell downstairs kept ringing, and it occurred to her that she might not have heard it before. She flew down the steps, barely taking the time to lock up the attic, one prayer, one prayer only, resounding in her mind. When she opened the front door, her uncle was there.

"Thank God, dear girl, thank God," he said, and let out a long breath, as if he'd been holding it the whole time.

31

He was being sent out of the country. For how long he couldn't say exactly, but it was sure to be weeks, maybe months. Budapest first, then Warsaw. Then maybe Moscow. Victor's words as he spoke were urgent but low, and Anton had to lean in to hear fully what he was saying.

"Months?" Anton repeated, thrusting his hands into the pockets of his overcoat, which he'd worn on the day of his arrest. It looked strange, surely, to be wearing one in the middle of May, yet he couldn't stop trembling and was glad for its warmth. He'd been shivering for weeks, it seemed, inside that cold cell — four, to be exact, according to Victor — and it probably didn't help that he'd lost so much weight.

"I know it seems like a long time," Victor replied quietly, turning away from the grayish building with no windows from which both men had emerged only minutes earlier.

There was a formality in his posture, yet in the shadow of overhead leaves, his features beamed with a joyful affection.

Anton's gaze drifted a moment, misty all of a sudden. "Of course, I understand, Victor. We would love to see you. Anytime."

They parted with a fleeting handshake, one designed for the eyes that no doubt were watching them. There was so much that Anton wanted to say, *needed* to say, but he knew this was not the right time. Instead, he stood there very still, watching Victor as he darted across the street to catch a trolley. Then he drew in a long breath and began in the direction of home.

Slowly, he walked, taking his time. As much as he burned with desire to see his wife and daughter, his legs were weak, and they couldn't carry him any faster. Besides, he needed time to think, to process what he could hardly believe himself. He had just been released from a place that no one ever emerged from to see the light of day. No one.

He owed Victor his life. That was for certain. Yet it seemed implausible that Victor had single-handedly put a stop to the daily interrogations, the prewritten statements that they were trying to force him to sign, and that he had arranged for Anton's unconditional release. Had the Security Police grown tired of his resistance? That was even more unlikely.

Certainly, he had not caved. No matter what they threatened him with, he had confessed nothing. He would have never admitted to those preposterous charges — that he had plotted against the Party, that his wife had intended to harm a Soviet officer because they were counterrevolutionaries, enemies of the people, bourgeois loyalists. To do so would have meant death. So in one interrogation after the next, Anton held steadfast, sticking to the same set of facts. He had purchased a gun simply for his wife's protection. The shooting had been an accident. He even went so far as to state that he was, in fact, a staunch supporter of the new regime, and although not a Party member himself, he had always sympathized with the cause. Yet even that did not seem to abate the tide that had turned against him.

Three days after his incarceration, they had transferred him to a basement cell, where he was held in complete darkness. He was given no food or water, and there was one daily bathroom break with a loaded gun at his back. He could feel the cold steel poking him between the ribs as he made his way to the Turkish toilet at the end of a long hallway lined with metal-sheeted doors.

A tall, wiry man whose face bore a perpetual expression of indifference came into his cell every morning. Not bothering with greetings or even so much as an acknowledging glance, he would drag the sole chair from the corner of the room and position it directly in front of Anton, who usually sat leaning against the wall.

"You will die in this cell, or you will confess to the charges before you," the man would utter each time, stretching his legs out to indicate that he was in no rush at all. "This here is your only salvation."

Out of his breast pocket, he would extract a folded typewritten paper and a pen. "You can sign it now if you'd like. Personally, I think it would be wise. Later you will beg for the opportunity, but it will be too late. Because by then your fate will be sealed. You will be facing the firing squad, or you will be sent to dig up the Danube Channel for the next fifty years. Either way, you will never see your wife or daughter again."

Still, Anton refused. He knew that admitting to the crimes they were accusing him of would guarantee him a trip to the wall, regardless. There would be no trial, no pardon; he would never see the outside of this prison. Yet the man came back, day after day. Each day, he left in frustration, swearing and threatening more. Then one day, Victor arrived in his place.

"Leave us," he ordered the guards who had unlocked the three bolts to let him in. "Take a cigarette break, and close the door behind you."

He swiveled the chair around and placed it near Anton, just as the interrogating officer did every morning. His steel-toed boot grazed Anton's leg as he bent down to whisper:

"Anton. How did this happen?"

Anton managed a small, resigned smile, his first one in days. "Victor, I am so happy to see you. Somehow I knew that you'd come."

"Don't be happy, Anton. This is quite a serious situation you have gotten yourself into. Start at the beginning. And don't leave anything out. I need to know every detail."

And so Anton began, without any sort of suspicion that Victor had already been briefed before his visit and already knew the gravity of the charges. That a plan had been set in motion, a plan of which he could know nothing for the time being if it was to work.

"You are very lucky that your wife is alive,

that you are *all* alive, you know," Victor remarked in a pensive tone when he was finished, and Anton nodded sullenly.

Yes, he knew only too well what happened to people like him, people of his background caught in circumstances far more trivial. A casual remark, a whisper to a trusted friend, an offhand comment, and you could be permanently silenced. He knew several people who had disappeared in the middle of the night, never to be seen or heard from again. Their families had not even been given an explanation for their disappearance, much less a body to bury. Death was all around, and the lives of people like him were cheap — that he knew.

"Well, it's done with, at least for now," Victor resumed in a low voice, leaning in closer. "I've arranged for your dismissal. They have agreed to a fine, a substantial one, but it's the best that we could hope for under the circumstances. You will have to turn over the firearm to the police, of course."

For a moment, Anton stared at him in disbelief. It was not possible that he would be let go, not after all that he had been subjected to, after all he had seen in this place. But looking at Victor and the faint smile that played on his face, he grasped that he was not mistaken. And so he would be set free, after all. But at what cost? What was the cost of a life such as his?

Anton was aware that he had grown hot, his hair damp around the temples. He tried to cobble together something to say but found that he could not. What words would be sufficient at a time like this? What words could render what was inside his heart? What he wanted to do was to fall at Victor's feet, to kiss his boots. He nearly did, but just then, there was the click of the peephole, and one of the guards looked in.

"Is everything all right?"

Not glancing in the direction of the door, Victor made a dismissing gesture. Anton rested his forehead on his bent knees to hide the wave of emotion that had overtaken him. It was only when he was certain they were alone again that he looked up, his eyes brimming with tears.

"Be careful," Victor said, already on his feet and buttoning his leather coat. He picked up the chair and placed it back in the corner. "It's not entirely over, you know."

"I will, Victor. I will live the rest of my life to repay you. I will do all that I can to show you my appreciation. No price will ever be enough."

"You already have, Anton," Victor replied, rapping his knuckles on the metal door. "It is I who am repaying you. The debt was on my part."

The guard stood at attention and saluted Victor as he walked out of the cell. Then the door slammed with a harsh clang, and the last thing Anton heard before the familiar silence engulfed him was the sound of Victor's boots echoing down the empty corridor.

32

"My friend, what a surprise!" Natalia heard her father say in the entryway, full of such buoyant energy that one might think King Michael himself had stopped by for a personal visit. The front door clicked shut, and another voice followed, one that she recognized instantly.

"Anton, it is so good to see you."

"It's been a long time, hasn't it?"

"Yes, it has, it has, indeed. I've been traveling a bit, as you know. I'm sorry I couldn't come sooner."

The voices drifted away from the foyer and became less distinguishable as they moved into the house. Five months too late, Natalia thought. Her father had been waiting for Victor for almost half a year.

Her heart, however caught in a flutter, was filled with an acute indignation. How many times had her father checked the mailbox hoping for a sign of life? She almost pitied him now, the way his voice betrayed no anger at all, no reproach whatsoever, for being so utterly forgotten. Well, not Natalia. Her mother had gone out on her Sunday errands, so no appearance was required of her at all; she could just stay up here, read a book, be spared some superficial excuses that only her father would believe. Yet no more than ten minutes passed before a feeling of a different kind overtook her, and she found herself standing in front of the mirror over her dresser, examining herself disapprovingly.

The brush caught in her curls, and she winced as she tugged it all the way through. Her hair, which had darkened to a chocolatey auburn, was so thick and long now it was impossible to tame, evidently much like the rest of her. Peeling off her nightgown, she glanced at the mirror in profile, thinking as she had over the months past that she hadn't one thing to wear. The onslaught of changes had come rapidly, more rapidly than their budget could be stretched to allow for a new wardrobe. It wasn't unusual in such moments — when catching sight of the full blooming of breasts, the rounding of hips — to have the strange sensation that she wasn't looking at herself at all but at a complete stranger.

Rifling through her armoire, she settled on a navy-blue dress with a lace collar that made her green eyes look almost blue and that had once been loose enough around the torso that it still allowed her some room to breathe. She slipped on her gold ballet slippers and gathered her hair in a loose ponytail. *Cool and collected,* she commanded herself, coming down the steps quietly, save for the volcano that had erupted in her chest. Halfway down, she nearly changed her mind and turned back around, but Victor had already spotted her through the open French doors.

"Talia," he called out to her, smiling affectionately, holding out his hand over the back of the sofa.

She stopped, her palm suddenly moist against the wooden banister as her other hand came up in a gesture of hello. Now there was no choice but to continue the rest of the way. Slowly, she descended to the bottom of the stairs and approached the doorway to the parlor.

"Talia, how have you been?" Victor asked, his lips curling up in that small, ironic smile of his. "How's school?"

"School is great," she lied, lowering her eyes. School was, in fact, far from great, but she did not think that he wanted to know the details. He was just trying to make polite conversation.

Oh, how she hoped he wouldn't notice her obvious discomfort, the sudden heat that rose to her cheeks! She looked ridiculous, no doubt, standing there as if a hole had opened at her feet and she was about to fall into it. He, on the other hand, had never looked more at ease, in his white silk shirt opened casually at the collar and dark gray trousers. No tie. His black hair was slightly longer, wavier, but still perfectly smoothed back from his forehead. Casually, he crossed his long legs and extracted a silver lighter and a pack of cigarettes from his pocket. The lighter clicked several times as he cupped a deeply veined, sculpted hand around the flame, like that belonging to a count in a baroque painting. She watched him take a long drag and hold in the smoke for a moment before exhaling it through half-parted lips.

But why in the world had she not stayed upstairs? It had been something insignificant, something so absurd now — a small retaliation she'd planned, to act indifferently, making him pay for his absence. A mistake that had backfired, for she was now suffocating in the tight grip of her dress.

Then, as if things could get any worse,

her father's voice cut through the room, jolting her out of her stupor, and to her utter embarrassment, she heard him say, "Talia, darling, if you're just going to stand there, would you mind bringing in some ice water, please?"

"No, please, don't bother. I don't want to impose. Besides, I can't stay long," Victor replied, looking directly at her, causing her blood to spike again to the very tips of her ears. "Thank you anyway. I just wanted to drop by to see how your father was doing."

Her father, Natalia could not help but notice, was doing more than well at the moment. He had not seemed so animated, so full of enthusiasm, in as long as she could remember. As if he had not heard Victor at all, he was already on his feet and was crossing the length of the parlor with the sprightliness of an adolescent.

"I have a perfect wine that I have been saving for a special occasion. I can't think of a better time to enjoy it! Just give me a minute while I go grab it from the cellar."

"Please, Anton. I really cannot stay. Maybe another time."

It was as if all the air had gone out of the room. For a moment, he stilled, and then he turned and walked back toward the coffee table, with shoulders slightly drooped and his bright smile faded. When he sat down again, neither her father nor Victor spoke, and in the ongoing silence, Natalia sensed a startling change. She could not recall a single time when the two of them had been at a loss for words.

And the other odd thing: Victor seemed intent on ignoring her. He'd barely spoken two words to her, had hardly even acknowledged her presence. A shard of terror ran through her as she wondered if somehow he was able to read her thoughts, but then she realized that couldn't be, and the terror melted into a slight sadness. Memories tugged at her, glimpses from years before — the way he used to twirl her around in the entryway when he came to visit, the way he sat so still while she played her piano, as if he would never tire of it. Once, down by the lake, where her mother had sent him to keep an eye on her while she swam, she'd told him a joke. It was something she overheard in line at the grocer's, and even though she didn't fully understand it herself, he laughed as if it was the most amusing thing on earth. "Talia, you are one funny girl," he had said, shaking his head as they sat side by side in the dewy grass. "You are going to break someone's heart one day." But now it was as if she wasn't even in the room. All of Victor's attention was focused strictly on her father.

"How are you feeling?" he asked now, leaning forward onto his elbows, his gaze intent on Anton's face. "I've been worried about your health. You looked so thin last time I saw you."

"Oh, I'm getting by. Despina has been feeding me well, even though it's not easy these days. The shelves are empty, you know. It's impossible to get fresh bread if you're not in line by four in the morning. She insists on going herself so I can get some extra rest. Rest for what? I ask her, but she refuses to let me go. It's hard for her, you know."

Victor nodded. "These are strange days, Anton. How's the store?"

Anton waved his hand in a *don't ask* sort of gesture. "Business is practically non-existent. Most days, I will have five, maybe six customers, just enough to keep the doors open. But what else can I do? That shop is my life, Victor. All in all, it still gives us enough income to live better than most. Once in a while, when there is a little extra cash in the register, I go to the speculators and get a little meat, some eggs. A luxury these days. And I thank God for it —"

"Anton," Victor interrupted, "do you

remember what we talked about the last time? The day you were released? You must be careful. Keep a low profile. Make do with what you have, and stay away from the speculators. Better to live on bread alone but to live free."

"But there are other things as well, Victor. There are piano lessons for Natalia; they cost a small fortune, but she plays so beautifully now. And I still like to surprise Despina with something nice once it a while, so —"

"Anton, I'm afraid you are not listening." Victor's tone was suddenly impatient, clipped. "This is precisely why I stopped by. To tell you, to *warn* you . . ." He paused to clear his throat or maybe to find the best words. "There is a file on you with the police and at Party headquarters. An open file, Anton. No more piano lessons, no more trips to the speculators, no more presents. You have to be careful. Can you promise me that?"

"Sure, Victor," he answered, looking into the flameless fireplace. "I understand. I thank you for all that you've done for us, but I don't think you should worry."

"Please, promise me, Anton. Give me your word that you will do as I ask."

For a moment, only the sound of children

outside was audible, a voice from a window calling their names. Victor looked suddenly drained, the sharp angles of his face sagging a little, making him look years older. Her father, too, looked crestfallen.

"You have my word," he replied softly.

Victor nodded then, satisfied or relieved or maybe both. He placed the cigarette pack back in his pocket and reached for his hat at the edge of the sofa. There was something painstakingly slow in his movements, as if they required more energy than he possessed.

He can't be leaving yet, he just got here, Natalia thought with a flurry of panic. But her father was already on his feet and coming up to Victor, holding his arms out. When they embraced, something passed between them, something so tangible that Natalia felt it from across the room. They stood like that for a while, motionless, with their dark heads bent together in silence.

"Take care of yourself, Anton," Victor said, pulling back but keeping one hand on his friend's shoulder. "Please give my love to Despina. Tell her I will never forget her lamb stew. Talia," he called out, shifting his gaze abruptly in her direction, "look after your father here. Take care of him. He is the best man I've ever known."

He looked straight at her when he said it. This time, she did not look to the ground, she did not look away, but she held his eyes, green and steadfast, a mirror of her own. A moment? A minute? How long was too long? She did not know. Something was dissolving in the pit of her stomach, a hot liquid spreading through her limbs like a poison.

Don't go, she nearly blurted. *Don't leave. Can't you see that he needs you?* But the words wouldn't leave her lips, and it came to her with a sobering jolt that Victor was leaving for the last time, that they would not see him again. She glimpsed this simple truth in the knowing smile that passed between him and her father as they walked toward the foyer, in the way Victor touched the rim of his hat with his index finger in the open doorway. She watched still the chiseled line of his shoulders as he turned and walked down the stone steps into a defiantly sunny October afternoon.

Please turn around, she prayed, *please,* but he did not — there was no wave good-bye, no last gesture, there was nothing at all. Leaning against the black-lacquered door, her hand grasping the edge with all its might, she listened to the sound of his steps on the pavement below until they faded

away, until he rounded the corner and disappeared in the pedestrian crowd.

33

February 1954

"You left the fire on all night?"

Squinting in the near darkness, Natalia sat up and tried to adjust her eyes. The fire had indeed all but gone out, the last of the flames lost in a bed of embers. It was cold already but not nearly as much as it would have been upstairs. Anyway, she loved sleeping down here on the sofa, surrounded by the maroon walls and the gleaming marble and the last of the fine valuables that for mere seconds, while the serenity of sleep seeped from her body, made her feel that everything wasn't so different.

"You've just wasted three days' worth of wood, do you realize that? Have I not asked you to put out the fire and go to bed?"

She sat up straight, and the woolen shawl Despina had knitted for her slid off her shoulders to reveal a wool cardigan, and underneath it a long flannel nightgown. She

311

sighed, pushing her feet into her slippers.

"I'm sorry, Mama. I was reading and fell asleep. I'll put on some tea."

As she got up to go to the kitchen, rubbing her icy hands, she shot an involuntary look in the direction of the log basket. Fewer than a dozen, to be sure. And only February. At least they weren't the only ones who would have to bridge the rest of the winter on a few pieces of wood.

In the first two weeks of the year, every store in Bucharest had run out of logs entirely. People took to chopping down trees in parks, on poorly lit streets in the middle of the night, before the police patrols arrived. All over town, men in overcoats were hauling their stolen tree branches through slush and snow, slithering along in the dark on icy sidewalks with ladders and axes, and all the trees in Bucharest were just barren stumps.

Her father simply did not have it in him to do it. "Trees have souls just like people," he declared. "They do not deserve to share in our fate."

Instead, he began chopping up furniture, one item at a time. First there were the chairs in the dining room, all ten of them, followed by Despina's beloved Biedermeier table, which, in all its gleaming, majestic glory, had been the centerpiece of the household.

"We don't need it anymore," Despina professed, trying to keep her voice steady, her face indifferent. "This is not a time for dinner parties, and anyway, we only eat in the kitchen these days."

That got them through the first two months of cold weather.

Next came the furniture in the bedrooms. Natalia's delicate pale green armoire with brass knobs, the one she'd had since she was a little girl, was the first to go.

"It is too small for you now, Talia." Her mother had tried to comfort her as her father lugged it down the service stairs and into the courtyard. "You can hang your dresses alongside mine."

Natalia didn't want to make much of a fuss, to remind her mother that it was the very first thing they'd bought for her when she came home from the orphanage. She did not want to complain that it still housed a few of her little-girl outfits, dresses of velvet and lace that she had not worn in years but still secretly rubbed against her cheek once in a while just to remember what they felt like.

The rest of the furniture came in quick succession: bookshelves, the art deco table in the entryway, the coat stand, Natalia's desk with the old-fashioned Florentine frothiness that never looked more out of place in a barren room. She now did her homework in the kitchen by the stove. It was just as well, for it was the only warm place in the house, and besides, she lacked motivation to keep up with schoolwork. It seemed pointless to spend hours poring over geometry and physics and history when there was no food in their home and when most nights they slept with their coats on. When there was no hot water, no soap to wash with. Even the lights were automatically turned off at eight o'clock sharp, long before she had a chance to finish her daily assignments.

"You have to keep up with your studies so you can go to the university next year," her father reminded her whenever he caught her daydreaming over her books. "It's the only chance you'll have for a decent life. Knowledge is power, the only power that can set you free."

"But Papa, you know that all I really want to do is play the piano, and the music conservatory won't pay that much attention to my academic grades. Besides, they've changed the books, don't you see? All the history books — math and science, even —

have been altered. What is there for me to study? It's all a lie!"

Every time, she regretted saying such things to him. After all he'd done to get her into a public school, he didn't deserve it.

The year before, the Catholic school that Natalia had attended since she was seven was forced to close its doors. The nuns who taught there for decades had simply disappeared overnight. No one had any idea what had happened to them, but one thing was clear: they were disposed of without much fanfare or fuss. It was the same week the Ministry of Education announced that all students coming from private institutions — bourgeois children like herself — were permanently banned from attending public schools.

"What will we do?" mothers and fathers whispered as they waited for their children to be dismissed for the last time. "Are they to be left uneducated? Are they to beg in the streets for a living?"

In her own home, the same questions had bubbled endlessly from her parents' lips. For six months, they went unanswered, as her father begged and pleaded and paid fines and offered bribes to get her into a school, any school at all, even one outside of Bucharest. The reply — on the rare occasions when he wasn't actually hung up on — was always the same: *Not a remote possibility, you might as well wish for the moon.* Then, unexpectedly, the answer had changed.

It was precisely one week after she'd gone to the store to help out with inventory and found two empty glasses in the back room. Traces of brandy, thick as honey, still coated the bottoms as she brought them to the sink to rinse out. At the time, she'd thought nothing of it; people stopped by to see her father all the time, and he still greeted them in his usual fashion, no expense spared or effort forgone to make them feel welcome. Only a week later, when they received a letter from the Department of Education announcing that the ban on her public school attendance had been lifted, did she know undoubtedly whom her father had met with that afternoon.

It took her a couple of weeks after that to shake off the restlessness that had returned with a vengeance. She spent hours staring out the window or at a page in a book, unable to read any of it. Even her piano seemed to provide little solace, and shockingly enough, she found herself feeling a little bit jealous of her father, even though it was obvious that had it not been for her, the meeting might not have taken place at all. It faded in the end. There was nothing to hold on to, he was gone from their lives, and perhaps she was better off for it. She saw the whole thing now clearly, exactly for what it was, an unhealthy attachment to a man who would never see more in her than a little girl. Soon it was time to start her new school, and she never welcomed anything more fervently.

The first day was an overcast, muggy one, though for Natalia, everything was bathed in a pleasant light, brimming with new possibility. As she walked through the front gates, head held high, she vowed that this year would mark a new beginning, that she would work harder than ever and make the effort that was expected to her. She would rise to the occasion, for her father.

So absorbed she was that she barely took notice of the whispering voices growing in her wake, the bellow of laughter that erupted behind her as she passed the water cooler in the corridor, looking for her room number. It did not seem possible that she could be the subject of such amusement, for no one here knew her. No one knew her at all.

It was only when she paused in front of

her classroom that an intense uneasiness settled on her like frost, a suspicion that this day might not go as she had imagined. Nervously, she straightened the red pioneer scarf that all students were required to wear and smoothed out her uniform skirt. Inhaling deeply, she opened the door.

The room was smaller than she expected and crammed to capacity with rows of desks that extended all the way to the back wall. A swirl of noise enveloped her — voices and laughter and the thump of books. But then someone whistled at the back of the room, and instantly the din ceased.

Breathless with emotion, she inched forward, trying not to look at the gaping faces and curious eyes fixed upon her. She stopped in the middle of the room, unsure of where to go, praying that the heavyset woman with a hard-edged face scribbling furiously on the blackboard would turn around and say something. When she did, Natalia attempted a weak smile.

"Your desk is over there," the woman said curtly, without as much as an introduction, motioning with her chalk to a desk in the corner. "Yes, over there."

Holding her book bag against her chest as if it offered some measure of protection, Natalia walked to her seat. A moment later, the second bell rang, and the entire class rose in unison.

"Good morning, class," the woman uttered with a flat disinterest, huffing a little as she moved away from the blackboard and slumped down behind the podium desk. The back of her hand rose to her bleached hairline to sweep away a few beads of sweat, and Natalia couldn't help noticing the stain in the shape of a half-moon that had formed under her arm.

"Good morning, Miss Tima," the students answered lethargically.

"You may be seated."

A rustling of pages followed. Someone belched and did not say *excuse me.* At the back of the room, a pencil was being tapped on the back of a book, as if in tune with a melody.

"We have a new student today," Miss Tima said matter-of-factly, not looking up from the attendance ledger. "This is Natalia Goza. Natalia, please stand up."

She stood timidly.

"Natalia has been granted permission to attend our school. Please come up to the front."

She did as she was told.

"Natalia, before we begin our lesson today, I would like you to go around the room and pick up any trash that you see on the floor."

Strange how she nearly burst into laughter despite the nausea that rose in her gut. Was this some kind of a joke? Was this supposed to be a comical introduction? Certainly, she had not heard this right, she had misunderstood.

"Go on, then, we don't have all day," Miss Tima said, gesturing to the room with visible boredom. "Go on and pick up the trash so we can get started."

Still, Natalia did not move, staring with wide, uncomprehending eyes at Miss Tima, who clicked her tongue and shook her head disapprovingly.

"Yes, well, I see. We *all* see. A bourgeois princess like you doesn't pick up trash, yes? You have someone else do it for you at home? Well, not here. Here you will be picking up the trash for the class."

Lifting a ruler in her large hand, she began tapping it on the edge of the desk. "This is a perfect lesson for today," she went on, addressing the class now, sweeping the wooden stick out as if she was waving it over an orchestra. "An exercise in equality. Miss Goza is about to understand that she is no better than anyone else in this room."

It took all Natalia had not to run or to tell

this rude woman to go to hell. To pick up her own trash or worse. But then she remembered her father's face, how happy he'd looked earlier that morning, how proud he'd been that he could get her back into school. How could she run? How could she go home and tell him that all of his efforts had been in vain, that she had kicked away of her own will her only chance at an education?

Tears came fast, blurring her sight, making the room blend into a dance of shadows. She clenched her fists, her fingernails digging painfully into her palms. Then she did what she could hardly believe herself. Straightening her back, taking her time, she walked to the farthest end of the room and bent down. Crouching between the rows, she began picking up whatever she saw on the floor — bits of paper, a couple of broken pencils, a discarded bread crust that looked like it had been there for weeks. When she reached the front, she went down the next row and did the same.

Someone laughed in the back of the classroom.

"Silence!" Miss Tima shrieked, slamming the ruler down on her desk with a force that made every shape in the room grow still. Then she went back to correcting her papers. She only looked up again when from the corner of her eye she spotted Natalia standing nearby, holding the trash bin in her quivering hands.

"Finished, then?" she said. "Good. Let's begin our lesson. Natalia, you may return to your seat."

Natalia thought she would never live past the shame that burned inside her when the next day, and the day after, she was asked to perform the same task. But to her own surprise, she did. The humiliation she had felt on that first day lost its bitter edge as she taught herself how to do whatever was asked of her with a blank mind and a blank heart, as she forced herself to feel nothing, to think nothing, to execute the task, get it done, today, tomorrow, *survive*. After a while, the students no longer snickered as she bent down by their desks to pick up their garbage. They no longer threw wads of paper at her as she slithered along, biting her lip, her eyes pinned on the classroom floor.

In time, Natalia was no longer an interesting diversion, a curiosity. She was just Natalia, the girl whose parents had been labeled class enemies, whose father had been labeled an exploiter of the people, bourgeois, a capitalist, and for whose sins his daughter would pay, at least every morning in this classroom before instruction began.

34

She did not know what drew her with such force to Saint Paul's Orphanage that afternoon. There was nothing in particular that she hoped to find. In fact, she was a little afraid of what she might discover there, what she might dig up. Nearly four years had passed since she had come across that letter in her father's safe, and still she thought about it more often than she liked. She couldn't remember how many nights she'd fallen asleep replaying those lines in her mind — those lines that wouldn't give her peace.

I do not wish to disturb the life to which she has become accustomed.

Well, it had certainly accomplished just that. Whatever her life was now, whatever had become of it, it was punctuated with a simmering, pestering curiosity that gnawed at her night and day. It was strange, she realized now, how as a young child she'd so easily managed to cut herself off from her past. She had made herself numb to it, indifferent. But that letter had opened up the door to ghosts she'd long buried. For four years now, she'd been haunted by them. They lurked everywhere, inside her dreams, underneath the surface of her everyday life, like dirty little secrets.

But this has nothing to do with you now, Talia, she often chided herself for this absurd preoccupation. *This has no bearing on your life now.* She knew only too well that there were more important matters that required her full focus, like the fact that her dream of attending the music conservatory had just gone up in flames. It had not been a surprise entirely when the rejection letter had come in the mail. She'd seen the answer already on the faces of the auditioning committee, when at the end of her recital, they examined her application and their expressions shifted from pure enchantment to helpless disappointment. It had broken her heart at first — her heart and her will and, worse even, her faith in herself — but after months of wallowing in self-pity, she decided that she would not give up on her piano.

For years now, she'd been in love with jazz, and she'd heard that although it was banned from being played publicly, it was still very much alive in a budding under-ground movement. The idea seemed crazy (and risky, at that), but if she practiced enough, if she really committed, maybe someday she would find a place for herself in its midst. In the meantime, she could earn a little money by giving lessons — there were other avenues, other paths, as long as she didn't quit.

Yes, there were more pressing matters bearing down on her life. But the more she struggled to put the letter out of her mind, the less she succeeded. What if there had been other letters, more inquiries? Could there have been? She didn't think it likely. After 1945, when Romania was cut off from the West, it would have been impossible to get any correspondence into the country. If there had been more letters, if there had been more attempts to find her, the chain would have been severed there. But what if that wasn't true? She recalled the times she'd wanted to ask her uncle if he knew the circumstances of her adoption and now regretted not doing it. Then again, it would probably not have gotten her very far. Whatever Stefan knew, he would take to his grave. Nothing would ever come between him and his undying loyalty to her parents.

It seemed that if there was anything more

to know, there was only one way to find out. She would have to go back to the place where it had all started.

Later that afternoon on the trolley, Natalia could still not believe her own impulsiveness, the way she'd simply hopped on at the last moment without any sort of a clear plan. She rode standing up, the city and its usual mélange of sun-scorched parks and soot-stained facades going by in a blur as she counted the years. Thirteen years had passed since she'd last seen the inside of that place. Thirteen long years in a different life, a life before food lines and rationed electricity.

Once, she had ridden past it by chance. It was right after the war, and the buses were not yet running regularly, so she and her mother had taken a cab to go someplace. She remembered her mother talking to the driver, saying something about the interminable winter, how a bomb had left a gaping hole in the center of town. And then she'd stopped in mid-sentence. At the silence, Natalia looked up from the book in her lap and followed the trajectory of her mother's gaze. There, underneath the metal scaffolding, the place that contained her earliest memories lay in a state of decay.

"Remember, Talia?" her mother said softly as the place grew smaller in the rear window.

Of course, she remembered. She didn't think it possible to ever forget. How could she forget the faces of those dirty, desolate children crying late in the night, their lice-infested uniforms, the musty courtyard that smelled perpetually of garbage, the daily watery soup? But of all this she said nothing. She shrugged instead, trying to appear indifferent, hoping that her disinterest would discourage her mother from wanting to discuss it further. They never spoke of it again. No doubt, cab drivers in the future were instructed to avoid that particular street, to take a different route no matter how much it added to the fare.

At the next stop, Natalia decided to get off. It was not the station closest to the orphanage, but she needed to walk for a bit, to collect herself. As she did, her thoughts returned to the one question that had driven her here, the one she'd never been able to answer. Why had the people who'd given her life chosen in the end to live a life without her? In the past, for brief moments when she tried to imagine it, all the convenient reasons were there. They were young, maybe they were hungry, they were burdened with the responsibility of being parents. She pictured them as a pair of drifters, moving from flat to flat, destitute and starving, struggling to survive. Maybe she'd been a mistake, an unfortunate turn of events. Maybe they'd done their best before giving up, letting someone else do the job. Yes, it had been easy not to think about them. Until she'd stumbled upon that letter, no other possibility had even entered her mind. But now here she was. Now, of her own will, she was the one chasing the ghosts.

At the intersection, she studied the street sign and turned the corner, feeling her pulse quicken a little. A few pedestrians rushed past her, their heads hung low, hands in their pockets, oblivious to the fact that she was walking so slowly that nearly twenty minutes later she had not yet come to the end of the block. When at last she reached her destination and looked up, she was surprised to see that the building looked more or less exactly as she remembered. Only the metal scaffold and the dark blue placard that read *Saint Paul's Orphanage* was absent, but otherwise the building appeared unaltered.

Timidly, she stepped through the wood-framed gate, expecting to come face-to-face with an onslaught of children, but the courtyard was silent. She had come late and unannounced. And now it seemed absurd that she was here at all. She'd come hoping to find — what? That the orphanage director would invite her in and hand over a sealed file? One that undoubtedly her parents had paid a great deal of money to sink into obscurity?

She turned to go and was nearly at the gate when a door clicked open behind her, and a slant of light fell in her eyes. In the bleak light, an officer marched toward her, frowning as he adjusted the brim of his cap. For a moment, she thought he was coming for her, to interrogate her, ask what she was doing here. But he hurried right past her without a single look. The front gate slammed shut, and as she pressed her back to the wall to hide in the shadow, she saw that the entrance to the main building had been left ajar. For five minutes, she waited, then quietly slipped inside.

The hallway, much like the exterior, seemed eerily unaltered, with its chipped pale green walls and smell of ammonia and checkered linoleum tiles that squeaked beneath her hesitant steps. As she made her way toward what she vaguely recalled was the director's office, she tried to go over what she would say. How would she explain why she'd come? Would the old woman recognize her after all these years?

She paused in front of the door, took in a breath. Quickly, before she could change her mind, she pressed down on the door handle and entered. As her eyes roamed about the room, taking in what she was seeing, she froze in confusion. An enormous rectangular table which took up most of the space stood in place of Mrs. Tudor's old, peeling desk, and seated around it were a dozen or so men wearing military uniforms. There were clipboards and files scattered all over the table, and a tape recorder was placed right in the center, next to a half-filled water carafe.

"I-I'm so sorry," Natalia stammered as twelve pairs of eyes shot up to her in unison. "I must be in the wrong room, I must be . . ." She took a step backward. "Please excuse me."

One of the men, an elderly one whose breast was covered in decorations, swiveled his chair around to face her. In the harsh artificial light, his white hair looked almost silver, as did his neatly trimmed beard, which he rubbed pensively as his eyes bored into her. He examined her with his cold, blue eyes as if she was some kind of rare insect, one he contemplated either squashing under his foot or setting free.

"Young lady, what are you doing here?" he said sternly after a moment.

"Excuse me, sir," Natalia repeated in a fluster. "I didn't mean to interrupt. I was just . . . I was looking for Mrs. Tudor, the director of the orphanage. I'm sorry to have barged in."

"Orphanage? What orphanage?"

The officer to his right cleared his throat. "Yes, General, she is right. There was an orphanage here, before the war. Part of the building was destroyed in the bombing. The wing that housed the children's dormitory and kitchen, to be exact. And the archive room, too, plus a couple of the classrooms."

"So, what is it that you want?" she vaguely heard the officer address her again.

What happened to the children? Where are the children? she wanted to scream. *Where are the nuns, the cook, the teachers?* But all she could do was stand there as dread seeped through her like ice water.

"I was one of the children here," she mumbled, so softly that the officer cupped a hand around his ear.

"What's that?"

"Before the war, I was one of the children here. I was one of the orphans who lived here for a little while."

"Well, this is a government building now. We do not know anything about the orphanage. And you are trespassing on an official meeting," he said with detachment.

"I'm sorry. I'm sorry for disturbing."

And then she was running. She turned and ran as fast as she could down the corridor and through the courtyard that had once been her playground. She ran, not looking back, not bothering to shut the gate behind her, down the street and farther still, until a sharp jab in her side forced her to stop. As she leaned against a wall, waiting to catch her breath, she gazed up at the darkening sky and thought of the children. The children.

It wasn't until much later, when she retraced her way back to the bus stop, that she was able to dry her eyes. Whatever traces of her past remained, whatever secrets had been confined within those walls, they had gone up in flames along with the orphanage. The thread did end there; it was severed for good. Right before turning the corner, she glanced back once more at the building that for a brief period of time had been her home. She gazed at it for a few moments, trying to imprint it in her mind. She knew she would never see it again.

35

"Someone was here asking for you today," Natalia announced as she dove eagerly into a plateful of roasted chicken.

Plump, golden meat melted in her mouth, so tender that she let out an involuntary gasp. On the rare occasions when her mother was able to get a fresh bird at the butcher's, the first supper was always a feast. In the days that followed, there would be a row of dishes carefully crafted using every leftover morsel and ending with a soup made solely from the bird's carcass. But the first meal was always a rare treat, and Natalia hated having to bring up anything unpleasant at a time like this.

"Did he leave a name?" her father asked.

"He said he was a city inspector. He was conducting a census and wanted to know how many people live in our home. I told him he would have to come back when you were home."

Her father looked up from his plate. She thought she saw him pale a little. "Natalia, you know you are not to ever answer any questions about our family, you cannot —"

"Yes, Papa, I know. I asked him to leave. He said he would come back another time."

A silence passed during which her father nodded slightly, then took several more bites before placing his fork down.

"I had my biggest order in years today," he said, his features brightening a little. "Someone came into the store and bought ten thousand sheets of premium envelopes, just like that. I helped him carry the boxes out, helped to load them in the back of his car."

Despina's eyes rose from her own plate, wide with surprise. "So who was he, Anton?"

"He said he was from the ministry, which one I didn't catch. A clerk of some sort, I suppose. He seemed quite interested in our inventory. Said he would be back next month to place another order. Then he paid for the envelopes in cash. In cash, Despina. Who does that anymore?"

"I don't know," she said after a contemplative moment, bringing the glass of water to her lips, and Natalia knew what she was thinking. This meant a little more food for a while, *better* food, some fruit, perhaps, fresh eggs. It meant that they could loosen their rations a bit. All in all, it was the best news they'd heard in months.

"Anyway, what does it matter? That's wonderful, Anton," her mother went on cheerfully, standing from her chair and beginning to collect the plates that had been scraped clean, the flatware. "Timing couldn't be better. I haven't been able to sell anything at the flea market this week. Our great leaders' wives seem to have grown tired of silver fineries, it seems, even ones they can pick up for mere coins."

"Despina, please . . ."

"Oh, I know, Anton. I know. She knows, too. She's there helping me every Wednesday, remember?"

She winked at Natalia, who returned a small smile from across the table. It was true, what her mother was saying. They had good weeks and bad weeks at the local *talcioc,* and this last one had not been particularly good. But week after week, they kept going regardless. More often than not, it still brought in some much-needed cash, and she no longer minded the excursion as much as she had in the beginning.

A month earlier, when they'd gone there for the first time, Natalia had wanted to vanish into thin air. Trailing her mother through a sea of women who had laid out their most precious wares on coarse blankets in the middle of a vacant plaza, she'd prayed that God would just make her disappear, cut her out of the scene unfolding around her like a painter might varnish out one segment of his canvas. It was hot, and they'd waited a while in a spot under a tree they'd been lucky enough to get. Her mother wore one of her pretty dresses, which had mortified Natalia even more. The way she stood there straight-backed, her hair loose, shining in the sun as if she was some kind of a sorceress. A woman had walked over, peered down at their open valise. "That," she said in a deep Russian accent, pointing a red-varnished finger at one of her mother's stoles, and her mother had bent down and lifted it out.

It made her chuckle now to recall her foolish pride, the pure rage that had ignited inside her when that woman ran her fingers back and forth over the fur, flipping it over to feel the silk lining, not even looking her mother in the eye as she handed her a few bills. Because, she realized now, the important thing, the only one that mattered, was that they *had* things to sell. They still had her mother's furs and snakeskin bags and hats fashioned in Vienna and Paris. They had silverware and china. And even if all these things combined were now worth only a fraction of their true value, they still had enough to keep them eating for years.

But she couldn't stop counting, tallying up in her head what belongings remained, which would go next. She never could.

Early the next morning, there were knocks at their door. The sound came from some distant place, as if it followed Natalia from her sleep, and she sat upright, a little disoriented, glancing at her clock. It was just past seven. Who would be coming by at this hour on a Sunday? She didn't know how long the knocking had been going on, but it didn't seem like anyone else was going to answer, so she got out of bed and tiptoed downstairs. In the foyer, the floor felt like ice beneath her bare feet as she ambled to the door and looked through the peephole.

The squat, suited man who had come asking for her father the day before was back. He was standing at a slight distance, politely holding his hat against his chest, but there was something intrusive in the way his eyes darted about the house, examining the iron sconces, looking up as if he took great interest in how high the roofline was, how fine the stucco walls.

Natalia took a step back and let the flap of the peephole come down with a clang. She did not care for the look of that man. What did he want? Why was he here at this hour? Well, if he didn't know that this was not a proper time to be dropping by, she certainly wouldn't be the one to inform him. Blazing with irritation, she started back up the stairs and was nearly at the top when she practically ran into her father.

"Talia, who was that?" he asked, smoothing back his disheveled salt-and-pepper hair. If there was anything at all to give away his fifty years, it was that his once pitch-black hair was now threaded with silver. That and a slight sagging of the shoulders which she noticed only recently.

"Oh, that . . . well, no one, really," she answered unconvincingly. "I don't think it's anyone . . . anyone important, I mean . . ." She trailed off, for her father was already flying down the steps, his burgundy silk robe fluttering behind him.

She was supposed to bring the man something to drink. "A drink?" she mouthed to her father in dismay. A drink, after the way he'd barged in, hanging his hat in the foyer without invitation?

"Yes, a glass of water." While he was changing, her father had whispered. If she didn't mind going back down.

Well, she did mind. She minded a great deal, but there wasn't anything she could do about it now. Without bothering to offer any sort of a greeting, she marched straight to the kitchen, where she filled a glass of tepid water from the sink. Then she brought it into the sitting room, where the man had already made himself at home on the sofa. When she plunked it down on the coffee table, it made a loud thud, louder than she intended.

"Ah, thank you," the man murmured, not looking up from the contents of his briefcase which lay open right next to him. He perched a pair of glasses on his bulbous nose and dug into one of the silk-lined side pockets. "That's very kind."

At last, he fished out a silver pen and a small pad, in which he began to scribble furiously, frowning in contemplation every few moments, pushing his glasses higher. When he was done, he stood up, and with the pen and paper still in hand, he circled around the back of the sofa, letting his short fingers brush over the velvet upholstery. A moment later, he was standing in front of the china cabinet, tilting his head this way and that, studying the objects inside. The whole time, he kept scribbling in his pad.

"Excuse me, is there anything I can help you with?" Natalia blurted, unable to contain herself any longer. "Something to satisfy your curiosity?"

The man did not answer. He did not look at her. Only his fingers kept moving, tracing invisible lines over the hand-carved surface of the cabinet, the white-and-gray marbled fireplace, the leather-bound books on the shelves.

"Do you play? Your mother?" he asked, turning to her abruptly as if he was just now noticing that she was in the room. He picked up a stack of sheet music from the sideboard and began leafing through it. "Is there a piano in the house?"

Something rose in her throat, bitter, like old coffee. She looked down at her hands, praying that her father would come down at once and kick this ill-mannered man out of their house. She hated his florid, sweaty face, his shameless eyes which kept roaming greedily over her mother's possessions, things that had been in her family for generations, as if they were on some cheap sales display.

"Oh, that," she said coldly. "Yes, there is a

piano upstairs. It hasn't been tuned in years. It's just furniture, really."

He regarded her flatly, as if he'd paid no attention, and then his face spilled into a coarse grin, displaying a full range of tobacco-stained teeth. "Your father's store, is it near here?"

It was too much to take, so she turned and stormed out of the room, whirling right past her father, who had appeared in the doorway in a pair of khaki trousers and a white linen shirt. The look she shot him was supposed to convey her outrage, but his eyes did not take hers in; they were somewhere else altogether.

At the top of the stairs, she slumped on the last step and strained to hear the conversation that ensued. Her father had not closed the door, and she could make out nearly every word. The man was asking endless questions, about the properties her father had owned before the war, the store, the horses that had been taken away when the stables were nationalized two years ago. He was asking how many bedrooms they had, how many baths, whether the maid's room was occupied. What was in the attic?

After a while, Natalia got up and ran to her room. She threw herself on her bed and turned on the radio. Not a moment longer could she listen to this man who was interrogating her father, scribbling furiously in his notepad, cataloging their entire lives. Not a moment longer could she listen to her father's tone, so resigned and expressionless, as if the battle had already been lost.

36

January 1955

She woke in the middle of the night, trembling, and had to focus on taking deep breaths, in and out, steady and slow, to unknot the dread in the pit of her stomach. She had dreamed of a family gathering, her cousins and aunts all clustered together around their oval dining table. The sun trickled innocently through the lace curtains, shards of light reflecting in the crystal wineglasses, the perfectly set silverware. There was a fragrant lamb stew in one of her mother's china bowls, ensconced in its dark, thick juices. At the other end of the table, delicate pastries no larger than her thumb made her mouth water. There was fresh lemonade that her mother made from her own lemons in the garden and bottles of wine just corked, their foil labels shimmering in the afternoon light. Across the table, her father was laughing. *What is so funny, Papa?* she'd asked, laughing along with him, and then abruptly she woke up. His eyes were the last thing she remembered. In her dream, they twinkled and danced like when she was young.

Night after night Natalia dreamed of her old life. Fractured, hazy recollections tortured her endlessly; they would not give her peace. Well, she did not want to remember. She did not want to remember her childhood home, the veranda with its scent of lilac, the hum of traffic, her room with huge windows looking out over the sycamore trees. Her piano, above all. She hated all the nostalgia that came along with it, all the pointless regret, the heartache. She would have given anything to wipe out those memories, burn them to ashes. At least then she could live in the present, in the here and now, which she with her own hands had brought into being. For had she not been the one to let that man into their home? Had she not been to blame for all that followed?

Natalia closed her eyes tightly to stop the room from spinning. How would she ever forget the look on her mother's face that day, when the inspector returned with a police escort and official papers to put them out on the street? How would she ever forget her expression, wild with disbelief, pleading silently for it not to be true? Her father staring in the middle distance, not speaking, not moving, as if someone had turned off a light switch?

"You are being moved to a communal flat across town," the inspector had told them. "A very nice one, indeed. You have two hours to pack your belongings."

What had been in his smile in that moment? Guilt? Satisfaction? Whatever it was, she'd been the only one to see it. Her father had disappeared by then. Only his physical form had remained at the foot of the steps — slumped, ashen, still. And her mother — her mother had been screaming.

Natalia turned to the wall. Her eyelids were too heavy for her to keep them open, her head too heavy to lift off the pillow, her heart too heavy to face another day. She had begun drifting off again when she was startled awake by the sound of an object hitting the other side of the wall, just above the davenport in the family room that was also her bed. Then another. A door slammed so violently it made the windows rattle. She heard a man's voice, hostile and thick, then a woman's pleading, sobbing. "Please,

Dima, please, Dima, please, Dima. Please, stop."

Natalia pulled a pillow over her head to drown out the noise. Heavy footsteps pounded the hallway, coming closer, but continued on to the front of the flat. A moment later, the front door slammed, then silence. She knew it would only last long enough for him to go down to the corner *tabac* for a fresh bottle of gin. She hoped she could sleep through the rest of it.

A knock at the door awoke her sometime later. She looked at the pendulum clock and realized that it was morning. Groggily, she swung her legs off the sofa and went to the door that separated their two joint rooms from the rest of the apartment. A woman in a floor-length flannel gown leaning on crutches stood before her, looking at her suspiciously. Half of her face was a dark bruise, her hair still coiled in curlers.

"Hello, I'm Ioana," the woman said, not smiling, not extending her hand. "My husband and I occupy the rooms next to yours. I just wanted to make sure that you are aware of the house schedule. It is posted on every door."

"Yes," Natalia muttered. "I know."

"Well, we haven't seen much of your family, so I just wanted to make sure you know there are no exceptions. None at all. If you miss your scheduled time, you don't get to use the bathroom. Or the kitchen." She stared obstinately at Natalia.

"All right," Natalia said in a flat voice. "Thank you for letting us know."

Like Natalia and her parents, the couple was new to the flat. She had overheard her mother say that they had moved in just weeks before and that because the husband was a Party journalist, they had secured the largest of the six bedrooms, next to the kitchen and the bathroom. The remaining two bedrooms were occupied by a young nurse who worked the graveyard shift and never left her room during the day and a woman in her late forties who was employed at the oil refinery and spent all her free time warming up crowds in pro-Party rallies.

That was all Natalia had been able to learn about her neighbors in the few days since their move. That was more than she ever wanted to know. These were the people she was forced to share a roof with, a man who beat his wife every night and a Party informer who glared at her with open hatred when they crossed in the common area and who probably wanted nothing more than to see her family put on a train to a forced-labor camp. How would she learn to breathe, move, eat, sleep, *exist* among them? And for how long? Suddenly, the rest of her life seemed like a very long time. She curled herself around a pillow and closed her eyes.

It was late evening when she opened them again. The flat was unusually quiet, save for the faint sound of the radio coming from the next room, her father no doubt turning the dial back and forth trying to tune into Radio Free Europe. In the near darkness, she glimpsed her mother arranging their salvaged silverware in a china cabinet with a broken glass front, removing them one by one from the sole trunk they'd been allowed to bring.

Her father came in. Struggling to keep his voice low, he said, "They say it is only a matter of time before the West will intervene. The atrocities going on here cannot continue much longer. Do you know what they call the border that stretches between us and the rest of Europe? The Iron Curtain, Despina. The Iron Curtain. Help will arrive soon, you will see."

Her father, like her, disbelieving. Then going back to his room and turning out the light.

How much time passed like this? She wasn't sure. Days, at least, as her mother reminded her constantly. Every morning, when she laid her cool hand on her forehead and whispered in her ear, "Talia, come, you have to eat something," she knew that another one had passed. How could she explain that she never wanted to open her eyes again, she never wanted to eat, wash, move again? She could not, of course. For them, she had to find a way to set her body in motion. For them, she had to find a way.

It wasn't until her mother threatened to pour cold water on her that she actually did it. She rose reluctantly, even if in her heart the last thing she wanted was to upset her mother, to drive her mad with worry. Sliding her feet inside her house slippers, not bothering to throw a robe over her nightgown, she followed her mother into the common area, where a plate of toast and a mug of tea had been placed ceremoniously on a wooden table covered in plastic. Taking a bite, chewing listlessly, Natalia let her eyes wander about the room.

The flat was not quite as dreadful as it had first seemed. It had been elegant once, she could tell, designed in a classic Edwardian style, with thick, beveled glass French doors, expansive windows, and an intricately designed parquet floor. But years of neglect had caused the windowsills to peel, the walls to become darkened with soot, the gleam and richness of the wooden floor to subside underneath the layers of grime. It certainly did not help that the living room had been dissected and barricaded, each family claiming its stake with wooden dividers and rugs hung from clotheslines. Yet something about this dilapidated flat moved her. It was an invalid, a cripple in need of acceptance, in need of embracing. Like her, it willed itself to remain upright, to maintain some semblance of its former splendor.

After breakfast, Natalia helped her mother clear the dishes and bring them to the kitchen at the end of a poorly lit hallway. They were still rinsing the cups and setting them to dry on the counter when that woman Natalia feared the most burst through the swing door.

"Time's up," she said, without as much as a greeting. "Didn't you see the schedule?" She stood there in a greasy apron draped over a bright dress, pointing to the sheet of paper taped over the stove.

"Yes, we are just about finished," said Despina, not looking up from her dishes, which she continued to scrub vigorously.

The woman's eyes stretched as wide as one might imagine possible, and a new shade of pink rose to her already florid face.

"Comrade, this cannot happen again!" she exclaimed, waving her chubby hand in the air. "There are demonstrations that I am required to attend every Saturday, do you understand? Every Saturday afternoon, and I cannot be a minute late!"

They bundled the dishes haphazardly inside their drying towels and hurried out without saying a word. The woman's voice chased them all the way to the end of the hallway.

"That's right! Who the hell do you think you are? Your days are over, madam! They are over! Soon you will be shining my boots at the front door!"

The first thing her mother did back in their rooms was to go close the windows. Then she drew all the curtains shut.

"Do not speak to that woman ever. Do not say a word," she remarked to Anton, who was rustling through the pages of his newspaper, searching for news that did not exist. "Do not even let her hear you whisper. She means to cause trouble for us."

"Oh, let me be, Despina! I can say what I want in my own room. That Communist bitch can go to hell!"

Her mother glared at him, horrified. Then she went into the other room and turned the radio on full blast.

■ ■ ■ ■

Weeks passed like this. Weeks before they were able to reemerge from their paralysis, their stunned inertia. By the time they began gravitating back toward a routine, Natalia had already gotten used to fitting her daily tasks into predetermined time slots. She learned how to bathe in tepid water, making the most of her allotted ten minutes, how to clear the table and wash the dishes before the other flatmates barged in with their pots and pans, their pig fat and wilted carrots, to cook on the stovetop that only her mother bothered to clean. She learned how to keep her voice at a whisper, to convert her face into a mask that betrayed nothing other than casual detachment, to shrug when an insult was hurled her way. Most important, she learned how to convince her mother that she wasn't hungry, she was never hungry, for their savings were quickly dwindling.

Ever since the day her father had been forced to relinquish ownership of the store along with the home he had built with his own hands, he'd been looking for work. He had looked anywhere and everywhere, but no one would hire him. He applied for jobs as a store clerk, then waiting tables and driving cabs, even working a pretzel cart on the street corner.

"I am still young, I can perform any job," he told shopkeepers and restaurant managers and store clerks.

"Do you have working papers?" they all asked him. "Are you a card-carrying Party member?"

"No," he'd admit. "My right to work has been revoked, but I am willing to do anything. Whatever you need, just ask me. I used to own a chain of stores once. I can be quite resourceful, you know. Just try me out. You can pay me whatever you are able to."

Each time, the conversation ended more or less the same way. "Not worth the trouble, I'm afraid. I'd be in an awful mess myself if I hired you. Good luck. I hope you find something, somewhere. Not here, though."

He did find something once in a while, day jobs that no one wanted which barely paid enough for a day's meal and a trolley ride home. He sold lottery tickets at the corner kiosk next to the sports stadium, swept sidewalks, helped unload delivery trucks at the few restaurants still open in town. The only people who hired him now were old friends, people from his past, from the old days.

And still, those jobs were a blessing. When he was able to come home with a little cash in his pocket, Despina took the bills and counted them carefully. Then she hurried to the outdoor market to buy a few vegetables, some fresh eggs before they ran out, trying her best to put together a meal that would revive her husband's dwindling energy, his splintered spirit. For there was only one thing Natalia's mother was determined to do, and that was to maintain some measure of normalcy in their home, even though nothing about their new life was normal. For that, however, her mother was prepared to fight with her last breath. She would fight as she had since that day during the war, when they rode in darkness on a train full of wounded soldiers, looking ahead, only ahead, for anything that was still possible.

For Anton's fiftieth birthday, Despina figured out a way to bake his favorite tart, even though no one had seen any fresh fruit in Bucharest in more than five years.

"I have an idea," she whispered to Natalia that afternoon in early June. "Come with me." Handing her a straw shopping bag, she grabbed the house keys and headed for the door.

"Are we going to the open market?" Natalia asked, perplexed, knowing that their weekly budget had run out days ago.

"Not really. We are just going for a walk. Just a stroll around the neighborhood. You and me, alone."

Natalia eyed her suspiciously but followed anyway. It was, indeed, a perfect summer day, and she didn't mind the walk, even though her mother seemed not to welcome much conversation. Walking slightly ahead of her, she stopped at the corner and waved for her to hurry. A moment later, they found themselves on a remote cobblestone street where a multitude of trees cast long shadows in the afternoon sun.

"So here we are," Despina said.

"Where?" Natalia asked, still confused.

"Look around, darling." She swept her arm out toward the street, and some mischievousness played in her eyes.

Then, all of a sudden, she saw it. Branches of cherry trees heavy with fruit hung over the gated fences on both sides of the sidewalk. The street was littered with fallen cherries. A small, astonished cry came from her lips. She watched her mother begin to collect the fallen fruit, bending and straightening as she moved about, tossing the cherries into her burlap bag as if it was the most natural thing in the world.

"That bag of yours is mighty full," she joked, glancing back at Natalia, who stood there clutching the bag to her chest.

In an instant, Natalia caught up and looped her arm tightly through her mother's. She rested her head on her shoulder, and they walked like that for a while, lost in their thoughts, passing the dancing shadows on the sidewalk to the next street, where more cherries lay scattered on the ground, ready for the picking. The summer sky embraced them, so blue, the color of hope. It wasn't much, but it was enough to make her feel thankful. Thankful, indeed, that she still had her family and that at the very least, her family would enjoy some splendid pastries.

■ ■ ■ ■

THREE:
VICTOR

■ ■ ■ ■

37

August 1959

Natalia had promised Lidia that she would be at her place no later than six, but with the buses not running on time, it was clear she would never make it by then. Her cousin, her dearest friend, was hosting a small birthday party at her new apartment. She had invited a few friends from the national bank where she had been working for the past two years, people she wanted to introduce to Natalia.

"Please, Talia, just this once, be on time. I think you might find it worthwhile," she'd teased, nudging Natalia with her elbow as the two of them sat on a park bench sharing an orange soda the previous Sunday.

At first, Natalia had said she had something to do that day, that she was busy. But Lidia kept insisting, deploying her full charm, laying out every reason why she could not miss out on this gathering, she simply could not. "Don't you think you're too old to be without an admirer?" she'd said more directly, when it seemed that she was making no progress. "You're twenty-two, Natalia, for God's sake!"

And so in the end, Natalia had agreed to go.

It took nearly half a day and two buses to get to Lidia's house. She lived now in one of the city's outlying sectors, where housing blocks erected after the war stretched on for endless kilometers. Each time Natalia visited, she had trouble finding her cousin's flat and often got lost in the maze of pathways that connected one identical concrete giant to the other. Most of the time, it seemed to take nearly as long as the commute itself to find the right wing, the right stairwell, the right door.

At least Lidia was lucky enough to live on her own. She was the master of her destiny, Natalia mused with a twinge of envy as she rode on the first bus amid a mass of crammed bodies. In five years' time, she herself would probably still be living at home. The export produce hall where she worked barely paid enough to sustain the three of them, much less a separate residence. But she was in no place to complain. Luckily, she'd been able to secure a transfer from the cooperative farm twenty kilometers outside of Bucharest where she had been putting in twelve-hour shifts for the better part of the year. At least she no longer had to put up with the foul-smelling train rides, the lack of sleep, the field workers leering at her, brushing up against her, laughing at her puritan pride. She no longer had to endure the sun beating on her back as she harvested potatoes in an open field, the bitter cold that followed in the winter months when by sundown she trudged back to the train station unable to feel her legs.

No, the warehouse where she now worked was a dream by comparison. Her job, too — cleaning and sorting pears and peaches and apricots, then loading them onto the platforms of trucks that took them directly out of the country — was less taxing than she'd imagined. Even though she had little memory of what all that fruit tasted like, she enjoyed the feel of it in her hands, soft and plump and fragrant in full season.

The bus screeched to a halt, and as the doors swished open to let on a new wave of sweltering commuters, Natalia realized that she was about to miss her stop. Clutching her bag against her chest, she carved a path to the front and descended hastily in Piazza Romana, mere blocks from where her father's store used to be. From there, she crossed Magheru Boulevard to the connecting trolley line, where she sat on a bench and waited, watching the activity unfold on the periphery of the square: gypsies selling flowers, pretzel vendors and cardboard squatters begging for coins, and mostly pedestrians, hurried, preoccupied, frowning at the ground. The trolley was late as usual, and a half hour later, she decided to walk.

From time to time, she glanced behind to see if the trolley was anywhere in sight, but there was no sign of it, so she continued ahead in no real hurry. A few blocks later, she noticed a café across the street with red-and-white umbrellas, where a few patrons were seated around wrought-iron tables, talking casually, enjoying the balmy late-afternoon sun. The softening rays trickled through the thick branches of a large oak in the center of the terrace, casting glints and dancing shadows on the checkered table-cloths. How lucky, she thought, to be able to sit in a place like that, to enjoy a bowl of ice cream or a cold beer on a hot day.

Not for people like us, she reminded herself. Those tables were reserved for a select few, officers and Party leaders, government workers. She sighed, watching the people on the terrace a little while longer, when all of sudden, near a fountain in the far corner, a woman caught her eye. What Natalia first noticed was her wavy blond hair, so long that it covered the back of her chair. As she moved, those golden waves shimmered in the sun, cascading over her bare shoulders.

Natalia was mesmerized. No one had hair like that anymore, no one she had seen in recent years. The girl laughed at something her companion said. She threw her head back and let out a bellow, then quickly covered her mouth, catching the curious stares of the other patrons. Trying to stifle her laughter, she leaned over the table, and the mass of blond hair tumbled over her face. The man sitting across from her laughed, too, as he stubbed out his cigarette in an ashtray. Then he stood and took out a few bills from his pocket, which he counted and placed under the ashtray. Before he walked away, he leaned over the woman's chair and, tucking a golden strand behind her ear, kissed her cheek.

Natalia did not know why it moved her so, whether it was the tenderness of his gesture or the way the woman smiled at him as if they shared some kind of secret. And in that moment, she realized what her heart already knew. That man was Victor.

She stared at him as he made his way

toward the door of the café in large, confident strides. On his way, he paused to say something to the waiter standing nearby with a tray in his hand and a white napkin draped over his forearm. The waiter bowed slightly and smiled as Victor disappeared inside.

All her blood seemed to have seeped into the ground through the soles of her feet. The bag in which she had packed a change of clothes for the party felt too heavy, and she let it drop to the ground. Leaning against a wall, she watched the blonde across the street extract a compact mirror from her purse and apply a fresh coat of lipstick, tilting her delicate, heart-shaped face toward the sun. Something shot through the pit of Natalia's stomach like acid. She needed to get away, immediately. *Go, walk, now,* she commanded herself, but her legs wouldn't obey.

With all her effort, she reached down and picked up her bag. Slinging it over her shoulder in an unladylike way, she began moving, marching unsteadily down the sidewalk. She picked up her pace, her body pitched slightly forward in a direction she did not know, no longer toward the bus stop. And then she heard him.

"Talia! Talia, please stop!"

Again, she quickened her step, gazing at her feet, only at her feet, concentrating on putting one in front of the other. For a moment, she considered running but then realized there was no point, really. He would only catch up with her. When she stopped and turned quite abruptly, he was so close behind her they almost collided.

"Talia," he said, bewildered. "It's really you. Why are you running from me?"

She looked up into his face, feeling as though the air had stilled, and her first thought was that she was trembling so much that he would see it. A flash of anger tore through the web of shock and embarrassment and confused feelings.

"What do you want from me?" she blurted recklessly. "Why are you following me?"

He took a small step back, shocked by her tone, but his eyes remained on her. "It really is you," he repeated, as if he couldn't bring himself to believe it. He grinned unsurely, his eyes seeking hers, but Natalia's were not smiling.

"Why are you following me?" she said again, icily.

He looked as if he was trying to compose himself, to find something to say, a justification for chasing her for nearly two blocks. It was obvious that her coldness had taken him by surprise. Well, she was no longer the sweet, passive girl he remembered. And he was certainly not the dazzling young man he used to be.

His smooth black hair was streaked slightly with gray at the temples, and he looked thinner, somehow smaller than she remembered, even though he still towered over her. Even in her heels now, she barely reached the top of his chest. His angular features, which once used to make her think of a Roman gladiator, had softened a little, but his eyes were unchanged, despite the soft lines threading underneath them. They were still piercing and sharp, like uncut emerald.

"I thought . . . I hoped it was you," Victor said quietly. "I didn't mean to startle you."

"Yes, well, it is me. Natalia, remember? And do you recall my parents? Anton, who you once said was like a father to you? Who needed you most when you vanished?"

He watched her wordlessly, stunned, as though she had thrown cold water in his face.

"Ah," she went on bitterly. "What difference does it make to you? Why would you care what's happened to us since we last saw your face almost a decade ago?"

In his long stare, Natalia saw a trace of

sadness and something she had never glimpsed before: fear. Perhaps he had always feared this moment, this exact moment when he would have to reckon with his past and be forced to make amends, excuses. But she would not be the one to give him redemption.

"Yes, my father . . . my father hasn't worked since the time he was imprisoned. Did you know that? Since that time that you were kind enough to secure his freedom. For what? Freedom to lose it all, to be discarded like he never mattered, to pass his days wondering when he will be released from the hell that his life has become? While you dine in expensive restaurants without a care in the world? Places like that will not hire my father even to wash dishes or mop floors. Did you know that, Victor?"

She couldn't go on. She was breathless. Tears were choking her throat, and she swallowed hard against them, for she would not let him see her cry. For a moment, she thought she'd been too direct, too brutal, and that he would lash back at her. But he just stood there, not saying a word. His silence fueled her fury, spurring her on.

"I didn't think so, Victor. You do not know me, you do not know *us,* any longer. Why don't you go back to your friend? No doubt, she's waiting for you."

He seized her arm then, unexpectedly and so forcefully that she almost lost her footing. *Don't touch me!* she wanted to scream. Instead, she turned to face him, squaring her shoulders, rising to her maximum height. Her eyes went up to meet his, unafraid. He was squeezing her arm so hard that she was certain his fingers would leave an imprint on her skin.

"You — you do not know," he stammered. "You do not understand. You were so young, and I . . . I did all that I could." He released her and ran both hands through his hair, then sat heavily on the low concrete wall behind them. "You do not know what it has cost me."

"I know what it's cost my father. Not having you there anymore."

He inhaled sharply, held in the air as he looked in the distance. Good. She hoped it hurt. She hoped he felt a mere fraction of her anguish. The same way she had felt when he walked out of their home and she quivered for a last glance from him, for a wave good-bye. Those moments, that schoolgirl crush, belonged to another world. That girl had perished long ago, together with her last image of him rounding the corner after leaving their house.

All of a sudden, she felt deeply tired, as though all her strength had poured out of her body, leaving her a hollow shell. Slowly, she lowered herself onto the wall next to him.

"Look what's become of us, Victor. Look what your beloved Party has made of us."

Those words, Natalia knew, could secure her a lifetime in a Gulag camp when spoken to a man like him, but she didn't care if he turned her in, if the Security Police took her away right now and blindfolded her against the wall. Her life had stopped being hers a long time ago.

"Natalia, what do you know of my life?" he said now, his own voice on the edge of breaking. "What do you know of the things I've seen, that I've had to do, since we parted?"

She looked at him then as if seeing him for the first time, her eyebrows knitted together in confusion, in anguish, in longing. She touched the spot on her arm where his fingers had been just moments ago, like a branding iron.

"I died, Talia. The young man you knew died a long time ago. I am only a ghost."

She wanted to ask him what he meant, to explain what had happened to him, but she did not have the chance. The click of high heels interrupted her, and when Natalia looked up, she saw the young woman from the restaurant coming toward them, her blond waves bouncing in the breeze. She stopped right in front of them and smiled unsurely at Natalia.

"Victor?" she said in a perplexed tone, her gaze shifting between them.

Her feet were spaced slightly apart, and Natalia could not help but notice her exquisite leather pumps. Her mother, she recalled, had shoes like that once. An awkward moment stretched interminably before Victor scrambled up to his feet and took a few steps toward the woman.

"Darling, this is Natalia, an old friend. I was close to her family once. We haven't seen each other in years." Then, turning to Natalia with visible discomfort, he said, "Talia, this is my wife, Katia."

38

There had been no noticeable change in the weather that year, no gradual blend into the colors of fall, and if Natalia had missed the turn of the seasons, it was because time was passing over her like a cloud. One evening, she emerged from the produce hall a little late and was stunned to see that it was already dark. Wrapping her raincoat tightly around her, she began walking briskly, realizing that it was early November and that judging from the chill, snow might soon arrive. At the corner, she waited along with a few other pedestrians, watching her breath billow out in trails of vapor, when suddenly she heard her name.

"Talia."

She paused but did not turn. *Perhaps I should run,* she thought. *If I was smart, if I knew what was best, that's what I would do.* But then she did turn, slowly, deliberately, and he was there right beside her in a fraction of a second. His coat collar was turned up, shielding most of his face. Only his eyes were visible, acute, filled with unrest. Natalia glanced past him to see if he was alone, if anyone had followed him, but she saw no one who looked suspicious. There were no men in trench coats hiding in the shadows of buildings, only a few civilians buried underneath mountains of clothing, passing them by in a hurry.

"Can I walk you home, Talia?" he asked softly.

"No, thank you. I was on my way to the bus stop."

"Would you like a ride? I can —"

"No, Victor," she interrupted, shaking her head sternly. "I don't want you to give me a ride or to walk with me. Whatever it is you intended to say, you've already said it."

Tilting his head to one side, he measured her, narrowing his eyes a little. "Are you afraid of me, Natalia?"

It took her aback, the directness of his question. Perhaps that was what he thought, that she wouldn't speak to him because she was afraid. Well, after all, he was a man to be feared. If she had any sense, she certainly would be.

"Victor, I am grateful for all that you've done for my family. My father loved you once like a son, so it isn't my place to judge. But you don't know me, you don't know *us* anymore. That was a lifetime ago."

It was simply a statement, honest and final, not requiring a reply. She hoped it would be enough to make him go. Why wouldn't he leave her alone? Why was he still standing there as though he expected her to go on, to say something more? She knew it wasn't the first time he'd waited for her. She'd seen his car before, parked at the curb some distance away, far enough where it would blend in with the rest of the traffic. But it wasn't until a few days ago that he approached her, came up to her like this in the open. Still, she didn't have anything to say to him. What was there to say after all this time? It angered her, the image of him on that terrace, sipping his brandy, laughing with that woman. That woman who was his wife.

"I don't know what you want, Victor. To pick up where we left off? You want to come over for supper like you used to? I'm afraid you wouldn't like our food, even though my mother does all she can to make the best of a few potatoes and some pork fat. We haven't been able to get fresh bread in weeks. I can't remember the last time I had some meat."

A shadow passed over his face, something that might have been pity or remorse, and she wondered for the first time if it was forgiveness that he wanted from her. Well, she wouldn't be the one to give it to him. The choices he'd made, the life he'd built on victims and corpses and fear, was of his own doing. It was his to own.

"You can't come here anymore, Victor. It's isn't wise. Isn't that why you went away in the first place? Why you disappeared from our lives all those years ago?" She paused, swallowed hard. "Please leave, Victor. Turn around and go. Whatever you think you know about us, about me, you do not."

"You're wrong," he said then.

Ah, he did have a voice. It was raspy and strangled and entirely strange to her.

"I do know you, Talia. I've known you since you were a little girl. I used to listen to you play piano so beautifully, do you remember? I thought, she is gifted. She will be a great pianist someday. Who else knows that about you?"

He might as well have reached out and slapped her. Yes, her piano had been the most precious thing in her life until it was ripped out of her hands. Her solace and her gift had been stolen from her. By people like him.

"Yes, I played beautifully once," she said sadly. "Before my piano was taken away from me, along with everything else we had."

He sighed then and looked at the ground as if he might cry. It was then that she noticed the dark circles under his eyes, the tiny brackets around his crooked, sad smile. The years had matured his face, embroidered it with some sort of a majestic quality, yet turned back the clock at the same time. There was an air about him that reminded her of the Victor of her childhood days, when he still lived in the loft above her father's store.

"I know other things, too," he went on, undeterred. "I know how much you loved those gold-and-ruby earrings your father gave you when you were seven, that you read *Anna Karenina* at least a dozen times, that you do not like stuffed peppers no matter how well your mother prepares them, that your special hiding place when you were little was underneath your father's desk at the store. I know that your favorite day of the year was Christmas Eve, when he took you and your cousins for a sleigh ride on Kiseleff. I know how you looked at me when I left your house that day, after your father was released from prison. You were fourteen, Natalia, *fourteen,* and I was still a relatively young man with unshakable convictions."

Tears were streaming down her face. She hated herself for not being able to hold them back, to control her emotions. How was he able to do that, to bring everything back with such startling precision? She'd tried so hard to forget that other life, to lock it away in a place where it would no longer disturb her. It had not been easy, but somewhere along the way, she had managed to do it. She'd buried those memories until he'd come along uninvited and let them all out into the light. Until with his words alone, he'd resurrected what had been long dead.

She opened her mouth to speak but could say nothing. Instead, she just stood there shaking her head, not bothering to wipe the tears from her eyes, until Victor reached out and traced his thumb lightly over her cheek. It felt like a jolt of electricity. Something dissolved inside her, softened the shell around her pounding, miserable heart. Against her own will, she leaned her face into the soft leather of his glove, and he drew her near, slowly, cautiously, until her forehead rested against his chest. He pulled her closer still, until she could hear the thumping of his heart through the layer of his coat.

"Let's go somewhere, let's get warm," he said, resting his chin on top of her head, but she could not answer, could not move.

I want to stay like this forever, Victor, she wanted to say. *I want to stay like this and listen to your beating heart, your cruel, misguided, merciless heart.*

39

He was there again the next day, leaning up against a silver Volga, a Soviet luxury car reserved for diplomats and high-ranking state officials. When she came out of the windowless warehouse talking with a few of her coworkers, she tried not to smile, but despite her best intentions, she raised her hand. It was an instinctive gesture, and it happened before she had a chance to consider that he might take it as an invitation.

In an instant, he was at the bottom of the steps, his gaze searing through her as she came down the rest of the way. Behind them, two girls halted their descent and watched them with unconcealed curiosity. She heard their hushed words, their stifled giggles, as Victor reached out and slid off her headscarf, then traced his fingers lightly over her hair, taking in the whole of her face. Embarrassed, she pushed him away a little. He laughed then, a soft chuckle that made her feel adolescent, unsophisticated.

"Hello, Talia," he whispered, smiling in a way that made the crinkles around his eyes more pronounced.

"Hello, Victor."

Without asking, he reached out and took her backpack. This time, she did not object, and they began walking. Despite the cold, she felt as though she was burning up. Another night, walking with him side by side with no destination, the leaves tinged with frost crunching under their feet.

"I have something to tell you," he said after a while. They stopped in front of a poorly lit café with a torn awning. Inside, a couple of old men were sharing a drink at the bar. There were no other customers.

"Would you like something to eat?" he asked.

Natalia shook her head no. The thought of food was distinctly uninviting. Her stomach was tied up in knots, much, it seemed, like every cell in her body.

"A drink, then."

It was not a question. It was a statement. Without a reply, he opened the door and stood aside, waiting for her to step in. As usual, his self-assuredness unnerved her, the way he assumed that she would do whatever he said, as if there was no other option. The bells above the door tinkled faintly as a portly middle-aged man in a white apron bounded up to the doorway.

"Victor Dimitrov, what a pleasure!"

"Hello, my friend. Glad to see you are open this evening."

"Your table is always ready for you. Please, this way."

The man's lips remained stretched in a smile that seemed frozen, exposing his prominent reddish gums. As he ushered them in, past the bar and the cluster of empty tables, Natalia caught his long, appraising glance, and she suddenly shrank within herself, wondering if other women in Victor's company had traversed this wooden floor that was badly in need of waxing.

They were shown to a roomy candlelit table at the back of the room, where she sat down stiffly in one of the two chairs. She'd insisted on pulling it out for herself, but now that she was seated, she didn't know what to do with her hands. At the bar, the men looked half-drunk and engrossed in conversation, completely unaware of their presence. One of them leaned over the other's shoulder to say something or steady himself, and they both laughed heartily.

"You don't have to worry," Victor said, sensing her discomfort. "I don't bring anyone here. Least of all my wife."

Ah, his wife. The mere mention of her was enough to halt her breath. There were things she did not want to hear about, that she wasn't ready for. She did not know what hurt more just now, the mention of his wife or the other women, the ones he presumably did not bring here. Did his wife know? Did she ignore his indiscretions? A bitter wave of jealously rose in Natalia's throat as she imagined her sleeping next to him, her ivory skin and shimmering blond waves under his touch. She imagined the others, too, the ones with whom he also shared a piece of himself, all but his imprisoned, guarded heart.

I am less than that, she thought. *I am only a glimpse of his past, a reminder of his bygone youth.*

Rising slowly, she picked up her bag.

"Talia, where are you going?"

She stood in front of him, feeling light-headed, trying to extricate the right words. *Good-bye, Victor,* was what she needed to say but could not. She just stood there paralyzed, fighting her tears, gritting her teeth.

"Victor, I don't know what I'm doing here," she managed after a few moments. "I really need to go. I must get home."

"No. You cannot leave now."

Before she could take a step away, he reached out and grabbed her wrist. It was a gentle grip, imploring more than forceful, but its suddenness frightened her nonetheless. Moving back to her chair, she sat down as the waiter returned with a water carafe and two empty glasses, which he placed ceremoniously on the table.

"Two vodkas. Your best, please," Victor said, his gaze not leaving her face, and the waiter nodded and vanished again in a hurry.

"Talia, I really need to talk to you," he began when they were alone. "I wanted to explain . . ."

She closed her eyes then, not so much to hide her torment as to show him that she did not want to hear it. *Don't say anything, Victor,* she wanted to beg him. *Don't apologize or explain things away. Do not diminish what seeing you again has meant to me.*

"It isn't necessary. We've gone over it, and I wish you'd just —"

"Talia, do you know who Ivan Vasilovich is?"

Of course, she knew who he was. He was a prominent Soviet official, one of the first Russian military attachés to install himself in the Royal Palace after King Michael's abdication. In those chaotic early days, when the young monarch was stripped of his citizenship as well as his properties and forced into exile, Ivan Vasilovich had proclaimed himself minister of internal affairs. He was responsible for arresting and deporting thousands of people, for wiping out the king's entire cabinet virtually overnight.

"Yes, I do. I know about all the great things he has done for our country. He is in the history books. The revised ones, at least. What about him?"

"Katia is his daughter."

He paused to extract a pack of cigarettes and matches from his breast pocket. As he lit one, leaning his elbow on the table, his face hardened a little, and for an instant, she regretted her sarcasm.

"A great man, indeed," Victor said. "An accomplished, dedicated man. Very spirited. So spirited, in fact, that he went home to his villa on Kiseleff every night and beat his wife and daughter senseless. He used a crowbar once, a fireplace iron, an empty whiskey bottle, but most of the time, he resorted to the metal buckle of his military belt. Of course, I did not know any of this when I began working for him at the ministry. I met Katia sometime later when she came to our office to drop off his wallet one morning. She was wearing a shawl over a sleeveless dress, and when she handed me his wallet in the reception area, it slipped off her shoulder. That was when I first saw the bruises."

The cigarette twisted in his fingers restlessly. He stared at the lit tip before taking another drag. The waiter arrived, set down the two glasses of vodka, and went back to the bar.

"Ivan Vasilovich wouldn't let her out of his sight. He brought her along on every trip we took, to Warsaw and Sofia and back to their hometown of Leningrad. I went on those trips, as did his entire staff, on trains where we would occupy all the available cars. We became quick friends, Katia and I. One night, I heard her crying in the corridor of the sleeper compartment, right outside my own door. I slipped outside, asked her if she wanted to share some of my vodka.

"There was a boy in her life, she told me. He was a medical student, the son of a peasant, whom her father ironically did not approve of. He had greater plans for her, it seemed. The problem — as she spelled out to me with such pathos — was that this boy was the love of her life. She could not imagine a future without him. In fact, her precise words were that she would not live without him, and something in the way she said it, so resolutely, made me shudder. A moment later, she reached for my flask and took a large swig from it. 'Don't worry, it's only life,' was what she said before she went back to her compartment.

"A week later, I stopped by their home on Kiseleff to drop off some papers. It was late when she opened the door, and at first I did not recognize her. Her entire face was a purple bruise, her eyes swollen, one of them entirely shut. 'He found out,' was all she said. 'He is sending me to a boarding school, back in Moscow.'

" 'When?' I asked, shocked to see her in such a state. 'In a week,' she told me. There was something about her that broke my heart as I reached out and took her hand. I looked at her beautiful, desecrated face, and I said, 'Katia, come by the office tomorrow. There's something I want to talk to you about.'

"Three days later, I returned to their home with a bouquet of flowers, an enormous box of chocolates for her mother, and the best Russian vodka I could find for her father. He greeted me in the doorway with great enthusiasm, seemed genuinely happy to see me. 'Come in, my boy,' he said. 'Katia told me you would be coming by.'

" 'Yes, sir,' I replied solemnly. 'There is something of great importance I would like to discuss.' "

Victor paused to reach for his vodka glass and took a good gulp. He was no longer looking at Natalia; he was staring at the blank wall behind her.

"Two months later, we were married. A grand wedding with five hundred people in attendance. Every dignitary, every government official and military attaché was there — you can imagine. We danced in the ballroom of the Athenaeum Palace, which her father had secured for the occasion. We smiled at each other and cut the first piece of our seven-tiered cake as everyone cheered and raised their glasses filled with the best champagne delivered from France. Later that night, after our car dropped us off at the new villa that was our wedding present, she changed out of her gown while I poured myself a tall drink.

"As I stared into the flames of our marble fireplace, she came up behind me, quiet as a cat, stunning in a black dress. She put her arms around me, rested her chin on my shoulder. We stayed like that for a while, Katia and I, and I knew what we were both thinking. She was free, free to be with her doctor, and I had an undeniably bright future ahead of me. We had both gotten what we wanted. 'I love you, Victor,' she whispered in my ear. 'I'm going now. Don't wait up for me.' Then she kissed my cheek and flew out the door."

Natalia watched him crush his cigarette in the ashtray and throw back the remnants of his vodka in one shot.

"And that's how it's been, Talia, between my wife and me for the past five years."

For a while, they were both quiet, the silence between them crowded with so many things unspoken. Victor reached across the table and took her hand. She tried to pull it away, but his determined grip, the weight of his fingers, held it in place. Slowly, he raised her palm to his face, and there it was, the warmth of his skin, the moist softness of his lips underneath the trace of stubble.

"Look at me," he said, but she could not, afraid he would see in her eyes what she no longer had the strength to conceal. But already his glance was penetrating right through her fissuring mask, and she thought, *I cannot stop him, there are no barriers he cannot break, it is my soul that he wants.* When at last she raised her eyes to him, he smiled, a hopeful, knowing smile, and everything around them disappeared.

40

In the communal bathroom down the hall, Natalia gently placed her bag in the corner and flicked on the lights. Washing her hands underneath the trickle of cold water, she examined her image in the tarnished mirror. Her face was flushed but really no different from this morning. So much had changed since then. She had never felt more different, more *altered,* yet none of it showed. Still the same green eyes that slanted a little at the outer corners, the same long auburn hair, so thick that it had become an annoyance to wash. The same fading beauty mark at the top of her left cheekbone. Still the same face that somehow had managed to blossom despite the years of poverty, the despair that clung about her like the damp, thick air of a midsummer storm.

It wasn't until recently that Natalia had come to see that she was, in fact, pretty.

She was not beautiful in a blatant, indisputable way like her cousin Lidia, but she possessed a kind of appeal that was less intimidating, more approachable, the kind of attractiveness that drew boys to her instead of causing them to flush red and run for the hills. But it wasn't until she'd stood face-to-face with Victor that she'd seen it so plainly. She had seen it through his eyes.

When did you become so beautiful, Talia. Let me look at you. Just let me just look at you.

No, there was nothing there to betray the revolution inside her heart.

Quietly, she tiptoed back to her room, leaving her shoes outside the door. Not turning on the lights, she went to the armoire and dug inside for her nightgown, then changed in complete darkness, careful not to make a sound. When she fell backward onto the embroidered cover of the davenport, she stretched her arms out wide, as wide as she could, like a bird in flight. Her eyes traveled up, toward the invisible ceiling. It took her a moment to realize that she was smiling in the dark.

Even now, alone with her thoughts, she could not steady the beating of her heart. Who was he? Who was this Victor who had reentered her life as suddenly as he had left it all those years ago? It didn't matter. She did not want to know about his life, his ambition, his pain, his loves, his deeds. She didn't want to think about all that had happened in the years that stretched between them like an unconquerable abyss.

What do you know of my life? he'd said to her that afternoon when somehow he spotted her from the café terrace. *What do you know of the things I've seen?* Well, she knew more than enough. She had heard about what people of his kind did in cold blood. How many arrests was he responsible for? How many deportations to forced-labor camps, to Siberia? Was his face the last those poor prisoners saw before they were turned to the wall?

The thought cut through her, making her shiver. But even as her mind recoiled in terror, her heart was already running ahead, galloping, leaving the rest of her behind. *The heart takes what it wants, it sees no reason,* she'd read somewhere or heard someone say. Well, if that was true, she wished she could tear it out of her chest, smash it to pieces, let the blood flow out of her, her blood that was poisoned with him.

But it would be of no use. He would not stop coming to see her no matter how many insults she hurled his way. He was a man for whom no obstacle was enough, a man who took what he wanted, whenever he wanted, not bothering to ask permission. *Well, I am not his for the taking,* she thought. *I am not an amusement, a diversion, a pretty girl who trades herself for his protection.*

And yet, and yet.

Hours later, as early dawn trickled in through her window, casting a sliver of light on the threadbare rug, Natalia had still not slept. She felt as though she'd never sleep again, as a thousand images of Victor flooded her, jumbled and out of order, causing her to career from exhilaration to distress and then back again in the course of a second. She was too tired to fight them, too tired to keep them at bay, so she let them wash over her like waters from a broken dam, she let them pull her out to sea, drowning her in their wake.

Victor. Victor of long ago, Victor on the street, calling out her name. Victor's eyes, his sadness, his steps close behind. His regret in the palm of her hand. Victor in a threadbare shirt in a heated argument with her father at the dining-room table. Victor in the leather coat of his youth, tall, powerful, breathtaking. Victor's gloved hand, wiping away her tears, whispering, *Let's go someplace warm.* And later, Victor's face quivering in her hands, quiet, silent, intent. His breath against her cheek, obliterating all, obliterating the past and the future, obliterating all but that one single moment.

There had once been a glorious summer day, a day before the war. She could smell the freshly cut grass, she could feel the sun's rays on her pale skin, the shorn blades tickling her feet in her mother's garden. He was there alongside her father at the wooden picnic table, and they were having a cognac, poured plentifully into tiny snifters. Her father had whispered something in his ear, something that was meant for just the two of them, and Victor threw his head back and laughed. From the corner of her eye, she had watched him shyly, for she was a mere girl, and he was a man in the best years of his life. She could still hear that laughter, robust and unrestrained, rolling in waves over her mother's rosebushes. And his voice, which had felt to her like home.

41

"I must talk to you," Natalia said.

"Of course, sweetheart. Let's talk."

Victor took her hand and placed it on his chest. He liked to do that, almost as a way to convince her that his heart was hers, that it beat only for her. She pulled her hand away gently and placed it in her lap. Someone strolled past the bench on which they sat at the edge of Lake Herastrau, beneath a willow tree heavy with the silvery bloom of early spring. She moved away from him a little. Some distance was necessary for what she wanted to say.

"I want to talk to you about my father."

"Yes?" he said cautiously.

She looked down at her hands as if she was searching for the right words. He had a way of intimidating her, even when they were close like this. "I don't want him to ever know about us. About *this*, Victor."

His eyebrows went up in surprise. It

wasn't something she was accustomed to seeing on his handsome and guarded face.

"He isn't himself these days," she explained, clearing her throat uncomfortably. "He hasn't been for a while, really. I'm not sure that it would do him any good to see you again. After all this time." There. She'd said it. It was out in the open.

"You really believe that it would be so bad for him to see me again?" He sounded hurt, as if he had not considered the possibility. As if he'd forgotten how much had happened in the years since they had parted.

Natalia shook her head miserably. "Most mornings, he leaves before sunrise. My mother has given up trying to get him back to bed, to keep him in the house. When we ask him where he's going, he says he has errands to run, he can't sit around idly all day."

Victor watched her intently from underneath his thick, black lashes. His gaze traveled toward the ripples spooling out over the lake, and he rubbed his chin pensively. A shard of light trickled through the branches above and fell across the edge of his jaw, over his hair, setting ablaze a few silver strands. The band on his finger gleamed in the light, too, mocking her.

"What errands?" he asked quietly.

"Well, that's the point, Victor. Just the other day, when I was helping him find his house keys, he wished me a good day at school. I haven't gone to school in years."

"So where does he go?"

She sighed. How could she explain that he simply disappeared for hours on end? That they had no idea where he went? Just last Wednesday, he had returned home well after midnight. Her mother had been out of her mind with worry.

"Oh, but I'm sure it's nothing," she said now with feigned nonchalance, wishing she hadn't brought it up at all. "He's probably just visiting old friends. Probably hanging out at Stefan's."

He measured her again in that precise way, as if he was trying to read beyond her words. Then he looked away. Something about his reaction, the way he stiffened beside her, comforted her in an odd way. Perhaps he did care, after all. She had not considered that Victor might still miss her father, that for him he was more than just a relic, a faded memory.

"Do you still think about him? My mother?"

A sad smile passed over his face. "Of course I do, Talia. They are still dear to my heart, despite what you might think. And the way it appears."

She challenged him with her eyes. She knew she shouldn't, but she couldn't help herself. "Do you, now?"

"Yes, I do," he said tersely.

At last, she had managed to ignite something in him, a spark. It gave her a small sense of satisfaction knowing that she could do it.

"I'm not going to have this conversation with you, Talia. You know how I feel about your family, that I would do anything in the world —"

She did not know why she laughed. It came unexpectedly, surprising even her. She did not mean to ridicule him, but did he still actually believe in his devotion to her family? From what she could see, from what she could judge from the expensive linen jacket and tailored trousers, his only dedication, his sole loyalty, had been to himself.

Recklessly, not caring how he might take it, she blurted out, "And what about you, Victor? Do you believe in what you do? Do you still believe in your cause? For I have seen what it has done to my family. I've seen what it has done to my father. He has been stripped, Victor. Stripped of his wealth and his home and his livelihood. But worse than that, he has been stripped of his dignity and his will to live."

He looked stricken. No, more than that. He looked as though she had lodged a blade in his heart. His face remained very still, but she saw the trembling of his hand as it came up to rake his hair. She had gone too far this time. Perhaps a small part of her had wanted to.

She reached for her purse then, desperately wanting to flee, but the flap was open, and all its contents tumbled out, scattering at the foot of the bench. Bending down, she began picking them up one by one, her house keys, her rouge, the small bottle of French perfume and the gold Bulova watch that Victor had recently given her for her birthday. Gifts that she had accepted from him graciously, not having the heart to remind him that she'd never be able to wear them. That she couldn't wear them at home, for her mother would surely ask where they came from, and she couldn't wear them at work, for she might have been stabbed in a back alley for less.

"What about Despina? How is your mother?"

This time, it was Natalia who looked up in surprise. Her purse lay open on the ground, irrelevant for the moment, forgotten. A slight gust kicked up as he reached down and took her arm, then pulled her back onto the bench next to him. She shivered, and he removed his jacket and enveloped her in it.

"You need not worry about her," she answered after a silence. "My mother will continue to make our lives as comfortable as possible, as she smiles at the strangers we share our home with and shrugs when there is no food and washes our clothes in the communal tub by candlelight. She collects fallen fruit from sidewalks, did you know, and makes three meals out of two eggs and a little flour. My mother is fine."

It was not meant to appease him, yet there it was, a faint smile. Was he amused by their circumstances? Did he find some twisted comfort in what she'd said? He who lived in a beautiful villa with a marble fireplace and gleaming parquet floors and a butler who vanished on command, only to reappear at the chime of a bell? It struck her then, the perversity of life, where one day you lived in an attic with no food and no light, and then the next in one of the city's grand villas. And all it took was a war to reverse it. All it took was trading one's misfortune for another's. She stood up and tossed his jacket at him.

"Talia, please. I'm sorry I've upset you.

Don't go."

But she was moving down the path, putting one foot in front of the other, and it took all her strength to do so. It had been nothing at all for him to catch up with her, for his arms to go around her shoulders, to hold her in place.

"I'm sorry," he whispered in her hair. "I know how hard this is for you."

His proximity had the exact effect it had each time. It splintered her resolve and infuriated her, all at once.

"I have to go, Victor. Please. Please, let me go."

"No."

There was something in his eyes, something that resembled despair and a raw neediness as he spun her around to face him.

"Talia," he whispered, leaning in and smoothing a strand of her hair behind her ear. "Talia, I only wish that I could."

What are we doing? she wanted to scream. *What am I doing here with you?* But she felt the warmth of his palm on her cheek, and his fingers pressed ever so slightly into her flushed skin as he cupped her face and drew her to him. Their eyes locked for a brief moment before his hand dropped away and his mouth was on hers. A wicked flame blazed through her, jolted her, catapulting her to a place she didn't know, and she felt herself falling, raining down from the sky in a million shards of light. He reached around, and his hand was in her hair, pulling it backward, loosening her braid. The strands fell apart, they coiled around his fingers. A whimper came from her lips, something that sounded like pain, and he released her. He dropped his head to the crook of her neck.

They stood like that for a while in the deserted park, with only the chirping birds and rustling leaves for company. She could feel his warm, jagged breath on her collarbone and wanted desperately to say something. *I'm all right,* she thought would be appropriate, or something else, something entirely different. *How will this end for us?* were the words she wanted to utter. *How will this end, Victor? Will a day ever come when I can walk down the street holding your hand, when I can smile at you openly, when I can rest my head on your shoulder without fear of being seen?*

42

"I want to take you on a trip to the Black Sea."

The sheer canopy fluttered in the warm June breeze, matching her quickening pulse as she heard his words. The first time she had seen that canopy, stretched like a horizon against the serene paleness of this room, it had made her dizzy with jealousy. But his lips and his hands had been there immediately, and they blotted out the room and everything in it, they blotted out the sun. In the months since, she had taken less notice of the oasis of peach and lilac hues, of delicate lace and sheer silk, that Victor's wife had assembled with the utmost taste. Like a thief stealing away in the night, she chose to focus on the immediate, only on what was hers for the taking, no more.

"For a few days," Victor explained. "I want us to spend the whole time on the beach, maybe go dancing at night. I know a great hotel in Constanta. It's very secluded, just a few short blocks from the beach. They have a great restaurant, too, one of the best at the sea, so we wouldn't have to leave the place at all."

Natalia was dimly aware that she was biting her nails. That she was fiddling nervously with the piped edge of a silk pillow.

"Well, what do you think?" he asked, pulling her into his arms and giving her one of his crooked, playful smiles that still had a way of making her knees go numb.

Truly, she did not know how to answer. It sounded out of this world, of course, three days alone with him, uninterrupted. Three days without his work commitments, his trips, his wife. But she did not think it was possible. What would she tell her parents? How would she account for a three-day absence at work?

"I don't know, Victor," she said. "I'm not sure this is the best time."

He sighed and pulled his arm out from underneath her. It came to rest on his chiseled chest that seemed to defy his forty years. "Can't you think of a way?"

"No, Victor. What excuse could I possibly come up with? You know how my mother is. I may be able to explain our evenings or even a full Sunday at Lidia's — but three days? What excuse could I possibly come up with? And what about my job?"

He sighed and sat up straight, leaning against the backboard. On the round bedside table, a crystal clock with a silvery dial was ticking away.

"Victor, I don't know what you want me to say."

"You know, Natalia," he snapped, "after all we go through to be together, I thought you might put some effort into it, that's all."

He threw the covers off and marched directly to the bathroom, slamming the door behind him. A moment later, she heard the shower running. A ribbon of steam floated up from underneath the door. She couldn't remember the last time she had taken a hot shower. Most nights, she was lucky if there was a trace of lukewarm water by the time she stepped into the tub, after all the other tenants had had their turns.

But it wasn't this blatant oversight on his part that bothered her so. This was the first time he'd spoken to her in such a tone. After that day in the park, there had been no more accusations or words hurled in anger. It was as if that fight purged them both of what lay hidden inside them, what had been gnawing away at their souls for nearly a decade. The bitterness she had carried around for years, the guilt that perhaps had burdened him for even longer, all inexplicably vanished. What followed had been more blissful than in her wildest dreams. It had been more than she ever envisioned love would be, for there was no doubt they were in love, that he loved her, even though he never said it. Yet she was happy just with the knowledge of it. It was enough to be near him, to feel his lips upon hers, breathe in the scent of his skin. And for a while, he, too, seemed content with as much. But recently, his need for her had started to take on an overbearing quality, his demands on her time nearly tyrannical, his passion overwhelming. When they were together, Victor demanded her very breath. All of herself she gave with a full heart, but soon she began to fear that it would not be enough for a man like him. For somewhere along the way — she wasn't quite sure when — things had begun to change.

For a couple of weeks now, he'd been surly with her. She wasn't sure how it had started, if it was something she'd said. A couple of times, he cut her off in mid-sentence. Often, it seemed that he wasn't even listening as he smoked incessantly and frowned at the ceiling.

Maybe he'd grown tired of the whole

thing. She had not considered this possibility. Well, it had been nearly eight months, after all. Eight months of twisting their lives for mere moments together. Maybe that was it. All the excuses and planning and last-minute arrangements had become too much for him. It had become complicated. More than that, it had become dangerous.

All along, she'd known what was at stake for him, how not only his career but his very life would be in jeopardy if word got out about their relationship, about his association with someone like her. The Secret Police were notoriously merciless in dealing with members of their own rank, especially ones like Victor who had been around for so long and knew so much about the inner workings of the bureaucracy. In his world, made up of only black and white and no half shades, she would be merely a pawn, a reason to silence him. And how she feared for him! Every day, she feared that the rope Victor had spent so many years braiding with his own hands could at any moment now be coiled around his neck like a noose. Wasn't that the reason he always looked behind when they walked together, his peripheral vision acute even when he seemed to be focused only on her?

Of course, it had not been easy for her,

either. He did not know what it cost her, sneaking around to see him, meeting him on street corners in the dark, in alleyways where no proper young lady should go. He did not know what it did to her pride, coming to the flats of his friends who were out of town for the day, waiting around the corner from his house for his wife to leave and go about her day so that she could steal a few moments with him. "All we have is friendship," he told her. "We are good friends, Katia and I." Yet he shared his meals with her; they shared a roof. She didn't have to sneak around for a glimpse of him, for a single word of affection.

"I have to go, Talia," he said now, stepping out of the bathroom in a navy terry-cloth robe. He moved about the room, seemingly preoccupied. He went to the dresser and rifled through his wallet, then flung open the armoire and examined his impressive collection of silk ties. His hair was perfectly slicked, and he smelled of fresh soap and expensive shampoo, the kind you could only find in exclusive export shops.

"I have a meeting in an hour at the ministry. And Katia should be back soon, although she would probably offer you some tea if she found you here."

He had meant it in jest, to lighten the

mood, perhaps, but it had the opposite effect. No words could have wounded her more. How could he make light of their situation, as if her being there meant nothing to him? She wasn't like one of his other women, a meaningless diversion. Or was she? The thought slammed into her, and she couldn't stop it from forming. Rising slowly, she swallowed against the tears forming in her throat. And along with her tears, she swallowed her pride, her pain, her love and disdain, her jealousy and self-loathing.

As calmly as possible, she said, "Yes, Victor, I will go now. I'll let myself out the back door. Before I go, I'll wash the bar glasses and empty your ashtray. I will erase every trace of my presence, so that your wife will never know I was here."

And then she was on her feet, gathering her stockings and dress from the chair in the corner, where they'd been tossed with such abandon just hours ago. In her nervous haste, she knocked over a glass of water, and it clattered to the floor. That was all it took to make her burst into tears.

"Talia, I'm sorry. I'm sorry," Victor murmured, coming to her and encircling her waist. "I shouldn't be so rough with you. I just want to spend a few days with you, that's all." Gently, he caressed her hair, looped it over her shoulder. "Do you think you might find a way to make it work? Could you try? It would mean so much to me, you know."

She wiped her eyes with the heels of her hands, and he, too, reached up and stroked her face, cupping her chin tenderly as if she was a child. This was beyond what she could handle, beyond what her twenty-three years had equipped her with. How could she say no to him? How could she ever deny him anything at all?

"Yes," she murmured against her better judgment. "Yes, Victor, I'll go to the sea with you."

He bent down and kissed her hard then, pulling her to him possessively, and she willed herself to kiss him back the same way, grasping his hair, with an intensity that masked her desperation. For a moment, he hesitated, startled, she supposed, by her ardor, and then he lifted her as if she was no more than a feather and, smiling down at her with some wickedness, carried her back to his bed.

Once again, she was lost in him, lost as she wanted to be in the only thing that was simple — the hard curve of his back under her fingertips, his mouth on her quivering skin, burning through her like wildfire. Over

410

and over, she murmured his name like a chant, yet still she couldn't drown out the voice in her head, the voice that would not quiet, mocking her mercilessly.

Yes, Victor, I'll find an excuse. I'll lie to my parents. I will deceive the only people in the world who need me, for you. I will cheat, I will steal, I will do anything for mere days with you. I have already lied, and I will do it again without remorse, without shame.

43

Lying for Victor was easier than she thought possible. It astounded her, really, the ease with which she sat across from her parents in the communal area of the flat and told them about the rally she was expected to attend over the weekend.

"It's in Timisoara," she said casually. "I will have to spend two additional days on the train, of course, but they will provide us with lodging and food. All my coworkers are going."

"Oh?" her father said. "What is the rally for?"

"Well, you know, Papa. It's a pro-Party rally. It's a chance for young people from all over the country to come together in support of our great leaders. Of course, you know I cannot refuse to go. I am expected to be there, you understand."

And there it was. The perfect lie, laid out before them. Flawlessly executed. She

412

chewed another bite slowly, looking at her plate.

Of course, she expected her mother to raise a number of objections, to ask about lodging, where they'd be staying, if there was a phone number where she could be reached. Natalia had not thought in advance about how she would answer any of these questions, but she was off to an impressive start. Three days with Victor alone. That was all she needed to think about.

Fortunately, her mother did not probe a great deal more. By the time they had finished supper, her father said he felt tired and was turning in for the night. But he did not go straight to his room. Pushing his chair back, he walked to Natalia and held his hand out to her. When she reached for it, he pulled her to her feet and embraced her with such force that she could not draw a breath.

"I love you with all my heart, dear girl," he whispered in her ear.

"I know, Papa. I love you, too. Sleep well."

Still he wouldn't let go of her. He kept holding her like that, and she thought how strange he was, how emotional. She was only leaving for a few days, but she realized it was the first time she would be doing so since the war.

Eventually, she pulled away from him, and, smiling as serenely as she could manage, she said, "Let's go to the Hippodrome soon, Papa. Watch the horse races, when I get back. What do you think? Just you and I, like we used to."

He said nothing, but in reply, he took her hand and kissed it, held it against his lips for several moments before letting it go. "Just like we used to, my love."

Then he turned and went to his room.

Later that night, as her mother flicked the dial on their small black-and-white television searching for a movie, Natalia set aside a couple of dresses, her sandals, a straw hat — most of her entire summer wardrobe. From under the davenport, she extracted a small valise and began stacking her things inside it. Her movements slowed gradually, until they came to a full stop. Crumpling a cream slip to her chest, she turned to her mother.

"Mama, I want to tell you something. I don't know how to tell you, though."

But her mother wasn't listening. Her gaze was fixed on the small screen, where the image of Rita Hayworth had materialized among the thin, vertical lines that passed over the screen. Flipping her cascading hair, she smiled coyly at the camera, which zoomed in on her dazzling face, and Natalia let out a small, startled gasp. Right there, looking directly at her, was the mother of her youth. As a child, she'd grown used to people commenting on the uncanny resemblance. Yet it wasn't until this moment, as her eyes drifted from the famous American star to her mother and back again, that she realized how much her mother had changed, how altered she'd become over the years.

Despina, too, seemed oddly melancholic and dropped her head against the sofa rest. Rain drummed quietly on the windowpane as Natalia curled up on the sofa next to her. On the screen, the images flickered away, changing the room from bright to dark to bright again. A man in a black tuxedo was smoking a cigar as he stood by the fireplace. Rita was seated at a table nearby, sipping a glass of champagne. She stood, and, lifting a stole from the back of her chair, she shimmied toward him in a cream silk gown, diamonds catching a glint of light, illuminating her flawless skin, her deeply rouged lips. This might as well have been her mother once, free of complications, before food lines and nights without fuel and hot water.

For an instant, before she nuzzled against her, Natalia studied the softened lines of her profile, her hair gathered at the nape and sparsely threaded with silver, the fragile, curved slope of her shoulders. She was beautiful still, her mother, but in a way that resembled a fractured porcelain doll, one that could shatter into a million pieces in the slightest gust of wind. It stunned her, this fragility that she had not seen before. Her mother had always seemed larger than life, formidable, the pillar of their family, the one who had kept them together through war and illness and uncertainty and loss. It hadn't occurred to Natalia until now that anything on earth could alter her. She realized suddenly that telling her about Victor might not be the right thing to do. That as much as she wanted to let the truth out into the open, she would have to keep it to herself, at least for a little while longer.

"Mama, are you sure you don't mind me going?" she asked instead.

Her mother got up and turned off the television. She sat back down next to her and took both of her hands in hers. When Natalia lifted her gaze and looked into those soulful eyes, she was surprised to see that they were filled with tears.

"Talia, your happiness is the only thing that has ever mattered to me. You know that, don't you?"

"Yes, Mama, I know," she whispered, a little confused. Did her mother suspect she had lied to them? That it wasn't her cousin or work friends she'd been spending all this time with, that, in fact, she hadn't seen Lidia since last Christmas?

"I love you more than anything in the world. You are the most precious thing in my life. You always have been . . ."

"I know. I love you, too, Mama."

"Don't forget that, Talia. Do you promise me? Do not forget how much you mean to me. You have made my life truly beautiful."

Natalia smiled, falling into her arms. "It's only three days, Mama. I'll miss you, though."

44

For hours, she'd been awake. The hands of the grandfather clock would not move fast enough, a full rotation, then another, the sound of its faint rusted chime bringing her closer to her three days with Victor. Through the window, a weak light started to filter in, but it was still too early to rise. Her straw valise had been packed the night before and was waiting by the door. Into it she had haphazardly tossed just the bare necessities, even though Victor had warned her to bring some warm clothes as well, since the weather at the seaside was unpredictable.

In any case, her clothing choices were rather limited, and all she really cared about bringing was a silk dress the color of roses that shimmered around her like liquid when she moved in it. It was a hand-me-down from Lidia, but in it she looked older and downright glamorous, much like the actresses in the movie last night. As she gazed at the ceiling, she imagined Victor's reaction, his lingering glance before walking to her slowly and sliding the spaghetti straps down the length of her shoulders, letting his fingers graze her skin. Two more hours, the pendulum said.

Only a few days had passed since she'd last seen him, and yet he was all she could think about. He had told her that he'd be busy, that there were work commitments he had to take care of before they could leave. But he had not even come by her work, and he had not tried to call. It wasn't like him to be out of touch for so long. She tried to conjure his exact words when they parted. What was it that he had said to her?

"Be at the pastry shop around the corner from your house at seven o'clock sharp. If we get to Constanta in time, we can watch the sunset from our hotel balcony."

That was what she needed to focus on. That and, more immediately, how she would manage to slip out of the flat without waking her parents. She knew her mother would fuss and insist that she eat breakfast before the long train ride. Her father would ask again where she was going, and she did not have the heart to repeat it a second time. No, it was best if she was gone by the time they were up.

In the budding light of a welcome dawn, Natalia got out of bed and made her way quietly to the bathroom down the hall, locking the door behind her. It was not her family's allotted time, but she knew everyone would still be asleep at this hour. Hastily, she splashed some cold water on her face and brushed her teeth, then combed her hair a dozen times and clipped it back in a silver barrette. Daylight had already spilled into her room by the time she tiptoed back in to change and grab her valise. Her eyes traveled over the room, making sure everything was in place, before she flew out the door, her heart in a mad gallop.

Leaping over the steps, two and three at a time, then past the row of metal mailboxes, she burst through the entrance door and into the street. She had never felt more alive, her whole being blazing with excitement, and she practically ran to the end of the block, though when she got there, her feet stilled. There wasn't a soul in sight anywhere near the pastry shop, only a few pigeons pecking crumbs from the sidewalk, scattering off at the sound of her steps. Nervously, she checked her watch. She was on time, not a minute late, as Victor had insisted. She let her suitcase drop onto the landing and leaned against the wall. Had she misunderstood the place? The time? She was sure she had to be here at seven o'clock sharp.

Another twenty minutes passed with no sign of him. Then an unwelcome thought slammed into her: What if he had changed his mind? She couldn't bring herself to consider it, yet as the minutes ticked by, it seemed more and more like the only possibility. Closing her eyes so that she would no longer have to look at the empty street, she sat there breathing in and out, trying to calm herself, but she could not keep her mind from reeling. How long could she wait? What would she tell her parents if he didn't come after all and she had to go back inside? Would she tell them that she had spent the better part of the year lying to them? That she had been naive enough to fall for a man nearly twice her age, someone in whom they had once placed their trust and affection?

Suddenly, she heard an engine, almost as in a stupor, at the end of the block, and Victor's car came into view. She stood and inched toward the edge of the sidewalk, everything too stark and too jarring, no longer romantic in the full light of morning.

"Hello, Talia, I'm sorry I'm late," he said, getting out of the car a moment later and coming around to take her suitcase. "Have you been waiting long?"

"Well, a bit, but not long," she lied, forcing herself to smile. More lies, more covers. But she did not want him to know how mere seconds earlier, she had been certain she would never see him again.

"Hello," he repeated, and, holding open the passenger door, he planted a hasty kiss on her lips. With a further drop of her heart, she noticed how disheveled he looked. Days must have passed since he last shaved, and his eyes were bleary, with dark circles beneath them. It was the first time she had seen him out in public with his hair not perfectly glossed.

"I'm ready," she said, glancing at him unsurely, feeling a little short of breath. Sinking into the tan leather seat, she slid off her scarf. Victor jumped in beside her.

"Late, darling. Need to get going," he muttered, checking his watch and popping the shift into gear.

Over cobblestone streets and around sharp corners, their car sped away. It began to drizzle, and he turned on the windshield wipers. For a while, there was nothing but the scrape of rubber over the glass, back and forth, back and forth, smearing the summer dust in a semicircle as Natalia's head throbbed painfully.

He still had not spoken a single word by the time the maze of intersecting boulevards, with their hurried pedestrians, cheaply made domestic cars, and clattering streetcars, began to thin out. Soon the side streets turned into wide thoroughfares lined with concrete tenement blocks that stretched interminably under the hazy morning sky. And then those disappeared, too, and they were traveling on a smaller two-lane highway that cut through a vast open field, passing nothing for kilometers but an oil refinery and a factory that manufactured automobile parts for export. The entire time, Victor's eyes remained fixed ahead, both hands gripping the wheel.

"Victor, is something the matter?" Natalia heard herself saying at last, unable to contain her anxiety any longer.

He gave her a sideways glance, not answering, not smiling, but his hand reached across and grabbed hers unexpectedly. He squeezed it so tightly that she almost let out a cry. It was meant as a sign of affection, she was sure of that, but it only made her more nervous. She went back to staring out the window, fighting back tears, tears that she was afraid would propel them into an unwanted exchange. He did not have to say much, after all. The truth hung between them, requiring no useless utterances. Surely, if he opened his mouth, he'd say that he loved her still but that this was their good-bye. Their last time together. Perhaps he'd even change his mind and turn the car around, head back to the city. It was best, she decided, if she kept silent about her misgivings until they got to the sea. It gave her time to think, which she needed desperately — time to figure out what to say to him once they got there, how to convince him that she'd try harder, make more time for him, do whatever on earth it was that he wanted.

A plane roared overhead, slicing through the grayish overcast skies, pulling her like a magnet out of her daze. She leaned forward, looking up through the windshield, and caught a glimpse of it as it passed over, leaving behind a trail of exhaust. It reminded her of the Luftwaffe fighters during the war, when they flew so close over the rooftops that she could make out the SS insignia on the underside of the wings. Another plane passed, flying even lower, closer to the highway. Several minutes later, a third one.

A few kilometers farther on, they came to a crossing. As the car slowed and came to a stop, she thought it was strange that there was a traffic light out here in the middle of nowhere. By now, there should have been nothing but green pastures and patches of pine trees, the salty scent of the sea piercing the air.

She turned quite suddenly, all of her being shifting in this one move toward him. "Victor, are we on the right road?"

Again, no answer. She glanced behind, trying to make out the highway sign they had just passed, but it was too far back. The light changed, and Victor stepped on the gas, moving through the intersection, but instead of gaining speed, he veered the car to the side of the road. In the distance, the outline of a concrete building shimmered against the skyline. She did not know what it was. The adrenaline was pumping through her so fast that she felt faint.

"Talia, there is something I have to tell you."

His words seeped through her like water. *Here we go, then,* she thought. She observed her own hands as if they belonged to someone else, the way they balled into fists, trembling. Her throat was closing around her breath.

"We are not going to the Black Sea," he said.

"No." It fell from her mouth like a stone.

"So where, then?"

"We're headed to the airport. I'm taking you to the airport."

Before she could say anything more, he reached across her lap and tugged open the glove compartment. From it he extracted a brown envelope. After opening the flap, he pulled out a small green booklet, which he held out to her. Natalia stared at it but didn't take it.

"Do you know what this is? This is your passport. I'm taking you to the airport. You are leaving the country. Today."

It did not register right away. Whatever he had said to her did not sink in, for her mind was elsewhere. She was thinking about their last afternoon together, when he'd begged her to come along with him as if the world might break apart if she refused. As if his very existence hung on her saying yes. But now he was saying these terrible, incomprehensible words — that he was taking her to the airport — and she was whiplashed back into the moment. She stared at him, at the thing in his hand, and she burst into laughter. She was laughing uncontrollably, hysterically, as if she had lost hold of her senses. Was this some kind of cruel joke? Was this how he was planning to get rid of her? She was laughing still when he reached his arm

426

out over her shoulders, clamping them firmly.

"Stop it, Talia. Breathe."

"Why are you doing this?" she croaked, gurgling her words.

"Talia, this isn't a game. I am not trying to deceive you. This is your passport. This, here, is a plane ticket. You're going to the United States, to New York City."

"It's not possible," she said, because she knew that it couldn't be. No one left from behind the Iron Curtain. No one other than state officials, the president and his trusted aides, the highest members of the Security Police. And a ticket to America would have cost a fortune. Even Victor, with all his military connections and his wife's wealth, couldn't have pulled this off.

"Your plane leaves in two hours," he insisted. "There will be a three-hour stop in Munich. That's where you will board the Pan Am flight that will take you across the ocean. To New York City."

She looked at the green booklet that he placed in her lap. So slowly that her hands were barely moving, she picked it up and opened it. There was her picture, a recent one, her name, address, nationality, date of birth. On the next page, there was a small stamp in the middle of the page. It was an entry visa from the United States embassy.

"I don't understand, Victor. I don't understand any of this. If you don't want to be with me, if you don't want to see me any longer, you could just say so. There's no need for this, for this elaborate . . ." She paused, bile rising in her throat. She felt like she was going to retch.

"This is not my doing, Talia. I'm just helping you get on that plane."

Something snapped inside her, hard, like a brittle branch. "This is insane!" she screamed. "I am not going to hear another word of this!"

The door handle stuck, and she jerked it forcefully to get it to open. Then she was out of the car. If her legs were not shaking so badly, she would have run. But all she managed to do was stumble a few feet, reel against the direction of traffic. She knew he would come after her; it seemed the only constant. She was always running, and he was always catching her, bending her to his will.

"Talia, stop."

"Let go of me!" she spat, trying to free herself from his grasp. "Let go of me now, you bastard! Go back to your Russian wife and your despicable job! I should have never looked in your direction! I despise myself for spending one moment with you!"

On his face, as he began pulling her back toward the car, she saw no emotion, only a trace of something hard, unyielding. Somewhere along the highway, he had become someone else, someone cold, detached, vacant. He had become a machine, a robot executing a task. It was more out of terror than anger that she raised her free hand and slapped him. It was enough to make him halt, but he did not release her. She slapped him again, harder this time. This time, he did not flinch, for he was ready for it.

"Talia, look at me!"

There was nothing left in her. There was no trace of strength or anger, there wasn't anything in her at all, as he shook her shoulders, forcing her to look in his eyes — those beautiful eyes that she had adored for almost her entire life, which now felt like daggers in her heart.

"You are getting on that plane today," he said sternly as if he was issuing a command. "Do you know how many people would risk their lives for this chance? Have you not told me how you were tired of hating, you were tired of living this life? This is it, Talia. This is your only chance to have a different life, one that is worthy of you."

"What about my parents, Victor?" she

cried, unable to stop shaking. "How can you think that I would ever leave them? How could I leave my father when he is so weak and lost these days, my mother who needs me now more than ever? How could you think I would ever abandon them?"

He let go of her. His hands fell to his sides. Gently now, evenly, he said, "They know, Talia. Your parents know. Your mother made me promise that I would get you on that plane."

It felt like a blow to her stomach. The bones in her legs seemed to have melted, and she had to grab on to the edge of the car door so she wouldn't sink to the ground. When had Victor had a chance to speak to them? Before this morning, he did not even know where they lived. He had not seen them in a decade. They had known nothing of her relationship with him. No, it didn't make sense. He was lying to her.

Raising her cold, hard eyes to him, she said, "So what about us? You came after me with such determination, and this is how you want to finish it?"

"There is no us, Talia. There can never be *us*. We've already had the best that we could hope for."

There it was at last, the truth unvarnished and brutal, the truth she'd always sought in his eyes and never seemed to find. So she had been right after all. Her instinct had been right. He had never loved her, and he didn't care how much he was hurting her now. He had played with her like a toy, a trinket, and she had let him. It was too much to absorb, and she dissolved in a torrent of sobs. Not bothering to cover her face, not caring how she looked in his eyes, she sank to the ground and wept openly while he watched. After a while, he came and crouched down next to her, leaned his head against the car door.

"Think about it, Talia," he said when there were no tears left, when all that remained of her despair were dry, quivering gasps. "Think about the possibilities. This is the only way that you could help your parents, truly help them. You can send them money when you get a job. Perhaps they can join you later. I could try to help with that, you know. They are old now, they are no threat to the state. Either way, you can have a life, a future in which you don't have to hide and look over your shoulder at every turn. That's all they ever wanted for you. Do not disappoint them."

He was right, of course. Whatever Victor had done to get her the passport, however he had paid for the ticket, he was right about that much. There was no future for her here. Other than with him. And he did not belong to her, never had. He had made that very clear.

"Will you go? Talia?" It was odd, the way his voice fractured when he said her name. It sounded like he was saying it for the last time. "Will you let me take you to the airport? There isn't much time left."

She wiped her eyes and straightened up, gazing off into the distance. She felt void, tampered with, hollowed from the inside out. This was all too much; it was happening too fast. Her senses were disabled, and she knew that she couldn't trust them.

"There will be the next plane. I need more time. To think."

"This is the only plane, my love. This is the only plane if a hundred were to follow."

45

Victor's hands were gripping the steering wheel, and he was looking ahead, straight ahead, as they sped down the side road that intersected the main highway. Next to him, she sat with her knees drawn up, her forehead resting against them. She was no longer crying, she just sat there shivering despite the heat and humidity, which even at this early hour were unbearable.

There was an awful smell coming from outside, something like fertilizer and gasoline intermingled. It was the only thing on which she could pin a sense of reality. It was persistent enough to let her know she was not trapped inside a dream. Still, she had not given up hope that any moment she might awaken and breathe out with relief, realizing that she was in her bed. That her parents were in the next room, still asleep. Her thoughts would drift to Victor then, as they did every morning while her lids still fluttered with sleep. She would see a different face from the one before her. A different set of eyes from the ones looking at her now.

As he spoke, his voice calm but austere, she became aware that it was the last time they would be like this, sitting together side by side. He was saying something about what she should do once she got to New York City, where she needed to go. There was someone she needed to see the moment she landed. He pronounced a name, an English-sounding name that she had never heard before.

"How do you do it?" she said, interrupting him. "How do you turn yourself off like this, like a light switch?" It wasn't meant as an insult; she really wanted to know. She wanted to know so that she might attempt it herself.

"Talia, let's not say anything. I beg you, let's not spoil our last moments together."

She laughed, a hollow, bitter laugh. "Our last moments together? What do they mean to you, Victor? Why should they matter at all?"

"You're wrong," he said softly. "Soon you will understand that."

They rode without saying another word the rest of the way. A few kilometers later, they pulled up along a narrow strip of asphalt that lined the length of a domed building with rows of vertical windows. In front of the massive glass doors, a dozen or so policemen with patrol dogs marched up and down. Victor turned off the engine and got out of the car. He came around to her side and flung the door open wide, then stood there holding his hand out to her.

"You cannot park here!" a guard with a rifle slung over his shoulder shouted, waving his arms as he marched menacingly toward them. Victor took a badge out of his shirt pocket and flashed it impatiently, not looking in his direction.

"Oh, I am so sorry, sir," the soldier muttered in a very different tone, coming to a halt. "Please, let me escort you inside."

"It's not necessary," Victor growled. "I know exactly where I am going."

Natalia thought this might be her last chance to escape, to run back to her old life, her old home, which already seemed so far away that she might have already crossed over continents. *I can still reach out and touch his face,* she thought. *I can drop to my knees and beg him to let me go. I can scream in front of the airport employees, in front of the guards.* But it would do no good, she knew. Victor was going to put her on that plane the same way he had put people on trains to the Gulag camps. No pitiful pleas would break him down or get him to change his mind. There was nowhere to run anyway, and her body would not move. Somewhere along the road, she had lost her resolve. She took his hand and let him help her out of the car.

Extracting her valise from the trunk, not letting go of her elbow, Victor ushered her into the building. They moved along at a clipped pace, crossing through a maze of interminable corridors, stopping only at checkpoints along the way where her passport was checked, her valise ransacked. Several times, guards rushed toward them with hands held up, shouting for them to stop. Each time, Victor flashed his badge, and instantly the guards stood aside, practically bowing as they passed through. One of them clicked his heels and saluted him, a military salute that looked out of place as a disheveled, glum-looking Victor in civilian clothing waved him off.

At the end of the last hallway, he led her down a flight of concrete steps that opened into a large carpeted area. When they reached the bottom, he released her arm, and she wandered away from him a little, her gaze scanning the airless space, taking in the dozen or so people who sat scattered among the rows of chairs. An elderly white-haired man was reading a book. A young woman with bleached hair was bouncing a crying baby on her lap. Sitting underneath the row of windows that spanned the length of the room, a young couple who looked distinctly Western in their clothing were whispering, absorbed in conversation. But it was what stretched beyond them that she couldn't look away from. Although she'd never seen a runway before, she knew from magazine pictures that that's what it was.

She stood there without moving, thinking that this strip of land would be the very last thing she would see of her home, of the city of her birth. How was it possible that her parents had known all along? That they had not only known but helped Victor arrange this? It was astounding that the three of them had been accomplices, that they had planned everything without her knowledge, without the slightest regard for what *she* wanted.

But if that was what they truly wished for her, she would do it. She would do it for them, for her mother and father. If it made them happy, if it made it possible for them to live the rest of their days in peace, she would not hesitate. Deep down, she knew that what Victor had said was true. He never would have acted without their approval and blessing. For Victor, there would always be that invisible thread that connected him to her father, despite the passage of time, despite class differences, despite even death itself.

It was with this last thought in mind that she turned to him and said, "You don't have to stand guard to make sure I get on the plane. I'll go."

Wearily, he came to her and stopped a few feet away, far enough so that she could not touch him. After fishing inside the pocket of his trench coat, he took out the envelope containing her ticket and passport. It quivered slightly in his hand as he held it out to her. She thought his lips quivered, too, or perhaps he mouthed something wordlessly. When she took it from him, his hand dropped limply to his side. So this was it. Well, she would not make it that easy for him.

"What am I supposed to do for money, Victor, once I get to New York? Sleep under a bridge? Eat out of garbage cans? Have you thought about that?"

"There is the letter," he answered with a start, as if he had just remembered it. "There is the letter I was telling you about earlier, in the car." His hand disappeared once more inside the trench coat and extracted a smaller envelope, this one of thick, creamy stock.

"Remember what we talked about? Wait to open it on the plane. When you are in the air."

She stared at him, then at the letter. When had he mentioned a letter? She had no recollection. Then again, the entire morning had been a blur. She slipped it inside her skirt pocket alongside her passport and ticket.

"Any more surprises, Victor? Anything else you have in store for me before I vanish off into the sunset?"

He exhaled deeply, closing his eyes. A strand of hair fell across his face, and he brushed it away. Beyond the window, an airplane was rolling on the tarmac toward them.

"You think that you are being just?" she went on, her voice low but fierce. "You think that what you are doing is out of loyalty to my father? Is that how you justify to yourself that you simply wanted to get rid of me, to dispose of an unnecessary complication? Well, you found the perfect way. To break free while still looking noble in my father's eyes. Congratulations, Victor. You're very smooth."

He stared at her then with eyes so dark they looked bruised. She could no longer stand to look at them, so she turned back toward the window and watched the plane as it taxied.

"Forgive me, Talia," he said then, a little too loudly, for every one of the passengers who had lined up in front of the oval metal door turned to look.

It threw her off kilter. She expected a more discreet reply or the concrete, impenetrable wall that she had been pounding against since early this morning. When he reached out to take her hand in both of his, she flinched and wanted to pull it away, but then she saw the muscles of his chest rising and falling, rising and falling under his shirt, and she could not. As he had done before, in another life, in another time, he brought her palm up to his chest and rested it against his heart. It thrashed wildly underneath her cold, damp fingers. He held it there still as tears welled in her eyes, as her other hand came up to trace his cheek unhurriedly from his silver-threaded temple to his square jaw, as if to imprint the contours of his features beneath her fingers.

He seized her hand then and pressed it hard to his lips. For a brief moment, her pulse leaped, spurred on by a glimmer of hope that there was a part of them she could still salvage, that this was not the end, this was not the last time she would see his beautiful, stoic, unflinching face. She lifted her wet eyes to him and smiled, despite herself and all that she was feeling. And then the moment passed.

He let go of her. He looked smaller, diminished, suddenly a middle-aged man for whom the best years of his life lay behind him, as he turned and walked away. Deliberately, as if it took great effort, he made his way up the stairway to the corridor above, the corridor that would lead him out of the airport and back to his old life.

Natalia listened to the echo of his shoes on the concrete steps even after she could no longer see him. And there it was again, that image of a younger Victor fading from view, disappearing in a crowd of pedestrians as she stood watching in the doorway of her childhood home, thinking she would never see him again.

46

She was gliding. A feather caught in the breeze, floating through space. Not flesh and bone but the vibrations of sound, Duke Ellington's notes from a decade long gone spilling all around her in a mad swirl, cascading, and she with them. She was one with the music, everything perfect in the capsule of this moment, everything serene. If only she could stay like this, nestled in the echo of those sounds emanating from within. If only.

The plane dropped again, jolting her, and she sat upright. For nearly two hours, she had been on this flight to Munich, but she had yet to get used to this motion, this vertical jarring that sent swells of fear right through her core. She still did not know how she was able to board at all, how she found the nerve to walk down the tarmac and climb the unsteady metal steps, how she sat idly and watched as the jet pulled away from the gate and rolled down the concrete strip, slowly at first, then with dizzying speed, before ascending into the somber late-morning sky. The entire time, she watched the whole thing unfold passively, with no emotion, as she would watch a movie, as if it was someone else's life that would change irrevocably when the wheels lifted off the ground.

Yet somewhere in mid-flight between the city of her birth and Munich, her senses began firing again, like bolts of electricity spouting through the severed end of a telephone wire in the dead calm after a storm. Little by little, she became aware of the shadows playing on the white ceiling of the cabin, the blinking red lights, the backdrop of white and blue and perfect symmetry surrounding her. She became aware of her own hands, white and lifeless in her lap, the dull ache in her ears. The pulsing of her heart, the heaviness lodged in its beats. Victor. Her parents. The three of them had made up her entire world, and she had lost them. She did not know what awaited her at the end of this flight or the one that would take her across the Atlantic. She did not know what her life would resemble tomorrow or an even an hour from now. All she knew was that it would go on without the people she loved.

Sometime later, when she looked up with eyes raw and veiled with dried tears, the striking blue outside her window made her gasp. Clouds in the shape of animals, cotton-candy pink and translucent, moved past her, some close enough that she thought she might touch them if she reached out. A shard of light slashed across the horizon, like the edge of a sword glinting at high noon, and the plane tilted toward it, flooding the cabin with a light so bright that she had to shield her eyes. By now, her parents would know that she was in flight somewhere above the Alps, above a range of mountains that did not belong to her homeland. *She's free,* Victor might tell them, sitting across the table or perhaps standing in their doorway, loosening the collar of his shirt, raking a hand through his hair.

Would the three of them shed a tear together? Would it be a tear of loss or one of relief? *Your parents know. Your mother made me promise that I would get you on that plane,* Victor had told her in those final moments, while he stood before her in flesh and blood, not yet a chimera, not yet a haunting presence that would become distant and faded with time. She had looked into his eyes, solemn and detached, already looking ahead to a life without her, and she had believed him. This was what her parents had wanted for her, and no matter what Victor had said or done to convince them, it was the one thing that gave her solace. *You have made my life truly beautiful,* her mother had said, and Natalia realized now that it had been her good-bye.

Setting foot in the Munich airport was like sliding into another world, a strange, magnificent world that stunned her with its brilliance. A sea of ruby-red carpet opened before her as she emerged from the airless tunnel, clutching her valise as tightly as she might a battle shield. Above her, rows of lights punctuated the cathedral-like dome, casting a soft glow on the floor-to-ceiling windows in which she glimpsed her own sphinx-like image amid the beehive of activity. It took her a moment to realize that she wasn't, in fact, standing still, she was moving forward ever so slightly, pushed forward by the crowd.

A kaleidoscope of colors and forms exploded before her as she made her way down the vast corridor that connected one terminal to the next, more conscious than ever of her aloneness amid the swarm of people. At kiosks between the hushed waiting areas, Swiss chocolates in gold wrappers gleamed at her invitingly, and bottles of Coca-Cola stacked three high behind a refrigerator's glass reminded her of an advertisement she had once seen in a foreign magazine. On adjacent shelves were rows of tins — identical save for the labels — of *Brazilian Coffee* or *Espresso, Premium Cocoa* or *English Black Tea,* welcoming her like eager children standing in line at a matinee movie. Dried fruit sparkled in ribbon-tied cellophane, and snail-shaped pastries arranged in boxes with transparent lids beckoned with glazed sugar and the promise of something forbidden.

At the end of the walkway, she turned the corner as if in a trance and encountered a further assault on her senses. There, spread out across a large circular area, were several duty-free shops, so brightly lit they would have been adequate for a surgeon's work, flaunting boxes of French soaps and perfumes and foreign liquor. Beyond the immaculate shop windows, women in high-heeled shoes tilted their heads this way and that over display cases, men leaned impatiently against white marble walls, checking their watches. Female clerks in black smocks smiled invitingly among shimmering multicolored silk ties and cashmere shawls that were displayed artfully behind the cash registers. For a moment, Natalia considered walking into one of the shops, simply to take a closer look, perhaps to steal a touch, but then changed her mind. Instead, she looked away from it all, a little embarrassed, aware that she had been gaping wide-mouthed like the foreigner she was, a girl from behind the Iron Curtain who had never seen such things.

Someone bumped into her from behind, making her jump. A man in a sports coat the color of dishwater mumbled what must have been an apology in German, his gaze shooting in her overall direction but flying past her, perhaps to the plane he was about to miss or the business appointment he was late for. She smiled to indicate that it was all right, but he had already moved on. Clutching her valise, she resumed walking a little bit faster. She passed a couple who were kissing passionately against a wall, no doubt saying good-bye, but the girl wasn't crying at all, she was laughing, her head thrown back gleefully, her arms draped around the boy's neck, and Natalia realized it wasn't a good-bye at all, it was a home-coming. A woman trotted by quickly with her head held high, her chestnut hair loose and fluttering behind her like a curtain. She

447

was trailed by a young boy, no older than ten, who was gesticulating and whining in a language Natalia did not understand, perhaps complaining about a toy his mother would not buy for him.

They were all going somewhere, these people. Somewhere beyond this merry-go-round of shiny distractions, families were waiting, and lovers, and life. But not for her. There would be no arms to embrace her at the end of her journey, no warm meal to comfort her, no words of love whispered in her ear. Yet something strange had happened in the time since she had entered this new world, this opulent, nearly frantic world that left her breathless. She did not know what it was, but a new sensation had sprouted in her heart, something that fluttered at her rib cage like the wings of a hummingbird. It wasn't anything that might obliterate her grief entirely, but it was enough to carry her across the airport, to the Pan American terminal, where the plane that was to take her over the ocean was taxiing to the gate.

Another flight, another row of seats, these light blue with white covers draped over the headrests. Seat belts, lights, another runway, the roar of engines, and the speed that halted her breath, then open sky, immense and interminable.

This flight turned out to be not as calm as the first. The pilot's voice came on several times to announce that they would be through the worst of it soon, that there was nothing to worry about, they were just experiencing turbulence from a storm down below. But Natalia was no longer frightened. She was no longer daunted by the sudden rising and dropping, the floor quaking, the luggage bins rattling overhead. She was beyond fear. All she was acutely aware of now was distance, distance that she could feel in her bones, in the air she inhaled. It was pulling her forward and stretching behind her in equal measure, like a long prison wall that she might surmount irrevocably, only once.

All around her, people shifted in their seats, conversing with one another, exchanging stories of their travels, reading newspapers, writing postcards, drinking champagne from plastic flutes. Champagne on a plane. Who would have imagined such a thing? She would never know what it was like to live with such carefree nonchalance. Her America would never be as easy as this. America. Her new home. What did it look like? She closed her eyes, trying to imagine it, its lakes and rows of mountains, its cities and bridges and steel-and-glass skyscrapers glinting in the sun, but nothing came to mind. Only a void was there and a sweet, sweet pull, a release of thoughts and limbs and mind that she vaguely recognized as sleep.

Sometime later, a drop in altitude caused her eyes to snap open. Bewildered, she sat up in her seat, squinting against the stark daylight, which, despite the passing of hours, had refused to dull. There was a quietness now in the cabin as many of the passengers had slipped into their own slumber behind elliptical masks, and she felt herself loosen a little, grateful to be shielded from the scrutiny of their glances.

Gingerly, she reached inside her skirt pocket and felt around for the smaller envelope that Victor had handed her when they parted what felt like a lifetime ago. It was still there, alongside her passport and ticket, its sharp corners grazing her finger-tips like the blade of a dull knife. More than a dozen times, she had intended to take it out and read it but lacked the courage. Now the moment had come, for it wouldn't be long before they landed. *It's time,* she told herself, and her fingers gripped the envelope more firmly, pulling it out in one swift move.

Several sheets of paper fluttered out when she tore it open. More than she realized at first, typed in her native tongue — translated, perhaps, by someone British or American, someone whose name she had never heard before. There was something else in that envelope, too, something dark green, which tumbled onto her lap. Holding it up to the light, she studied it for a few moments, its markings, its seals and serial numbers. *One hundred American dollars.* She was holding more money than she had ever seen in her life. Careful not to bend it, she placed it back in the envelope and slipped it inside her pocket.

Then she picked up the pages and began to read.

May 20, 1960

Dear Natalia,
My name is John Fowley. I am an attorney living in New York City, where I have been practicing law for more than fifteen years. Although you do not know me and have probably never heard of me before this day, you may find it hard to believe that in a sense I know you.

In my profession, I have written many letters, informing people about divorces and deaths and wills, but none of those letters was as complex as this one is. And so please forgive the length, since I start at the beginning.

In 1945, at the beginning of my career, I was working at a small family law firm here in Manhattan. One February morning, a young couple — no older than thirty, I guessed — walked into my office. In deeply accented English, the young man told me that they didn't have much money but that he had been told I was a fair attorney, one who could be retained for a reasonable fee. I already had numerous cases on my desk and could have easily sent them on their way. But something in their demeanor was so grave that I could not help but offer them a seat.

Proudly, yet with visible emotion, the young man went on to tell me that he and his wife — the frail young woman sitting next to him — had escaped the Romanian Pogrom, the rounding up and killing of Jews in Romania, four years prior.

I had, of course, heard about what had taken place in Europe during the war, about the atrocities in Poland and Hungary, about Jews being sent to so-called work camps. Worse rumors than that circulated, rumors that no one believing in God and human decency could fathom to be true. Yet here was this couple telling me that they had fled exactly that. He told me that it wasn't until six months later — after hiding in a friend's attic — that a train took them out of the country with just the clothes on their backs. "Fascinating story," I told him. "But how is it that I can help you?" Nothing could have prepared me for what I heard next.

He told me that when they fled, they were forced to leave their daughter behind. He said that she was in Bucharest and was now seven years old. They were separated from her when she was not yet four. At first, she was at an orphanage, but now she was with a new family. She had been adopted.

It was for the first time in my professional life that I found myself at a complete loss for words. What could one say about such things? I tried to focus on the facts. They had fled an unspeakable situation, that much was clear. How they ended up in the United States, in New York City, was not of much importance to me. What was of the essence was that they had a daughter caught behind the Soviet line. No money or influence in the world would break through that barrier.

As if reading my thoughts, the young man told me that he had been working on the docks six days a week and had done some other jobs as well, driving delivery trucks, busing tables. He said he had saved a little money and would get more. The family that adopted her was well-off and owned a chain of stores around Bucharest. He wanted to know what he would need to offer people like that to get his daughter back.

He was asking me how to get his daughter out of the occupied Eastern Bloc. From a family who had adopted her legally.

I told him it was impossible, that it couldn't be done. He looked at me then with eyes so anguished that I told him that I'd look into it but that it might be a long while before I could find out anything. In the meantime, I informed him that he should save all he could.

I handed him a set of papers to fill out in order to start a trust. I explained that the funds placed in it would be held in your name, that I could help him invest it so that it would multiply over time, that when you were of legal age, we would try somehow to get that money to you so that you could use it to get to the West. It was a long shot, but that was the best advice I could give him.

He nodded and took the papers. We shook hands, and I told him to come and see me in a month's time. Three weeks later, he was back. Then three weeks after that. Months turned into a year, then two, and he kept coming to see me regularly. His trust kept growing, little by little, as did our camaraderie, blooming eventually into a full friend-ship.

On one occasion, we shared a beer at the bar across from my office. He told me then of the pain he had suffered, of his wife who still cried herself to sleep every night, of the heaviness that hung between them. He told me how much he missed her, how much he missed them, the couple they once were when they were a young family in love. They'd come to America, he explained, because there was nothing left for them back in Europe, not even each other, and I told him that I understood, offered him whatever words of comfort I could summon. As the evening wore on, I shared a bit of my own struggles. It helped him, I think, on some level to know that he wasn't alone, and we parted outside with an embrace.

After our beers that night, some time passed before I saw him again. In fact, it was nearly two years before, unexpectedly, he came back. There was a joyful energy about him that I had not seen before. We didn't bother with pleasantries.

"I have figured out how to get her out!" he told me excitedly. He said it wasn't their daughter that the money should go to but the state of Romania. He had been talking to a few people in the Jewish community. Apparently, Romania had a secret arrangement with the state of Israel to export Romanian Jews out of the country. "Can you believe this?" he said. "They trade people for money, like they do cattle or oil. So I thought, why not her? Why not our daughter? If the Romanian government will accept money for her freedom, then we can surely get her out."

He had already received many donations from people of means who were willing to contribute. He wanted me to look into the matter, do some research, and said he'd pay me for my time.

I told him that we were friends, that I would not charge him a dime and would do all that was in my power to help him. I wanted to warn him not to get his hopes up. It was a long shot, and even if it was true, who in that country could help us arrange such a transaction? Who would even dare to speak to us of such things? Yet at the moment, I didn't have the heart to point out the obvious. This was by far the happiest I'd seen him. He tipped his hat to me as he left my office that day, and his smile said more than words ever could.

Many years passed after my friend's jubilant visit, years of trial and failure, of multiple attempts to reach the right people, to get our offer into the right hands, with no progress at all. All the letters I'd sent to the Romanian government went unanswered, and I'd long given up trying to get an audience at the Romanian embassy. With my friends, I spoke very little of these fruitless efforts, and we were seeing less of each other now. Though I still managed the couple's trust, I could tell from the slight disinterest with which they asked me about it that they, too, were losing hope, that the money meant little to them now. "Do with it as you wish," my friend told me on more than one occasion. "I cannot bear to speak of it any longer."

Then, one day something remarkable happened. One of my letters came back, "Return to Sender" written on the envelope in English. Had it not been for this simple marking, I probably would have tossed it into the wastebasket, but as I turned it over, I saw that the envelope had been opened and reglued with a visible strip of tape before being mailed back overseas. For once, someone had not only read my letter but wanted me to know that they'd taken notice.

I opened it fervently, and there it was, my original letter addressed to the Ministry of Affairs, all three pages of it detailing in simple, straightforward terms why I was contacting them, what I wanted to achieve, the sum of money I was willing to pay. I looked inside the envelope. There was nothing else. And then I saw it, a small notation at the bottom of the last page, a scribbling in red ink.

Numbers. A series of them, separated by dashes and colons in groups of four or five. It took me a while to realize they were the routing number and account number of a bank in Switzerland.

I know that much of this may not make a great deal of sense to you, Natalia. It hardly makes sense to me, though I've lived long enough to know that once in a while, destiny has plans for us that we might never have imagined. Sometimes stars do align, and in the most mysterious ways.

Of what had been set in motion that night I vowed that I would not speak to anyone. I simply did what needed to be done. Why I chose to do it in secret I cannot quite say. Perhaps it was fear that the whole thing was only a sham, that the money would be lost or squandered. Fear for that couple's heartbreak. Above all else, that was something I could not risk laying on the doorstep of people who'd already suffered so much. Fortunately, however, our efforts were finally successful.

When you arrive in New York City, please contact me immediately at either of the numbers provided on my business card, which I have enclosed. We will then go together to the bank on Madison Avenue in Manhattan, where I have opened a safe-deposit box in your name. You will not find a fortune in it, but it will be enough to get you on your feet, give you a start. The rest of what was in the trust was transferred into that undisclosed Swiss account on my instructions. Those were the funds that secured your freedom.

Inside the box, you will find an address in Brooklyn. Make sure to go there soon; do not wait. I hope that you now look forward to a future that will fulfill your dreams.

Most sincerely yours,
John Fowley, Esq.

She hadn't realized she was weeping until she looked down and saw that her tears had moistened the pages in her lap, blurring the words in several places. It seemed as if she was watching herself from somewhere above, through someone else's eyes, this once stoic girl shedding so many tears.

Maybe she felt ashamed that in all these years, she hadn't given these people — these people who had given her life — more than a thought. When she'd found that letter years ago in her father's attic, she'd been so eager to put it out of her mind, to dismiss it as if it meant nothing, as if those words were nothing to her. *It was with a heavy heart that I had to set her free so that she might live, so that she might have a chance at life, even as it meant the end of mine.* She'd exiled them out of her heart, closed the door, bolted it shut.

It was cool inside the cabin, yet a warmth was spreading through her, like a shot of sherry on a cold winter night. It wasn't out of neglect that they'd left her that night; it was out of love. Fate had rolled over them like the tide, a deluge they hadn't been able to stop. So they'd done the only thing they could do, raising her above the turbulent waters before the sea could pull them all down into its depths.

Then, as now, there had been a sacrifice.

Immediately, her thoughts shot back to the night before, to those last moments with Anton and Despina, the only parents she'd really known. It wasn't exactly their words that were reassembling now in a different light but the silence between them. She understood now what had been in her father's eyes when he held her in his arms before turning in for the night. All that they had been to each other, all that he had wanted to give her and had not been able to, all that he wished for her still, was there in his misty gaze as he kissed her forehead for the very last time.

And her mother. Not for a moment had there been a crack in her armor, a tremor that might have given away what was to come. She had played her part perfectly. No doubt, days before, when Victor had shown Despina the letter that had inexplicably landed on his desk, she had silenced her heart and said, *Do it. Do it, Victor. Get her out of here. Get her to a place where she can have a better life. Return her to them. It is just.*

Be strong, Talia, she would whisper now if she could. *Be strong and don't look back.*

I will try, Mama, Natalia thought, tears flooding her anew. *I will try even though I do not know how I will get by without you, without my papa, my savior, my knight in shining armor.*

You have made my life truly beautiful, her mother had said, and Natalia realized now that perhaps it had not been a good-bye after all, but an affirmation, something she could keep locked inside her heart forever, like a pearl.

Inside the aircraft, flight attendants began ambling up and down the aisles, asking passengers if they would like some water or coffee or tea, if there was anything they needed on this last stretch of the flight.

Rustling in their seats, stretching their arms, men and women rubbed their bleary eyes and looked out at the sky, where a softness had at last seeped into its persistent azure, tingeing it gold.

Natalia sat silently and waited, although for what she wasn't sure. Perhaps she expected a conclusion of sorts, the words *The End* to flash before her like at the close of a movie, although she knew one would not come, for this was not an end but a beginning. Perhaps she expected a physical sign of some kind, a bolt of lightning or the sound of thunder, something to mark the slow descent into her new life, but all that stretched before her was a void, and all she heard was the wild hammering of her own heart.

Then suddenly, down below, she spotted something that she had only read about in papers. She had never seen a picture of it, but she knew what it was. A statue, dark green and proud, welcomed her, and the torch in the statue's hand beckoned her to her new life, to her new existence, which she now knew was a gift. So much awaited her down there in the land of light and promise, so much that she embraced with a feeling of grace and, above all, with love.

47

On a stoop on a sycamore-lined street, she sat clutching her purse, the leather strap moist in her clenched fists. In the hours just after sunrise, she watched children brushing past her in a swirl of laughter, the corner fruit vendor hauling out a variety of produce in crates under the bright awning — an explosion of orange and red and green, a Cézanne painting. She watched the sun rise higher still in the sky, the pavement shimmering with heat in the noon hour, people wearing baseball caps and construction gear lining up along the length of the block in front of a restaurant called a pizzeria which was yet to open. And she watched one building in particular, a prewar brownstone with noisy air-conditioning units and a rusty old fire escape zigzagging the length of its five stories, people coming and going through a door that was poorly painted.

Three mornings in a row, she'd walked

here from the tiny apartment she'd rented just off the waterfront, in this lively borough of Brooklyn. It seemed impossible that in the ten minutes it took to get here, she could so utterly lose her nerve, yet there she was, running off each time, feeling defeated, paralyzed by anxiety, cowardly. On this morning, however, Williamsburg burst into a new energy of sorts, signaled at first by little flags appearing in the windows. By ten o'clock, people were streaming out into the street by the dozens, children bearing more little red-white-and-blue flags, an outpouring that reminded her of the marches she'd had to participate in back home, although there were no somber faces here, and only cheerful voices engulfed her. Whatever this was, she was caught up in it, emboldened, restored in her courage, enough that she sprinted quite suddenly across the street. Nonchalantly, she hovered near the entrance, and when the door swung open, she caught it in time.

"Thank you, sir," she offered in her best English with a smile. So little she remembered from school, and although she'd been poring over her instructional books, she still felt unsure of even the most basic phrases. "I lost my key, and I can't find it." The man, however, did not seem to care about an explanation; he was already off, his mind on other things.

Ten, fifteen minutes had passed since she'd reached the third landing, and still she hadn't been able to take one step toward the apartment door. It was hot in here, hotter than outside, and she leaned against a wall, unbuttoned her blouse at the top, and blew air into the crevice between her breasts. Through a narrow window, a beam of light pierced the darkness, landing right at her feet. She ran her fingers through the dancing dust particles, scattering them momentarily. She wondered if she'd come too late to mend what had long been broken. As she was turning to leave, she heard sounds on the other side of the door, and she became still.

The door pushed open. Again, there was some clatter, voices, an object hitting the floor. Then a figure emerged. A pair of pale, moonlike eyes met hers, and she had to grab on to the railing.

"I-I'm sorry," she stammered. "I think I've made a mistake."

But she couldn't quite move because of the way the boy was staring at her. At first, she thought it was because of the unbuttoned blouse, and she clasped it shut, but the eyes only darkened, and he retreated inside, crushing a paper cone hat into his fist. He was about to slam the door when Natalia raised her hand.

"Wait," she said. "Wait a moment."

"I'm not going with you!" the boy shouted, red-faced now, ferocious. "I'm not going anywhere. You can't make me! You can't make me, you hear?"

Another child appeared behind him. Then another. All aged between five and ten, two boys and a girl. They stood together with the first boy as a group, a unified front, an army ready for battle.

"I'm sorry," Natalia repeated. "I must have gotten the wrong apartment . . ." She dug in her purse for the piece of paper bearing the address, but she couldn't find it. "I'm looking for a couple," she began again bravely. "Maybe you can help me?" she said to the children, who hadn't budged an inch.

"Our father isn't here," the littlest one said, as if she'd rehearsed this line beforehand without fully understanding it, holding her chin high. She had a slight lisp, and her hair, in pigtails, was as light as spun gold. "He's on a construction job in Rhode Island. He's bringing us presents."

"Be quiet, silly," the elder boy said, nudging her a little. "Didn't I tell you not to talk to strangers?"

He put an arm protectively around the girl's shoulder, and she leaned toward him, biting a plump, rosy lip. All eyes returned to Natalia, piercing, expectant. Then another silhouette appeared behind them, and they all turned slightly and moved out of the way, making room.

"Kids," the woman said. "Kids," and then she stopped.

She wasn't much taller than them. A lithe figure in a green, flowy dress, her abundant hair piled high in a bun, a few reddish highlights framing her face. In the bleak light of the hallway, she looked younger than she probably was — with high cheekbones and luminous, flawless skin — though when she stepped forward, Natalia could see the tiny lines curving around her mouth. In her hands, she carried a bouquet of daisies that had been tied together with a red, white, and blue ribbon.

"Can I help you, miss?" she said with a warm, friendly smile.

"Yes. Yes, I'm here because . . . I'm looking for . . ." Natalia swallowed hard against the knot in her throat. All the words she'd carefully rehearsed beforehand had left her, flown from her memory. She only knew a handful of them anyway, hardly enough to cobble together something this complex, but then she realized that she didn't have to. If she'd indeed come to the right place, there was another way.

In Romanian, so softly that she could hardly hear her own voice, she said, "I've been sent here by a mutual friend. A man by the name of John Fowley."

The bouquet slipped from the woman's hands.

She had sent the kids away. She'd given them money to go buy lunch, pizza and lemonade, and ice cream afterward from the street vendor. Then they would go to the park. Enough for a feast, fit for a holiday, and they left in a cloak of excitement, no longer paying attention to the unexpected visitor.

"Some wine?" she said after she'd locked the door and come back into the kitchen timidly, a stranger under her own roof. She looked extremely pale.

Natalia felt quite light-headed herself and wanted to suggest sitting down, but she said nothing.

From a cupboard in the kitchen, the woman extracted two glasses, filled them high from the ruby-colored jug she brought out of the fridge. She placed them on the table, where a pair of brass candleholders cast reflections on the slightly scarred wood which had been nevertheless polished to a high shine. There were flowers here and there set in old jam jars, and the sofa and chairs had been recovered in a thick brocade cloth, though the cushions had long lost their plumpness. It stirred her in an odd way. Her own flat back in Bucharest had been tended to with the same care, the same intent to disguise its modesty with a few lovely details.

"They say Chianti should be served at room temperature, but I never quite got used to that, you know?" the woman said. "I guess for me, wine in the warm weather should be served cold, like the muscat we used to drink in the Moldavian countryside. I never grew to like the fancy ones here, you know, even though you wouldn't believe how many there are . . ."

When Natalia took the glass from her hand, their fingers brushed, and the woman stilled. She grew as stiff as a statue, including her face. Only a tiny gasp came from her lips.

It wasn't anything like Natalia had imagined since descending from that plane all of two weeks ago, counting the days, going over in her head how this would unfold, what she would say. No, this encounter was strewn with silence more than with words; it lacked the drama that she had envisioned. They were just two women, two strangers, with hair of almost the same hue, sharing a drink.

"They seem very sweet," Natalia said after a silence. "Your children seem very sweet." But she could still feel the way their eyes had fastened on her as their mother counted up the money, digging inside her purse. Maybe they'd already sensed who she was, *what* she was — not just an afternoon visitor but a hand grenade tossed at the heart of their family. "You don't have to tell them. About me."

The woman smiled as if she understood something quite suddenly. On the tabletop, she clasped her hands, but even so, Natalia could see they were trembling. Her lips were quivering, too, and Natalia realized that it wasn't lack of emotion that she'd witnessed but a colossal effort to keep it in check.

"They are not what you think. Yes, I love them dearly, I love each one of them, but . . ." She shook her head a little as if she couldn't quite find the way to explain, a hand coming up to her temple, rubbing it a little. Then her gaze lifted. "I am their foster mother, you see."

It changed after that. Whatever barrier had been there before was broken down enough that they could talk to each other a little more freely. Natalia felt her resistance melting away, and she began opening up about the remarkable circumstances that had brought her here, how she'd left her home with no more than the clothes on her back and little idea of where she was going. She went farther back in time and described all that her family had been through in the years after the war, how much their lives changed, how much they'd lost yet still had in one another. How in her heart she hoped, she *knew,* they'd all be together again. About Victor and what he'd meant to her, she said nothing. She couldn't speak or think of him yet without a hole opening up in the pit of her stomach. Thus, the rest of the afternoon passed in a blur, and it was only when daylight began to fade into a glowing dusk that she fell silent, realizing she'd done most of the talking.

"What about you?" Natalia said. "Tell me something about you. About you and your . . ." She didn't know what to call him, what word to use. "Your husband."

"What would you like to know?" the woman replied gently.

"I'm not sure." She paused. "Perhaps

something about the children?"

There was no answer. A long moment passed, and the woman rose from the table and walked away, disappearing into another room. When she returned, there was something in her hands. She did not sit back down but stood next to Natalia's chair and placed the object on the table. It was a piece of cloth, something dusty rose, made of cotton.

Even before touching it, Natalia's heart leaped into a full gallop. She extended her hand, ran her fingers over the fine texture, over the ribbon of lace and silk piping adorning the edge. And then she picked it up.

A child's bonnet. Her hands quivered as she brought it close to her face. She placed it next to her cheek, inhaled, groping for a recognizable scent. There was nothing there, the scent was long gone, but she was overcome by something else, and she closed her eyes and crumpled the cloth in her hands, aware only of the pulse batting in her throat.

A dark boiler room, too hot, too humid. A basement window. The flurry of snow looked like fireflies, and the three of them had been hiding for hours. Outside, street-lights, dim in the late hour, the sound of breaking glass. *Be brave.* Someone had said to be brave. But it was all right, she was safe, even if it was cold out on the street and she wanted to go home. She wanted to go home.

"I don't know," Natalia began. "I don't know if I'm ready for this." Her heart felt like it might burst through her chest, and a sharp panic seized her. "I don't know if I can do this," she repeated, and began rising from her chair, gripping the side of the table, but a hand steadied her. It fell squarely on her shoulder, and she no longer had the strength.

The hand traveled up to her cheek, along her temple, where her pulse throbbed like mad. And then she smelled it, the scent she'd been seeking. It was there, clear and stark like a bright light in a dark forest, a forest she'd been lost in and seeking her way out of for nearly twenty years.

48

In the months after Despina and Anton adopted her, Natalia had been plagued with endless night terrors from which only her father could rescue her. Night after night, when she woke screaming, clutching her pillow for dear life, he would run into her room and gather her into his arms. "I'm here, darling," he would whisper, holding her tightly against his chest. "I'm always here. Tell me what's frightened you. Tell me what you're afraid of."

She could never remember what the precise thing was. All she recalled was her father caressing her hair, listening intently as the words flowed out of her, rushed, tremulous. When she had calmed down, he would stand up and make a gesture with his arms, wide and upsweeping, as if he meant to catch those bad dreams in his grasp. Then, going to the window, wrenching it open, he would fling them out into the dark.

Sometimes her mother would come into the room, and seeing him standing there beneath the billowing curtains, she would shout, "Are you out of your mind, Anton? You'll both catch a chill!" But neither Natalia nor her father would utter a word. All that mattered was that whatever had disturbed her sleep would not be coming back — at least, not that night.

Those old demons. They never released her entirely, even long after the nightmares had ended. So much of her life, she'd been evading their grip, dodging their shadows, only to find that here, of all places, as the evening wore on, they were scattering off of their own accord, with no more resistance than dandelion seeds blown by the wind.

The kids had come home long ago, and the woman had fed them dinner and put them to bed. Now it was just the two of them in the quietness of the living room, nervously speaking over each other and silent at times, with only a few candles for company, the contours of furniture barely visible beyond the flickering flames.

The woman seemed suddenly wistful. Straightening herself up on the sofa, she let go of Natalia's hand, which she'd been holding most of the night. There was something in her that seemed to go soft, a loosening of a shell that she had built around herself.

"Oh, Natalia. If you only knew. It was a terrible time. A time . . ." She ran a hand over her hair, leaned forward onto her elbows. "It was a time when I thought that I would not live. There was so much pain in my heart — your father's, too." She paused, her voice breaking.

"Tell me."

After lighting new candles, she settled back down, reached for a blanket thrown over the edge of the sofa, and pulled it over their laps. She remained quiet for a moment longer.

"Whatever it is, whatever happened, tell me. I need to know."

So she began softly, going back to the beginning, to that fateful night that had dictated the course of all their lives, that night that had changed everything.

There had been no dream of America in those days for Zora and Iosef. Back then, as the young couple muddled through the bleakness of their early life in Geneva, their only preoccupation had been how to get back into Romania, even though it had been only by a miracle that they'd escaped on that outbound train. It was early in the war, and neither of them had considered that returning might just be a fantasy, a feat less conquerable with each passing day.

A kind man using a cane despite not being so old had met them at the railway station, a friend of Stefan's from his law-school days whom he'd met as an exchange student and with whom he had continued to remain in touch. The Swiss government wasn't allowing many non-POW refugees into the country by then, and although no longer in hiding, they soon found themselves, despite their host's good nature and hospitality, in circumstances not a great deal different — living in a tiny room with an old-fashioned washbasin, directly above a defunct flower shop which the man owned. After his wife passed away unexpectedly, he'd explained to the couple that first night over a simple supper, it had saddened him too deeply to set foot inside it, and so he'd closed its doors. He couldn't even begin to handle all the details that his wife had managed so superbly, and it was too much of a burden on his time, at any rate.

Only for a moment, Zora and Iosef exchanged a look before extending their offer. The hard work and long hours in restoring the shop, they insisted, could be a bandage to their wounds, not to mention a way to pay for their room and board. When their host agreed, they had clinked glasses and thanked him profusely, grateful for this small blessing.

Thus had passed the first six months, about which time Zora recalled little but a daily fourteen hours of work. Once they'd reopened the shop for business, exiles and expatriates, people much like themselves who'd escaped Hitler's wrath, trickled in and out without pause, and their own stories of heartbreak — of loved ones they'd lost and ached to reunite with — kept them going from one day to the next. All had made it to safety by some divine intervention, and in the dawn hours, as Zora and Iosef cut flowers and wrapped them in paper, their patrons' good wishes fueled them with an energy and will to survive that they'd almost lost.

It was this slight tilt of optimism that had caused them to take chances, to do things that had little odds of success, without seeing the obstacles that lay in their path. Zora, for instance, had been secretly sending letters to a second cousin of hers back in Bucharest, afraid to tell Iosef for fear that he might object to the dangerous plan. Danger had long stopped dictating her choices, and by now, all that mattered was that this cousin of hers — an oil-company executive who was always going in and out of the country — had agreed in unclear terms to smuggle Natalia out on his next trip. If he declared that she was his child, she'd urged in her fevered writing, that she was in fragile health, that she had lost her mother (this part, at least, was true), they might just agree to let him bring her along, even if it was only to Hungary, then, closer, to Austria.

How she'd get from Geneva to the Austrian-Hungarian border, which was swarming with SS guards, she'd never considered, any more than that Natalia, being now seven, might not be keen on going anywhere with a man she didn't know or remember. The whole thing was crazy, not well thought out, bound to fail. Somehow she knew it in the pit of her stomach, yet when she received word that things had not gone according to plan, that even her cousin's last-resort attempt to bring Natalia into the Swiss embassy had gone awry, her sorrow had returned with a vengeance, taking even deeper root in her heart.

For more than a year, she had been barely able to sleep. By then, she found it hard to get through the day or rise in the morning, even harder to help in the shop, and she barely showed her face downstairs anymore. Then, just like that, as she was sliding back into an abyss of apathy, a letter from Stefan arrived one day, and a flutter of purpose burst anew in her heart. Yes, she couldn't be with her daughter, she couldn't touch her or awaken feeling her body beside her, she couldn't brush her soft cheek with her fingers, but at least she could do this one thing. Even if she was to live a lifetime without her, even if she never set eyes on her again, she could give her this one gift, which, unlike any other, was still within her grasp.

Things did go according to plan this time and with a swiftness she had only dared to pray for. Penicillin was scarcer than ever, tens of thousands of soldiers were dying in the absence of it, yet as luck would have it, their Geneva landlord, whose shoulder she'd so often cried on, had volunteered since his retirement for the International Committee of the Red Cross and had ties in some Western circles. And the one thing she knew was that while the Red Cross could not return her daughter to her, it could at least deliver the one thing that could save her life.

She survived. Only by a few days, but she did, and for a while, Zora felt restored in her hope, brought back to the land of the living — though that was short-lived. Once the euphoria faded, she found herself caught again in a cycle of prayer and desperation, waiting for yet one more miracle to materialize, another window to open.

One day, the war ended as abruptly as it had started, yet for Iosef and Zora, there was no great triumph, only another dead end. As they listened to the news on the radio that day, they wept in each other's arms bitterly, knowing that all was lost. Their hope might have survived the war, four long years of it, but it was not strong enough to breach that barbed-wire border, the Soviet blockade that would now confine their daughter forever within its depths.

Then and only then did America become a possibility. It had opened up to them like a new oasis. In America, where a new international circle was forming, where the United Nations would be headquartered, they would be able to regain their spirit, their power to fight, and that was all they needed to bind them together again.

Zora was quiet now, as her voice had gone raspy. She took a sip of her tea and set the mug down, not saying anything more. There was no need, for Natalia knew from John

Fowley's letter what had happened once they arrived in New York with their hopes pinned on a prayer, only to fight another onslaught of disappointments, of closed avenues, of dwindled faith.

"So you see, Natalia," Zora whispered. "You were never far from us. All this time, you were here within our souls, every day, every year. Leaving you there had been the hardest thing imaginable, but if we had not, none of us would have survived. Despite it all, in my heart, I always believed I did the right thing."

"And these children," Natalia said in a choked whisper. "You cared for them after the void I had left."

Tears spilled over onto Zora's lovely cheeks. "For both me and your father, they've been our salvation. We took them in when they were very young, the youngest two just babies, and somehow having to care for them strengthened our marriage. Mended over time what had been broken between us. To love is much easier than to despair, even when all of your hope has been burned to ashes. Though I do think that keeping that love alive has brought you back to me. I know this with all of my being."

A silence passed. They held each other

tightly, cheek upon cheek, their hair inter-mingled in a tangle of reddish tendrils, and as the light of dawn brought the room back into focus, the demons that had haunted Natalia most of her life seemed to be receding.

She met him a week later, on Rockaway Beach in Queens. Why she'd chosen this spot Natalia wasn't sure, knowing only that she needed the open air. As she sat at the edge of the water, the deep burgundy of her dress (the one she realized only now with a slight detachment that she'd packed for Victor) was like a flame against the paleness of the sand. Clouds hovered above, so low that she could practically taste the rain droplets, but she was content to be there with this vastness sprawling before her, looking out at the horizon, where the sky and the ocean met in a clean silver line.

She did not wait long. In the distance, a shape grew as it came toward her, and she knew it was him, and if she hadn't been sit-ting down, her knees might have given out. Self-consciously, she observed him from the corner of her eye, smoothing sand from her lap, not wanting to stare. As he came closer, she was surprised to see he was different from what she'd imagined — not at all the towering frame that on that cold winter day had carried her on his back in the bitterness of a Romanian winter, hiding in shadows, dodging the guards. A slim man of medium height in dark rolled-up jeans, a slight effort in his walk as his bare feet sank in the sand, though he did his best not to show it. Yet when he lowered himself next to her, he took on a different dimension, and she grasped that life force resided not in a mountain of a body but in something a great deal more powerful: a will of spirit.

"Natalia," he said, kneeling, gripping his thighs as if he was trying to steady himself. "Natalia."

She couldn't look at his face, so instead, she kept her eyes pinned on his hands. They were a workman's hands, marred by labor, too rough to be smoothed and restored with ointments or creams. Years of hard work were scored on their surface, and something leaped inside her, not because of how rugged they looked but because they were so much like hers. The same long fingers with round, ample nail beds, the same webbing of veins. She felt a little less shy, and she did look up then and saw more of the same. His eyes were the color of hers, shaped the same way, with that same tiny expression crease over his right eyebrow. The same bottom lip, round and full, thicker than the top. She never imagined that it could be like this, that she could see her features carved so symmetrically in another creature. Only his hair was a different hue.

Iosef attempted to reach for her hand but then drew back immediately, as if afraid to touch her. She, however, was no longer afraid of what this moment was for them both, and she reached over and took his hand in both of hers. Such completeness in this simple gesture, there seemed to be no reason for words, and so they sat there for a while, silently, staring at the rolling waves.

"There is a God," he said after some time. "I could die in this moment a happy man."

She laughed, with a trace of unease. "Now, Iosef, after all this time, I think there is a much better reason to hang on."

The way he looked at her, with such awe, was almost unbearable. Then, from what seemed like thin air, something materialized in his hand. He placed it before her, right in the sand, and she just looked at it for a few moments, knowing that when she picked it up, she would be peeling away another layer, revealing another truth.

A journal of sorts, old, with a cover curling around the edges. There was a mug stain in the shape of a half-moon right in the center, and the spine had been secured with a glossy band of tape. There on the first page, a photograph had been pasted, a black-and-white of a baby girl with darkish curls and fat cheeks, wearing a familiar bonnet.

She brought the notebook up closer, closer still as she turned the page, and another, taking in the multitude of handwritten verses. There was a date at the top of each poem, exactly the same one, save for the year.

"I wrote these for you," he explained. "On your birthday, each one. The first one was when we were still in Bucharest, hiding out in Stefan's attic, thinking it would be a matter of days before we could get you back. But then time stretched on, so long and so torturous, and the only way I could stay sane was to write them."

He let out a tremulous breath and looked into the distance. "Even after we left Europe and came here, even after I'd given up trying to find a path back to you, I kept writing them. For your mother, there were the children then, a reason to rise in the morning, more than one person to pour all of her love into, but for me . . ." He paused. "This was the way I could keep you alive. By imagining what you looked like, how you had changed, what your life was like at every stage."

Natalia couldn't find words. Instead, she flipped to the end of the journal, ran her finger over the last cluster of verses, swept a few grains of sand from the page. Then, with a held breath, she began reading:

What is a life if without you,
The only thing that gave it meaning?
How to endure another day,
Without your sweet breath upon my cheek,
    your eyes near?
And in the end, when I am laid to rest,
Without your hand upon my breast,
What will my last thoughts be if not of you,
My darling girl of long ago?

"I keep feeling this is a dream," Iosef said when she'd regained her composure. There was wonderment in the way he regarded her, as if he still couldn't believe she was there, right at his side. As if she were an apparition bathed in a halo of light. No one had ever looked at her like that.

"Yes," she replied, meeting his gaze. "It is a bit of a dream. And so we'll dream it. With a little courage, we can dream it for the rest of our lives."

His arms went around her suddenly,

unreserved, and she hugged him back the same way. To have been loved so fiercely, by so many! Could anyone be so lucky? She'd never felt anything like this — a mixture of joy and of pain, two emotions so entirely opposite yet in this moment never more harmonious. The past and the future, colliding.

"Thank you," she told him. "Thank you for sharing your poems with me."

There was so much more that she could have said, yet somehow no more was needed. They stood, stiff from sitting so long. She kissed his cheek, once, twice, then turned back toward the ocean. It was time to go — they'd been there for hours, it seemed — yet they remained motionless, gazing at the waves as she nestled against him, close to his beating chest. Then she felt the softness of a different set of arms — arms that could have only been Zora's — closing in over her shoulders, the warmth of her cheek brushing against her chin. She did not know where she'd come from, but she was there, as were the children, the little girl in a spin of cartwheels, her blond hair brushing against the wet sand, the boys tossing a Frisbee behind them, laughing and teasing, calling them to come join in.

EPILOGUE

New York City is the place that I have called home for one year. Tonight, on the anniversary of my arrival here, I am sitting in my bay window watching the ships pass the Williamsburg Bridge. It is a proud moment, indeed, but a nostalgic one as well. Sadness seizes me as it does at times, unexpectedly, cutting my breath. *But why do you feel this way, Talia?* I ask myself as my gaze drifts upward toward the lights twinkling on the bridge. *Why such melancholy?*

There is no reason, really, for I know only too well that happiness does not come without a price. I should not lose sight of all that I have been given, for who could have imagined that in this crowded, bustling city I would find such contentment? It isn't much, the reason for my bliss. But it is enough for the moment. It is enough to play untuned pianos in dimly lit jazz bars downtown, to watch the pleasure the music flow-ing from my fingertips elicits in people's smiles. It makes my eyes water to hear their applause, their pleas for more, the astonishment that I see from time to time on a face in the crowd. And when an offer comes unexpectedly to play in a larger bar, a more well-known one this time on the island of Manhattan, I am flooded with the conviction that this is what I am meant to do for the rest of my days and that I am lucky indeed and very much honored to have been granted the chance.

But tonight my thoughts are not on my music. They drift instead over the ocean, to a place where a large portion of my life remains frozen in time. In my mind's eye, I see the two-room flat I shared with the people who raised me, as vividly as if I was still there. I think of them, still asleep at this early hour. Soon they will wake and gingerly make their way out of bed. My father will slip his feet into his worn leather slippers and look at the clock. He will make his way to the bathroom down the hall in his silk striped pajamas, the same ones that he has worn since I was a little girl. My mother will wake, too, and she will come into the family room and sit on the davenport that used to be my bed. Burying her face in my old pillow, she will try to absorb the traces of a fading scent.

Days, maybe weeks later, a worn, battered envelope stamped by the U.S. Postal Service will lie on the buffet in their family room. With trembling hands, my mother will reach for it and tear it open but then set it down, not quite ready to read it. She will know already what it says. My pleas for forgiveness repeat themselves in every letter I send them, along with most of the money I earn in tips. They are laden with promises, my letters, promises to come back for them someday.

I will send for you, my carefully scribbled words say. *I will be back for you and my papa whom I adore with every fiber in my body. Take care of him. Take care of him and of yourself until we shall be together again.*

And she will smile, my mother, she will smile with affection and pride, knowing that I have meant every word of it, that I will part the seas to get back to them.

Months will pass still, perhaps half a year, before another letter reaches them. In this one, I write of the miracles that surround me everywhere I turn. Long past the time when I've stopped staring at the brightly lit storefronts, at the well-stocked butcher shops and bustling coffee shops, one sight still stirs me most. As I sit on a bench some days, book in hand, amid lush trees and buildings jutting over the dark green borders of Central Park, I cannot help but gaze at the people. They are just ordinary folks going about their lives but with such quiet optimism on their faces, with such bounce in their steps, their shoulders squared and confident, their voices assertive and not hushed. Of all the wonders of New York, its inhabitants are what amaze and inspire me most. There have been many letters like these, letters that detail every aspect of my life, each thought or astounding discovery.

Yet there is one that I cannot write, one I have started and stopped so many times that I've lost count. It's not that I struggle to find the right words but that it's taken me a while to learn how to divide my heart into two clear halves, and so I must keep it to myself. Because there is this other half now, this sliver of light that was born out of darkness, that was given back to me when I thought all was lost.

Zora and Iosef, my blood parents. It is no secret that I have come to love them, that I've loved them from the moment Zora opened the door that late afternoon in July and the bouquet of flowers fell from her hands. Iosef, with his stern eyes and skin etched by a life lived too hard, Zora, with her gentle voice and the grace of a swan, even their three foster children — they have become my friends as much as my family. And so we go on. We spend Sundays in Prospect Park, and we stroll across the bridge at night just to see the Manhattan skyline sparkle and shine like something out of a storybook. Zora cooks me the most astounding dinners — golden-brown roasts sprinkled with spices, pasta with clams, dishes which she insists are quite ordinary though they explode in my mouth with a flavor so rich that I want to weep. And we do weep, though mostly we laugh. In their tiny kitchen, we talk about things we will do, places they want to show me, wonders I am still to discover in this heart-stopping city that is our home. But always I see what is in their eyes. I see what they've lost, the years, which not even I can bring back for them.

Lately, I've set out on a journey to do just that. I paint in the gaps, I infuse them with life, with *my* life, in colors vivid enough to turn back the hands of the clock. The little girl, the adolescent, the budding woman. With every triumph and loss, with every heartbreak, I build a bridge over time, back to the people whose love I still feel so acutely. Even Victor is there in parts, Victor who broke my heart yet gave me the biggest gift in return. Victor, my childhood friend, my first love, whom I will never forget through all the loves that will follow, though I have long forgiven him, as he asked me to do on that day long ago. In my tales, we all walk together at last, we are a universe, we are one.

How can I write of such things?

In the end, I settle simply on this: *I am happy, Mama. I am truly happy, and I dream with conviction, here in a place where all dreams are possible.*

What else must be said? It is all she needs to smile every day when she rises in the morning and draws the sheer lace curtains away from her window. It is all she needs as she looks up at the sky of early dawn, to know that I am looking at the same sky, that we live under the same bright dome, and that as long as we love each other and hold on to what God has given us with such tenderness and mercy, our bond will never perish.

■ ■ ■ ■

THE *REAL* GIRL
LEFT BEHIND

■ ■ ■ ■

THE TRUE-LIFE
EVENTS BEHIND
THE GIRL THEY LEFT BEHIND

Although anti-semitism had been on the rise in Eastern Europe for well over a decade, my novel begins with the Bucharest Pogrom, which took place in January 1941, when the anti-Semitic extremist faction known as the Iron Guard pillaged Bucharest's Jewish sectors in an effort to gain political power within General Antonescu's fascist regime. Thousands of Jews were dragged into the streets to be beaten, tortured, or killed. Accounts of atrocities included a group being brought to the city slaughterhouse half-conscious, where they were hung on meat hooks and left to die. It was during those brutal three days that my mother, much like Natalia, was found on a doorstep terrified and half frozen, and brought to an orphanage. Inside the pocket of her beautiful velvet dress, a simple note was discovered: *In anguish and despair we release this child into the hands of God, with hope and faith that she may be saved.*

The mystery of my mother's origins haunted me for many years growing up in California, where I moved with my family from Bucharest as a young teen. Somehow the biological grandparents I would never know always existed in my imagination, alive in a sense. What had happened to them? Did they survive those terrible days of the massacre? If so, what kept them from ever finding their daughter again? It wasn't until 2011, after the loss of my own father, that I began in earnest to set the events on paper, to form a conclusion, however fictional, to a story that indeed had no real-life ending.

About Anton and Despina, my adoptive grandparents, and their own heartbreaking journey, I changed very little. The grace and dignity with which they faced every adversity was evident in the few years I spent with them and perhaps taught me the greatest lessons. I am never far from the tiny communal apartment they were forced to share after the war, where for much of my childhood I was imbued with their spirit and appreciation for the beauty of everyday life despite its many imperfections. It is for them in many ways that this novel was written, as a tribute to the sacrifices they made until the end of their lives, when the daughter they'd so lovingly raised bid them farewell to pursue a better life in America.

It is important to note that although my mother did not leave Romania in the same dramatic way as Natalia, tens of thousands of Romanian Jews did — their freedom bought with cash via clandestine transactions with the Romanian government. These agreements, formed initially between the state of Israel and Romania with the help of the U.S.-based Joint Distribution Committee in the late 1940s, became known as the "gentlemen's agreements" in the 1950s and were kept secret from the Romanian public. Under Ceauşescu, the transactions expanded to include Romanians of German origin who wanted to return to their homeland. It is rumored that by the summer of 1978, these payments rose to as much as $50,000 U.S. per person depending on age, education, and profession. This selling of people was a unique and disturbing occurrence in modern history, the effects of which were felt not only by those ultimately granted exit (many waiting ten years as unemployable political refugees) but also by the country as a whole, as the unbalanced distribution of travel visas added to the underlying anti-Semitism still present within the country.

To weave Romania's turbulent and complex history into a work of fiction did not come without effort, and in the process, I was grateful to be guided by a number of resources. Of particular note are *Balkan Ghosts: A Journey Through History* by Robert D. Kaplan; *Rumania 1866–1947: The Oxford History of Modern Europe* by Keith Hitchens; *Kiss the Hand You Cannot Bite: The Rise and Fall of the Ceauşescus* by Edward Behr; and *The Ransom of the Jews: The Story of the Extraordinary Secret Bargain between Romania and Israel* by Radu Ioanid, director of the International Archival Programs Division at the United States Holocaust Memorial Museum. Equally valuable was the chronicle of Ion Pacepa, former chief of the Romanian Secret Service, who in the aftermath of his defection to the United States in 1978 exposed in *Red Horizons* some of the most corrupt schemes devised under the Communist regime.

Today Romania has risen from four decades of darkness, reemerging once more as a thriving European nation. Yet the shadows of its past still remain. They are ever present in the eyes of the elderly, which speak louder than any monuments about what they have endured, and fought for, and withstood.

"In anguish and despair we release this child into the hands of God, with hope and faith that she may be saved."

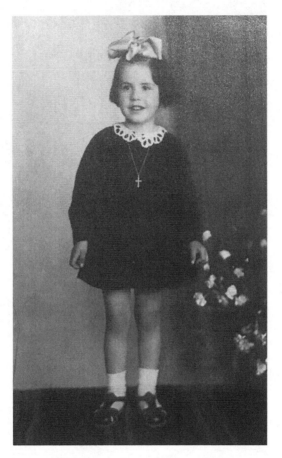

Roxanne's mother around the time of her adoption

While the journey of Roxanne's biological grandparents was rooted in her imagination, the hardships suffered by her mother's adoptive family was sourced in truth — picking up, in a sense, where the other one ended — with the same underlying themes of resilience and courage in the face of tyranny.

Despina, late 1920s

Anton, 1930s

Despina and Anton shortly after their marriage, 1930s

Despina and Anton, 1940s

Anton, Despina, and Roxanne's mother, around 1944

Octavia (Despina's sister) with her daughter and Despina with Roxanne's mother, mid-1940s

Roxanne's mother at age six, 1945

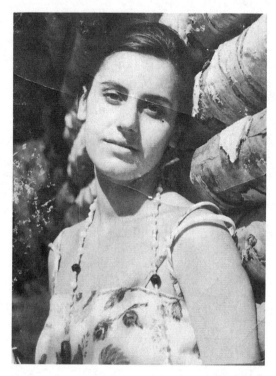

Roxanne's mother in her early twenties, 1960s

*Despina and Anton on their fiftieth
anniversary, 1980s*

ACKNOWLEDGMENTS

To see this novel in print is truly a dream come true, so I must begin by thanking a few individuals in particular: Ms. Johanna Castillo, my editor, for her meticulous and poignant guidance, for helping me elevate the story in ways I never imagined possible, and above all, for giving this novel a home. Ms. Sarah Cantin, for embracing this project with such enthusiasm and shaping it into its final format; I have been honored to work with you both. I am equally grateful to my agent, Ms. Elizabeth Copps of Maria Carvainis Agency, who generously offered her time, support, and creative input, and believed in my writing through the highs and lows of this journey. You are my champions.

I would also like to thank the rest of the Atria team who have helped bring this book into the world, as well as my first readers, Heidi Epstein, Cris Genovese, Michelle

Childers, Jodi Stewart, Denise Miller, and Annie Manfredi for muddling with me through the early drafts and giving me their unvarnished feedback. To my dear friend Laura, who always manages to put a smile on my face and my sister, Arina, for her encouragement and comforting shoulder — I could not be luckier to have you by my side.

Huge gratitude goes to my children, Luca and Dominic, for their patience, and especially to my husband, Philippe, my love, without whom this novel would not have been completed. Thank you for living this book with me, for your tenacity, for believing.

Last, I must thank my grandparents, Anton and Despina, who live in my heart every day, and my mother, Alexandra, whose engaging and colorful storytelling planted the seed for this novel. You are my guardian angels. I love you.

ABOUT THE AUTHOR

Roxanne Veletzos was born in Bucharest, Romania and moved to California with her family as a young teen. Already fluent in English and French, she began writing short stories about growing up in her native Eastern Europe, at first as a cathartic experience as she transitioned to a new culture. Building on her love of the written language, she obtained a bachelor's degree in journalism from California State University, Northridge, and has worked as an editor, content writer, and marketing manager for a number of Fortune 500 companies.